For Kaveh

Published in the United States by St. Martin's Griffin, an imprint of St. Martin's Publishing Group

TRUTH OF THE DIVINE. Copyright © 2021 by Lindsay Ellis. All rights reserved. Printed in the United States of America. For information, address St. Martin's Publishing Group, 120 Broadway, New York, NY 10271.

www.stmartins.com

Interior art: spiral © Oleksii Lishchyshyn/Shutterstock.com; ink splatter © enjoynz/Getty Images

Kaveh's portrait illustration by Stanley Chow

The Library of Congress has cataloged the hardcover edition as follows:

Names: Ellis, Lindsay, 1984– author.
Title: Truth of the divine : a novel / Lindsay Ellis.
Description: First Edition. | New York, NY : St. Martin's Press, 2021. | Series: Noumena ; 2
Identifiers: LCCN 2021021152 | ISBN 9781250274540 (hardcover) | ISBN 9781250281838 (signed edition) | ISBN 9781250274557 (ebook)
Subjects: GSAFD: Science fiction.
Classification: LCC PS3605.L46773 T78 2021 | DDC 813/.6—dc23
LC record available at https://lccn.loc.gov/2021021152

ISBN 978-1-250-83022-7 (trade paperback)

Our books may be purchased in bulk for promotional, educational, or business use. Please contact your local bookseller or the Macmillan Corporate and Premium Sales Department at 1-800-221-7945, extension 5442, or by email at MacmillanSpecialMarkets@macmillan.com.

First St. Martin's Griffin Edition: 2022

10 9 8 7 6 5 4 3 2 1

ALSO BY LINDSAY ELLIS

Axiom's End

TRUTH
OF THE
DIVINE

A NOVEL

LINDSAY
ELLIS

ST. MARTIN'S GRIFFIN
NEW YORK

AUTHOR'S NOTE

The following serves as a content warning, and as such contains some spoilers. If you feel that you aren't someone who benefits from or needs content warnings, I suggest you skip this section.

There is much discussion in media criticism circles about the ethics of portrayals of suicide and self-harm, particularly the tendency to romanticize it. Indeed, I have had some very bad nights as a result of certain pieces of media framing suicide as a sad thing that happens, but maybe sometimes the noble thing to do, especially for those of us who have metaphorically pissed our pants at the Grammys (looking at you, *A Star Is Born*). But romanticization or no, any depiction of suicide, attempted, contemplated, or completed, can make someone who already experiences those tendencies to fall back into the ideation pit. Depiction of an act need not be romanticized to trigger negative effects, especially if the viewer/reader goes in unaware.

On the flip side, as a writer you never know what will be harmful for others, and just because someone feels hurt or is triggered by your work doesn't mean you've done anything wrong. I don't like the idea of certain subjects being "off limits" either as a writer or a reader, and I think we should allow ourselves to write about messy, difficult, and painful situations, including sympathetic characters engaging in acts of self-harm or acting in unethical or even abusive ways. Armed with this foreknowledge, the onus is on the reader to decide if this material might be harmful to them.

One of the main themes of *Truth of the Divine* is trauma, and it contains depictions of post-traumatic stress, depression, addiction, alcoholism, domestic violence, and a wide smattering of manifestations of mental illness such as panic attacks. The book includes depictions of suicidal ideation, suicidal planning, attempted suicide, completed suicide, and violent self-harm. The book also contains depictions of racism, xenophobia, Islamophobia, racially motivated violence, anti-Semitism, and a few incidences of racial slurs. While the book doesn't contain anything that I would consider sexual violence, it does contain some uncomfortable sexual situations (and no, I don't mean with aliens, sorry—not yet, anyway).

I include this warning not because I want to dissuade anyone from reading but to inform the reader of content they may not otherwise anticipate, especially given the relatively light tone of the first installment of this series. If indeed you do feel like any of the above might be harmful to you, I suggest you postpone reading this book until such a time that that is no longer the case.

THE UNIVERSAL DECLARATION
OF Human Rights

WHEREAS disregard and contempt for human rights have resulted in barbarous acts which have outraged the conscience of mankind, and the advent of a world in which human beings shall enjoy freedom of speech and belief and freedom from fear and want has been proclaimed as the highest aspiration of the common people,

WHEREAS the peoples of the United Nations have in the Charter reaffirmed their faith in fundamental human rights, in the dignity and worth of the human person and in the equal rights of men and women and have determined to promote social progress and better standards of life in larger freedom,

WHEREAS a common understanding of these rights and freedoms is of the greatest importance for the full realization of this pledge,

NOW, THEREFORE THE GENERAL ASSEMBLY

proclaims this Universal Declaration of Human Rights as a common standard of achievement for all peoples and all nations, to the end that every individual and every organ of society, keeping this Declaration constantly in mind, shall strive by teaching and education to promote respect for these rights and freedoms and by progressive measures, national and international, to secure their universal and effective recognition and observance, both among the peoples of Member States themselves and among the peoples of territories under their jurisdiction.

United Nations General Assembly in Paris
10 December 1948

T O P S E C R E T # TOP SECRET

SUBJECT: LIST OF ALL KNOWN INDIVIDUALS OF SPECIES AMYGDALINE ("PEQUOD") AS OF
JANUARY 1 2008, LISTED BY NUMBER, ESPERANTO CODE NAME, FUNCTION (IF KNOWN),
CASTE (IF KNOWN), AND STATUS (IF KNOWN)

Inarajan, Guam Event-"Fremda"
February 26, 1971

```
AG-ETI-001 - "Ĉefo"     technocrat   caste: Oligarch  status: d. (9/20/2007)
AG-ETI-002 - "Esperas"  diplocrat    caste: Oligarch  status: RNSC Building 112
AG-ETI-003 - "Brako"    stratocrat   caste: Similar   status: RNSC Building 112
AG-ETI-004 - "Kruro"    stratocrat   caste: Similar   status: d. (10/7/2007)
AG-ETI-005 - "Celo"     diplocrat    caste: unknown   status: RNSC Building 112
AG-ETI-006 - "Feliĉa"   diplocrat    caste: unknown   status: RNSC Building 112
AG-ETI-007 - "Okulo"    technocrat   caste: unknown   status: RNSC Building 112
AG-ETI-008 - "Scivo"    technocrat   caste: unknown   status: d. (9/22/2007)
AG-ETI-009 - "Lema"     unknown      caste: unknown   status: d. (11/4/1973)
AG-ETI-010 - "Anaso"    technocrat   caste: unknown   status: RNSC Building 112
AG-ETI-011 - "Vespo"    technocrat   caste: unknown   status: RNSC Building 112
AG-ETI-012 - "Idealo"   unknown      caste: unknown   status: d. (2/14/1989)
AG-ETI-013 - "Kontako"  unknown      caste: unknown   status: d. (9/30/2001)
AG-ETI-014 - "Intenci"  technocrat   caste: Aristocrat status: RNSC Building 112
AG-ETI-015 - "Loĝi"     technocrat   caste: unknown   status: d. (9/22/2007)
AG-ETI-016 - "Sperta"   unknown      caste: unknown   status: d. (11/4/1973)
AG-ETI-017 - "Proksima" stratocrat   caste: Aristocrat status: RNSC Building 112
AG-ETI-018 - "Ekbrilo"  unknown      caste: unknown   status: d. (6/11/1997)
AG-ETI-019 - "Arĝento"  technocrat   caste: unknown   status: RNSC Building 112
AG-ETI-020 - "Blanka"   unknown      caste: unknown   status: d. (1/4/1973)
AG-ETI-021 - "Anaso"    stratocrat   caste: unknown   status: RNSC Building 112
AG-ETI-022 - "Allogas"  technocrat   caste: unknown   status: RNSC Building 112
AG-ETI-023 - "Vorto"    diplocrat    caste: unknown   status: RNSC Building 112
AG-ETI-024 - "Flanko"   unknown      caste: unknown   status: d. (9/30/2001)
AG-ETI-025 - "Komenci"  diplocrat    caste: unknown   status: RNSC Building 112
AG-ETI-026 - "Jaro"     diplocrat    caste: unknown   status: RNSC Building 112
AG-ETI-027 - "Fiŝo"     unknown      caste: unknown   status: d. (2/14/1989)
AG-ETI-028 - "Birdo"    technocrat   caste: unknown   status: d. (9/22/2007)
AG-ETI-029 - "Domo"     diplocrat    caste: unknown   status: RNSC Building 112
AG-ETI-030 - "Stelo"    propagandist caste: Aristocrat status: RNSC Building 112
AG-ETI-031 - "Krias"    propagandist caste: Aristocrat status: RNSC Building 112
AG-ETI-032 - "Kaŝi"     diplocrat    caste: unknown   status: RNSC Building 112
AG-ETI-033 - "Nebulo"   diplocrat    caste: unknown   status: RNSC Building 112
AG-ETI-034 - "Cimo"     unknown      caste: unknown   status: d. (6/11/1997)
AG-ETI-035 - "Problemo" technocrat   caste: unknown   status: RNSC Building 112
AG-ETI-036 - "Dika"     diplocrat    caste: unknown   status: RNSC Building 112
AG-ETI-037 - "Nokto"    unknown      caste: unknown   status: d. (9/30/2001)
AG-ETI-038 - "Dolĉa"    technocrat   caste: Aristocrat status: RNSC Building 112
AG-ETI-039 - "Pensu"    technocrat   caste: unknown   status: RNSC Building 112
AG-ETI-040 - "Belto"    unknown      caste: unknown   status: d. (6/11/1997)
AG-ETI-041 - "Akvo"     technocrat   caste: Aristocrat status: RNSC Building 112
AG-ETI-042 - "Verda"    technocrat   caste: unknown   status: d. (9/22/2007)
AG-ETI-043 - "Libro"    technocrat   caste: unknown   status: RNSC Building 112
AG-ETI-044 - "Povi"     unknown      caste: unknown   status: d. (9/30/2001)
AG-ETI-045 - "Ekstra"   unknown      caste: unknown   status: d. (2/14/1989)
```

Altadena, California Event-"Ampersand"
August 23, 2007

AG-ETI-046 - "Scio"   technocrat   caste: Oligarch   status: RNSC Building 127

Altadena, California Event-"Obelus"
September 20, 2007

AG-ETI-047 - unnamed   stratocrat   caste: Similar   status: d. (10/10/2007)
AG-ETI-048 - unnamed   stratocrat   caste: Similar   status: unknown
AG-ETI-049 - unnamed   stratocrat   caste: Similar   status: unknown
AG-ETI-050 - unnamed   stratocrat   caste: Similar   status: unknown

TOP SECRET

PART 1

IT'S A FOOL WHO PLAYS IT COOL

January 7, 2008

ARTICLE 14.1 Everyone has the right to seek and to enjoy in other countries asylum from persecution.

December 14, 2007

𝕿𝖍𝖊 𝕹𝖊𝖜 𝖄𝖔𝖗𝖐 𝕿𝖎𝖒𝖊𝖘

A Third Option

To answer legal questions regarding the rights of extraterrestrial intelligences, we must think outside the box.

BY JANO MIRANDA

This week, protests in the capital spilled into violence as demonstrators in front of the White House, demanding accountability, clashed with police. The Cheney administration has seen a steady stream of resignations ever since President Cheney took office, and despite record-low approval ratings for the new president himself, he still refuses to address the topic at the center of these demonstrations: The people want to know the truth about First Contact.

I don't condone what violence there has been, but we have to admit that the upset comes from a legitimate place. We still know almost nothing about the alien presence on Earth. Two months after President Bush resigned in disgrace, no new information has been released from those in power. What scant crumbs we do have at this moment come from the leaked memo that precipitated Bush's resignation in the first place, the so-called Fremda Memo, which was published by my friend and colleague Nils Ortega via *The Broken Seal.* This memo effectively told us only that there are so-called ETIs (intelligent extraterrestrials) in federal custody, and they either cannot or will not communicate with us. But the purported reason for the delay in the release of what has up until now been confidential information isn't the assumption that the public at large can't handle the truth but instead the lack of legal status for any living ETIs inside the United States.

The de facto presumption right now, communicative or no, is that any intelligent extraterrestrial beings have existed and continue to exist in a sort of legal gray area, enjoying no real legal protections and beholden to no human law. Those on the left cry out against the former, those on the right cry out against the latter. And the rest of the world is similarly hamstrung, waiting and holding its breath to see what the United States will do, as the United States is, for the moment, the only country that actually knows what it is dealing with.

Regardless of what gets revealed about any ETIs, our first priority should be our own protection. A system of natural personhood was designed for humans, and we do not know what the consequences might be for allowing aliens, which, for all we know, possess vastly different intelligence and abilities from our own, into that system.

However, we likewise cannot assign extraterrestrial beings the legal status of animals, or of property. Protecting ourselves from abuses does not mean we should open the door for the abuse of others, now that we appear to be members of a galactic community. But that doesn't mean we need to extend to any hypothetical extraterrestrial being, knowing absolutely nothing about their culture, their intelligence or even their civilization, the full scope of natural human rights. What then would follow? The right to citizenship? The right to vote? The right to marry? To own property, to play the stock market, to run for office? It may seem laughable, but in the United States, any natural person, provided they are of proper age and not in some violation of the law, can access some or all of these rights.

So the discussion has us at an impasse; either we grant ETIs, knowing absolutely nothing about their similarities or differences to us, full human rights, or we grant them no rights. The idea that these are our only two options strikes me as odd because part of what makes us human is our ability to problem solve, to innovate.

I would like to suggest a third option.

"Hey, anyone home?"

Cora blinked, shooting to attention. "Yes."

"Did you hear the question?"

"Yes." She blinked again, trying to snap out of the mind fog that had been plaguing her all morning. The fluorescent lights in this conference room were the frequency of knives. "Scio has declined to speak."

Sol shot her a millisecond of a glare, then faced the brigadier general seated on the other side of the conference table. "If he says he's not going to talk to us, that's pretty much that for the day."

Brigadier General Whatsisfuck didn't even look at Cora, which had been par for the course for this meeting and also fine by her. This guy was only the last in a long line of government bureaucrats she'd had to reassure everything was fine and the world isn't ending while also gently telling them no, the aliens do not want to talk to you. State had been fine—they'd been polite, and only came knocking once. Homeland Security were low-key awful, but at least they kept it short and to the point. NASA were actually cool, she enjoyed those guys. The Department of Energy even showed up at one point; she had no idea what that was about. But the Department of Defense, they were the worst. Not only would they not take *no* for an answer, there were so many of them, none of the different departments ever communicated with each other, and they just kept showing up with the head of whatever new ETI task force they'd formed this week. This one was called something like . . . National . . . Security . . . Intelligence Force for Who Gives a Shit? She was so tired.

"I know it's a strange situation," said ROSA director Sevak "Dr. Sev" Ghasabian, flanked on his right by Cora's aunt Luciana. A fiftysomething with sharp features and a head like a cue ball, he preferred *Dr. Sev*, just in case anyone was unclear on which degree he'd completed. "I know you're on a tight schedule, but the best we can suggest is that one of them might be more amenable if you come back tomorrow."

"When I flew out here, it was my understanding that some face time was going to happen with one of the, um, *amygdalines.*"

The brigadier general, a square-shouldered man who looked like a Boy Scout wearing age makeup, still ignored Cora. She wondered if it was because of who she was, since he was being noticeably dismissive to Luciana, too. Perhaps it was because they were members of the Ortega family, and her father, Nils Ortega, was presently the biggest force of chaos on this earth besides the aliens. Given that they were the only women in the room, it could also be shameless misogyny. Or both!

"Scio didn't agree to it, though," said Cora. "Dr. Sev agreed to it, and I asked Scio if he would do it. He declined."

Finally the brigadier general spared her a glance—Porter, his name was, which she only caught once her vision de-blurred enough to read his name tag. "But we have no way of verifying that, do we? I find it highly questionable that an unqualified teenage civilian is the only 'communication intermediary' between extraterrestrial intelligences and the American government."

That lit an anxiety fuse inside her. She wasn't a teenager, and *no one* was qualified to be a communication intermediary, but that didn't mean he hadn't pressed just about every insecurity button she had.

"What is your goal, exactly?" asked Dr. Sev.

"To appraise the capabilities of the ETIs. But moreover, we need to know if any of them intend to use those capabilities." Porter sighed, and Cora could all but see the rails switching routes in his mind. *If Scio won't talk, perhaps Esperas will.* "There are two subgroups within the Fremda group, each with their own representative, correct?"

"There are not two 'groups,'" clarified Sol. Sol Kaplan was in charge of the relatively small CIA contingent at the Riverside National Security Complex, which numbered somewhere between three and thirty, Cora wasn't sure (and half the time, she didn't know who was CIA and who just looked the part). "There is one group, and one . . . *individual* amygdaline we keep in seclusion."

"And that would be 'Scio.'" Porter sounded almost as uncomfortable with Ampersand's Esperanto code name as she was. Unlike Esperas, who *might* sometimes communicate through a computer-based translator, Ampersand preferred his human intermediary, and unless one considered annoyed glares a form of communication, Ampersand refused to communicate any other way.

"Yes," she said, leaving it at that. She didn't want to give this man any ammo to confirm his suspicions of how out of place she was here. She was a college dropout with no training and no certifications and was only given top-secret clearance after Ampersand's refusal to communicate without her stretched for an entire week before they panicked and let her into the club. So here she sat, underqualified, underpaid, and completely unappreciated. But she kept on, kept enduring this workplace, not only because a recession that was rapidly tumbling into a depression meant that jobs were scarce but because it was the only way she could guarantee access to Ampersand. Not that it was doing her mental health any favors, since the space aliens were also the root of most of her ills.

And if this headache was any indication, her condition was not improving.

When she'd seen a psychiatrist, she could not tell them what had actually happened to her three months ago, that she had been kidnapped by an alien Similar, a "militarist," and held as ransom. She could not say that a twelve-foot monster had skewered her with its meat-hook digits, driven them straight through her body and into the cold ground. She could not tell the doctor that there were two weeks of her life after that that she did not remember.

So she told the psych a story about being kidnapped by a *human* person, an ex of some sort. He had held her under threat of violence, and when she fought back, he stabbed her several times. She'd survived the ordeal, but now there were nightmares. Nightmares and panic attacks and random bouts of crying and irritability and all sorts of fun times that had not been there before.

This, however, was a gamble of a story to tell, because if someone were to ask to see the scars, she would be found for a liar, because there were none. Ampersand was very good at operating on the human body like it was a machine, stitching her ambulatory sack of meat and water back together like a mechanic would repair a car. Good as new, no one would be able to tell it was ever in an accident.

The diagnosis came back as post-traumatic stress, but since it was still in its early stages, the prognosis was actually pretty good if she began treatment for it now. The psych had suggested that Cora begin therapy immediately and had given her a script for Prozac—treatments she could not begin and medication she could not take, because she could afford neither. ROSA did not offer benefits, and although still technically just below the poverty line, she now made too much money to qualify for California's state-run health care system, MediCAL, leaving her in the limbo between with no health insurance.

"Help me understand the issue," said Porter, addressing Sol. "The issue is . . . both parties refuse to be in the same room with each other?"

Everyone looked at Cora, and she tried to blink away the nuclear explosion going off in extreme slow motion behind her left eyeball.

"Only one of them has expressed a preference, and that's Scio," she said, "but yes, he won't even consider being in the same room as Esperas, and Esperas controls access to the rest of them."

"Do we know why they won't be in the same room together?"

Again everyone looked at Cora.

Oh, she knew why, all right. Unbeknownst to the other humans in the room, Esperas had a special hate-on for Ampersand owing to his failure to disclose his relationship to the leader of the group of Similars who had been hunting them last year, code name: "Obelus." The same Similar who had nearly killed her.

"We think it has something to do with one of their cultural taboos," she lied. "I'm not entirely sure."

"But Esperas does not have a dedicated interpreter like Scio does," observed Porter. "Why is that?"

Cora glanced at the clock on the wall. This meeting was scheduled to end five minutes ago. Why was this man being so goddamn tenacious? Also, could eyeballs spontaneously explode? It felt like she was about to find out.

"It's a matter of preference," she said. "Scio feels like he needs an impartial intermediary to speak for him to better ensure that his meaning is getting across in the way he wants."

"And Esperas does not?"

Esperas doesn't care, thought Cora. Esperas had the luxury of hiding behind his own Similar, his "heavy," and no one could *make* him talk to anyone. It had been assumed last year that both of the Fremda group's Similars, their only form of protection, had been killed by Obelus. Cora found out later that was only half-true, as Brako, the one who had been thought killed at NORAD, survived, and was now just fine.

"Esperas has never requested a human intermediary," said Dr. Sev.

"Then if Esperas is not here, why has Scio declined to speak to us?" asked Porter. "As I understand, between the two, Scio has been a much better source of intelligence. So if he has declined to meet with us, I'd like to know why."

This guy was like a fork raking over the chalkboard of her nerves, and she could feel the beginnings of a meltdown. She tried to focus on breathing normally while Dr. Sev offered some placating half truth to General Brigadier. *Not now,* she told herself. *Not now, not now.*

"Please understand," said Dr. Sev, "we are dealing with intelligences we largely don't understand. Sometimes they behave capriciously, and we do not know why."

"I flew all the way out here, and you've kept me waiting for two days—surely there can be some way we can schedule an interaction."

"He said he wouldn't do it, whether Esperas is here or not," said Cora. She could hear the blood thumping through her skull. She was genuinely beginning to worry this was a prologue to an aneurysm.

"Yes, but *why*?" If her eyeball were about to explode, this man would be the detonator. "What is his reasoning?"

"I . . . I'm not sure," she said.

"Come on, we know you have an excuse," said Sol, frustrated. "Let's hear it."

In the three months she had been an employee at ROSA, Sol had never disrespected her that overtly. Even the brigadier general looked uncomfortable. Sol seemed to realize he'd stepped over a line, and corrected himself. "I mean, I'm sure he has an excuse. He always does."

But the spiral had already begun, the last Jenga block holding the tower in place pulled out, and she was collapsing. "He's busy."

"Busy doing what?" asked Sol.

"I don't know. Excuse me," she said, barely holding it together. "I need to use the restroom."

"We're not finished," said Sol.

"Please excuse me."

She didn't make it to the end of the hallway before she started running. By then, the bomb had gone off, the tower was collapsing. She fled to the nearest single-stall bathroom and had only just shut the door behind her before her breathing turned into audible shrieking so loud that anyone passing by could hear it. She fell to the tile floor, wrapping her arms around her midsection, begging her traitorous windpipe to quiet down. *Sol will hear it, he'll hear it, and he'll take your clearance! He's been looking for an excuse to revoke your clearance, he wants you gone, stop stop stop!* This was the third one inside of a week.

Her throat burned, her eyes watered, and she grabbed fistfuls of hair in the hope that the pain would provide some sort of stopgap, short-circuit the panic. She pulled and pulled, then dug her fingernails into her skull until she felt moisture on her fingertips. She was so deep in her own torment that it was only now that she fleetingly wondered if Ampersand was feeling this, too.

Dynamic fusion bonding was what he called it, the way that members of an amygdaline "phyle" bound themselves to each other. Dynamic fusion bonding was the crux of amygdaline social structure, with members of a phyle called *symphyles*. Symphyles were bound to each other in the familial sense, if not the alien equivalent of the biblical one, which she was pretty sure would be the case if these guys hadn't evolved past reproducing the old-fashioned way. Ampersand had told her that when he had attempted to fusion bond with her, he had expected it to fail, because he was a sleek and sophisticated 650-ish-year-old cyborg alien technocrat Oligarch and she was a lowly human, a being of meat and hair. And yet now here they were, bound together, 'til death do us part.

The ability to sense each other's "state" was also a part of the package, only there was no rhyme or reason to how intensely they felt each other. Sometimes he couldn't sense her at all, sometimes it was, in his words, "*mildly debilitating.*" She hoped now was not one of those times, hoped he wasn't feeling his own alien equivalent of this tempest.

Then she realized someone was talking to her, a voice in her ear. It had spoken to her several times, and she hadn't been coherent enough to respond.

"Dear one, come to me."

She tried to get words out, but they weren't coming. She could barely comprehend what he was asking.

"Dear one, come to me, I will stop it."

"I can't," she garbled. "I can't. Someone will see!"

"I can stop it."

"Someone will see!" she all but shrieked. "I'll lose my clearance. Sol is always looking for an excuse to revoke my clearance, if they see me like this! *If they see me like this!*"

There was a ripple on the tiled floor in front of her, and then a cloak of invisibility melted off a liquid metal plate. He must have slipped it under the door. It took a few dozen breaths before she could tear herself away from the wall, collapse onto the plate, curl into a fetal position, and let the liquid metal sweep over her, enveloping her in darkness.

When the metal unwrapped, the panic was still going strong. Her eyes, used to the bright fluorescent lights, could hardly see in the dark of Ampersand's quarters. She rolled off the plate, her vision still swimming, her skin still prickling, her breath still coming in rapid bursts. Her vision coming in fits and starts, she could almost see Ampersand standing over her—giant by human standards at over eight feet tall, even with his forward-leaning center of gravity like a silver velociraptor. Long clawlike fingers floated over her, a head that was somewhere between a dragon and a praying mantis looked down at her.

"Do you consent to be medicated?"

"Yes," she pleaded. "Yes, please, make it stop, make it stop!"

He placed his front four fingers of his left hand together, a small, syringe-like device forming at the tips, and he inserted it into her neck. The effect was immediate. It didn't stop her hyperventilating, but it did pull back the prickling of her skin, the swimming of her vision. "I'm sorry," she managed, her breath still fast and shallow, but slowing down. "I tried . . . to stop it. I didn't . . . want it . . . to affect you . . . I'm sorry."

He removed the syringe, the extensions on his fingers melting back into him. He stood still for a moment, as if recalibrating, and then lowered his body right next to hers. Ampersand didn't "sit" like a human. More than anything, it reminded Cora of a deer, arms tucked neatly

flowed through him like blood. From his fingertips, he produced three drone lights that hung in the air a few feet over her. She'd seen him use the drone lights a few times when he was studying something, and they were among her favorite tricks in his arsenal. Since amygdalines were so much more sensitive to light than humans, his ideal working lights were soft and pleasant to her eyes. They hung in the air like marble-size suns, but the light was soft, like warm red fireflies.

He demonstrated what the monitors looked like to her, which were indeed so thin she could barely see them. Each looked like a human hair, but one that shone iridescent like an oil spill. He used the side of her temple to enter her head. The tips of the needles he used were so sharp that she didn't even feel a pinprick.

"I have a question," she said when he was between threads. "On top of monitoring me and my symptoms, you said you wanted to study the nature of our bond. What did you mean by that?"

"*There are characteristics of our bond not found in any inter-amygdaline fusion bond that has been observed.*"

"What kind of characteristics?"

He produced another thread, stringing it taut in front of her eyes, then moved to her right temple to insert it. "*As of right now, the biggest mystery is the empathic nature of our bond.*"

"What do you mean?" she asked, keeping her jaw locked, moving her lips as little as possible.

"*The ability to sense and share mood swings, this is unheard of in dynamic fusion bonding.*"

"I thought dynamic fusion bonding meant you could sense each other's 'energies.' You can tell if symphyles are nearby, if they're alive or dead."

"*Yes, but dynamic fusion bonding is not an empathic bond. We cannot sense each other's emotional states as you and I can. This side effect is unprecedented.*"

He finished the thread, and she moved to look at him. "Really?"

"*Really.*"

"Do you have . . . any idea where it comes from?"

"*None.*" He pulled another thread taut, and moved back to her left temple. She stilled. "*My hope is to find out what part of your brain it is rooted in.*"

"Why *my* brain?"

"*We have a sample size of one, and an experiment we cannot re-create; there is much I can only extrapolate, but given that this side effect is unprecedented and you, as a natural human alien, are the only variable that has changed, I surmise that the basis for this side effect lies in your brain.*"

She turned to look at him as he finished a thread. "What do you want to do about it?"

He nudged her head back onto its side as he made another injection. "*Eliminate the side effect so that we are no longer affected by each other's moods.*"

"Oh."

This was a lot. She'd assumed the empathic aspect was a normal part of the deal; it had never occurred to her that they were in any way unique. In a way, that made her feel even worse; her nascent mental illness creeping into his mind wasn't only a bug of being bonded to *her*, it was the first and only time he'd experienced anything like that at all?

And of course, it ran both ways; there were times when the wall between them was particularly thin, and she would feel some external force invade her. Sometimes it was deep despair, but more often, it was fear, terror, anxiety. Overstimulation from simply existing on an alien planet with its thin atmosphere, its violent weather, its sharp, bright, overbearing sun.

But on the other hand, it wasn't like there weren't any benefits; for one, she didn't have to explain every goddamn thing anymore. If he said something offensive, he could intuit it without her having to explain it. It had likewise made him a quick study on the art of physically comforting her; before, she'd had to give him specific instruction on exactly where and how to touch her, which was not only tedious but wasn't particularly enjoyable, like training a robot that was designed to put cars together how to pat you on the head. But their connection removed the need to explain what was good and what wasn't, what helped and what didn't. If he touched her in a way she wasn't crazy about, he could sense it, and he wouldn't do it again. If he did it in a way she liked, he added it to his toolbox without needing to be instructed to do so.

He finished with the thread and stood up to half height, keeping his back parallel to the floor. "*I have finished this round of implants. You may prepare for sleep. I will monitor you awake, then asleep, then I will depart.*"

Cora went into the bathroom, did the toothbrush and face wash rigmarole, then returned to her bedroom where her pajamas lived in a canvas IKEA box on the floor. Ampersand was still there, taking up half the room, looking at nothing in particular, standing between her and her pajamas. She sighed. How to handle this? Ask for privacy? It didn't really matter, did it? A clothed human to him was just a natural alien with a jacket on.

Amygdalines were, even by the standards of their own species, completely asexual. With the exception of their Genomes, they were born sterile, and even their ancestors didn't experience sexuality the way humans do, because a human will, of course, fuck anything. But more than that, she knew he'd seen her naked before, likely quite a lot. After Obelus had ripped her open, there was that period of two weeks that Ampersand had kept her to himself that she did not remember, two weeks that he'd spent doing god knows what repairing her. It was not likely that he had done so while she was clothed.

She walked right by him, removed her baggy jeans, and replaced them with even baggier pajamas right in front of him. She hadn't weighed herself, but she'd dropped at least two sizes in the last three months, and was going on three. She just wasn't interested in food anymore.

She put her bed back together, crawled in, and turned off the lamp on her bedside table, disappointed to see that he'd already put his soft little drone lights away. And then, he just stood there, half height, back still parallel to the floor. Staring at her.

"So I should just go to sleep?"

"*Yes.*"

"Okay."

She waited to see if he'd back away, or move forward, or sit down, or do anything other than hover next to her bed, staring.

"Good night?"

"*Good night.*"

He kept staring.

Okay. She turned onto her side, back to him, but she could feel him staring. She was sure that he had some unfathomable algorithm that he was running that was mapping out the incredible complexities of this living computer, her human brain. She knew that him standing there, staring at her, was not the equivalent of a human doing the same.

But he kept just fucking staring at her.

"You are uncomfortable."

She sighed and sat up to face him. "You standing there is uncomfortable, yes."

"I am here to monitor you."

"I know that, but standing next to my bed and staring at me—"

"I will sedate you."

She huffed. "It's still uncomfortable."

"What would be comfortable for you?"

It struck her then, the image of the two of them in a hospital bed three months ago. She'd simply asked him to get in the bed with her because of some visceral, yearning need to be physically close to this being that was so alien. They hadn't repeated that moment since.

She backed away from him, toward the wall. She pictured herself asking for what she really wanted and was hit by a splash of shame at the thought. "It would be more comfortable if you weren't standing," she said, hoping he'd take the hint.

He cocked his head to the side slightly, then moved toward her. *"I am concerned my body resembles the source of your trauma."*

"You mean Obelus?"

"Yes."

She had a slight twinge of nausea at the thought of Obelus, one she tried to expel with a breath. *He's dead. He's dead. He's gone.* But it was true that Ampersand more resembled Obelus than he did any of the rest of the Fremda group, most of whom were much smaller and svelter than he was. He wasn't completely wrong about that. Still, while the thought of Obelus gave her the anxiety, the fear, the nausea, the thought of Ampersand did the opposite. "I won't feel trapped."

He moved closer, almost over her in that fluid way that he moved, unbound by the laws of gravity. He tucked his left arm under him in that deerlike posture, half cocked on his side, then carefully, like he was testing the temperature of the water, placed his right arm on the other side of her, tucking her up next to his chest.

Yes, correct, this is correct, this is where I should be.

It was as though there were two halves of herself that had been vibrating out of sync that were finally on the same frequency. Smooth, calm, correct. She had her arms tucked up against her chest like a mummy, unsure what was appropriate. Then, she decided, *fuck it.* She wrapped her left arm around his midsection and pulled herself close to him, felt the texture of the carapace on his back. The closest analogue to the way his skin felt was sharkskin from a bamboo shark she'd once touched at the Aquarium of the Pacific, the slightly rough texture, the way it didn't slip around like human skin, the firmness underneath.

With that sense of rightness, that sense of comfort, that sense of safety also came the shame. What if someone saw this? What would people think? What if people knew that this went beyond not being horrified by this but actually *liking* it?

She'd felt somewhat asexual ever since she'd met Ampersand, perhaps a side effect of the fusion bonding. She'd gone to a couple of gay clubs to try to hook up with a girl, but struck out there. Then she'd gone to a regular bar and found a guy, some white-collar bro-bro who worked for an insurance agency or something. He had a name like Paul or Chad or Dave, a receding hairline and a round, ruddy, meaty face that could have been twenty-five or forty-five. She'd gone home with him, let him have his way, in part because she was drunk but also because she wanted to see if she could feel something. It was dry and unpleasant and painful, and Paul or Chad or whatever his name was invaded her mouth with his tongue like he was a sandworm of Arrakis. She didn't even spend the night with him.

That wasn't affection. That wasn't satisfying. This was.

Oh, God, this is so fucked up.

"You are anxious."

She opened her eyes, hugged him tighter. "Just thinking. Good anxious. I . . ."

"I will sedate you."

"No!" she blurted. "You can sedate me in a few minutes, but I just . . ." She tried to push through that sense of shame. *He isn't human. He's not going to judge this like a human would.* "I feel safe here. I feel like this is helping."

That was true, wasn't it? One of the hallmarks of PTSD was a loss of a sense of safety. Ampersand was, aside from the Similar Brako, the most powerful being on the entire planet. His entire body was effectively its own city fueled by some unfathomable matter/antimatter core that was capable of generating enough power for every major city in the country combined. Sometimes it was overwhelming to think about all the things she did not know about this body he inhabited. And here he was, in bed with her, telling her, *I will help you, I will treat your illness.*

"I don't know when you'll be back here," she said. "I just want to enjoy being here a little while longer."

"A part of my study was intended to be therapeutic. If this is therapeutic, then we shall create a schedule, and I will come here every night."

She pulled away, looked up at those luminous amber eyes inches away from her own. "You will?" *This is so fucked up. Why do I like this? I should be with a human. This is so fucked up.*

He ran his long arachnoid digits over her scalp, and she shivered. *"I will arrive two hours before your scheduled sleep time, and I will stay here with you until you sleep."*

She thought her heart might burst from gratitude, and she hugged him. "Yes, yes, I'd like that."

She pulled her face back into his midsection, the "chest" for lack of a better word, where a collarbone would be on a human, and closed her eyes. She tried to plug that little spring of shame that kept burbling up, and he continued caressing her head, the back of her neck, then the top of her back.

Please don't stop.

She allowed herself a few minutes before she looked up at him and said, "You can sedate me now."

He put his four forefingers together, so like the forelimbs of a spider, and that syringe-like device appeared. *"This will make you sleep deeply. You will not have nightmares tonight."*

At that, she nearly cried. He could have given her a billion dollars, a private island, a full scholarship to the best school in the country, all the praise that the masses were heaping on her father, folk hero and soldier for truth; there was nothing she wanted to hear more than *you won't have nightmares tonight.*

He injected the sedative into her, a warm sensation followed by darkness that took a few minutes to take effect. *I love you,* she thought, not for the first time as she drifted off to sleep. *I love you, I love you, I love you.*

3

A series of text messages from Sol woke Cora before her alarm did, demanding that she "get in here" because "we are in deep shit." She sighed, allowing herself another five minutes in bed. Yes, things had gone poorly yesterday, but that didn't mean Sol was not prone to hyperbole.

Sol asked her to come to Conference Room 110, the glass-walled prison cell where yesterday's shit show had occurred. Dr. Sev was there, his demeanor much more austere than his usual *que será* approach to life, the universe, and everything. Luciana was there, too, as well as her longtime coworker and probably closest thing Luciana had to a friend, Stevie. The whole thing felt like a parent-teacher conference was imminent.

Stevie had a light brown skin tone, sharp features, and curly black hair, a person so petite she looked elfin. She looked at Cora in the way that anyone would when they were about to have an unpleasant interaction with a coworker, but with Luciana, it was more personal. Four months ago, her aunt was the closest thing Cora had to a normal friend outside of people she knew from the internet, but then came the Fremda Memo and Luciana's likely involvement, which she maintained to this day was nonexistent. It wasn't active animosity, but the comfort was gone. The trust was *definitely* gone.

"Hokay. So," said Sol, taking a seat and gesturing for everyone else to do the same.

"Am I fired?" asked Cora, speaking before thinking.

No one reacted, save Luciana, who placed a hand to her forehead.

"See, shit like that is why we are here," said Sol. "The way you handled yourself yesterday was unacceptable and unprofessional. And that shit right there—unprofessional."

"Yes, yes, I know. I'm sorry." Cora took a seat across from Sol.

"What happened?" asked Dr. Sev.

"I really wasn't feeling well yesterday," said Cora, opting for the half-truth route. "That man kept pushing, and I'd been feeling nauseous beforehand. I felt like I was going to be sick."

"Then you should have said something," said Luciana. "Don't just run out halfway through a meeting."

Cora nodded, but didn't say anything. She had clung to some resentment toward her aunt in the weeks following ET-gate, but lately she'd wanted to figure out how to repair the rift in their relationship. Still, how to even begin to have that conversation? She more or less knew *what* the problem was, but had no clue how to fix it, and now sure as hell wasn't the time.

"I'm *trying* to work with this situation," said Sol. "The president granted you top-secret clearance because Scio won't communicate unless it's through you. Fine, we understand that, but that doesn't mean anything if Scio won't communicate *period*. That combined with a rash of unprofessional behavior—"

"It makes it hard to continue justifying the level of clearance that you have," said Dr. Sev, saving Cora from however callously Sol was about to phrase the exact same thing. "It was quite the task to convince the powers that be to give you clearance at all."

"I understand."

"This keeps happening, you're out," said Sol flatly.

"I understand."

Sol fiddled with his lanyard and shrugged. "So, on a related note, in part because of Scio's increasing reluctance to communicate with us, the DOD has recommended to President Cheney that the official information release be pushed back. Again."

Dr. Sev sighed, and Cora caught that the likely reason for his serious mood wasn't so much her personally as it was the whole situation. "When we asked what the reason was for the info release being delayed, the administration came back that a lack of communication does not inspire confidence, and they are concerned that the information they have may not be accurate."

"In effect," said Stevie, "they're being pissy because Scio won't talk to them."

Cora leaned back in her seat. "What is it they want?"

Everyone looked at each other uncomfortably, as if hoping someone else would be the one to deliver the unhappy news. Finally, Luciana bit the bullet. "They want the DOD to take over the whole operation," she said.

Cora's face went slack. "Why?"

"Because these bleeding-heart liberals over here don't take a firm hand with the multidimensional cyborgs," said Sol, nodding to Stevie, Luciana, and Dr. Sev.

"The president wants the military to oversee everything from now on," said Dr. Sev. "They are looking for any reason to do so."

"That's why Brigadier General Porter was being so . . . pushy," said Luciana.

"Fuck no," said Cora. "If the issue is Scio not talking to them, the military taking over is *not* going to help matters. Hell, if they do take over, he might—"

"He might what?" said Sol, now on alert.

"He might just *leave*," said Cora. "You know how he feels about 'militarists.' If they walk in and say, 'Hey, this is a military operation now,' he'll just say, 'Okay, cool, bye!'"

Dr. Sev rubbed his hand up his face, parking it on his perfectly bald head. "Are you sure about that?"

"Well, we haven't discussed this exact scenario, but I'm fairly confident that's how he'll feel."

"Then they need to hear it from him," said Sol.

"But why? Why would they think the DOD taking over would be a good idea?"

At this, Dr. Sev looked livid, an expression that seemed completely foreign on him. Luciana sighed. "Based on what we have learned through our friends at the CIA"—she nodded begrudgingly to Sol—"it really boils down to politics. The Cheney administration needs to put on a big-man act in order to compete with the Third Party."

"Like remember in the '90s how everyone was like, 'Vote for me, I'll be tough on crime'?" said Sol. "Well, it's like that, but now it's 'Vote for me, I'll be tough on aliens.'"

If there was any color left in Cora's face, it was gone now. "But . . . they don't even know what they're dealing with?"

Sol snorted. "This is America. When has that ever stopped us? Let me put it this way; it traveled up the line to the secretary of defense, whom you'll remember you had a little tête-à-tête with back at NORAD, not only that Scio figured out English in the space of less than a month but that Obelus learned it in even less time."

"More noteworthy," added Stevie, "that Obelus was able to break into enough levels of encrypted correspondence that he was able to locate a CIA caravan with basically no paper trail."

Cora suppressed a shudder at the memory of that caravan. Four CIA agents had been tasked with transporting Cora and the Fremdan Genome, a collection of what Ampersand had described as "genetic material," which turned out to be a living, breathing alien *person,* to an undisclosed location, but Obelus had found them before they got there. Cora and the Genome had been the only ones to make it out alive.

"What does that have to do with defense?" she asked, shaking the memory off.

Again, that awkward silence, like her hamster had died but no one wanted to break it to her.

"Let me put it this way," said Luciana. "They are not thinking in terms of *defense.*"

It took Cora a moment to see what Luciana was getting at. "Oh my God."

"What Obelus did, while terrifying, could potentially be repurposed by the military," said Dr. Sev.

Sol chuckled humorlessly, adding, "If an ETI can break into NORAD after following a trail of badly encrypted emails, an ETI can probably find bin Laden."

Cora didn't react, stunned that it was being floated anywhere, at any level of government, that the Fremda group could be used for military purposes. But wasn't it more naive to be surprised? Of course they were thinking like that. *This is America.* Besides, she couldn't say she hadn't had thoughts like that. Not "find and kill bin Laden," exactly, but if Ampersand put his mind to it, he could do some terrifying things, and he was in no way beholden to human scruples.

But by that same token, he could also do some good things. Great things, even. How many of humanity's problems could be solved by technologies it was well within his capacity to innovate?

But, of course, extrajudicial killing would be the first thing they'd think of, wouldn't it?

Cora looked at Sol. "What do you think?"

"Well, I would love to know where bin Laden is. I would love to personally shove my foot down his throat and put it out the other side."

"And I think . . ." Luciana shook her head, momentarily at a loss for words. "I think Scio wouldn't agree to it. But if he did, something about the U.S. military repurposing alien tech to decide who lives and who dies doesn't sit right with me."

"That's not a road any of us want to go down," said Dr. Sev. Sol's expression indicated to Cora that he was totally humoring the idea of going down that road.

"But why is it the DOD that's being loudest?" asked Cora. "If Cheney's so desperate for a political win, can't you just ask him to, like, cure AIDS or something?"

Luciana's, Dr. Sev's, and Stevie's eyes all popped as if they hadn't considered that but, my, what a marvelous idea! Sol, predictably, ignored it. "Well, you know what, the CDC is the one agency that doesn't seem to really have any interest in getting in on this. But the Cheney administration is in a tailspin. They're being threatened in a *primary*. An incumbent has never lost a presidential primary before. So they are desperate, and there are those within the administration putting out feelers on how to turn these incredibly powerful ETIs into an asset. And, of course, the best and most obvious way to do that is through the military, and they are chomping at the bit to get in here. So if you really think that's a bad idea then you need your buddy to get out here in person in front of Brigadier General Porter, and explain why."

· · · · ·

"*I will not.*"

Cora released an exasperated sigh. As time went by, he'd only gotten more obstinate about face-to-face meetings, even though she'd made the trek to the other side of the complex to ask him in person. When she (or anyone) entered his lair, it involved a labyrinthine level of bureaucracy, several key cards and a fingerprint scanner, and even some amount of paperwork. It was even worse when Ampersand went in and out. Perhaps that was why he was being so difficult; the simple act of existing was, for him, a huge pain in the ass.

"No one here wants you to work with the military," she said. "But it's possible the military might take the whole thing over, and they might try to . . . push you to do some of their dirty work for them."

"*I would not.*" He wasn't really looking at her, parked on the floor as he usually was, loafing like a cat and focusing on nothing in particular. He wasn't doing nothing; whenever he had that distant, unfocused look it meant he was focusing on something within his internal systems, his own projects, a domain that no human may enter.

"I *know* that. But you need to meet with this general, come physically tell him why you won't do it."

"*You are perfectly capable of relaying my message in my absence.*"

"That only works up to a point; as far as they're concerned, I could be making it all up. They need you to be there *some* of the time to make sure that I am truthfully relaying what you're saying."

"*I have no interest in direct engagement with militarists.*"

"I know that, but I need you to physically get in front of them and tell them."

The light of his eyes coagulated, pooling like droplets of glowing orange oil in black water until they combined into luminous focus.

She crouched down to his eye level. "Look, to be honest, I'm not really worried about their bureaucratic bullshit, but I am worried they might decide I'm not necessary. If you won't talk to them whether I'm here or not, then I'm extraneous. I know I don't technically need to work here in order to interact with you, but . . . the economy's in free fall, we're heading into a depression, I need this job. And at least as long as I'm here, that gives both of us more bargaining power. I'd rather be here if you need me."

Ampersand seemed to consider this, the focus in his eyes pulsing ever so slightly. Then, he rose to his feet. "*What will assuage them?*"

"Aside from having this conversation in person where you tell them in no uncertain terms that there is absolutely no way you will work with the military, they have a list of things they say they need to run by you before they can do an official information release. In person. As a show of good faith."

He approached her in that slow, almost snakelike way that he moved, his attention rerouting from his internal world to the real world. She'd told him a while ago he didn't need to ask permission to touch her anymore—at this point their relationship didn't warrant that level of formality. He raised a finger, placing it on her neck and grazing it upward along her skin, a little too gently. She flinched and giggled. "Sorry, that tickles."

She felt a similar sensation from the other side of her neck—a surprise attack from his other hand, and she giggled and shied away from him. She started to correct him, but then realized he was doing it on purpose. This was him being *playful*. She shot an eye at the security camera in the corner, dark and barely visible, but its lens shining at her. She hoped there was no one on the other side of that camera who could see this.

"You are anxious about the situation. Would it lessen your anxiety if I meet with them?"

"Yes."

"If you wish it, dear one," he said, pulling his arms back into his neutral posture. *"For you. Not for them."*

January 18, 2008

HOUSE COMMITTEE JOINS JANO MIRANDA TO TALK "PERSONHOOD THIRD OPTION"

WASHINGTON—The House Committee on Science, Space, and Technology Chair Carolyn Wang (D-WA) and Vice Chair Ryan Mellin (R-GA) joined Jano Miranda of the Aristotle Institute for Human Rights to discuss the Select Committee's work. Established in 2007 as part of Hillsdale College, the Aristotle Institute is committed to "combining philosophy and technology to create a constructive debate and authentic dialogue in order to meaningfully outline what it means to be human, and how we should define personhood in the 21st Century."

The Chair and Vice Chair spoke about options regarding the potential legal status of autonomous extraterrestrial intelligences, and the recent recommendations outlining a special set of legal standing and personhood rights for potential nonhuman intelligences as they might differ from rights for humans.

4

"Calm yourself."

"Sorry."

She took a deep breath and pushed herself closer to him. It had been a couple of weeks, and what was at first exciting had become routine. Ampersand would arrive around 10:00 P.M. and stay with Cora until she slept. She used the opportunity to turn it into an information exchange, walking him through certain aspects of human culture, and in turn, he answered her questions about life, the universe, and everything, and sometimes he wasn't even frustratingly coy about it. It felt like a relationship. A *friendship* form of relationship, of course. A friendship-relationship. Yes.

He had her all but pinned up next to the wall as he always did, his body on one side of her and one hand on the other. She glanced at that hand, arguably the most alien thing about him, mere inches from her face, and once again was struck by the thought that this was not normal, and she really should not be okay with this. The four digits on the top were structured more like human fingers, with the two on the bottom on either side; the "thumbs" bore a striking resemblance to the forelimbs of a spider. His fingers weren't attached with dozens of metacarpals but seemed to her more like hydraulics attached at a ball joint, held together up to the "knuckles" with a film that looked like a layer of skin rather than a meaty palm as seen in humans. It should be horrifying, but it wasn't. Maybe humans could get used to anything with enough time.

"You can sedate me whenever you want."

"You will sleep tonight without sedatives."

Cora's eyes shot open. The light sedative he'd been using every night put her into such a deep sleep she didn't dream at all, let alone have nightmares. "Oh."

Sleep without sedatives. She hadn't had nightmares in weeks because she hadn't slept without sedatives in weeks. Now it was time to go back to normal, and that scared her a little bit. Shouldn't that be good, though? Why be scared of normal sleep? Wasn't she *more* vulnerable when he sedated her? This was the same being, the same body, that had captured human beings (including her) and played with them like toys, and here he was running the tips of his fingers over her head trying to soothe her, a stack of pillows she'd pillaged from her mom's house propping up his giant head, his body all but cocooning hers. And yet *sleep* was the intimidating thing in this scenario?

"*Sleep now, dear one.*"

She felt a warmth in her chest at the sound of his pet name for her, what he called a *hypocorism.* "Do you ever sleep?"

"*I sleep.*"

"When?"

"*When I must.*"

She nodded and closed her eyes. What the hell was wrong with her? She was half-naked in bed with a thousand-year-old (or 650-year-old, depending on how you measured time), eight-and-a-half-foot-tall alien cyborg, and the thing she was afraid of in this situation was the act of going to *sleep*?

She released a breath, trying to push out her anxiety with it. Going off sedatives was inevitable. Nightmares were a part of life. This was fine. This was necessary to figuring out a permanent solution. "Okay . . . just . . . don't make me stay in it."

"*I don't understand your meaning.*"

"I mean, don't leave me alone in my head longer than you have to. If I'm having a nightmare, wake me up when you have the data you need."

"*I will, my dearest.*"

Her heart did a little flip. *My dearest!*

From what she could tell, amygdaline names were less "names" as humans conceived them so much as labels that had to do with one's relationship to the speaker and were very tied in with their caste system. One wasn't addressed as "Steve" or "Karen," so much as "Mom" or "bro" or "*senpai.*" At first, Ampersand had addressed her with an impersonal "*you*" or "*interpreter*," but after the dynamic fusion bonding, it was "*dear one.*" Was "*my dearest*" an upgrade?

She felt the impulse to respond, "I love yōu," because it was true. She had come to terms with that by now—*love* was the word for it, as it would be for any friend, only this friend happened not to be human. This was Aristotle's *philia,* a dispassionate virtuous love of function. Not of passion, *never* of passion. But she knew he wouldn't return the sentiment, at least not verbally, and that would ruin the moment. Instead, she closed her eyes and said, "Thank you."

There was no shame in this. No, people would not understand, but they didn't know and did not need to. After all, it wasn't like they were fucking.

It wouldn't be the worst thing in the world.

Her eyes shot open at the thought, a thought she had been trying really very hard not to have. But really, it was just a thought, not a terrible one, it wasn't like they were going to act on it. The thought didn't send any warm flush between her legs, didn't make her cheeks grow hot.

But still, it wouldn't be the worst thing in the world.

How would that even work?

Humans are inventive. You've said it yourself. Humans will fuck anything.

This thought should be revolting, but now that she was beginning to humor it, she couldn't help but think, it wouldn't be the worst thing in the world. He'd be gentle, he'd be considerate, he'd likely be a quick study. Unlike Bill or Frank or Chad, he wouldn't use her, he wouldn't be centering his own pleasure.

Brain, brain, please, I am begging you, stop these thoughts please stop stop stop.

It wouldn't be the worst thing in the world.

Where the hell are these thoughts coming from?

"*You are agitated.*"

"No . . ." Her lie was so bad, even a space alien wouldn't be convinced by it.

"*You are anxious.*"

Okay. Strange how speaking for him and effectively being the diplomat for his words hadn't made speaking diplomatically *to* him any easier. "I'm just thinking about, um . . ."

Getting fucked by a space monster.

She winced. "You're not doing anything wrong, I'm not made uncomfortable by *you,* but the idea of . . ." She dared a glimpse down her body, how close they were, the way his arm had her tucked near him like she was an egg he was incubating. "Someone seeing us like this. I don't think they'd understand. I guess I have some shame at the idea."

"*I understand.*"

She drew into herself, worried she might have offended him. "Please, don't think I don't like being with you. I do, but it's . . ."

"*I have shame, as well.*"

Her eyebrows popped, and she looked up at him as he raised his head so he could look down at her with his big almond eyes. Those beautiful amber gems that glowed softly in the dim light filtering in from the parking lot outside. She never would have imagined he would admit to experiencing something so, well, Catholic as "shame." "What are you ashamed of?"

"*I desire you.*"

At this, she felt like she might implode, like her eyeballs were sinking back into her sockets to avoid the conversation, her eyelids trying to slink off her skull. "What . . . what do you mean?"

"*I desire to know you.*"

"Oh," she said, relaxing a little. "You mean . . . high language?"

"*Yes. I desire to know you. You are a natural, an alien, an animal, but you are my symphyle all the same.*"

She let a breath out. Okay, not *that* kind of desire, not in the human sense. Amygdalines had three forms of language—Pequod-phonemic, the spoken "common language" (and its written corollary); "network language," a variant on common that was transmitted through internal networks; and "high language," about which she knew little, only that it was a much deeper form of communication than the other two, and one that humans were completely incapable of. "You've never really explained it to me, what high language is."

He tilted his head slightly to the side, running his fingers along her hairline until they stopped at the base of her skull. "*High language isn't truly a language at all. A language is a medium, and medium is the only way humans have to communicate ideas. Spoken language is a medium,*" *written language is a medium, music is a medium. High language is the absence of medium."*

"I don't think I understand."

"A medium is not an idea. A medium is a means to communicate an idea. It is an interpretation of ideas, of concepts, of your lived experience. But through high language, my consciousness experiences your consciousness as you experience it, and vice versa. There is no medium."

She looked away from him, burying her face in her pillow to take this in. When she'd first known Ampersand, she had feared that he *could* actually read her mind, and it was only his perpetual cluelessness that eventually convinced her that he could not. But in this context, the idea that he'd actually thought about it, on some level *wanted* it, horrified her.

What could possibly disgust him more than truly knowing what it was like to be human? To exist inside *her* human body? To actually know her evil impulses, her sprawling self-loathing, her disdain for her coworkers, her embarrassing attempts at songwriting, the weird shit she (used to) masturbate to? Perhaps he had a desire to *know* her as a result of dynamic fusion bonding, but that didn't mean he really *wanted* it.

Who would?

She shuddered, tense as a cord about to snap, and she could tell that something similar was going on on the other side of the wall. "Why is that a source of shame?"

"It is the product of a diseased mind."

She relaxed her posture, confused, and looked up at him. "You mean me?"

"My mind."

"What do you mean?"

"My brain is damaged, as is yours, but mine far worse, irreparable in many regards. Within the Superorganism, there are resources to repair some forms of trauma, but no resources to repair damage as extensive as mine. In our Superorganism, I would not be suffered to live. I did not believe the attempt to fusion bond with you would succeed, but it did. If Esperas knew . . ."

"I . . ." There was a part of her that was offended. He categorized his decision to bind himself to her as the product of a sick mind?

"We are different species. It is perverse. It is bestial."

There it was, the word she'd been avoiding. She pressed her cheek into the nape of his neck. *Bestial.*

"*But this desire cannot be acted on, regardless. You are incapable of high language, so my desire to know you can only remain a hypothetical desire.*"

She didn't know why the thought was so frightening, the "absence of medium." Maybe he'd die wondering what it would be like to remove the medium between his mind and hers, but it didn't matter; it couldn't be acted upon.

Not like *her* weird impulses.

She shuddered. Ugh, if he got in her head, then he'd *see* the thoughts she'd just had, that she'd just considered . . . *whatever,* and thought, hey, maybe that wouldn't be the worst thing in the world. What would he think of that?

"At least we can't act on these . . . desires," she whispered. "Maybe that's for the best."

She tried to relax and go to sleep, tried to reassure herself of what felt like something of a consensus—that these thoughts were okay to have, because it wasn't like they could be acted on, anyway. It was for the best. But even so, as she began to doze, she got the sense that that wasn't what he wanted her to say.

5

Cora got the email for an all-hands meeting that morning at around 4:30—"ETI LEGAL STATUS CONGRESSIONAL INQUIRY." She had known this was coming for months, as had everyone at ROSA, but as with so many other concerns, it was a can kicked down the road. Sooner or later, the legal status of ETIs on Earth (and more specifically, in the United States) was going to have to be clarified, but it wasn't something anyone had particularly worried about until an idea called the Third Option started gaining traction.

It had been first pitched by a law professor named Jano Miranda, a young constitutional lawyer with a gift for public speaking. The Third Option, a proposed law that would create an entirely new category of personhood, led to the creation of the nascent Third Party, a bipartisan movement that branded itself as a "repudiation to the establishment." Miranda's advocacy for the Third Option had put his star on the map in a big way, but nobody, not even Sol, had seen the surging popularity of the Third Option becoming so relevant as to merit a congressional hearing so soon.

"It's Julian," Sol told Cora before the meeting started. "He really thinks he's got a chance against Cheney in the primary, so this is the horse he's going to ride into battle." He meant Todd Julian, the junior senator from Illinois. A libertarian-minded sort (who, regrettably, had also said nice things about Nils, which was how Cora even knew of him), Senator Julian was the biggest champion for the Third Option in the Senate.

So this meeting was a big deal. Ampersand could not do this one remotely.

With some prying, Cora talked him into going through the rigmarole of leaving his lair, out of Building 112 and into Building 127, and into the conference room, flanked by military entourage. Try as they might to stay cool and professional, the people working here, military and civilian alike, couldn't help but stare on the rare occasion that Ampersand came out, their eyes darting between the girl and the giant monster that walked behind her like he floated through water. She entered the conference room in front of him, but stopped dead when she saw who had already arrived. Luciana, Dr. Sev, and Stevie she had expected. Other amygdalines she had not.

Esperas never, *ever* came out, but there he was on the other side of the giant white room, likewise flanked by military entourage, a few of his underlings, the two propagandists, Stelo and Krias (or as Cora had nicknamed them, Woodward and Bernstein), and bringing up the rear, the Similar, Brako.

Oh no.

She felt something clawing against the metaphysical wall between her and Ampersand, like being pricked by emotional briars. Cora glared at Sol, which he duly ignored, instead calmly addressing his human coworkers. Did he not understand what a breach of trust this was? That by doing this, he was pretty much guaranteeing that Ampersand would never agree to meet with them in person again?

Those briars pricking her from the other side of the wall dug in harder, and she looked at Ampersand as some army private nervously closed the conference room door behind him. She felt the air change around him, grow thicker, his invisible defenses rising like spikes.

"*I was not told they would be here.*"

She turned to him and mouthed, "I didn't know," hoping Esperas didn't catch that. There had been a time when Ampersand had been the only one of the Fremda group with an algorithm to decode human language, but that was no longer the case. She wasn't sure if the rest of the underlings had it, but at the very least, Esperas and Brako had it, so she could no longer speak to Ampersand in confidence in front of them.

"Okay," said Sol, taking a seat at the head of the table in front of the flat-screen while everyone else sat along the length of the table. Cora was the only human in the room who stayed standing. "Everyone at State, everyone in Intelligence, and everyone in DHHS agrees that any legislation surrounding ETI personhood directly affects you, and therefore you need to be a part of these discussions. First and foremost, our two group leaders—Esperas, Scio—do you understand what is being discussed in the upcoming hearings?"

Esperas took a moment, then responded in Pequod-phonemic, a translation appearing on the flat-screen behind Sol:

[The debate is between two political ideologies, one of which seeks to grant exoterran intelligent individual beings rights equivalent to a human, one which seeks to grant exoterran intelligent individual beings a restricted set of rights.]

"Good. Scio, do you understand what is being debated?"

Something was wrong. Something was very wrong. She could feel it, both through the wall between them and through basic human intuition.

"*I was not told Esperas would be here.*"

"He understands," she said.

"Okay, so with that in mind, we need to know where you stand on the issue."

Both Esperas and Brako were watching Ampersand now. They could tell something was wrong, even if none of the other humans in the room picked up on it. Esperas spoke, and the flat-screen translated:

[My stance remains one of noninvolvement. The humans will choose laws which are best for them. I do not seek to sway your lawmakers one way or the other.]

"Okay," said Sol, looking at Cora. "Rebuttal?"

"*I was not told Esperas would be here. He can see the disease.*"

She'd never seen Ampersand like this, never felt his emotions so thoroughly override his self-control. She tried to stay focused, but she was having a hard time staying put together herself. He wasn't answering Sol's questions, so it was on her to come up with an answer.

"Scio feels that, among other things, he should have the right to control his own space. The problem with the Third Option is that it would preclude, among other things, the ability to own property, the ability to control wealth, the ability to participate in any kind of civic activity. He'd effectively have to have a human chaperone in order to stay within the United States, and if the United States decides that's how to deal with ETIs, most other countries will follow suit."

"So he opposes the Third Option."

"Correct." She glanced at Ampersand, standing behind her with that slight sway. It was barely an inch in either direction, but noticeable to her and probably blindingly noticeable to Esperas. She had to get him out of here.

"So we have one side that doesn't care, and one side that opposes the Third Option," said Sol. "If we have one indifferent, and one in opposition, that tilts to me that we are in opposition."

"I'm in opposition," said Stevie, more confident than Cora had ever seen her.

"I'm in opposition, too," said Luciana.

"I . . . respect Esperas's stance," said Dr. Sev. "I think it is something to consider, that ultimately what our laws do is irrelevant to them. However, my concern is that restriction of rights, any restriction of rights, carries with it the potential for abuse. I am in opposition."

"To state the obvious," said Luciana, "they are never going to pass full personhood for ETIs as long as they don't know what they're dealing with. Do we know why they keep kicking back the official information release deadline?"

"I honestly don't," said Sol.

"Sooner or later, the public has to learn what they're dealing with," said Luciana. "Have we learned nothing from the last three months?"

The room quieted. Esperas and the others stayed stone still, all but Ampersand. An inch to the left, pause, an inch to the right, and on and on. Cora wanted to say something to soothe him, but there was nothing she could do that everyone in the room wouldn't see.

"We need to give them legal names," said Stevie. "All of them. That's the first step. The release could happen any day now, we can't introduce them to the world with Esperanto code names."

"You've never given a thought to what their legal names would be?" asked Cora.

Dr. Sev leaned back in his chair. "Every human name correlates to some history, some ethnicity. There isn't a single name we could give them that doesn't come with some implication. Imagine the optics of naming one of them Christopher Goodman in a country with a history of forcing the indigenous people to adopt 'Christian' names in order to appear more 'civilized.'"

"They can see. I can't sleep. The Similar will find us. They will not suffer my disease. They will kill us."

"I guess we could do something shitty and obvious like name them after U.S. presidents, not like we could piss people off more than we already have," said Sol.

"But anything else is going to stick out, too," said Luciana. "African names, Indian names, that's appropriation. Chinese names, that's—"

"Fallen American Empire," said Sol. "Bad idea. Anything that 'sounds' foreign to WASPy American ears is a bad idea."

"I can't sleep. They will find us. They will kill us."

Cora tried to hold her breath, clenching and unclenching her fists. She was beginning to sway, too.

"Maybe we should incorporate their Esperanto names," said Stevie. "Keep it simple."

"So, what, 'Scio . . . McGillicuddy'?" Sol snorted.

"Esperanto still comes with implications," said Dr. Sev. "Esperanto is completely based on European languages. It was invented by a Polish man."

"They can see, they can see my disease."

"How about Xethorp?" chuckled Sol. He was the only one laughing.

"This isn't funny anymore," said Luciana. "They need advocacy. *Real* advocacy."

Cora's eyes were watering. She didn't think she could keep her breath quiet much longer. She looked at Brako, and for an instant, she saw Obelus in his place. *We have to get out of here! They'll kill us!*

"I'd like . . . He'd like to be dismissed," Cora managed.

"Is it really more important to you that we hide every state secret than do the work we're supposed to do?" asked Luciana, either not hearing her or ignoring her.

"My job is to gather intelligence and report it back to my agency," said Sol. "My job has fuck all to do with alien advocacy."

Then, the dam broke. Not Ampersand, not Esperas or Brako, not even Cora, but Woodward and Bernstein, the two propagandists. They stepped forward with a short spurt of Pequod-phonemic, translating on the flat-screen:

[ASYLUM.]

That was when all hell broke loose. Ampersand swayed so hard he nearly hit the wall. Every human in the room started talking over each other at once. Esperas and Brako turned their attention from Ampersand to the two propagandists, who broke away from the rest of the underlings. The pair moved to the other side of the room, catty-corner from Esperas and Brako, who were bobbing their heads in bewilderment. More Pequod-phonemic screeching, *loud* Pequod-phonemic screeching:

[ASYLUM. ASYLUM. ASYLUM. ASYLUM.]

Then it became clear what was happening; this wasn't a coordinated request, this was a rebellion. None of the Fremda group except for Esperas and Ampersand were supposed to communicate with humans, but Woodward and Bernstein had apparently decided enough was enough; it was time to break out of their rigid caste system.

[ASYLUM. ASYLUM. ASYLUM.]

Stevie was on her feet in a second, ushering the two toward the door nearest to them. All of this happened so quickly that no one had noticed Ampersand's initial stumble, but everyone saw him collapse onto the floor.

[ASYLUM. ASYLUM. ASYLUM.]

Cora jumped in front of him as he struggled to stand back up, straining like a four-hundred-pound bird that had been shot out of the sky. She grabbed the sides of his head below his eyes, tilted his face toward hers.

[ASYLUM. ASYLUM.]

The screeching continued even after Woodward and Bernstein had been ushered into the hallway. Brako and Esperas turned their attention to Ampersand. Esperas moved behind Brako, and spoke:

[That one is diseased. That one is dangerous.]

"Come on, we have to get you out of here," said Cora, straining to lift Ampersand's head up in the hope it would help him stand. "Someone open the door!"

Everyone stared at her, dumb, even their military escorts, until Luciana leaped to her feet and opened the door directly behind Ampersand. Cora grabbed him by his wrists and pulled him toward the open door. Out of the corner of her eye she saw Brako make a move toward them, then felt a forceful electromagnetic blast, one that shielded her but hit Brako, shoving him against the opposite wall and pushed him right through the drywall.

By now, Ampersand was coherent enough to move, but not coherent enough to do much else. He was trying to slip into invisibility as Cora dragged him down the hall, bewildered humans gawping as patches of his body slipped in and out of invisibility, sliding all over him like splotches of paint.

The Similar wasn't following them, even if half the Department of Health and Human Services was, alongside their dopey military escort. She made it to the door of his lair, bypassing most of the usual rituals. First the door key card. She could do this, she could hold it together. Second door, thumbprint. Fuck the fucking paperwork, the bureaucrats could handle that. Then they made it inside, and she closed the door behind them.

"Take us out of here!"

Out of the carapace on his back slid the liquid metal casing that he used to transport himself within the Earth's lower atmosphere. It slid over him as he lowered himself to the floor, pulling her close as he lowered into a crouch, covering them both in the liquid metal and in darkness.

Then she opened her eyes, and they were on the floor of her bedroom, the setting sun sending bright red rays through the dust that hung in the air. She took in a loud gasp of air, pushing Ampersand off her. The gasp, the loud noise, frightened him, she could feel it.

"Come on, it's okay," she said. "Get on the bed, it's okay."

He did as she said, but only just. He didn't pull into his neat little roost like he usually did, but instead sprawled, curled away from her like an injured falcon backed into a corner, ready for a fight. His massive consciousness, the half-organic thing that controlled the unfathomably complicated machine of his body, had utterly collapsed in on itself.

The wall wasn't thick at the moment, but it wasn't thin, either. She sat down on the bed next to him, and felt an instinct prick her from the other side of the wall. *Danger! Danger! Alien monster!* His fingers curled, ready to attack.

"It's okay," she said, her voice trembling. "You're safe. It's me. You're in my apartment."

Those eyes didn't feel like the eyes of an intelligent being. They felt like the eyes of an animal. A prey animal looking at a predator. *Monster. Flesh-eater. Pugilist. Militarist. Flesh-eater. Don't eat me, don't eat me, don't eat me!*

"It's me," she said, trying to keep her breathing steady so she wouldn't slip into panic with him. "It's me. You're safe with me."

She closed her eyes to steady herself, to gain some perspective, hoping that her attempts to calm herself might act as a flotation device for the drowning man. "You need to sleep."

She didn't know how she knew this. It wasn't just his odd, seemingly random assertions, "*I can't sleep, they'll kill me.*" It wasn't just the decades of trauma piling onto each other that had triggered this, it was exhaustion.

Do you ever sleep?

I sleep.

When?

When I must.

He needed sleep, same as any living thing did, but he didn't. He had to stay vigilant. Earth was too dangerous, too wild, too full of terrors for him to allow himself to sleep.

"You need to sleep," she said. "You'll be safe, I'll watch over you."

There was a war going on in there, the prey animal afraid for its life against the intelligent being that knew he had pushed himself too far for too long and had collapsed into exhaustion. He would die if he didn't sleep. Cora hugged herself, and sat down on the floor, giving him space. "Hey Jude, don't make it bad," she sang, leaning against the side of the bed. She closed her eyes, focusing on the lyrics, focusing inward. "Take a sad song, and make it better . . ."

He didn't understand music, not really. Even the meaning of most lyrics was lost on him, but it wasn't really meant for him; it soothed her, it helped her be the flotation device he could latch onto.

It took her several hours, the involvement of her guitar, and several repetitions of the Beatles' kindest and gentlest repertoire, but eventually, she convinced him to sleep. By this point, it was long past dark, and her phone was still at work. No one had come knocking, so however he'd hacked the surveillance in his lair must have convinced the powers that be she was still in there with him.

Ampersand hadn't made room for her on the bed except for a small sliver barely big enough to sit on. But the moment he closed his eyes, the moment she felt him slip from consciousness, she felt a connection sever. A dull thrum of terror she'd been feeling for months, ever since he'd bonded himself to her, had desisted when he fell asleep.

That dull thrum of terror wasn't hers. It had never been hers. It was his.

She pulled a couple of pillows and the comforter down onto the floor with her. All this time, she had been worried about how her post-traumatic symptoms were affecting him, it had never occurred to her that it might work the other way around. How much of her symptoms came from him?

No, not all of it. Not even most of it, that much she could tell. The feeling of being out of place in her own body, the body that had betrayed her by giving in to such violence when Obelus had skewered her, that trauma belonged to her. But that wasn't all there was to it.

We've been going about this all wrong.

Why had it taken her so long to see it? It was ironic that Sol and the others were even bothering to discuss the personhood issue at all. They didn't see the Fremda group as people, victims of unimaginable traumas; they saw them as automatons to be mined for intelligence, as political problems that needed solving. Then there was the issue of their caste system—none but Ampersand and Esperas may speak to the human, and Esperas was the gatekeeper to all the rest of the group. But the group was clearly unhappy. The group was suffering. The ones that were not committing ritualistic suicide were now in open rebellion. While she could advise the well-intentioned bureaucrats of the U.S. government, she couldn't help the Fremda group if Esperas was keeping them under lock and key.

But she *could* help Ampersand.

She opened her laptop and began typing furiously. First and foremost, she had to get him away from Esperas, far away, preferably in a different country. Then they needed to create a living space he felt in control of. Cora, like so many, had taken for granted that "secret U.S. government compound" was the only place they *could* live, but there was nothing saying they had to stay there. And if Ampersand were to ask for asylum in another country, maybe the Americans would stop being such dicks about the extending-human-rights issue here.

Then they could formulate a real treatment plan, actually work toward healing. Not just for her but for both of them. He didn't know how to help himself, and the experts on amygdaline psychology were a hundred light-years away, and even then their solution was apparently "euthanize the broken one." But he was not a hundred light-years away, he was on Earth—a planet of belligerent, violent flesh-eaters, yes, but compassionate, empathetic problem solvers, too. Trial and error, probably lots of trial and error. But they would figure something out.

At last, she was beginning to see a way out of this. *It will get better,* she thought. *We will find a way to make you safe, and then we'll make it better.*

6

Cora awoke with a sensation of pure terror, her heart pounding and the back of her throat on fire. It didn't feel like the nightmares, it was more like she'd had her mind wrung out like a washcloth before being released from the prison of the subconscious. This was being thrown into a black hole of icy water, miles from shore, swirled in its maelstrom of terror and loss, unable to see anything, unable to feel anything but fear and ice.

It only lasted a few seconds before she was fully awake, still on the floor, fighting her way out of her duvet. She shot up, her skin cold and clammy, and looked over the edge of her bed.

Ampersand's eyes were open, his head jerking and bumping against the wall as if he didn't even realize there was a wall there. She hopped up next to him on the bed, placed her hands on the shell of his back, and closed her eyes, trying to get a bead on what was going on in his head, but only sensed more chaos.

"It's okay, you're with me," she said. "You're safe, you're with me."

It was here that she became acutely aware that something was very wrong, and not in the way it was yesterday during the meeting. Something was existentially wrong. Still moving with jolting, halted movements, he stood up on shaking legs, pushing past her like she wasn't even there.

"Ampersand," she said. "What's going on?"

He moved to the window, and in a flash, the metal edges surrounding the glass glowed. He removed the window altogether, pulling it inside and dropping it to the floor. Then he wormed himself outside and up toward the roof.

Cora didn't waste an instant, tearing out of her apartment and to the stairwell that led to the roof. It was barricaded by an emergency exit that promised an alarm if breached, but she knew it was broken, as her frat bro neighbors used the roof constantly to get high. She burst through the emergency exit onto the roof, looked around, and had she been capable of feeling relief in that moment, she might have felt it to see Ampersand there, carelessly visible for any and all to see, his gaze to the heavens. But she could sense through the wall that there was no relief, that they would never experience relief again.

It would all be over soon.

She looked in the direction he was looking, and within seconds, the sky opened. It was small at first, blinking like the blip of a shooting star, but it expanded, a bright light like a hole was being ripped in reality itself. It looked like how she imagined a nuclear blast might appear if it went off in the sky, the night still black but the light brightening the landscape like an outdoor floodlight. But she could sense it was much farther away and much larger than a nuclear blast. It was already the size of Jupiter. A thousand Jupiters. It was already the size of the sun, a hundred suns. Her simple, human self wanted to ask, "What is that?" But through the wall she could feel the answer: *I don't know.*

"We have to get out of here," she said, grabbing his arm and tugging it. He didn't move, and she found she could sense what was happening. This was a burst of energy, far away but inescapable, faster than sound, faster than thought. This was a supernova, a blast of energy so powerful that nothing in the solar system could possibly escape it. It would mow through everything—first Jupiter, then the outer planets, then every asteroid, then Mars, then Earth, then the inner planets, and finally, it would obliterate the sun. There would be nothing, and even if they moved right this second, nothing on Earth, human or alien, was physically capable of escaping this.

Then, as quickly as the tear in reality had opened, it receded into itself, the energy pulling back into its concentrated mass, an inverse big bang. The light dimmed, and then it disappeared.

She clung to him tighter. "Are we going to die?"

"*I don't know.*"

She actually did feel something like relief to see that he was still capable of speech. "Ampersand, please, what was that?"

"*A large release of energy.*"

"Where was it?"

"*The origin of the blast is approximately forty-four light-minutes away.*"

"There was no way we were going to escape it," she said, eyes still skyward, her retinas burning in the spot where that light had been.

"*I don't see the shock wave anymore. Whatever caused the blast reabsorbed the energy back into itself.*"

He finally moved, and she saw that some of the characteristic luminescence had returned to his eyes, that he was able to focus. He was swaying a little, not dissimilar from the way he had been moving yesterday. She moved in front of him, grabbed both of his forearms in an attempt to steady him. He was so big and so heavy, she hardly had any effect on him at all. She held back from asking where it came from, already knowing the answer: *I don't know.*

Now that the buzzing in her mind had calmed, now that she was out of the maelstrom of ice, she came back to reality, the reality in which they had just up and left ROSA yesterday without notice and in chaos. The reality in which they weren't the only ones to have seen the light in the sky.

She remembered the resolution she'd made before she'd gone to sleep, that they needed to get out of the country, away from Esperas, away from the U.S. government. She still believed it necessary, but that wasn't the responsible thing to do right this second. The world would be freaking out, and with good reason. Their great escape would have to wait.

"We have to go back to the security complex," she said, looking up at him urgently. "We have to tell them what we know."

He hesitated, then summoned his semiautonomous plate, turning her around, pulling her back toward him, and enveloping both of them in liquid metal.

· · · · ·

The next thing she was aware of was a banging sound, one that sounded like a human fist on a door. She opened her eyes, unfolding her limbs as the sleek liquid metal of Ampersand's autonomous plate slid back up under the carapace on his back. She'd barely gotten her bearings before the door swung open, both of them standing there stupidly like they'd been caught making out under the bleachers, and someone she didn't recognize stared both of them down angrily. Not ROSA, not even one of Sol's underlings—this guy was military, and he had about half a dozen other goons behind him.

"This is a breach of our agreement," she snapped before Ampersand could say anything. Normally, he would be beyond furious about this sort of thing, but right now, she could sense that the army breaking the agreement they had made with regard to his privacy was well below his bar of low priorities.

"We haven't gotten any response from you in hours," said the man, a guy in a soldier's uniform with a name tag that read Bishansky. An army corporal, from what Cora could tell. Of course the government had retained the right to bust into his space in an emergency, which, in fairness, this totally was. But that agreement had been made with ROSA, not with the army.

"Something just happened outside. Something big. A bright light. Does he know what happened?"

"Yes."

"How does he know?"

"He has drones." She turned to look at Ampersand, who was standing about three feet behind her, his body in profile and his head turned toward them in a half-antagonistic stance. Good. He could not afford to look weak right now.

"Is it alien?" asked Bishansky, his voice cracking. His soldier's veneer was slipping. He was afraid.

She took a breath, and when Ampersand didn't answer, she said, "He doesn't know, but probably. I need a moment to brief with him."

"Kaplan is on his way," said Bishansky. "All-hands meeting in fifteen."

"I'll do my job, but he's not going out there. It was a breach of agreement that you put him in a room with Brako and Esperas without warning him. He'll speak through me, but he's staying in here."

The muscles in Bishansky's jaw twitched, and he turned to leave. He tried to slam the door, but it was a heavy hydraulic thing incapable of being slammed. When the door latched, Cora let out a long breath and turned to face him. His posture relaxed, and his head drooped in a way that felt almost human. "Fifteen minutes," she said.

"*He did this. He is alive. He did this.*"

"Obelus?" she said on reflex.

"*He did this. He is alive. He was gone, he was dead, I felt it.*"

"Obelus?" she repeated, her voice firmer.

"*Not Obelus.*"

Why had her mind even gone there? Obelus was dead. She had *watched* him die. She racked her brain. Čefo had been his only other living symphyle she knew of, with the rest dying in the Fremdan genetic purge. Meaning that, excepting Cora, all his symphyles were dead.

Then she remembered that her math wasn't quite right. Before Obelus had died, and before he had fusion bonded with Cora, Ampersand had mentioned having had *seven* symphyles during his life, of which two, including Obelus, still lived. Now Obelus was dead, but presumably, the seventh was not.

She put her hands on the bottom of his head, where his "jaw" would be if he had one, bent him down to face her. "You mean . . . Your last living symphyle?"

"*He did this. He is alive. He was gone. I felt it as the blast hit. He was the blast.*"

"Ampersand," she said, trying to shake him and failing. It was like trying to shake a boulder. "What the hell are you talking about?"

"*Sending electromagnetic waves through space folds is a technology we have had for generations, but sending matter through the fold, that has never been accomplished in volumes greater than a few atoms. To send matter that large through a space fold, theoretically possible but far too dangerous to ever test. It would require far too much energy. He ceased to exist. I felt it, I felt him die. You felt it, too.*"

"I did," she said, now understanding her experience that was not quite a nightmare but something like it. His last still-living symphyle had ceased to exist when he folded space. It had felt like his death to Ampersand, and that feeling had been so intense, it crashed through his walls and went straight into her. But then they reappeared on the other side of the fold, once again made whole. Once again still alive.

"That's never been done before?" she breathed. "Ever, in the history of your civilization?"

"*To my knowledge, no.*"

"He's here."

"*Yes.*"

"For you?"

"*I don't know.*"

· · · · ·

Cora was the last to enter the all-hands meeting. The flat-screen was turned to CNN, on which a visibly shaken talking head was speculating on the bright light that had glowed for a few seconds and then stopped around 3:20 A.M. PST.

Luciana, who had one of the longer commutes all the way from Anaheim, was not in yet, but Sol was there, as were Dr. Sev, Stevie, several people who she assumed were CIA, and Brigadier General Porter. He was the only one who didn't look at her when she entered.

"Where is he?" asked Sol, muting the flat-screen.

"He isn't coming," she said.

"Why not?"

"Because you put him in a room with Brako and Esperas without warning him. You can talk to him through me, but he isn't coming out here."

"For how long?" asked Sol.

"Does it matter?"

"Yes, it matters."

"Indefinitely, then."

Sol's shoulders heaved in a full-body sigh, and she caught the two other CIA guys giving him hard looks.

"What was it?" asked Porter, directing the question to Sol, not Cora. Sol, for his part, looked at her, raising his eyebrows in request of a response.

"It was an energy burst," said Cora, "caused by a hole being ripped in space."

"An energy burst," Porter repeated.

"Effectively, we witnessed a miniature supernova. But, and I'm guessing human scientists can confirm this, the energy was pulled back into the . . . let's say 'hole' from whence it came."

"Are we in any danger?" asked Sol.

"From the energy burst, no, I don't think so. We would have if it had kept expanding, but something pulled it back. Some incredibly intense force, like a black hole."

"Was it alien?" asked Porter, finally deigning to look at her. She was beginning to see that it was Porter, not Sol and certainly not Dr. Sev, who was in charge here.

"Yes, it was almost certainly alien," said Cora.

"And what was the cause of this energy burst?" asked Porter.

"He says that they've known how to send electromagnetic waves through these folds in space for a while, but matter . . . while theoretically possible, he didn't know that it had ever been done. All he knows was that if it was done, it would take an incredible amount of energy to do it."

"So he's telling you that what we saw was an energy burst that resulted in a hole being ripped in folded space that was big enough for matter to pass through it," said Dr. Sev.

"That's what he thinks, yes."

Porter's expression was like the face of a cliff, and he wasn't bothering to mask the disdain he held for her. "What matter passed through the fold in space?"

"He thinks it was probably . . . a person," said Cora calmly. "Or persons."

The air became thick with sighs like steam escaping. She didn't know what they'd expected. Best case it might be a drone of some sort, and without that family connection, hell, Ampersand wouldn't even know whether or not that much was true.

"Whatever passed through this fold in space," repeated Porter, "he thinks it's definitely alive?"

"He's pretty sure."

Sol rubbed his face, ran his fingers through his wavy black hair. "Well, are we sticking with the typographical naming scheme? Asterisk?"

Nobody acknowledged the comment, or even looked at him.

"Or maybe 'at sign.' Is there a better name for at sign? Like does the at sign have a name? At sign is easier to actually draw than an asterisk."

"Is it another refugee or refugee group?" asked Porter, keeping his voice steady. "Or is it a representative of their civilization?"

"He doesn't know," she lied. "All he knows is that it's almost definitely amygdaline, not physeterine."

"Physeterine," said Porter as if he were pronouncing a foreign word.

"The name we've given to their sister species," said Dr. Sev. "*Hypothetical* sister species, I should say. There have been some witness testimonies of alien sightings that line up with how Scio describes amygdalines' 'transient sister species'—he calls them 'transients'—but we don't have any direct evidence they even exist besides hearsay."

"The technology to fold space is one only the Pequod Superorganism has, as far as he knows," said Cora. "Physeterines are interstellar, but they can't fold space."

She looked up at the television. It was midmorning on the East Coast, and the politicians of D.C. had been awake for hours. Senator Todd Julian was giving an interview. The TV sound was on mute, but the chyron at the bottom was bold and sharp:

JULIAN: "'ENOLA GAY' DROPPED ITS BOMB," DEMANDS ANSWERS FROM DHHS, CIA

"Enola Gay," repeated Sol. "I guess it's better than Asterisk."

• • • • •

Cora didn't see Ampersand for hours, nor did she hear from him. By now, she didn't even care if she was interpreting his wishes or meaning honestly to the people she was speaking to. She'd done her piece and told them as much as she knew, for all the good it might do them, which wasn't much. If they were going to get the hell out of Dodge, the time was now.

It was after 10:00 A.M. before she was able to get away, and getting back into his lair took even longer than usual, as she had to file paperwork in triplicate after it hadn't been filed last time. She half expected Ampersand to have already disappeared by the time she shut the second door to his lair behind her. He hadn't, but he was in mid-motion when she returned, and even in the dim light, she thought she saw the wisps of his semiautonomous plate disappearing back into him like liquid wings.

She shook her head, exhaustion diluting the adrenaline that had been keeping her going since she woke up. Now wasn't the time to demand where in the hell he had been. "The press has a name for them already. 'Enola Gay.'"

"*I have sent several communiqués, but none have been met with a response. I must prepare for the possibility that they are hostile.*"

She approached him, hoping that he would touch her to comfort her like he usually did, but he stayed stone still, arms drawn in.

"I'm really scared."

"*Rational.*"

"Is it possible he . . . they . . . were with Obelus?"

This seemed to shake something in him, and the defensive posture relaxed. "*That is extremely unlikely.*"

She watched him, unsure what to make of this. "You're afraid of Enola Gay."

"*I have very good reason to be afraid, as do you.*"

"Why?"

"*You see what he is capable of. But more to the point, I do not know what he wants. I do not know what would drive anyone to attempt an experiment so dangerous, so reckless.*"

"Is there anything I can do?"

"*I have been preparing for the eventuality we may encounter more hostile members of my kind.*" The carapace of his back slipped open on the left side as though his semiautonomous plating was about to ooze out, but instead he reached onto it and withdrew a device the size of a can of soda, and handed it to her. "*I have considered the possibility that you can protect yourself, in manners we have employed in the past.*"

It didn't look too dissimilar from the pill bug device the Genome had used to revive him after his own EMP had knocked him out, the one that Cora had thought of as a defibrillator. But this one had a more kidney bean shape with the same iridescent, off-white silver color and texture as amygdaline skin.

"*I designed this for human hands, in case of an emergency, the only means we have to defend ourselves against Similars, or those like myself inhabiting the body of Similars. It generates a charge pulse of the same type and frequency that Obelus employed against me.*"

"And that you used against Obelus to rescue me," she finished, turning it around in her hands.

"*Handle it carefully; pressure in the center will detonate it. It won't affect humans, but it will short out electronic devices. But you will not be able to test it.*"

"What do you mean?" she asked, careful not to touch it anywhere near the detonator.

"*If you test it, you will incapacitate me. I cannot afford to be vulnerable, not now. We do not have the luxury of testing it. If you have need of it, either it will work or it will not.*"

She turned and pointed what she assumed was the "barrel" of the pulse emitter toward the door. "So even if I aim at the correct target and it works, it might still affect you."

"*Correct. I do not know how precise the targeting will be, but I don't think it will be very precise.*"

She examined it, turning it over in her hands, and turned around to ask more questions, but saw that his semiautonomous plating was on the floor in front of him, and he was about to step onto it.

"What are you doing?"

"*I must depart. I have much to prepare. I have little time.*"

"No, please," she said, grabbing him gently by the forearm, at which he gave her a look so harsh she let go and stumbled back. He hadn't looked at her like that since they had first met. "Ampersand, please, we should leave."

"*The militarists are preoccupied. It is more beneficial that they believe me complicit and contained in this space. There is no benefit to leaving.*"

"I mean, we should leave the country altogether. We need to get out of the United States."

"*If your government feels that they cannot control my movements, that will only mean more difficulty for me. Moreover, it is likely that Enola Gay will land nearby; therefore, I cannot leave. It falls to you to make sure they don't realize when I am absent from my cell.*"

"You're never going to get *better* if—"

"*'Better' is a luxury we do not have. I must leave you now.*"

"Please," she said, her throat growing tight. "Please don't leave."

He looked at her not like he would look at his ally but an animal. Just one of the billions of flesh-eating aliens. "*The situation is changed.*"

He lowered himself onto the plate, the liquid metal slid over his body, and he disappeared. She watched the space where he had been, holding the pulse emitter like it was her bouquet after she had been dumped at the altar.

And once again, she was alone.

PART 2

LOVE HAS A NASTY HABIT OF DISAPPEARING OVERNIGHT

February 1, 2008

ARTICLE 6 Everyone has the right to recognition everywhere as a person before the law.

The Broken Seal

ETI Asylum Seekers Raise an Existential Legal Question

How do we define human rights for nonhumans?

By Nils Ortega
JANUARY 29, 2008

Hello, Friends and Strangers,

The Cheney administration has pushed back their official information release yet again. We at *The Broken Seal* have come into possession of documents that may contain an answer as to why, and, dear reader, even I was not prepared for this.

Two individuals of a species called AG-ETI ("amygdaline") have *requested* asylum. We know the two only by species code ("AG-ETI") and their numbers (30 and 31)—AG-ETI-030 and AG-ETI-031. The reason given for this is the same as it would be for any human requesting asylum; AG-ETI-030 and AG-ETI-031 "fear persecution in their home country" and specifically fear persecution "on account of at least one of five protected grounds: race, religion, nationality, political opinion, or particular social group."

Interesting.

Perhaps we can get into the deep, horrifying implications of this asylum request another day, but what we are dealing with in terms of more practical matters is the question of whether or not the Department of Homeland Security should treat AG-ETI-030 and AG-ETI-031 as legal persons. Should AG-ETI-030 and AG-ETI-031 have human rights, same as you and me? The only people who can decide *that* are the fine, upstanding folks in the United States Congress.

I do not envy the legislative body the deep existential debate that is to ensue in the weeks and months to come—it is doubtful that legislators have ever had to create laws with such profound existential implications. But here is the problem—the only thing we *know* about AG-ETI ("amygdaline") is what we can extrapolate from their name, which I'm guessing was given to them by some bureaucrat working for the Department of Health and Human Services in the 1970s.

The root *amygdal* comes from the Greek word meaning "almond." Was the name "amygdaline" inspired by physical characteristics, as animal names so often are? The word *rhinoceros,* for instance, comes from *rhinos* ("nose") and *keratos* ("horn")—literally, "nose-horn." I have seen speculation that "almond-like" means we are effectively dealing with a race of ambulatory spacefaring almonds.

But it could be more obscure than that—*amygdalin* is also the name of a naturally occurring poison found in peach pits, apple seeds, and, you guessed it, almonds. Are they somehow poisonous? It is also possible that the word refers to the *amygdala,* a part of the human brain responsible for regulating memory and emotion. This theory seems to be the most popular, concurrent with a growing number of people who believe that these alien beings are so named because they are able to influence human thought. Google searches for "amygdala hijacking" have skyrocketed in the last two weeks alone.

My intent, however, is not to speculate on what *amygdaline* means but to illustrate the sheer scope of our ignorance. How can we even begin to discuss extending human rights to nonhumans if we know absolutely *nothing* about them besides a name and a truly troubling asylum request from two of an unknown number—dozens? Hundreds? Thousands? We don't know! Perhaps if we did, our lawmakers might be able to make some informed decisions!

The issue of the asylum seekers cannot be addressed until Congress decides whether or not they should be treated as legal persons. And the issue of their legal personhood cannot be debated until we know detailed facets of the "amygdalines" and their civilization. But the Cheney administration has ostensibly decided to delay the official information release until after they decide what to do with their two "asylum seekers."

Do you see the problem here?

7

Cora jerked herself awake, turning over and smacking her pillow in exhausted frustration. The nightmares had resumed their regular schedule; sometimes they were the paralysis kind, but lately, they had been more violent. Tonight's was the rare combination of an "I have an exam I didn't study for" stress dream and being hunted by an *I Know What You Did Last Summer*–style serial killer.

Then she saw what had awakened her, a text message from Sol:

Enola Gay landfall—get in here NOW

This text was honestly better than the alternative, the one she expected to wake up to every day: *He's gone, where is he??* Every day was an exercise in bracing for the other shoe to drop when the powers that be realized he wasn't even where she told them he was.

When she got to work, everyone was running around like a bomb had gone off but no one knew where. They were in Conference Room 110 that morning, the very same window-walled room they had been in when she had first met task force brigadier general Porter. So it would figure when she arrived that at the head of the table sat, who else, task force brigadier general Porter. Since she'd dyed her hair blue last week (so she could have control over at least *one* aspect of her body and mind), he was much more prone to venomous glares.

The ROSA team, including her aunt, was there, too. "Where is Stevie?" she asked, taking a seat next to Luciana.

"She quit," Luciana whispered.

"Why?"

Luciana spoke low, so the military brass couldn't hear. "Press asked to speak to me. *New York Times.* I referred them to her, and she agreed to talk to them. DHHS said that she couldn't, so she quit."

"Where the hell is he?" came Sol's voice from behind her.

Cora gasped and stood up to face him. "You didn't say—"

"Move quickly, please!" said Sol.

She nodded and dashed past him, rounding the corner and into the other building toward Ampersand's lair, thinking, *Please be there, please be there.* More than once in the previous two weeks, she had gone into his lair to find it empty.

Owing to the nature of the emergency, the bureaucrats in Building 127 let her skip the paperwork (or rather, to defer it until *afterward*). She slipped inside, and there he was, on the floor, eyes unfocused. It felt as though he were playacting at nonchalance, like he had hastily gotten himself into this innocuous position right as she opened the door.

"They want to talk to you." She clasped her hands in front of her. "Please, it's been two weeks. Esperas and Brako won't be there. Please. For me. Just come outside, show them that you're still here, that you'll still cooperate."

"*I will comply.*" It seemed that he had been expecting this.

"What are you going to do?"

The nuclei of his eyes concentrated in to a furtive glow as he stood up. "*I must keep this brief.*"

She hadn't warned him that the meeting was mostly conducted by "militarists," figuring he knew. But when they entered the room, and he laid eyes on the brigadier general, she could feel the air around him thicken. Even stranger, however, Luciana and Dr. Sev were no longer there.

"Sit," said Porter, looking at her.

"I'd rather not," she said. "He considers me his inferior, and it's improper for an inferior to sit if their superior is standing." She was almost proud of how much this excuse she had pulled completely out of her ass sounded legit.

That seemed to appease the brigadier general. "Tell us what you know."

"*I have no more meaningful intelligence than you have.*"

"He says he doesn't really know anything more than what we told you two weeks ago."

"Would any of the other ones know?" asked Sol.

"*They know less than I.*"

"If he doesn't know, they don't know," said Cora.

"Cross-reference them, anyway," said Porter. "Cross-reference the propagandists. They at least have a history of being more cooperative."

"Have you attempted to communicate with Enola Gay?" asked Sol.

"He says he has," said Cora, "and he's been trying for the last two weeks. No response."

"Why?"

"He doesn't know why. He doesn't even know if Enola Gay is getting them. All he knows is that he's been trying and hasn't been getting anything back."

"How many are there?" asked Porter in a tone one might reserve for discussing terrorists.

"He doesn't know."

"Is this another refugee, or a representative of the Superorganism?" asked Sol.

"He doesn't know. Probably the former."

Porter looked at her as if she were a private he was about to order to do fifty push-ups. "We've arranged a transport. We want to take you out to Temecula to help us survey the site."

"*I do not consent.*"

"He says he won't do it," said Cora.

"We need intelligence, we need to know what to expect, we all need to know what we're dealing with."

"*I do not consent.*"

"He said no."

"Perhaps he misunderstands this as a request," said Brigadier General Porter, enunciating his consonants as if he were condescending to a waiter who had failed to understand his order the first time. "It is not."

Sol stayed stone still, but Cora's jaw dropped. Porter was not looking at her but at Ampersand as if to say he had given an order. Why was this order not being followed?

Then the air changed, that thick static that accompanied telekinetic activity, compressing her chest and making it slightly difficult to breathe. Everyone in the room felt it, their wet, beady eyes widening in confusion and a hint of fear. Brigadier General Porter slammed his palms on the desk, and he took in a breath to bark some order, but before he could, every window in the room shattered.

Pane by pane, one by one like dominoes, the windows fell down onto the floor like a hailstorm. As the last few bits of glass finished settling on the floor, the entire building rumbled. The glass on the floor clinked, then rose into the air, floating like raindrops frozen in time. Then, each of the million pieces of glass on the floor flew back into place, and there was a flash of heat. One of the general's people yipped as the heat licked her skin, and she jumped away from the windowpanes. In an instant, the glass melded back together, each pane back in its place, but the crack of each break now visible, a muddy macabre parody of stained glass. What had been clear, basic office-grade windows that looked into the hallway was now hot, blurry, and translucent.

"*I do not consent.*"

Then, Ampersand's cloak of invisibility fell over him, and he was gone. The only sign that he hadn't disappeared from the face of the earth altogether was the air that moved in his wake and the wobble of the door as he removed his giant invisible self from the room.

"He said no," said Cora.

Brigadier General Porter shot to his feet, slamming his hands on the table again as he glared at her. She glared right back. To think, there would have been a time not so long ago when she would have crumbled before a man like that. Now, this government bureaucracy nonsense all felt so petty. Porter left the room, and his subordinates followed, leaving Sol and Cora alone in the botched conference room.

Sol popped up his eyebrows as if he were about to drop an interesting tidbit of trivia, and stated, "I don't think that could have possibly gone worse."

He sauntered up to the broken and reassembled glass, licked his fingers, and then touched it, tapping it a couple of times. Then he exhaled loudly, shaking his head and jamming his hands into his pockets. "Welp, I guess you'll have to do."

Cora shook her head, the angry shell that had formed around her cracking. "What?"

"Have you ever been to Temecula?"

Organization

Angus Normandy

Dear Friends,

Calling all good Men and Women to Temecula CA, Pechanga Indian Reservation

The work of protecting our species and country has fallen to us, as it is clear our corrupt kleptocrat president has left us to fend for ourselves. No matter, and no reason to be afraid, as we are more than able to rise to the occasion.

We have a lot of work to do here in Riverside County. We need more people to pitch in the work of growing our ranks, spreading our message and building defense against the alien globalists. We have had non-stop people from Southern California, Nevada and Arizona coming by and giving us their support. They are showing a excitement to participate in defending our country, our planet and taking up arms, but it is not enough.

We need more good men and women to come and participate in the work. Come and be part of assisting the people in the defense of our world. We are peaceful, but we are armed.

The road is blocked into the Pechanga reservation by the government. Come join us.

The Lord has been good to us,

Angus Normandy, Chairman of the Gadsden Line

> 41 minutes ago   Like · Comment · Share

👍 144 people like this.

💬 View all 572 comments

Write a comment...

8

Temecula was about forty miles from Riverside, and usually this long stretch of highway wasn't clogged with that quintessential SoCal traffic. Today was a different story. Unlike with the Obelus Event, where only fringe internet crazies were convinced that aliens had landed, now everyone knew what was going on.

There was bumper-to-bumper traffic, the northbound scrambling to get away from Enola Gay, and the southbound consisting of every other genius in Southern California who had also decided to descend on Temecula. What should have been a forty-minute drive was crossing the two-hour mark. They'd been stopped dead at this spot close to their exit for a couple of minutes, a billboard on the side of the road that read "Prayer Will Save Us" looming over them. Cora wondered if the billboard was pre- or post-ET-gate.

"You seem different lately," said Sol.

"What do you mean?" From the way he kept glancing at her, she knew Sol could tell she was hiding something, a lot of somethings. There was a part of her that wanted to tell him everything, not because it would do any good but so she could tell *someone*.

"I don't know. Seemed like for a little while there you were starting to perk up. But since the Enola Gay light, you've been different."

She sighed and shifted her gaze toward the Taurus in front of them. "It's been a rough few weeks."

"Is he lying about anything?"

"How would I know?" she snapped, regretting her tone immediately. It was a reasonable question. Ampersand tended to lie, or at least lie by omission. "I don't know if he's lying. But . . . he might have omitted some things since you didn't ask the right questions."

"What is the right question?"

She leaned her head against the car window, running her finger over the pulse emitter she had in her jacket pocket, which she had on her at all times. It had been easy to sneak in and out of work every day since it wasn't made of metal in the traditional sense and therefore didn't set off the metal detectors. "You didn't ask if he knew *who* Enola Gay is, and he does know *who* Enola Gay is."

Sol digested this. "*Who* singular or *who* plural?"

"He doesn't know. Ampersand was singular, Obelus was plural. Could be either."

"How does he know *who* it is?"

"Enola . . . or one of the Enolas . . . is his symphyle. Like Čefo was."

"Jesus." Sol chuckled. "How many symphyles does this guy have?"

"Originally, seven. Now he's down to . . . the one."

"And Enola Gay contains the last remaining one . . ?"

"That's what he says."

"Well, I'm going to be uncharacteristically optimistic and choose to interpret that as a good thing. At least there's the possibility we aren't seeing a repeat of Obelus, where the new party is here to kill them."

She nearly snorted at that statement. Obelus being Ampersand's symphyle hadn't precluded all sorts of violence against alien and human alike. Cora thought of Vincent Park, Sol's junior agent who had been killed by Obelus. His death, along with the deaths of the other three CIA agents who had been with them in the caravan that day, had been so buried it was almost like they never even existed at all. Sol had made it clear in no uncertain terms that Vincent Park's death was never to be discussed.

"So what's he doing about it?" asked Sol.

"What do you mean?"

"I mean, he's obviously not back in his lair doing nothing. I mean, what is he really doing about it?"

She opened her mouth, rummaging her exhaustion-addled mind for an excuse. "I don't know."

"Cut the bullshit."

"I *don't* know, he . . ." She sighed, looking down at her upturned palms. "He isn't really talking to me. Only when you or Sev or someone forces it. It's like . . . being back in the Cheyenne Mountain bunker all over again."

Sol looked at her quizzically, but it wasn't a malicious or accusatory look. "What did your conversations look like before Enola Gay?"

The pit inside her was always there, a bottomless thing that invited dread by standing next to it. But that question pushed her right up to its edge, and she found herself suppressing tears. "He was trying to help me."

Sol waited for her to continue, but she just stared down at her palms resting on her lap. "Go on?"

She looked up at the traffic, which had slowed to a crawl now that they were finally off the interstate. They could walk on their hands and move faster than this. "He was piggybacking off my PTSD diagnosis, decided he wanted to cure it."

At this, Sol shot her an alarmed look.

"Nothing . . . unorthodox. He was trying to figure it out, what my symptoms were, what triggered them, what goes on in my brain when I have an episode, chemically. It was like . . . a side project of his, I guess."

Sol's expression of alarm cooled by, at most, two degrees. "What did he do?"

"I think it was brain scans or something. Like his version of an MRI." She had been entertaining the idea of telling him what else Ampersand had been doing (omitting the parts about him leaving his lair without permission, of course), admitting that he had been aping something that could be considered friendship, but the alarmed and borderline disgusted expression on Sol's face dampened her desire to tell him, or anyone. "But then Enola Gay happened, and he didn't have time for it anymore."

Sol's look of concern only intensified, and he turned back to the road ahead. "You can't cure PTSD."

Cora almost clapped back, "How the fuck would you know?" but she didn't see in him the snide sureness that often accompanied one of his assertions. He was looking ahead at the barely moving traffic, deep in his own thoughts.

"What do you mean?"

"PTSD is like cancer. You don't cure it. Maybe it goes into remission, but you don't cure it."

It was something she hadn't considered, a thought too ugly to touch, the idea that this might not be temporary. She'd taken for granted that the night terrors were a phase, that Ampersand had such a good grip on human physiology that he would figure it out, eventually find the right brain-button to push and push it, and the symptoms would go away. She had never considered that she might be broken for the rest of her life. That fear quickly turned into anger. "Are you just being shitty?"

Sol snorted. "What do you mean?"

"I mean are you just fucking with me? With this whole, like . . . 'you will always be broken' thing?"

"No," he said, his lip curling in offense. "Do you really think *that* little of me? I wouldn't joke about that. And besides . . ." He put the car into reverse, backing up far enough that the car behind him honked in alarm. "I didn't say anything about you always being a broken bird. I just said it's not something you can cure like it's syphilis. It's more compli-cated than that."

"It's just . . ." She was so tired of keeping her defenses up around him. If he was going to use this vulnerability to savage her later, let him. "I don't know what to do. I don't have any support, I don't have any money, I don't have any health insurance. And I don't know what sets me off, it just . . . happens."

"You mean your panic attacks?" he said, putting the car in park.

She looked at him, surprised to see sympathy on his face, some-thing she hadn't ever really seen in him before. Then she remembered the surveillance Ampersand had found in her apartment. "Have you been spying on me?"

"No," he said, smiling out of the corner of his mouth like she was making a joke when she was not. "You don't hide them as well as you think you do."

"How do I stop it if I don't know what will set it off?"

"Triggers are never as simple as movies tell you they are. It's not as simple as, 'Oh, I got raped at a Starbucks now I go into a panic-rage every time I see the Starbucks logo.' And when you have all these co-morbid conditions, sometimes triggers will be obvious, sometimes they won't be. A lot of the time, you won't even know what causes it."

He turned off the ignition, opened the car door, and tossed his head for her to follow him. "Hopefully, the Temecula towing company will be too busy to get around to my car."

"What are you doing?"

"I'm parking. It's quicker to walk at this point. We're only about a mile away from the police blockade."

Cora followed him toward the swollen mass of humanity gathering on the other side of the blockade, which blocked both the road that wound into the mountains toward the crash site and the extensive grasslands that surrounded it. On the right side of the highway was a giant casino that was visible even from a mile away, on the left side of the highway, a brand-new housing development full of expensive stucco houses that couldn't be more than a couple of years old, all against the backdrop of the California mountain wilderness.

The closer they got to the blockade, the thicker the crowd got. Both the Temecula PD and the Riverside County sheriff were completely overwhelmed, and even the tribal rangers from the Luiseño reservation adjacent to Temecula appeared to be lending a hand. Sol flashed his credentials to get past the police line, climbing on top of a police van alongside a couple of the sheriff's deputies to get a better look at the situation. He hoisted Cora up alongside him, and it was only up here that she got a scope of what was really happening.

There were hundreds, maybe thousands of people congregating over a big grassy field a few blocks west of the casino/resort, pushing up against the blockade that Temecula's Finest were trying to maintain. Some of them were already starting to get into arguments with the police.

"This is a fucking powder keg," muttered Sol under his breath.

Indeed it was. Cora had expected people more in the vein of the type who would welcome the alien enlightenment that was being held back by capitalism. But that wasn't the case at all. Sol pointed to one guy in the crowd, whispering to one of the deputies on top of the van with him, and the deputy hopped off the van and disappeared into the crowd.

"What is it?"

"That guy is packing," said Sol, nodding into the crowd. "I am concerned."

Cora looked down at the guy who was "packing," and he was pretty easy to spot—a white guy in a denim biker jacket with a big beard, he looked like a half-assed attempt at a biker, a Heck's Lesser Divine Entity, and he had a "Don't Tread On Me" flag sprouting up from his vest, flapping in the breeze.

"He is concealing—poorly—and carrying, but I'll eat my hat if that guy has a license," said Sol.

"How can you tell?"

Sol tipped his aviators down to look at her as if she had asked him an insultingly simple question, like if he knew where Canada was.

Then she noticed another face in the crowd, one that was staring right at her with a look of unmistakable hatred, even from a hundred feet away. He had thick, curly black hair that draped over his head like a lion's mane, an olive skin tone, and short black facial hair blanketing a long, triangular face. He was wearing a black jacket over a black sweater and black slacks, hands jammed in the jacket pockets, and he was looking at her like he wanted her dead, and was trying to figure out the quickest and most efficient way to do it.

"Where are our leaders?"

Cora looked away from Murderguy toward the source of the voice being carried through a loudspeaker. A man had hopped up on top of a Winnebago some three hundred feet from where she stood, using it as a makeshift stage. The crowd immediately responded to him, turning their aimless churlishness into cheering.

"Where are our leaders?" said the man again, now surer of his footing. The crowd roared their response, agreement, indignation. "And where is the truth?"

It was Jano Miranda.

"The biggest scandal in American history," cried Miranda into the loudspeaker, "and they stay silent!"

The crowd roared their agreement.

"Two celestial objects fall right next to a major American city, and they stay silent! Mysterious power outages all over our country and territories, and they stay silent! A light in the sky, the likes of which we have never, *ever* seen in all of human history—" At this, the crowd positively bellowed, and Miranda had to wait a few seconds before he could speak again. "And still they are silent! And here we are again, barred from the truth! Whatever is happening, out there, down here, it is clearly not over!"

God, but he was charming. Not in a big, boisterous way but in a vulnerable way, like he could make you feel that he cared about how your day went just by looking at you. He genuinely appeared to be afraid for the people in this crowd, radiated solidarity with them, the "us" united against a nameless, formless "them."

"We saw Enola Gay in the sky," Miranda continued. "We demanded answers, and we still haven't gotten them. And they did nothing to prepare us for this, even though they could have. Did they know this was going to happen? Did they know where? We don't know! But now the bomb is dropped, but what is the fallout? Like radioactive fallout, we can't see it, we can't feel it, but we know it's here!"

More outraged bellowing from the crowd. She felt Sol sigh next to her. "God-fucking-damn it, I hate it when they're good."

"Who do you mean by 'they'?" asked Cora.

"These fucking polemicists. You try working in anti-terrorism for a few years. This guy terrifics me both less and more. Less in that I think he's 900 percent less likely to strap bombs onto his chest and walk into a mall. More in that he's way smarter and more charismatic than the usual grifter."

"I don't even know that I'd call him a grifter," said Cora, transfixed. "I think he means it."

Miranda waited for the noise to die down enough that he could be heard, but not so much that he had lost the energy of the moment. He raised the speaker to his mouth and trumpeted, "*Truth is a human right!*"

The crowd parroted back, "*Truth is a human right!*"

It would be her luck that Miranda would borrow Nils's catchphrase. Cora deflated as "Truth is a human right!" turned into a chant. She looked back down in the crowd, and there was that guy in the black denim jacket looking her way again. "There's a guy over there doing a bad job pretending he doesn't recognize me."

Sol looked down, scanning the crowd, and upon seeing who she was talking about, his expression turned to alarm. "Shit."

"Shit?"

"Steer clear of that guy."

"Should I be afraid?"

"Probably," he said, speaking through clenched teeth. "Be careful. He's dangerous."

She stole another glance at the guy in the crowd just as he looked away, perhaps now realizing how utterly found out he was, but in that parting glance, she saw even more death in his eyes than she had earlier.

By now the "*Truth is a human right*" chant had devolved into the simpler "*Hu-man rights! Hu-man rights!*" It felt like that phrase meant something different now than it had earlier that morning.

Then, it was as if Earth's atmosphere split like a glacier breaking in two, and there was a crack like a thunder burst from less than a mile away, but the sky was blue and crisp and clear. The crowd fell silent for only a few seconds before the second noise came, this one deep and sustained, coming not from the direction of the crash site but seemingly from farther away in the mountains, like a giant a mile tall had blown on a tuba. The sound was so loud and deep in frequency it was as though the air itself had turned to molasses. Nearly everyone threw their hands to their ears.

"What the hell is that?" yelled Sol.

"I don't know!"

The shock wave came as the noise abated, not through the air but through the ground, rippling like a wake in water, sending little plumes of dust into the air and destabilizing everything, including the police trailer, which started to sway like this was an earthquake. Sol grabbed Cora and pulled her tight, and she grabbed him in turn, as much out of fear than for physical stability.

"Have you seen anything like this before?" yelled Sol over the din of the crowd.

"No, never!"

Then the mass panic set in, with half the people on the ground trying to run away, and the other half staying put, either too scared to move or excited to see what happened next, and in doing so becoming living obstacles to the people trying to escape. Thousands of people ramming past each other, but from what, to what? Even from her vantage point above the crowd, she could hardly tell where the epicenter of the noise was.

"Come on!" said Sol, breaking the embrace and grabbing her by the hand. She followed him without question, just as ignorant as to how dangerous it was to stay put as everyone else in this crowd was.

By the time they made it to the ground, a larger proportion of the people had joined the panic and decided to run. The direction people decided on was more or less the same direction from which they had come. Sol didn't go the direct route, probably because there were so many people that it was well beyond a safety hazard, but instead hewed toward the housing development on the other side of the highway. There was a gully between the highway and the wall that bordered the development. Once on the other side of the gully, he stopped, perhaps not realizing how many people were directly behind them. When he let go of her hand so he could turn around to survey the situation, a surge of humanity separated them, and before she knew what was going on, he had disappeared.

"Sol!" she cried, trying not to fall, as she knew there was a good chance if she did, she might not get back up. This was a stampede, and anyone who fell in front of it ran the risk of getting trampled. Two more bodies slammed into her before she regained her footing. "Sol!"

"*I am sending for you,*" said a mechanized voice in her ear.

Still trying to move with the flow of the crowd so she didn't fall down, she frantically scanned everything   rooftops, houses, the casino—for signs of Ampersand.

"Where are you?"

"*I am sending for you.*"

Without further instruction, the only thing she could think to do was to get out of the flow of the crowd, and the best way to do that seemed to be to get up next to the side of a building, where the crowd was thinnest. Only problem was there were no buildings nearby, just a massive stucco wall bordering the housing development. She pushed her way to the wall, then ran with the flow of humanity until she found a break in the wall that opened into the neighborhood on the other side.

Here she had to press through some people who had stopped and were standing in the goddamn way, obviously not residents but spectators who seemed content to stand back and watch the end of the world while everyone else ran for their lives. She nearly made it away from the crowd when she saw that someone was blocking her path, someone who stopped her short upon recognizing her.

It was the Murderguy who had been staring at her earlier, the tall, lanky man with his slender face and curly black lion's mane hair.

Reflective sunglasses now blocked his eyes, but even amid the chaos, he still wore that intense, vindictive expression. World-shattering alien shenanigans were one thing, but it was only now that she started to panic.

"Ampersand, I am in danger," she said, turning from him and making a beeline for the nearest yard. It was fenced, but at least it wasn't by a twenty-foot wall. "I need extraction."

"You must stay still."

She hopped over the fence into the yard, a nouveau riche McMansion with a pool and even a stone water element. She peeked back over the fence to confirm that, yes, he was still marching toward her. "I am still. Hurry!"

"At your feet."

She looked down and saw that a plate of liquid metal had appeared on the ground right next to her. She fell onto it, collapsing herself into as tight a ball as she could. She couldn't be sure, but she was fairly certain that the man might have looked over that fence just in time to see her disappear.

9

Cora opened her eyes inside a cave.

It was obviously not a natural cave, but rather more like what the result of an atomic bomb going off deep underground might look like. This wasn't a cave eroded away by time and water but by heat, the texture somewhere between recently cooled volcanic rock and glass. It was as though the earth had been scooped out by a shovel of fire. *So this is where you've been hiding,* she thought, sitting up.

"Where are you?" she asked, her voice bouncing off the smooth rock for several seconds. This space was like a small planetarium, perhaps the size of the telescope viewing area at the Griffith Observatory, but more haphazard than a perfect sphere, as though it had been carved out in a hurry. A few of Ampersand's drone lights hovered along the edges of the room, illuminating two passageways, one that led outside into the sunlight, and the other into darkness, another chamber perhaps. It was from this second, darker passageway that Ampersand emerged. Swaying, unstable. Terrified.

She shot to her feet and ran to him, placing her hands on the bottom of his head, guiding his head down to look at her. "I'm here."

"*Yes.*"

She closed her eyes and tried to sense what was going on, but the wall was thicker than usual. She could sense a garbled *something* not too dissimilar from what she'd felt the day of the breakdown in front of Esperas, but nothing clearer than that.

"Was that noise Enola?"

"*Yes.*" The nuclei of his eyes finally found their focus on her, and despite the thickness of the wall, she felt a sudden sharp terror. *"He is searching for me."*

"What was that noise?"

"Seismic pulse, designed to search for unnatural formations, formations like this one." His focus was dissolving, shattering into a thousand tiny shards of amber glass. *"He is searching for me. Careless, reckless. This region sits directly on top of a fault line."*

She tried to stay calm, tried to think of herself as the flotation device but was having a hard time keeping it together herself. He was so frightened. Had Enola found him, cornered him? Was he here?

And if he was, what was Ampersand afraid he'd even do?

"A fault line?" she repeated.

"Careless, reckless. The ground pulse is designed to flush me out, it is designed to detect hideaways like this, but this area is right on a fault line."

It took Cora a few seconds to see what he was getting at. "You're saying it could cause earthquakes?"

"It will cause earthquakes."

"We have to warn . . . we have to warn the U.S. Geological Survey. We have to warn people."

Ampersand's sway turned into a stumble. *"There is nothing they can do."*

"They can evacuate." She pulled out her cell phone—no reception, and almost dead to boot. "Where are we?"

"He is not responding to my attempts to communicate, but he is clearly trying to flush me out. He is searching for me. He is searching for both of us."

Okay, now she was afraid. "What the hell would he want with me?"

"He wants both of us. He wants us both dead."

"Ampersand," she said, taking him by the forearm, trying to guide him to the ground. "You're not okay; you need to relax for a second. Are we in immediate danger?"

His swaying worsened, and at first, she thought it was the beginning of another breakdown until she realized that she was swaying, too, and it was the ground that was making them do it.

It was an earthquake. A real one.

"We have to get outside!" she said, grabbing him by the forearm, but he didn't move. The luminescence in his eyes had dimmed to almost black. She had lived through a few earthquakes before, all minor affairs that didn't result in anything more than a short, quiet wobbling of various bric-a-brac and a ceiling fan waving back and forth. This was different, as if the earth had turned to water, and the ripples under her feet were challenging her to stay upright.

The next wave nearly knocked her off her feet, and Ampersand collapsed onto the ground, his head jerking and his limbs seizing. Not knowing what else to do, she fell to her knees and tried to soothe him, tried to get his head and his arms to stop making that jerking movement.

After about a minute, the shaking in the ground had calmed, but Ampersand's seizing had not, and Cora was standing on the precipice of a full-blown panic. She looked around frantically, as though there might be a key on the floor somewhere that would open the box containing the solution to this puzzle. All she saw was the second chamber, dark as ink. She bolted up, grabbed one of his light drones out of the air, and dashed into the second chamber.

This one was smaller, darker without the leaking light from the setting sun that spilled into the main chamber. Unlike the smooth, bare emptiness of the first chamber, this one was cluttered, the walls papered with what almost looked like giant honeycombs. So he *did* have material objects; it wasn't that he only needed the machines in his body and the computer in his head; he had other tools, he just kept them well away from human eyes.

It must be storage, she figured, but how it might be categorized, let alone used, was totally beyond her. It looked like a giant wolf spider had built a series of tunnels stacked on top of each other, dozens of them, but not of a material that looked like a spider's web, more like the thin outer layer of the human epidermis.

Something clicked in the other chamber, and she jumped, taking a moment to place the sound as another violent jerk, the sound of one of his limbs hitting the floor. She tried to shake it off, looking at these wolf spider tunnels, dozens of them. Loss of electromagnetic power was the one thing that could take down a Similar, which was why they were vulnerable to certain frequencies of electromagnetic pulse. Last year, during their battle with Obelus, he had given her a device that would speed the restart of his energy cores after an EMP had taken him out, a device that resembled a pill bug the size of a guinea pig.

If he was using this for storage, that thing had to be in here somewhere.

She approached one of the honeycomb tunnels, roughly the size of a child's cubby. That skin-like material seemed smoothed over in layers, covering something, but there was no way to find out what without ripping it off. Hand shaking, feeling like Willie Scott reaching her hand into a mystery hole to pull a bug-infested lever, she slipped a finger under one of those wispy thin layers of material, and hit upon . . . something. She pulled it out. It was a . . . tool. What comparison was there? It was more or less shaped like a cylinder with a jack on the end. She had no idea what it was, but it wasn't the pill bug, so she put it back.

By now, the earthquake had stopped. She tried a few more spider holes before, to her shock, she found what she was looking for. It was as she turned around, examining the pill bug carefully to make sure she had the right tool, that she realized she wasn't alone in this subchamber.

She saw the eyes before she saw anything else, reflecting the dim reddish light of the drone she was holding in her hand. Then the owner of the eyes stepped forward into the light of her drone, and she could see it in full. An amygdaline body, far smaller than Ampersand's, slightly shorter than Cora was. Eyes smaller and darker in proportion to the head than Ampersand's, further inlaid, and a crest on the back of its head that was less pronounced, but on full alert.

For an instant, she thought this might be Enola, lying in wait for Ampersand to become vulnerable so he could enact whatever terrible thing he had planned that made Ampersand so terrified. But no, this wasn't Enola. This was more familiar. It looked like Čefo's body. It *was* Čefo's body.

But this was not Čefo.

The next few seconds stretched into a year, and in that space, she knew. In the same way she had just known Ampersand had done something to her brain after he had rescued her. In the same way she just knew what was happening on the other side of the wall when he was having a breakdown, she knew.

Obelus.

She kept her eyes on him like prey trying to evade a tiger. The memories of the things he had done began nipping at her—that feeling of his claws going right through her, the thought of Vincent Park vanishing into a cloud of ash. All her memories were associated with Obelus's old body, that terrifying machine that stood at around eleven feet and was almost the size of a Cadillac, nothing like this frail, elfin little thing.

If Obelus was alive and in Čefo's body, that meant Ampersand had put him there.

Keeping her eyes on him, she placed the pill bug in the pocket of her coat and backed out of the chamber. Obelus followed her, keeping a distance of about ten feet between them as she backed away. She had left the pulse emitter Ampersand had given her for protection somewhere in the middle of the main chamber. All she needed was to get to that. And then, she'd have to test it. She'd have no other choice.

And then what?

She backed herself out into the main chamber, Obelus still stalking her, his head down in that familiar antagonistic posture like a bull about to charge. Ampersand had stopped seizing. His eyes were open, the light inside them flickering like a flame in the wind, but otherwise, he wasn't moving.

She stopped when the pulse emitter was at her feet and stayed absolutely still. Obelus stopped when he reached Ampersand, and took his eyes off her, speaking to Ampersand in Pequod-phonemic. When Ampersand didn't answer, Obelus spoke again, and then again. As slowly as she could, she lowered herself to the ground. Obelus's eyes were on Ampersand when she got her hand around the pulse emitter.

Then Obelus looked at her as he continued speaking in his language. He looked as though he expected her to respond. He spoke again, what sounded identical to one of the spurts of sound he'd employed to Ampersand a few seconds ago. Cora didn't move. Her animal brain was screaming, echoes in her body of the last time she had seen him. Vincent Park's face, and alongside it, a primal, almost violent urge for revenge. She wasn't thinking at all of Ampersand anymore. All she could think was that this might be her only opportunity to finish what she had started.

Obelus approached her, and then she heard a static in her ears. Then, a rolodex of words. "*Kezīhi befīti beneberikibeti gīzē 'ayini wisit'i mayeti ālichalihimi.*"

She froze, unsure if that had come from Obelus, or Ampersand. "What?" she whispered.

"*Lorem ipsum, vi estas same kiel anĝelo, via haŭto min ploras.*"

"I don't understand."

"*Object present purpose tangible natural purpose interrogative direct address—*"

"I can't understand you," she said, her grip tightening around the pulse emitter.

Obelus looked at her as though something inside him had clicked. And then: "*What have you done to him?*"

She considered that maybe she was wrong, that maybe she had panicked, that maybe this was not Obelus. Obelus was dead. She had watched him die. Ampersand had confirmed it. Hadn't he?

"*What have you done to him?*" Obelus repeated, stopping about three feet in front of her. "*What are you?*"

Going back over months of interactions with Ampersand, she realized that no, he hadn't confirmed it. She had *assumed* it. He had never confirmed it either way. This was Obelus.

But he didn't recognize her.

"*Did you do this?*"

Careful not to aim the pulse emitter at either Obelus or Ampersand, she inserted the pill bug into the other pocket of her hoodie. "I'm not the one doing this."

"*Do you know why this keeps happening to him?*"

Slowly, so as not to be mistaken for an intimidation gesture, she rose to her feet, and again, she second-guessed herself. Why had she been so sure this was Obelus? This being acted like he'd never seen a human before. Was it possible that this *was* Obelus, and that Ampersand had found a way to strip him of his memories? After all, he was perfectly capable of doing that to humans. Why not to his own kind?

"Has this happened to him before?" she asked, keeping her demeanor authoritative, but calm.

"*Many times.*"

"Oh, Jesus." She looked at Ampersand. This certainly explained a lot.

He'd been hiding Obelus from her, from *everyone*. No wonder he was so fucking scared of Esperas. "How do you know my language?"

"I have an algorithm that translates your language."

"Where did you get an algorithm that translates my language?"

"I do not know."

"Do you know what I am?"

"No."

She swallowed. "Do you know who you are?"

"No. Can you help him?"

She licked her lips and ran her fingers over the pulse emitter. She was barely keeping herself in check, one part screaming terror, another part pure animal rage. It would be so easy to finish what she'd started. It might be the only responsible thing to do. What had Ampersand accomplished by rescuing him, by keeping him alive? She'd thought he'd been overstating how "diseased" his mind was, but this was beyond immoral, it was stupid. It was deranged.

He wants both of us. He wants us both dead, Ampersand had said. He had not meant Enola was after him and Cora. Enola was after him and *Obelus.*

She closed her eyes, and released a breath. Furious as she was, afraid as she was, she didn't have it in her to do something so cruel as to kill Obelus while Ampersand was incapacitated. Not like this.

"I think I can help him," she said. "Will you let me try?"

"Please, help him."

Given that he didn't seem to remember ever seeing a human before, he likely could not read human body language or facial expression. Which was a good thing, because that meant he could not read the glare of pure and unrefined hatred she was shooting at him.

She knelt next to Ampersand, holding the pill bug in the same place she remembered the Genome holding it, high on the back near the neck. The carapace of his back was among the parts of him that were most insect-like, and though fused into one piece, it reminded her almost of the wings of a cockroach or a praying mantis. Something zipped, clicked, and his eyes shot open.

He struggled to sit up, not quite pulling himself into a roost, but staying half cocked on his side as he lifted his head like a cat disturbed from its nap. He looked at Obelus and then at Cora. She didn't even try to conceal her anger. "What have you done?"

Obelus said something to Ampersand in Pequod-phonemic, and the two had a short back-and-forth. Cora continued to glare at Ampersand, who eventually pulled himself up into a roost, tucking his forearms under him like a deer, looking at her like they were about to have a civil discussion about her grades this semester.

"What have you done?" she repeated, her voice trembling. "Why did you do this?"

"I told you that I would never allow Obelus to die if I could prevent his death."

She grabbed the pulse emitter inside her hoodie, and she saw his focus shift to her hand.

"That will not work if I do not allow it."

She saw that Obelus had inched toward her. "Keep him away from me!" she thundered, her voice bouncing off the smooth walls of the chamber for seconds.

Obelus backed away and said something to Ampersand. Ampersand stood up, loomed over her. *"I would advise you to be cautious. He has not seen a natural alien before."*

A geyser of rage made her shoot to her feet. *"Of course he fucking has!"*

Obelus started in obvious alarm, and Ampersand moved his body between his amnesiac symphyle and Cora, his movements now having recovered that gravity-defying grace that defined him, glaring her down with that antagonistic expression that he generally only reserved for "militarists." *"His memories are suppressed, not erased. Stressful situations could destabilize the dampeners I have placed on his memories."*

"Did you hear that, Obelus?" she said, glaring at Ampersand as she spoke, her voice quivering. "You don't know who you are? Well, I do. You are a murderer. A militarist. You just don't remember it."

"Stop this."

"You've already tried to kill me once, so you'll try again as soon as you get your memories back, and this time, you'll probably succeed. And you'll continue to torture him, and he'll be only too happy to let you do it as long as it means he gets to keep that one thread to his old life!"

The air in her lungs froze, her muscles locked, her jaw snapped shut as the invisible magnet held her firm, stopped her from speaking. His spider hands were forming a triangle in the way that they often did when he used his telekinesis, something he had not done to her since before they even started communicating.

"I can't . . . I can't stay quiet on this," she said, her air restricted like there were hands around her throat. "He's a murderer. He's a fucking war criminal. He can't be allowed to be free. I have to tell Sol."

"*No.*" He lifted her off the ground, her arms stiff as boards, and floated her over to him until she was eye level with him, hanging in the air three feet off the ground. "*You will not.*"

"So what are you going to do?" she asked, her throat still constricted. She was still too angry to be afraid. "Suppress my memories, too?"

"*If that is your intent, then I will.*"

She hadn't expected him to admit it so candidly, and at last her anger cracked, her expression faded from rage to hurt. *He can't mean that,* she thought, knowing that he absolutely did mean it. He didn't say things he didn't mean as a means of testing boundaries like a human might. And he'd already done it to Obelus. To his "Beloved." If he did it to Obelus, he'd do it to her without question.

"Holy fuck, you absolute monster," she whispered.

The constriction on her throat eased, and she floated to the ground, the stiffness in her limbs easing, the air in her chest flowing.

"*I will not allow my symphyle to fall into the hands of those who would kill or abuse him.*"

"*I* am bound to you, too!" she yelled, causing Obelus to cringe behind Ampersand. "I know you didn't mean for this to happen. I know you didn't really think that fusion bonding with a human would work, but it's done. If he's owed your protection, then so am I!"

She continued backing away toward the entrance of the cave, dimmer now with the sun having disappeared over the mountains. There was a part of her that wanted to beg for mercy, swear fealty, tell him that she would do whatever he wanted if he swore to take it back, tell her he didn't mean it, tell her that he wouldn't do that to her, not after all they'd been through. But her rage at that moment was still stronger.

She stopped where she stood, a few feet from the exit. "Go on. Do it."

He continued to watch her, hardly moving at all except to more solidly place himself between her and Obelus. She tried to reach past her own emotions to see if she could tell what was going on with his, but she couldn't. Hers were too strong, too staticky, and either way, the wall was too thick.

She took one step back, then another. He didn't stop her. Two more steps and she was in the passageway. Then she ran into the forest with no clue as to where she was or where she was going.

He didn't stop her.

10

The only clues she had as to where she even was were that it was on a fault line (which, in California, good luck narrowing that down), and it was nearish where Enola Gay's Martian horn of terror had blasted. So she was somewhere in the several-hundred-square-mile mountain wilderness between Temecula and Mexico. Cool.

She tried at first to go downhill, but the problem with that tactic was that it tended to turn back into uphill if one stayed in a straight line. That, on top of trudging through the thick underbrush of the cold mountain, made progress slow. The temperature was dropping quickly, and her coat was designed for brisk coastal winters, not mountain regions prone to actual snowfall.

After about an hour, the sun had nearly set, and she was becoming genuinely afraid. Fortunately, as the sky faded from pink to light blue, she found a winding paved road hugging the side of the mountains and followed it downhill. She still had no cell phone reception by the time her phone died.

Cora was not prepared for how dark it got, especially with the lack of moonlight this evening. The mountain was dark and freezing and terrifyingly silent, not even the distant sound or even light of civilization. There was some light pollution that probably came from the San Diego suburbs, but it was so far away as to be functionally meaningless. Barely able to see the road, she continued forward, following the texture of the road beneath her feet.

I should call Sol. I should tell Sol.

But what could Sol do? What could *any* human do? If any human (or god forbid, any "militarist") tried to compel Ampersand to do anything he did not want to do, well, his little charade with the broken glass showed how that would go.

She nearly slipped on a pebble she couldn't see, then kicked it, its delicate clinking the only other sound besides her footsteps. She'd been trudging for what felt like an hour and she hadn't seen a car, when there should have been a pilgrimage. She figured that the road must be blocked somewhere down the line, which meant she must be inside the containment zone where Enola Gay had landed.

She hopped up and down, trying to get her blood warm. Even if she did tell Sol, and then Sol told the powers that be, and the powers that be swooped down on this place, what would they find? Nothing; Ampersand would be twenty steps ahead of them, long gone.

She saw the light before she heard the accompanying sound, the hum of an engine. A *car*! And one that seemed to be headed right for her. She could see the headlights illuminating the road almost a minute before the vehicle itself came into view, and she stepped right into the middle of it, hoping the car wasn't careening up the mountain so fast that it hit her before it saw her. When it rounded the bend, it slowed to a stop immediately, and she winced, her dark-adjusted eyes unable to look at the car head-on. She wondered what a blue-haired girl alone in the dark on a mountain must look like to the driver. God, she must look like a ghost in a horror movie.

Or an alien.

The vehicle just sat there, its engine humming. She tried to tamp down the inherent terror of the situation and stood there almost guiltily, like she'd been caught by the janitor, vandalizing the high school after hours. It was a black SUV, lending credence to her suspicion that this was probably the feds and that, counterintuitively, those fuckers actually were on her side this time (sort of). Hell, she *was* a fed now.

The engine stopped, and the headlights switched from high beams to parking lights. Then the driver's-side door opened and a man stepped out. She couldn't see his face, but she could see his frame illuminated by the headlights, the tall lanky figure, the wavy lion's mane hair, and her blood, only having regained some of its warmth, froze in her veins.

It was the guy from the rally, the same guy Sol had warned her about.

The one who had looked at her like he wanted her dead. The thump of her heartbeat turned into a timpani, and she ran.

"Hey!" he called after her.

She didn't pause, running as fast as she could, which, considering the underbrush of the forest and the lack of light, was not very. She pushed through the dry brush, the twigs and briars ripping at her jeans and slowing her down. In less than a minute, she had made it out of the patch of brush to forest floor that was more covered with pine needles, but by now, she could hardly see, eyes still blinded from the high beams of the headlights, the lights from the still-parked car providing little help. But then she did catch a glimpse of another light—a flashlight.

He was coming after her.

"*Fuck!*" She continued into the woods away from the road, keeping low and letting her eyes adjust, the trees periodically lit by Murderguy's flashlight. She stumbled over a root once, then twice, trying to use her hands to feel her way through the trees. "Ampersand?"

No response.

"Ampersand, can you hear me?" She ducked behind a tree just in time for the light to glide over where she had been standing, like a prison spotlight. "Please, I think I'm in danger. Like, serious danger."

Still nothing, and despite the increasing sense that she was about to become the kind of victim of a rape-slash-murder whose bones were only found twenty years after the fact, she could not sense anything from Ampersand at all. The wall had turned to stone.

"Ampersand?" She tried to quiet her breathing, unwilling to speak louder than she already was. "Ampersand, please, can you hear me?" she breathed, lowering herself to her hands and knees. "Please, I'm begging you, answer me!"

Nothing.

She heard the crunch of footsteps on pine needles, and the spotlight came close, dangerously close. She saw a root creating a ledge that went farther down the hill and crawled over it, continuing her descent downhill.

"Hello?" said Murderguy, like he'd wandered into a store and was asking if it was open. Not a particularly loud or aggressive hello, nor a remarkable voice. A normal voice with a normal American accent. The spotlight glided right over her ledge. He wandered closer, the treads of his shoes crunching the dirt.

Why wasn't Ampersand answering her? The footsteps stopped, and she curled herself into a ball. Was Ampersand punishing her? Would he really cut her off in a situation as dangerous as this?

It was that thought that made her stop and wonder if perhaps he *couldn't* hear her.

The flashlight turned to the other direction, and she took a thin, shaking breath. Ampersand's earbud had line-of-sight range, but she'd known him to use it as many as sixty miles away, so she was nowhere close to the maximum range, unless he had left the area altogether. Was it possible that the hills had gotten in the way? Unlikely; they'd been separated by hills before, and the earbud had worked fine.

The flashlight shone back in her direction, and she held her breath, tightened the ball she was in. If it wasn't line of sight that had cut her off from him, maybe it was something else.

Maybe it was some*one* else.

When she opened her eyes, it wasn't Murderguy's flashlight that met her, not his eyes staring down at her, but a different set of eyes hanging in total darkness. There was no silvery iridescent skin surrounding those eyes. There was nothing but formless, black ink. She sucked in a sharp breath that bordered on a shriek, and sat up straight. Upon hearing her, Murderguy whipped his flashlight in her direction, fully illuminating the owner of those eyes.

It stood in a crouch about twenty feet away from Cora, barricaded on either side by pine trees, its eyes open wide, its head moving in a fluid, erratic way like a cobra following a charmer. It had the shape and form of a midsize Similar, larger than Ampersand by at least a foot, though crouched so low its back was level with the ground. But unlike every other amygdaline she had seen, this one was the color of pitch, its midnight skin shining like the shell of a beetle. Every inch of it was black except for its eyes, which sucked up the light from the flashlight and spat it back out like bright silver suns with purple and blue halos, its head down in the antagonistic position that Cora knew well. The bull about to charge.

It took one delicate step forward, and she heard Murderguy's breath catch in his throat, the light of his flashlight now shaking. It took one more step before it jumped, defying all laws of physics, a dinosaur that jumped with the speed of a flea. In a flash, its hand was holding her torso to the forest floor, and one of its feet had pinned her legs.

She screamed.

11

The tiny sliver of her mind still capable of thought wondered if this was Enola Gay, or if this monstrosity might be the much-demonized transient sister species. That this might not be amygdaline at all but physeterine, and she was about to get killed *and* eaten. Perhaps Ampersand had been right and physeterines had been on Earth all along, and Cora was about to discover that in the most gruesome way imaginable. Its movements were animalistic, nothing like the way she had seen Similars move in the past. Its gaze didn't belie intelligence any more than a machine did, half–wild animal, half-algorithm.

Murderguy must have dropped his flashlight in terror, either that or Enola had vaporized him. The flashlight fell in such a way that the only light cast onto the monster was reflected off a few trees, illuminating only its eyes, the rest of the creature shrouded in darkness. She couldn't see its hands, both of which were around her, encasing her like spiders the size of ceiling fans, clamping around her head, closing in on her orifices. "*No!*" she screamed, the only word she was capable of. "*No, no, no!*"

Enola paused, but not for her. Murderguy had caught his attention and was now hanging in midair not three feet away from Enola, whose sharp gaze regarded the man quizzically. Then the man fell to the ground, his muscles slack, his mouth and eyes hanging open.

Then both hands were on her again. She tried to grab for the pulse emitter in her hoodie, but was held fast by those shining black digits, the spider wrapping its prey. She continued to scream on instinct as it pried around her head, forced her cheek to the ground while she fought and struggled and screamed and cried. She didn't realize that it was focused on her earbuds until one of them was pulled out.

For the moment, its attention stayed on the earbud, not on her, one hand still holding her down and the other holding up the earbud for examination. Then, its gaze shot back down at her. It forced her cheek back down to the ground and shoved the earbud back in place.

"Ssssensnse. Auraralll."

A voice in her ear, a new one with a strange echoing effect that made it difficult to understand, like each word was being said twice a second apart, half overlapping. "Ssssensnse."

Cora jerked in each breath, looking up into the eyes of the monster, the only part of it she could really see. Its hands were on her, crawling up her neck, wrapping themselves around her torso, black widows about to inject their poison, suck her dry.

"Ssssensnse," said the voice. "Sspspeakk. Speak. Speak!"

"*No!*" she screamed, still sucking in quick, horrified breaths, tears now streaming down her temples. "*No, no, no!*"

"Speak!"

"I can speak!" she finally managed. "I can speak!"

Enola leaned in closer to her, inches away from her face, and she nearly choked on her shallow breath, gagged on it, cried out incoherently. "Ccallll yyourr mmasterr."

She was in a field again, Obelus was on top of her, his meat hooks inside her, extracting her viscera, the meat that made up her being, for that was all she was, meat to be butchered. She was begging Obelus, *No, no, no, please stop, please stop!*

"Call your master!"

The hand holding her midsection tightened, and she felt the fingers burrowing into her skin, the arms of the spider stabbing, clawing, ripping her in half. Blood pooling on the forest floor, her intestines spilling out. Blood, copper, shit, the smell of shit from her guts, ripped open, on the ground, on his fingers, everything, *everything*. She screamed, it was almost a word, but it wasn't quite a word, just a scream, a primal scream, the last sound she would ever make as the fingers wrapped around her head like vines, preparing to snap it off at the root.

"Where is your master?"

Then a telekinetic blow struck the creature, jerking her off the ground before the monster lost its grip, dropping her onto her side. On instinct, she grabbed her stomach to shove her intestines back inside her, tried to stem the bleeding. She heard a struggle, screeching in Pequod-phonemic. Ampersand's tinny voice, the other one's voice a strange, garbled heap of sounds. She grabbed her intestines from off the forest floor, shoved them back in, curled into a ball. She looked at her hands, looked for the blood, but there was none. Her guts had not been ripped out, there were no viscera all over the ground, no hole in her torso.

She got up on her knees and looked over to see the flashlight illuminating the two of them, Enola easily overpowering Ampersand, standing over him, the mass of a grizzly bear that moved with the speed of a grasshopper. Ampersand was on the ground on his back, writhing, struggling against whatever force Enola had placed on him.

Cora ripped the pulse emitter out of her hoodie, aimed at them, and fired.

The flashlight shorted out, and her vision went black. She heard a heavy *thud* and then only silence so deafening it made her ears ring. She pushed against the terror that was locking her muscles in place, crawling along the ground, feeling around where she thought the flashlight had fallen, all the while keeping her gaze on the inky darkness where Enola had been. She could barely see the silver white of Ampersand's skin, but nothing of Enola, not even his eyes.

After a few minutes of grasping, she found the flashlight. Remarkably, after she swapped the batteries and turned it off and on a few times, the flashlight came back to life, and she shone it in the direction the fight had been. They were both lying there unconscious, Ampersand on his back, angled to one side, and Enola lying prone on top of him. She nearly dropped the flashlight in horror at the sight of him, his hands especially, so uncannily evocative of that one most terrifying species of spider.

She stood up and moved toward them, keeping the pulse emitter aimed squarely at Enola with her other arm crushed against her chest. She practically made a running start at Enola and kicked him to get him off Ampersand, but he hardly budged. He probably had at least a hundred pounds on Ampersand, putting his bulk somewhere in the five-hundred-pound range. At just shy of four hundred pounds, Ampersand might have been easier to move if his bulk were more concentrated like a human's, but his limbs were so long, his head so big, and most of his weight was in his torso, so even moving that meant that the rest of him dragged along like so many balls and chains.

She got them a couple of feet apart before she decided, *Fuck it*. She turned the flashlight off to prevent it from shorting again, and shot Enola point-blank in the back with the pulse emitter. And then again. She kept shooting him until the pulse emitter had no energy left to shoot. Then she kept firing.

After a number of impotent clicks, she turned the flashlight back on and began looking around for a weapon. Any weapon. A shovel, perhaps. She wondered if a sharp stick would do. She wanted to kill it. She wanted it dead. If she couldn't kill Obelus, at least she could kill this one.

Now crashing from her high of terror, she was starting to feel nauseous, the thrumming of blood through her skull turning into a headache. What a barbaric thing to think. Her memory drifted back to a moment she had last year with Ampersand, one in which he had expressed confusion over why she hadn't killed him the first time an opportunity had presented itself. He was an alien, was he not? An unknown thing, a terror, a threat. And she had told him, *I wouldn't attack you when you're helpless. Even if I had known exactly how to kill you, I wouldn't have done it.* Why would she not extend the same grace to Enola?

The only help she could be at the moment was to make her way back through the woods to the cave, retrieve the pill bug, bring it back, and hope she was able to revive Ampersand before Enola came to. It had taken at least an hour to get all the way down here, but then she didn't have the benefit of a dead man's SUV to steal. Assuming he was dead— he'd *looked* dead when his face fell to the ground, eyes open and mouth slack, but she hadn't checked.

She approached him, noted that his eyes had closed even if his mouth hadn't, and his muscles were not completely slack. Now she could see him more clearly—a closely trimmed beard covering his long face, his chin and nose both forming sharp points. She felt for a pulse and found one easily. Enola had not killed him.

She dug around in his jacket pocket and found the key to the SUV, as well as a large pocketknife, which she gladly stole. She felt around in his pants pocket, and found a badge, one that was attached to his pocket with a clip. She pulled it out and was greeted with a big old PRESS at the top of the badge, directly beneath it a name and a publication: Kaveh Mazandarani, *The New Yorker.*

Oh no.

Oh *no.*

She returned his press pass, but kept the pocketknife and the key to his SUV, and for a fleeting moment humored the idea of finishing what Enola hadn't. She shook her head, disgusted with herself, and ran toward his vehicle before she could entertain that thought any further.

· · · · ·

Driving back up the hill to roughly where she had found the road cut her travel time considerably. Making it back to the cave was a little more difficult, but she remembered a few landmarks that she had noted just in case she did need to come back. Walking into the dark cave was an exercise in horror movie terror, the night sky black and both Ampersand and his soft little drone lights now gone. Her breath echoed against the walls of the cavern as she entered, one hand holding the pulse emitter, the other the shaking flashlight.

No sign of Obelus. She flicked her flashlight to either side of the cave, keeping the pulse emitter up like a gun, as if she were a cop entering a hostile perp's house. She'd always found that scene at the end of *The Silence of the Lambs* where Clarice entered Buffalo Bill's house terrifying, but right now she was feeling a new sense of empathy with Clarice. She kept her back to the wall of the cave so nothing could sneak up from behind her, her eyes on the pill bug in the center of the chamber where she had left it.

She tried to steady her hand and her breathing, eyes darting between the exit of the cave and that dark second chamber. After about a minute of no movement, she moved to the center of the chamber and knelt, still circling the room like a radar, and picked up the pill bug, keeping her eyes on the entrance to the dark second chamber the whole time.

"*Where is he?*"

Cora heard the voice before she caught the movement out of the corner of her eye, and she whipped around to see Obelus blocking the exit of the cave. On instinct, she raised the pulse emitter toward him.

"*Where is he?*" Obelus repeated, posture unmistakably antagonistic. "*I demand that you take me to him.*"

She wondered if he could tell how afraid she was, how loud her breathing was in this goddamn reverberant cave. "No."

"*Your kind cannot fathom him,*" said Obelus. "*My dear symphyle needs his own kind. He will only do harm to yours. Take me to him, simple creature. You are beneath all of this.*"

Even with his memories "suppressed," his vile personality was still intact. Perhaps there was much he didn't remember, but he knew their relationship within the amygdaline hierarchy, and in his mind, Cora was so far beneath them they might as well be using different units of measurement. *Simple creature.* Disposable animals. Nonpersons.

Vincent.

The adrenaline that had been gasoline on her terror was now gasoline on a plume of rage. This was still the same person, the same monster. The same *murderer.* She raised the pulse emitter toward him. Obelus clearly knew exactly what that was and what she was doing, because his antagonistic posture only sharpened, and he backed away. "*Why do you do this?*"

She stood up, shoving the pill bug into her jacket pocket, images flashing in her mind as answers to his question. Obelus disintegrating the blast door at NORAD. Obelus digging his claws into her body, ripping her to shreds. Vincent Park giving her the Yamaha guitar. Vincent Park half-conscious in the back of a van after an accident Obelus had caused. Vincent Park turned to dust.

"Because you killed my friend."

She fired, and the flashlight shorted, plunging her into darkness, and it was only here that she realized how poorly she had thought this through. That rage plume was immediately doused by terror. She heard something, perhaps Obelus stumbling. In a panic, she pushed the trigger, but nothing happened.

Fumbling, she backed away from him, spilling the batteries out of the flashlight, switching them around, and then jamming them back in, bashing them until the light turned back on, shining it at the cave entrance. Obelus seemed like he was righting himself.

Then something changed in Obelus's posture, his expression. His eyes flashed, focused. Something inside him that had been previously severed had now reconnected.

He recognized her.

She raised the now-drained pulse emitter, but before she could even press another impotent click, a telekinetic shove knocked it out of her hand, and a second one threw her onto her back, causing her to drop the flashlight. She scrambled to get it back, whipping it back toward the entrance of the cave, only to find it no longer blocked.

Obelus was gone.

12

Between her frantic scramble back to the cave, Obelus escaping, and making it all the way back down to the battleground without getting lost, it had to have taken at least an hour. She had thought her quest futile, that one or both of them would have regained consciousness and whoever got there first would be the victor. But while, to her shock and amazement, Ampersand and Enola had not regained consciousness, the third party had. She found him crouched over the two unconscious aliens, wincing at the light of the flashlight in his eyes as she approached.

"Get away from him!"

He shot to his feet. "What?"

At a loss for what else to do, she gun-pointed the pulse emitter at him. "I said, get the fuck away from them."

"What the—"

"Shut the fuck up," she spat, her mouth sticky from dehydration and her eyes prickling with exhaustion. He backed away as she approached him, head high, back straight, exuding the aura that yes, she could take his life away, and she'd do it, too. "You saw what this did to them, imagine what it would do to a human."

"I didn't see what 'this' did to them," he said carefully, like he was talking to a crazy person. "I was unconscious. Did that thing . . . ?"

"Yes, I said, shut the fuck up, or I'll fucking shoot you, too. Hands up." She continued toward him, and he put his hands up. Keeping the pulse emitter leveled at him, she turned the flashlight away from him, illuminating both Ampersand and Enola. Enola's eyes were open. Ampersand's were not.

"Don't move, don't say anything," she said, putting the flashlight down, but keeping the pulse emitter leveled at him. She took the pill bug out of her coat and pressed it to Ampersand's upper back, not taking her eyes off the man. "Get on your knees. Keep your hands up. Don't say a fucking word."

By now, his expression had turned cold. His eyes were striking, the color of jade coated in frost, even more menacing with the flashlight illuminating him from below as if he were telling a scary story at a campfire.

Ampersand stirred, and she nearly choked on her relief that he moved before Enola did. He regained himself much more quickly than she'd seen him do in the past after an energy pulse had taken him out. He hoisted himself to his feet, and Murderguy's cool demeanor broke. He took short, frightened breaths as his eyes darted back and forth between Cora and the alien monster that she had deliberately revived.

The moment his eyes came back into focus, they found Enola, and Ampersand practically fell on top of him. With zero delicacy, Ampersand ripped the shell off Enola's back. Then he started frantically extracting bits of his body, welding his fingers together and jamming them into his back like trowels into the earth.

This triggered some reaction, because Enola was suddenly spasmodic. At first silently so, then very *not* silent, making strange, natural-sounding garbling noises that were half-dolphin, half–dying goat, more like the Genome than any noise Cora had ever heard come from a true post-natural amygdaline. It was horrid, piercing, and echoed into the hills. Someone was going to hear this.

Ampersand tried to stop the bleating, but that only seemed to stop his airflow, and clapping one's hand over the speaking-holes of an amygdaline was lethal in a way that it was not to a human. Then, a protrusion grew out of Ampersand's fingers, something bigger and sharper than the syringe she'd seen him use so many times, and he stabbed—literally, stabbed—the thing straight into the back of Enola's neck.

That quieted him down.

For several minutes, Ampersand wrestled with the pitiful Enola, binding his forelimbs behind him and strapping his hind limbs under him. When Ampersand had Enola restrained to a point where he couldn't easily escape, he turned his attention to Murderguy like he was about to skewer the man. Murderguy's nostrils flared in terror, and he stumbled backward, falling down against a tree.

"Wait!" said Cora, moving between the two of them.

"He cannot be allowed to remember this."

"He recognized me."

Ampersand took a moment to consider this. *"You cannot question him here."*

Which meant they had a hostage. Great, another skill to add to the résumé. "Hands up. Keep your mouth shut," she said, shining her flashlight right into his face.

He raised his arms above his head, his expression compliant, but calculating. She moved away from Murderguy, gesturing for Ampersand to follow. When she was out of earshot, she whispered, "Obelus ran away."

It was obvious he assumed she had attacked Obelus, and she clarified, "I didn't . . . I didn't hurt him, I swear. I came back to get the pill bug to revive you, and when he saw me, he seemed to recognize me. I tried to use the pulse emitter on him, but . . . he seems to be able to manipulate electromagnetic fields." This last part she added with a hint of accusation. Non-Similar amygdalines weren't supposed to have any telekinetic capabilities like Ampersand did. Their bodies weren't designed for it. And yet Obelus had it. Meaning Ampersand had put it there.

"Recognized you," he repeated.

"I think whatever you were using to suppress his memories . . . failed."

Ampersand digested this inasmuch as a being without a digestive system can digest things. He took a moment to take stock of Enola, still mewling, still pitiful, and still horrible.

"What are we going to do?" It was as it came out of her mouth that she realized she had circled back to thinking of the two of them as a "we."

Ampersand looked at Enola for a very long ten seconds or so. *"He is unnaturally producing a chemical that changes his mind and body. That is why his skin has changed to this color; his bodily fluid is flushed with it. If he remains bound, he cannot produce more substance, and if I don't extract the substance from his system slowly, over a period of hours, he will die."*

She stood transfixed by the horrible, wretched creature. A part of her wanted Ampersand to put it out of its misery. "Jesus." She tore her gaze away, looked at Ampersand. "You'll take him back to the cave?"

"*It is my last secure safe location. I have to do a transfusion, and do it slowly.*"

"But Obelus . . ."

"*Obelus's life is in no immediate danger. If I do not do a slow transfusion to get this toxin out of Enola's system, he will die. I cannot lose another symphyle, dear one.*"

At this, something stung in her throat. The wall had thinned somewhat, and she felt his desperation. Three symphyles, all right here, and they all had to survive. Obelus could wait, Enola needed attention now, and Cora was the closest thing he had to help. Triage.

She looked back at Murderguy, who was looking at her as if she were a terrorist who had taken him hostage, half-afraid, half-disgusted. "Okay. I'll use his car to drive back up to the cave and tie him up somewhere and question him later."

"*Move quickly. I will not leave you alone with him until he's restrained.*"

Ampersand returned his attention to Enola, and Cora marched toward Murderguy, "gun" drawn, flashlight beaming directly into his eyes. "On your feet."

He sprang up, keeping his eyes locked on hers and not the "gun." Here was that expression again, the one she'd seen on him earlier that day, the one that betrayed a mind running through all the ways he'd like to hurt her.

"Hands behind your head," she said, hoping that it would make her look like she knew what she was doing. He complied. "Do not make a sound. Walk to your SUV."

Without pause, he obeyed, walking in front of her while she followed about three feet behind, holding up the gun that could not harm a human. Once they reached the car, she ordered him to open the back of the SUV.

Murderguy wasn't quite as tall as her frightened mind's eye had remembered him, but he was more than a head taller than she was, easily cracking six feet. He opened the rear of the SUV and returned his hands to the back of his head, returning his gaze to her, both unimpressed and expectant, as if to say, *What now, genius?* He didn't even look afraid; instead, he looked calculating. Like perhaps the plans to kill her might come to fruition in a different way from what he had hoped, but he still saw it working out in the end.

"Do you have any rope?" she asked. He opened his mouth, but she cut him off: "And don't lie, or he'll know."

That cracked his stone expression a tiny bit. This had been something she'd kept in her back pocket for a while; when in doubt, play off people's fears that aliens can read minds.

"No."

"Do you have any twine?"

His lip twitched as though he'd been hoping to evade having to tell the truth if she wasn't specific enough. "Yes."

"Do you have any duct tape?"

"Yes."

"Go get it."

He hesitated, hands still behind his head, and then he crawled inside the SUV, slowly, carefully. Too slowly. "Move it."

He pulled out a white cardboard box, out of which he removed a spool of twine and a roll of duct tape, which was nearly used up. She shoved the gun in the back of her jeans before his feet were even on the ground. Then he put his hands back behind his head, his expression a lake on a cold day with no wind.

"Hands together in front of you," she said, keeping her voice low and serious.

She tried not to touch his skin as her shaking fingers wound the twine around his wrists. She wrapped it no fewer than ten times, cutting the twine with his pocketknife after she tied a knot. Then, she tore off a strip of duct tape, and nearly slapped it onto his mouth, then covered his eyes with a second strip.

She pulled the pulse emitter back out, and jammed it into the small of his back to remind him it was there. She grabbed the nape of his shirt, and pushed him to the front passenger side of the SUV. She seated herself in the driver's side, turned the ignition, and the engine rolled to a purr. She switched on the headlights and looked back down into the woods.

Ampersand was hunched over with his back flat like a table, his head turned to her like a cat, his eyes on fire from the light of the headlights. She could see Enola now, the creature's legs folded under him, his arms jammed up behind him like the wings of a Christmas turkey. Then the fluid of his plate slid out of his back, over both him and Enola, and they disappeared.

Now she was alone. Alone with her murderhostage.

She took a minute to center herself, but this time, she noticed something—his iPod, plugged into the speaker of the car, that it was plugged in and playing, but the volume was low. Out of curiosity, she turned up the volume, and a white-guy-with-an-acoustic-guitar version of David Bowie's "Let's Dance" met her ears. It took her a second to really comprehend that, yes, someone would elect to listen to a sad guy with a guitar bastardize David Bowie. Seeming to intuit that she was looking at him, Murderhostage craned his head in her direction and shrugged. The motherfucker shrugged.

Maybe she should have killed him.

His entire playlist was like that. They were about halfway through Old Crow Medicine Show's "Wagon Wheel" before she found a side road near the cave. She hopped out of the car, opened the gate, and drove to the other side, closing the gate behind them and parking the SUV well out of sight from the road. Then she pulled him out of the car and started marching him into the woods.

Even though she now had a flashlight, it was difficult to march a grown man through hilly, wooded terrain when he wasn't able to see where he was going. He was breathing heavier now, perhaps from the exertion, but more likely because he was afraid. It certainly felt like a mob hit was imminent.

The second she had that thought, he slipped and fell down the hill a few feet, balling up on instinct, his back landing him against a tree with a strained "Mmph!" She gasped, instinctively moving to help him before remembering that he was supposed to be in fear for his life. "I guess that's far enough," she said.

She sat him up against the tree, now getting close enough to smell him. Whatever he was wearing smelled . . . expensive, like vanilla and leather. She tied him to the tree, a few strands around his waist, a few around his chest, and then a few around his neck. Was there a way one was supposed to tie men to trees? A method? Should she have googled it?

"Don't move," she said, as satisfied as she could be that he couldn't get away. The twine around his neck she had tied particularly tight, probably too tight; one wrong move and that twine could strangle him. She turned from him, heading back to the cave, hoping that the wrong move wasn't hers.

· · · · ·

She found them in the middle of the main chamber of the cavern, drones illuminating the cave with soft light. Ampersand was fastening translucent bulbous devices into the back of Enola's head, or at least she figured that they might have been translucent at one point in time—now they were smudged with a substance that looked like tar. The bulbs sticking out of the back of his head reminded her of the egg sacs of spiders.

Enola made a futile move to get away, but Ampersand caught him. He had a pile of the substance she had seen in the other room, the strange skin-like stuff he had been using as his honeycombs, and he was melting it into strips that looked like wide, thick belts. He took one of the strips, and she could feel the heat off it as he welded it to the floor, keeping Enola's legs tucked under his body. This was only the last of several of these belts that Ampersand had put in place to keep Enola restrained.

"*I have begun a transfusion.*"

"What are you transfusing *from?*" she asked, keeping her distance.

"*Myself. He has altered his chemical makeup to pump emotional nullifiers and hallucinogens into his brain along with basic glucose and other elements needed to stay alive.*"

"He's altered his brain . . . why?"

Ampersand kept his focus on his task, moving from Enola's head to whatever was under the "wing" of his back, seeming to rip parts out of him, reshape them, and jam them back in like lawn darts. "*I can only speculate. I assume this particular mixture is intended to keep his intelligence levels high while keeping certain sensitivities low or nonexistent.*"

He pulled at something on Enola's neck, rougher, angrier than Cora had ever seen him handle anything. Enola bleated out another couple of squalling noises before falling silent. But given the rigidity of his body, the way he was still trembling and struggling, he was obviously still conscious.

"Where would Obelus go?"

"*I do not know. If he has indeed recovered his memories, he will not want to be found.*"

Cora gawped at the sheer impossibility of the situation, unable to tear her eyes from Enola. "We are in over our heads. We need help."

"*No.*"

"You cannot handle *this* and hunt for Obelus at the same time!"

"*No.*"

"I'm scared. I'm worried for you, and . . . there's no way you can handle both Enola and Obelus, and I can't help you. We need outside help before Obelus—"

"*I cannot allow it.*"

"Is there something you aren't telling me? Yes, I agree, it would suck to pony up to all the secrets and lies, but the alternative—"

"*The alternative is death.*" At this, he looked right at her with the entirety of his focus.

"How . . ."

"*This incident would be the justification Esperas needs to have me euthanized.*"

"What?" she breathed. "He couldn't possibly . . ."

"*My removal has been his primary goal since he discovered the truth of my relationship to Obelus.*" His amber eyes flashed, and he returned his attention to Enola. "*With no definite stance from the American government as to our personhood, Esperas's understanding is that we have every right to deal with our own. He most certainly can, and he would.*"

She hadn't even considered how Esperas might take the news that Obelus was still alive; disrespectful as it was, it made sense for Ampersand to hide Obelus from Cora (in his alien brain, he'd see it as what she didn't know wouldn't hurt her). But Esperas already loathed him for keeping his relationship to Obelus a secret, endangering the lives of the entire Fremda group and resulting in the loss of their only other Similar. What would he do with the revelation that Ampersand had been keeping another massive Obelus-related secret? She didn't know the details of their respective destructive capabilities, but she did know that if it came down to a brute force showdown between Brako and Ampersand, Ampersand would lose.

"*Dear one, as you have observed, Esperas has little interest in remaining on this planet with your civilization. Esperas would have little trouble persuading his Similar to have me killed with the right incentive.*" He looked at Enola. "*I cannot imagine a better incentive than this.*"

"If Esperas attacked you, or killed you, there's no way the government would allow them to stay without—"

"*Esperas understands the legal situation, and he understands that there is nothing stopping him from exacting his own justice. If Esperas finds out that I have kept Obelus alive, if he sees Enola's condition at all, that will be all the justification he needs to have us killed, and his subordinates will cheer him for it. If you tell your militarists about this, you are consigning us both to death.*"

(2/1/2008 7:58 PM PST) Paris: Did you make it past the police blockade?

(2/1/2008 9:41 PM PST) Paris: The suspense is killing me. I'm trying to stay awake by watching Conan but I have to go to work in the morning and I'm fading fast

(2/1/2008 9:55 PM PST) Paris: ok I'm turning in, pls let me know what ET looks like ttyl <3 <3 <3

(2/2/2008 4:45 AM PST) Paris: kaveh are you okay? Please answer me

(2/2/2008 4:47 AM PST) Paris: Please please answer me, im legit scared, tried to call you on your main and your burner and they're both going straight to voice mail. What do i do? Do i call the police? You aren't supposed to be up there . . .

(2/2/2008 5:04 AM PST) Paris: Kaveh please call me!!!

13

Kaveh's main concern for a while had been when, not if, he was going to piss himself. He'd been in similar situations to this before—not tied to a tree exactly, but he had been detained with no bathroom accessible. In that earlier case, he'd had to soil the corner of the room he was sharing with his photographer, and they'd agreed to endure the stench of urine in the hope that it wouldn't come to having to endure the stench of that other form of waste humans are wont to produce.

In that earlier case, his hands had not been tied, so going some thirty-six hours locked in a room in Tabriz had not presented *such* a dire predicament. Even though he could still move his hands, the way Ortega had tied him up had made it impossible to reach his fly. But that wasn't the worst part—the twine around his neck, that was the worst part. She'd tied it so tightly that even a slight nod cut off his blood supply, and he hadn't been able to move his head in however long she'd been gone, somewhere in the vein of three or four years, by his estimates (or maybe a couple of hours). There was a pretty good chance he'd die of strangulation before he really had to have a come-to-Jesus moment on the whole pee issue, and then, *then,* well, at least he wouldn't have to bear the burden of that restraint.

Then he heard footsteps and tried to tune in to whether or not the steps were human. He couldn't remember what the alien footfall sounded like; there had been so much commotion, he didn't remember seeing them walk, except for once when Ortega had pulled the giant white one aside and asked if she could talk to it alone for a sec. Which, incidentally, what the fuck?

The footsteps grew closer, and now he could hear breathing. Definitely human, unless the aliens had the ability to shape-shift, too, which, sure, why not? They apparently had the ability to lift humans off the ground with their minds. Whites versus Blacks, big alien superpowered battles, and he had been unconscious for the best part, apparently? Probably an Autobots versus Decepticons situation. Maybe Ortega was an alien, too, a robot drone that took the form of a person he recognized, and the aliens had chosen this semi-obscure figure in his life just to fuck with him.

He could sense her crouched in front of him now, so close he could feel her breath on his skin, steeling herself for . . . something. Probably not a point-blank shot—people don't crouch for that, they stand like three feet away, shaking finger slithering its way over the trigger while they say things like, "It didn't need to come to this, Roxanne. You *made* me do this!"

She started to peel down the duct tape she'd placed over his eyes, which, given the length of time it had been affixed, had basically become one with his skin. He crushed his eyes closed as tightly as he could to protect his sensitive eyelids. She wasn't merciless, so it was only really, really painful. Finally, he opened his eyes for the first time in hours, and once his vision cleared, he got a look at her.

No gun, but she had his pocketknife drawn, and she was trying so, so very hard to look like a badass. But looking at her posturing, he wanted to shake his head. She wasn't a killer. She wasn't even a maimer. *What are you even doing?* he wondered for roughly the fiftieth time. *Are you under duress? Are you being mind controlled?* It didn't seem like either was the case, and either way, she wasn't the one he needed to worry about.

She didn't look much like Nils at all, with her round face and slightly upturned button nose a direct contrast to Nils's pert little beak. And of course that goofy blue hair, which in the darkness actually looked kind of ethereal, fitting, like what an alien's herald would look like, just left of human.

She cut the twine around his neck (thank God), and hardly breaking eye contact, she cut all the rest of the twine that was binding him to the tree, but not the twine that was binding his wrists and turning his fingers into cold water balloons.

"Get up," she said. Easier said than done when one had been unable to move for several hours and desperately had to pee. "Walk in front of me. Down the hill."

Kaveh stumbled like a baby ostrich standing for the first time, taking a moment to linger on her before he did as he was told. She was afraid of him, that much was obvious, but he couldn't really blame her. It was probably because of the stink eye he'd been giving Sol Kaplan back during the rally, that was weird enough, but finding her alone on the road and then following her into the woods? Yeah, in hindsight, that wasn't a good look. But what was he supposed to do? Yell, "Hey, did that hemorrhoid Kaplan abandon you out here in the middle of nowhere because that's sure what it looks like and yes I know who he is and yes I know who you are but don't worry about it"?

They walked in silence, save for Ortega occasionally giving him direction to veer to the right or left. After about five minutes, she said, "Stop." He wanted to plead his case to take a piss, which he could probably pull off even with his hands tied now that his arms weren't strapped to a tree, but his mouth was still gagged, and there was no way for him to gesture that he needed to pee in a way that she was likely to appreciate.

She got behind him and marched him forward, holding the back of his shirt. Then he saw where she was taking him—a cave. Clearly, not a natural one, as there were no caves in this part of the world, let alone the kind that opened with giant gaping holes in the side of a mountain.

The inside of the cave was perhaps thirty feet in diameter, rounder than it was square. The walls were glassy like obsidian, and at the center of it were the two aliens surrounded by a ring of dim light, a few dim light balls hanging in the air like fairies. The white one stood over the black one, which was lying prone on the floor, practically one with it. There was black bile all over the floor like tar, leaking out of the creature. It was grotesque.

"Sit down," said Ortega. He did as she said, and she tied the twine around his chest, locking his elbows in place, and this time, she tied his feet. Oh, if she only knew that in a different context, he would totally be into that sort of thing (although ideally not the one *being* tied up).

He backed himself up against the smooth wall of the cave and waited. Ortega moved close to the horrifying spectacle at the center of the chamber and sat down, drawing her knees up to her chest. Occasionally, she'd ask questions like, "How much more is there?" or "Have you ever seen that before?"

After about an hour, he saw a thin blue light emanating from the mouth of the cave. Sunrise was coming; he might live to see another day after all, whee. By this point, Ortega had started to nod off, and the white alien monster wasn't being so violent to the black one's body anymore. He dearly hoped the black ones were the Decepticons, because what he was beholding looked downright cruel. It was hard not to feel for the black one. It was affixed so firmly to the floor with so many harnesses of mysterious alien make, it could barely move.

A couple of hours after sunrise, the white one stood upright, its long stick fingers covered in what looked like tar. It backed away from the black one, and the black tar substance melted off its fingers like candle wax onto the floor. The black one had an elaborate system of glass-like bulbs now sticking out from under the wing-like shell of its back and what looked like hundreds of delicate wires flowing from those bulbs into the back of its head. The tar substance was everywhere.

The white one moved to exit the cave, and Ortega followed it. "Are you going to leave him in this mess?"

The white one stopped, turned, and looked at her.

"It feels cruel to leave him lying in his own filth like this."

It continued to look at her, its big gemstone eyes glowing. They seemed to catch the light of the morning sun, glowing much brighter now than they had during the night.

"Well, tell me how to clean it up."

The alien looked at her, silent.

"Will plastic gloves help?"

Still silent.

"I won't, but will soap hurt him?"

Kaveh shook his head in utter bewilderment. Okay, not Autobots and Decepticons. Maybe blackie had just had a rough night and his bro was doing him a solid. Kaveh had been there a time or twenty.

"If it's all biomatter, that means it's going to rot. I need disinfectant."

This time, there was a long pause between her words and . . . whatever she was hearing, then she grew agitated. "Wait, how is this my fault?"

what the pluperfect passive subjunctive fuck

The alien lowered its head a bit, its fingers curling up like it was one of those claw machines you try and fail to grab toys with.

"Why was he able to manipulate electromagnetic fields like that at all? Why did he even have that ability?"

The alien moved closer to her in what looked like a clear intimidation gesture. She didn't even flinch.

"Well, it worked! He ran into a human, and he protected himself. I tried to stop him, and I couldn't."

The alien was now standing right over her, and she had to crane her neck to look at it properly.

"Don't you dare blame this on me!" she said, nearly shouting. "You threaten my mind, let me wander off into the woods where you know Enola is running around somewhere, trust me with an untested weapon that you didn't know the full side effects for, and then blame me when a fail-safe you installed to protect Obelus from humans succeeds in protecting him from a human. He could have killed me!"

The alien's hands relaxed a bit, and he took a step back.

"It's a good goddamn thing, then! If he wants to kill anyone, he'll have to get creative." She looked over at Kaveh, sparing a glance for the condemned. "What about him?"

Oh merciful God, now that thing was looking at him with its horrible demon eyes. Both of them watched him, and it seemed to him that what he was looking at was one unit. The alien with its head down, cocked slightly, as if devising the most tantalizing way to be rid of the interloper, and the blue-haired girl who apparently had no compunction about yelling at the creature like it was her boyfriend.

"I think I would prefer you didn't do that no matter who it was," she said. Another moment of silence, the two staring at him. Then she said, "Okay."

She turned to look at the alien, and Kaveh thought he saw a flash of worry, maybe even fear pass over her features. "How would you kill him?"

!!!!!!!!

He nearly pissed his pants then and there. A part of him figured, why not? At least one's bladder can know peace before one dies.

That look of worry on her face heightened. "That's humane to you?"

The alien looked at Kaveh with those glowing hellhound eyes, redder now in the sunlight. It lingered on him for a few seconds, then the carapace on the creature's back cracked open, and what looked like liquid metal sheets spilled out of each side like satin, sliding like a living, viscous fluid down its legs and arms and neck, enveloping the thing in metal as it crouched down onto the floor, compressing itself almost like a giant bullet. Then, the metal-encased creature disappeared from sight.

Kaveh let out a shaking breath, then another, and watched as Ortega approached him, her expression completely blank. She pulled out the pocketknife, and he sat up straight.

I could take her, he thought. *The alien is gone, and she's not that big.* Even tied up, he stood a good chance of wresting the knife away, cutting himself loose, getting the fuck out of there. His breath hitched as she knelt in front of him. She held up the knife and stared at him, her expression still blank, dazed. Then, she took a long, slow breath. Her guard was down. He could do it—he could take her.

She lowered the knife and cut the twine around his feet. Then she paused, looking at him. She then cut the twine around his wrists, all the while maintaining that melancholy, blank expression. Finally, she folded the pocketknife and handed it back to him.

He didn't move for a few seconds before lifting up his hand to accept the pocketknife, backing even farther into the wall. He very slowly, very carefully, lifted his right hand to peel the duct tape from his mouth. He waited for her to say something, give him permission to speak, but she didn't say anything, just bowed her head a touch as if to say, *You win.*

"I . . . ," Kaveh started, pausing to see if he still wasn't allowed to speak. "I really have to pee."

She looked at him.

"Is it okay if I go . . . do that?"

She considered, then nodded, looking toward the monster lying in a pool of its own black bile at the center of the chamber. Kaveh hesitated, still suspecting this might be a trap, before deciding fuck it, he was going to die, anyway, if he didn't pee.

He stepped outside into the harsh morning sunlight, his muscles electric with a night of fear, still not quite believing this was real, not sure if unzipping his fly was a good idea. What if he got zapped with his dick out? Maybe that was exactly what they were waiting for, those sick alien fucks.

It wasn't even a good pee. It was the kind where when at long last the moment comes you've been holding it for so long that the muscles are like, *Nope, sorry, buddy! The storm surge is coming, we gotta keep these levees in place!* When he finally forced it out, it was more painful than a relief. It was only when he had finished that it occurred to him that now was probably a good time to run for his goddamn life.

He turned, half expecting there to be no cave entrance at all, but there it was, roughly human height. He could even see the unnatural smooth floor. Yes, now was definitely a good time to run for his goddamn life. But it wasn't going to happen. In Kaveh Mazandarani's inner struggle between self-preservation and curiosity, a struggle that occurred more often for him than it did for most people, curiosity was fated to win every time.

14

A headache was forming that felt like a toothy parasite was gnawing at her left temple from the inside as Cora stared at the monster in the center of the chamber. Ampersand had "drained" the "poison," but the creature still looked like it had been sculpted out of black ink, an apparent permanent side effect. The technique Ampersand had used to weld him to the floor had been crude by his standards, like straps melded one with the glass-like rock beneath him like a straitjacket made of black steel. The longer Enola stayed there, all but welded to the floor of the cave, the more the effluvium around him congealed, and it was becoming harder to clean by the second.

Ampersand had not given her any indication when, or if, Enola might regain consciousness, which was another thing keeping her paralyzed where she stood. What if he woke up? What if he started trying to talk to her again with that horrible voice? Ampersand had indicated that whatever cocktail had turned his body that color had also changed his personality, but she hadn't really seen anything resembling a personality; he felt like an animal, corrupted software, a glitching machine. She struggled not to think of Enola as an "it."

More pressing, she had no means of travel besides Murderguy's SUV, but at least she still had his key, so he wasn't driving anywhere. Then there was the issue of Murderguy himself, who had run outside "to pee" but had likely run off, as any sane person would do. Ampersand had been in such a hurry to hunt for Obelus that the only way she could keep him from doing something deeply unethical to this guy was to volunteer to take care of him, on the condition that if he

~*~*tried anything*~*~ he'd get zapped in the worst possible way. She'd assumed Ampersand had been exaggerating. She *hoped* he'd been exaggerating.

She'd already forgotten what his name was, save that it was long and kind of South Asian–sounding. Indian, perhaps? If she got back to civilization before he did, she might be able to figure out who he was based on what she knew about him. The fact that he worked for *The New Yorker* was a clue to finding out who he was.

Then she remembered; hadn't Nils had some affiliation with *The New Yorker*?

"Hello?"

Cora gasped and turned around, shocked to see Murderguy standing a respectful twenty feet away, palms facing her. Suddenly, the gnawing parasite headache exploded into a firework, and before she knew it, her breath was coming hard and fast, picking up speed with each inhale.

Fuck no, she thought. Now was *not* the fucking time for a panic attack.

"I don't mean any harm," the guy said, taking a baby step toward her, his eyes big and as innocent as a man his age was capable of. Thirty-something? At least thirty. Cora held her breath in an attempt to halt the hyperventilation and backed herself into the wall. Her body was screaming for air, outraged at the interruption of its regularly scheduled panic attack. She closed her eyes and held her breath tighter.

The next thing she knew, she was on the floor, and the pain in her head had now migrated to the outer left parietal bone, as if she'd been bashed in the head with a baseball bat. Murderguy was standing over her holding his hands up like he was being held at gunpoint, his eyes the size of small moons.

"Oh my God, are you okay?" He spoke with such terror that she was pretty sure that whatever had just happened to her, he hadn't been the cause of it.

"I'm fine," she croaked, an obvious lie.

Did I just fucking black out?

"Can you tell me who the president is?" he asked, crouching down a few feet away from her, hands still up.

She felt her head to assess the damage. It felt like she'd been clubbed like a baby seal. "What?"

"You just . . . had a pretty bad fall. It looked like you hit your head pretty hard. Can you tell me who the president is?"

She forced herself to sit up. "Dick Cheney."

He lowered himself to his knees and whispered, "Are you being held prisoner?"

Her breath was still shallow, and she was having a hard time concentrating on him at all. She leaned against the back of the cave, trying to shake it off, but her skull throbbed painfully. "No."

He nodded like a hostage negotiator on a particularly difficult assignment. "I know this might be out of your control," he said in a gentle voice, "but please don't kill me."

"Huh?" Then she remembered what he had overheard. "Oh."

"Whatever is going on, I might be able to help you. I think I'm probably already on your side."

"Don't worry about it."

"Don't worry about it?" He sounded offended.

"I mean, it was a conditional threat—if he's not around to protect me, he'd have to take extreme measures if you were to try to harm me. So . . . don't do that, and you'll be fine."

"*He?*" The man assessed her piteously as if he were talking to someone who spoke in tongues. "Are you . . . okay?"

She looked at him incredulously. *Do I look okay?* she thought. Then she remembered what had happened earlier in the day yesterday. What Kaplan had said about him being dangerous, why she had run from him in the first place.

"Who are you?" she asked.

He sat all the way down on the smooth floor with her. "My name's Kaveh."

Kaveh, she thought. *Kaveh of the long Indian-sounding name, who works for* The New Yorker.

Then it clicked where she'd heard his name before.

A journalist at *The New Yorker* had obtained documents detailing the detainment of her mother and siblings last year, a guy who'd sent said documents to Nils the second he'd gotten them. A journalist Sol had described as an unscrupulous "shitbag burnout." Sol had wondered why this guy had sent those documents to Nils instead of publishing them himself.

"You," she whispered. "You work with Nils."

His expression, which had briefly been one of professional courtesy, morphed back into fear. *Guilty,* that expression read. *Guilty, guilty, guilty.*

"Oh, God, you're going to go to Nils with this."

"No," he said, realizing his affiliation with Nils could be his death sentence. "I won't, I swear. I don't have any formal affiliation with him. I barely talk to him."

"Then why did you pass the documents about my family's detainment to him? Why didn't you publish them yourself?"

His mouth hung open, as though he was weighing the wisdom of a lie or a half truth. "I thought it would be the right thing to do. It was his family, not mine. And he was such a lightning rod, all eyes were on him. I thought he would get much more immediate results than I would have."

"All you did was give him more power to boost his own celebrity. You didn't have to go to him. It didn't have to be him."

"I'm sorry. I just didn't think about it like that."

She closed her eyes, reminding herself that regardless of his motives, the poor guy was terrified. "Have you talked to him since?"

"Not really, no. He sent me a thank-you note, though."

She opened her eyes to glare at him. "Are you still friends?"

"I'm not sure Nils has friends," he said with a nervous chuckle.

Her hand slid over her head and then joined her other hand in covering her face. "Don't worry," she said, voice muffled by her hands. "No one's going to hurt you."

He reached into his pocket and drew out a tiny flashlight, clicking it on. "I just want to make sure you don't have a concussion."

She wasn't sure what flashlights had to do with that, and she looked at him, skeptical.

"Just . . . look past me. I'm going to shine this in your eyes."

She did as he said. She was so, so tired, and the tiny sun burning her retinas made her want to go to sleep even more. "Are you a doctor?"

He chuckled. "Yes, I am, actually. A doctor of philosophy." He put the flashlight down on the floor, sitting it upright like a spotlight pointed at the ceiling. "So you can address me as Dr. Smooth."

Now that he was less terrified for his life, his natural charm came out, and he *was* charming. He clearly knew it, too. *Ugh, he even has the same degree Nils has,* she thought. She wondered if they'd gone to school together. "Why were you staring at me during the rally?"

"Honestly, it wasn't you that I recognized, it was Kaplan."

She blinked. "Oh."

"Yes, I do know who you are," he continued, "but honestly, I only connected the dots after I saw you alone on the road. I saw the same girl with blue hair that Kaplan had his tentacles all over earlier in the day in the middle of the road, and I was like, 'Hey, that's weird,' and wondered if maybe for some reason Kaplan dumped you out in the middle of the woods? Either way, I was going to ask if you were okay, but then I got a better look at you, and then I realized who you were, and I was like, 'What the hell is Sol Kaplan doing with . . . *her*?'"

"How do you know Sol Kaplan?"

"Well, a few years ago," he said, treading carefully, like his words were walking over a rope bridge made of rotting wood, "Nils and I collaborated on an exposé detailing the existence of a number of CIA black sites throughout Iraq, Syria, Pakistan, and Afghanistan, including allegations of torture and other such shenanigans. This exposed the identities of several CIA operatives, Sol Kaplan among them."

"I see."

"So now that I've told you who I am," he said, "do you think maybe you could tell me . . . what the fuck?"

She laughed hollowly. What to tell him? She did not know this man, a man with direct connections to Nils, a man who had run right to Nils the last time he'd gotten his hands on material related to her. What was to stop him from doing that again, but this time with something way, way more damning? What he'd seen with Enola was, to make a modest understatement, really fucking huge. But on top of that, she'd helped *kidnap* this man and then held him hostage for several hours. That was a class-A, grade-A, A+ felony. That could mean jail time. That could mean *decades* of jail time.

But looking at him right now, he didn't look like the narc type or the vengeful type. His terror now ameliorated, he looked like the journalist type who probably wouldn't let some light kidnapping get between friends if there was something in it for him. And what would a journalist want more than information as privileged and valuable as this? He wouldn't have gotten to where he was working for a publication as prestigious as

The New Yorker if he didn't know how to keep a secret. He could probably sit on this until the Obelus issue was squared away, and ideally until after they skipped the country. Her only hope for this not to backfire spectacularly was to get on his good side, so the smart thing to do would be to give him a little, let him see her as a source, and maybe he'd do as she asked on the promise that he might get more.

"This is Enola," she said, gesturing to the mess in the center of the chamber. "Which I am calling him for lack of a better name, but you can probably guess why I call him that."

"Wow," he said. "And the white one?"

"Ampersand."

"As in . . ."

"Yeah. It won't be his legal name, though. They haven't settled on that yet."

"And he communicates with you through . . . like . . ." He gestured to his temple.

"No, no. It's just an earbud."

"Oh," said Kaveh, seeming a little disappointed. *They always expect it to be telepathy.* "And where has Ampersand . . . gone?"

"He . . . went to take care of something."

His lips pursed. "'Something.'"

"Alien things."

He watched her as if he were waiting for the punch line to a bad joke. "You do understand that sounds extremely ominous."

"I give you my solemn oath that it has absolutely nothing to do with humans. It's . . . internal business. Nothing to do with us."

"How do you know that?"

"I know."

He looked at Enola. "Do they pose a threat to us?"

"No. I mean, they *could.* Like, you could pose a threat to me right now."

"Who held who at knifepoint?"

She allowed herself to crack a smile. "My point is, like, yeah, sure they could, but it isn't their intent."

"What is their intent?"

"Just . . ." Her worry for Ampersand reared back up. "Survive."

"I need to ask," he said, leaning toward her. "Your . . . Ampersand, for all intents and purposes, threatened to kill me, albeit indirectly."

"Only if you threatened my physical safety."

His expression grew serious. "Either way, I would really like to know, has he ever killed anyone?"

She hesitated, and noted his alarm at her hesitation. "He's never killed a human," she blurted. "I . . . can't really speak to other aliens he might have offed in self-defense, but not humans."

He eyed her, clearly skeptical. "I feel like there might be a caveat in there somewhere."

"No. I just . . . he told me he'd never killed anyone or anything on Earth. So no, he hasn't killed any humans."

"Untrue."

Cora jumped at the voice in her ear—a voice that was not Ampersand's.

"What is it?" said Kaveh, snapping to attention.

"He's talking to me," Cora whispered.

Enola's eyes were open, and he inclined his head toward them as much as he was able, causing Kaveh to jump to his feet. Enola looked like a sleeping dragon raised out of a pool of tar.

"Not true."

"What's he saying?" asked Kaveh.

"What's not true?"

"Our Beloved has taken the lives of many of your kind," said Enola. His voice was erratic, less computerized than Ampersand's, but the intonation was all wrong, jerking and placing emphasis on random syllables. "Every sample we have ever taken from your kind back to our Superorganism was killed by his order. You speak mistruth. Our Beloved has killed many humans."

"What?"

"What is it?" said Kaveh. "What did he say?"

Enola struggled to move his head toward them, but there was a strap over his brow ridge. His head was longer than Ampersand's, his eyes smaller in relation to the rest of his head, making him look more dragon-like than any of the others. Everything about this creature screamed predator. "I have acquired a little cousin. How is this possible? How is it done? You must tell me, little cousin, how did he do it?"

"How did he do what?" said Cora.

"HE SEEKS OUR OTHER COUSIN, OUR NOBLE OBELUS. NOBLE OBE-LUS IS BEING PURSUED BY MULTIPLE PARTIES. DOES OUR DEAR BELOVED KNOW? PERHAPS HE DOESN'T. NOBLE OBELUS AND HIS THREE SUBOR-DINATES, THE THREE SUBORDINATES DID LEAVE THIS PLANET, ONLY TO LEARN THAT NOBLE OBELUS STILL LIVED. THEY WERE INSTRUCTED BY THEIR SUPERORGANISM TO RETURN, WITH NOBLE OBELUS ALIVE AND INTACT."

"The Obelus Similars are still here?" She stood up, ready to bolt, like Obelus's three subordinate Similars might be hiding in the shadows.

"THE THREE OBELUS SUBORDINATES DO NOT SEEK TO KILL THEIR FORMER SUPERIOR; THEY SEEK TO CAPTURE HIM AND RETURN HIM TO HIS AUTOCRAT, ALIVE."

"Are they looking for Ampersand, too?" she asked. "Dear Beloved" could only refer to Ampersand.

"THEY HAVE BEEN INSTRUCTED ONLY TO RETRIEVE NOBLE OBELUS."

"What's he saying?" asked Kaveh. Cora ignored him.

"ONLY WHAT WILL OUR DEAR BELOVED DO WITH HIS OBELUS ONCE HE RECAPTURES HIM? KEEP HIM ALIVE, INDEFINITELY? I DO NOT BELIEVE HE HAS A PLAN. AND THAT IS GOOD, LITTLE COUSIN, FOR THEN HE WILL LET OBELUS RETURN TO HIS AUTOCRAT, AND HE WILL JOIN ME."

"Join you for what?"

"JOIN ME IN DEATH."

She was stone still, not believing what she was hearing. She could feel Kaveh staring at her, watching the look of growing horror on her face.

"SHALL YOU BE JOINING US, TOO, LITTLE COUSIN?"

Her eyes stung, and she backed away from the creature toward the mouth of the cave.

"FREE ME."

She backed away quicker, leaving a confused Kaveh behind. "No."

"What's he saying?" asked Kaveh, starting to get irritated. "What's going on?"

"He's asking me to let him go."

Enola's head jerked against the restraints, fast and unnatural, and at last, his eyes seemed to come into focus, more like Obelus's than Ampersand's. They had that oil-slick iridescence, blues and purples like a cloud nebula. "I ASKED YOU TO FREE ME."

"I can't do that, even if I wanted to, I can't. Please don't ask."

"IT IS NOT MY ENDEAVOR TO HARM YOU. ONLY TO ALLEVIATE MY OWN PAIN. THIS I CAN DO, BUT ONLY IF YOU FREE ME."

"I'm telling you, I can't."

"FREE ME." The voice was filling with static.

"I said no!"

Then the static turned into a cacophony, shrieking like a thousand untuned violins. She clapped her hands to her ears, screaming and stumbling outside.

"What is it?" Kaveh was beside her.

"Get it out!" she cried. "Get it out!"

"Get what out?"

"In my ears! The earbuds! Get them out!" she begged, the sound making her feel like she was detaching from reality.

Kaveh whipped out his pocketknife, flipped out a pair of tweezers. He said something to her, but she couldn't hear him. He gestured for her to get on the ground.

Cora fell to her knees, still clasping her skull, and then in desperation fell to her side, letting this absolute stranger who not fifteen minutes ago she'd bound and gagged do whatever he wanted to her with his pocketknife. He was saying something, giving instruction, but she couldn't hear him. Then he pinned her head to the ground. She clenched her teeth, clasped her hands together in front of her as the man knelt in front of her. "Please, get it out!"

She felt him begin to dig around in her ear canal, miss a couple of times, and then one was out.

"Got it," he said. "Turn over."

She did as he said, and surer of himself now, the second one came out quicker. He flung them on the ground like they were poisonous insects, and she half expected him to stomp on them. She sat up, rubbing the outside of her still-ringing ears with her knuckles. Kaveh picked up the two earbuds, wiry things that looked like metallic mosquitoes clasping invisible marbles. She could still hear the screeching hell noises emanating from them. She wished she were alone. If this strange man weren't here, she could cry like she needed to, but now it was taking every ounce of energy left in her to keep it in.

"Are you okay?" he asked. She didn't look at him, keeping her head down, grasping her elbows tighter, and nodded.

"Hey," he said, his voice gentle. But this time, it wasn't the careful, tightrope-walker gentleness of a hostage negotiator but warmer, more sympathetic. It frightened her. "Listen . . . I want you to know that I forgive you for the night of pain and torment."

Cora laughed, and a bit of a cry snuck itself in on the laugh, hitching a ride.

"I'm not going to say it didn't suck—it did—but I understand why you did it, and thank you for giving me the option to run free and make millions off your horrible secrets. But I'm not going to, not yet at least." He hovered his hand about a foot away from her back, like he knew touching her was a bad idea, but miming the act was fine. She found herself wishing he would drop the pantomime and touch her. "Do you think we could start over?"

Cora wiped her face, swallowing the stress that was begging to come out in the form of tears. "What did you have in mind?"

"Well, are you hungry?"

· 15 ·

It took about half an hour to get back to the Indian reservation that surrounded the mountains, and another half an hour to get back to Temecula. Still riding high off adrenaline, Kaveh made the drive easily, his blue-haired passenger in the back "trying" to "get some sleep." The sky was clear and blue, orange groves lining the road in perfect rows. This area of picturesque farmland was always green, but the winter rains made the whole valley greener than it was at any other point during the year. The brush on the mountains glowed with life, the grass verdant, the bushes on the side of the road dusted with millions of tiny yellow flowers. *Man, it's been so long since I've been in California,* he thought. *I never really appreciated California enough. Earth is beautiful. I hope it's not about to get destroyed.*

He chanced a look at the girl in the back seat, who appeared to have finally fallen asleep, her hands clenched tight around the hoodie he had given her as a cover, her brow furrowed like she was concentrating on a difficult math problem. Could he possibly be this lucky? That the most interesting story in human history just fell into his lap? Somewhere, a monkey's paw must be curling its finger.

He had expected the tourists to have fled, but despite a sizable crowd still congregating in the field near the blockade, Temecula seemed more or less back to normal, *War of the Worlds*–style doom horns followed by major earthquakes notwithstanding. After all, if aliens were going to invade, it was *probably* going to be in this general Area 51–adjacent vicinity, and if you can't stand a little earthquake now and then, you have no business being in California, anyway.

Kaveh found a secluded spot in the casino parking garage, responded to some very upset text messages from Paris, and then turned to examine his new "source," asleep and vulnerable in the back of his Land Rover. She was so hopelessly in over her head it would be comical if the stakes weren't so high, and he was fairly sure that once he got a better handle on the situation, that fact would play into his hands handsomely.

Then he felt a swell of something that it took him a moment to recognize as pity. He didn't buy for a minute that her "Ampersand" was off doing innocent alien things with no ill intent that she just-so-happened needed to keep secret, but the secrecy of it all was obviously eating her up. Easy as it would be to wear her down with a cultivated combination of charm, wit, and intensity, dismantle her like an old car and sell her for parts, it didn't feel like the right call here. This wasn't some Machiavellian mastermind, the type of person he'd dealt with and interviewed (and in some cases even worked with) so many times and who had made him so cynical in his own day-to-day life. This was just a girl, alone and afraid, a girl who knew things of great consequence like, for instance, if the world was ending anytime soon. He just needed to figure out the best way to extract what she knew.

"Hey."

She gasped herself awake, looking around the parking garage as if she were genuinely surprised he'd taken her back to civilization like he'd said he would. "Where are we?"

"Pechanga."

"The casino?"

"I figured it would be pretty empty, though it looks like I might have underestimated the local boomers' love of gambling. Do you want to go inside and get some food, or would you rather stay out here and take a nap?"

"I'll go in," she said, wincing and putting a hand to the spot where she'd hit her head.

Kaveh gathered his effects, hopped out, and rounded the front of the car to open the door for her. He raised his hands in deference, stopping short of saying, "Don't worry, I won't hurt you," as that sounded exactly like what someone who was going to hurt you would say. "Can I check your head?"

Still wearing that sickly, suspicious expression, she nodded. He ran his fingertips over a welt that felt like the back of a spoon. "Nice goose egg." He chuckled. She didn't smile. "I think this is probably superficial, though it's going to hurt for a few days. Do you feel nauseous, dizzy?"

"No, just tired."

He smiled reassuringly. "Let's get you some ice."

·　·　·　·　·

Cora stopped dead as soon as they stepped into the casino, the circus bells and slot machine beeps and whirs accosting her senses. He couldn't blame her; there was something about casinos that unmoored, demanded that reality be denied, and was only amplified by how absurd the last twenty-four hours had been. Kaveh looked at the overhead signs pointing to their options. Buffet? Hell no. Bar? Yikes. The steak house looked like the best bet for privacy, so there they headed.

Soon the two were seated at a table at the back of the mostly empty (and very expensive) restaurant at the newest, nicest casino/resort in Southern California, Cora sulking with a pack of ice gifted by the bartender on her head. Ravenous as he was, he urged the waiter to hurry things along and take their orders quickly. Cora's expression blanched when she looked at the menu. "I can't afford this."

"Don't worry about that."

"But—"

"It's *fine.*"

Kaveh, having decided he deserved it for surviving the night, ordered the most expensive thing on the menu, the eighty-dollar "Great Oak Surf & Turf." Cora ordered the eight-dollar "side of mashed potatoes." When the waiter was out of sight, Kaveh removed the earbuds from his pocket, those-spidery looking things that looked like futuristic ear cuffs, and placed them on the table between them. He was surprised their communication method wasn't anything much more sophisticated than a set of headphones. High-tech spidery alien headphones, yes, but headphones nonetheless. Headphones that presumably anyone could use.

Eeeennnnteresting.

After the food arrived, Kaveh tucked in, decimating half of his filet mignon and ripping into one of his two lobster tails like a caveman. Cora hardly touched hers, picking at the overpriced potatoes like it was workhouse gruel.

"Here," he said, moving to shunt one of the lobster tails onto her plate, but she recoiled from it like it was a live scorpion.

"No," she said. "I'm not hungry."

"When was the last time you ate?"

"It's fine, really."

"Please, take some of mine."

"No, really, I don't want it!"

This yanked a deep-rooted instinct in him, a lifetime of immigrant parents and aunties imbuing in him the importance of making sure everyone had gotten enough to eat, but something about the visceral way she reacted to the lobster told him there was more to it than just the typical faux modest "I'm a dainty little bird" affect endemic to The Whites, so he held his tongue.

She took another bite of her potatoes, swallowing it like it was cold medicine. She then noticed that he was staring at her, and averted her gaze back to the plate of potatoes. But of course he was staring. He couldn't help but stare. Here's the disheveled, blue-haired mess who talks to aliens. Her upper lip was slightly fuller than her lower lip, giving her a cute natural pout, and what he'd initially mistaken for frumpiness was really ill-fitting clothes on a willowy frame. If she washed out the Manic Panic and got a few hours of sleep, she'd probably clean up downright adorable.

It surprised him that this person whom he'd never expected to actually encounter in the real world was not a child but a young adult. Although in fairness, he was working off obsolete information by now, wasn't he? The memory of Cora that Nils had relayed to him had been of an ingrate teenager brainwashed by her sheeple, establishment-slave mother. *Let's see,* he thought, *Nils left in 2003, and she was sixteen then, so she's twenty-one now? Twenty-two?*

"Can I ask you something?" she asked.

"Shoot."

"Do you and Sol know each other?"

"No, why?"

She shrugged. "The way he talked about you, seemed . . . personal."

He forced a smile, putting his fork down. "And what did our friend tell you?"

"When I asked him who slipped those documents to Nils, he told me this guy named Kaveh Ma . . ."

"Mazandarani."

"Mazan . . . drani."

"*Mazan* as in 'was on,' *da* as in 'fa, a note to follow so,' *rani* as in Donnie, the lesser Wahlberg."

"Mazan-da-rani," she repeated, smiling shyly, looking up at him with hooded eyes. He suspected that the mispronunciation bit might have been more a calculated pivot to innocence rather than genuine confusion. "Sol said you were like this . . . well, the term he used was *shitbag burnout.*"

Kaveh snorted, nearly choking on a bite of fingerling potatoes. "I'm a fucking Rhodes Scholar!" he said, mouth still full. "And a bestselling author! I've won like two dozen awards, and I've been nominated for a Pulitzer!" He swallowed. "Twice! Fuck that guy."

"Why would he say that, then?"

"Because he's a fucking liar! And he hates me because I got him fired from his job torturing people." Was she actually surprised by any of this? Did she actually *like* that guy? "He's probably referring to the fact that I used to drink a lot. Like, a lot. He has no moral standing over me, so he has to go for the low-hanging fruit, because he sucks."

"Not anymore?"

"Nope, two years sober." He took another bite of lobster tail. "Now it's way worse, to be honest. Now it's carbs. I spend like half my expendable income at the Cheesecake Factory." That wasn't true, but lines like that made him more relatable. Saying "I have spent quite a lot of time in rehab" had a way of turning people off.

"I've never been to a Cheesecake Factory," she said awkwardly.

"Wow, you're really missing out." Either she didn't catch the sarcasm or didn't care to acknowledge it. "So why are they here?"

"They're refugees."

"Huh." Kaveh took another bite of overpriced cow. "Well, that's one thing we have in common."

She looked up, skeptical. "You're a refugee?"

"Well, I was when I was six. Now I'm a citizen."

"Where are you from?"

"I'm from LA."

Her expression hardened. It was cute.

"Well, not *LA*-LA. Really I'm from Palos Verdes."

She continued to glare at him. Cute, hard-assed glare.

"You know where Palos Verdes is, right? They were originally going to put USC there, but then some sadistic fuck decided it would be funnier to have the wealthiest underachievers in the state living in constant fear by putting it in South Central instead." Maybe it was the tied-to-a-tree-and-left-for-dead shenanigans, but he was enjoying giving her a hard time. "Okay, I'm just messing with you; I was born in the theocratic authoritarian fundamentalist state formerly known as Persia. But I grew up in LA."

"Iran?" she asked, and he nodded. "Your family had to leave?"

"After the revolution, we had a little bit of ye olde . . . grandfather getting executed for being the president of a university when the shah was in power, that sort of thing."

She blanched. "That's awful."

"Yeah, that *is* awful!"

"That was it? That was his crime?"

"Well, he had a lot of business and professional ties here, also spent quite a bit of time in the U.S. when he was younger, and said some nice things about American educational institutions in Persian publications over a period of a few decades before the revolution. That turned out to be an oopsie-daisy."

She looked at him, humbled. "So . . . you're an asylum case?"

"Hell yeah, I am, in *both* senses of the term." He popped the rest of the lobster tail into his mouth, smiling a self-satisfied smile. Amused though he was, his bad joke seemed to make her uncomfortable, so he decided to shift gears. "So where do you live now?"

"Riverside." She forced herself to take another bite. She had gotten through . . . maybe 30 percent of those taters. "And you in New York?"

"Usually, but my family owns a house in Yorba Linda where I'm staying while I write my book."

"They have a spare house for you whenever you move into town?"

"Right now they do. Investment property, but their last tenant lost everything in the crash and had to move back in with his parents or something. My mom was going to turn it into a short-term rental, but I was like, no, I want that house! There's no market for short-term rentals right now because everyone's broke. It's a huge schlep from LA, but it has the best backyard. I told her to try to rent it out after the economy bounces back. So right now, I'm basically just paying the property taxes on it."

"How many properties does your family have?"

"Investment properties, or properties in general?"

She blinked and then found an abyss to stare into a few inches to his left. Perhaps he'd spilled too much—the stuff about the Pulitzers, being a Rhodes Scholar, and reporting for *The New Yorker* was already a lot, but now she knew he came from money, and his family had a spare house for when the prodigal son needed to be on the West Coast in a nice-ass Orange County town like Yorba Linda. He didn't know much about Nils's family situation, but he did know that he never sent them any money.

"My family owns a few, but I only own my apartment in New York." Her bewildered expression told him that made things worse, not better, as if he were trying to insinuate *merely* owning an apartment in Tribeca was a sign of humble means. Like sure, my parents own six properties in the area (and a few more out of state) but me, I only got the one! "It's a . . . two bedroom."

"So what are you writing about?"

"Well, I wanted to get out of New York for the winter to work on a piece about some of the shenanigans in Hollywood, specifically some of the big names who use their power to, shall we say, take advantage of the talent, but then the, um, shit show happened last year—"

"ET-gate," she said derisively.

"And I've been a little distracted with that. A lot of people are looking for answers and demanding accountability. Hence Jano Miranda's Third Party showing up and putting up a real challenge to the establishment. But that's not the only group that's exploded in membership in the last few months—there was a big showing yesterday from this fringe group called the Gadsden Line. *Big* fans of Nils, those guys."

"Conspiracy theorists?"

"Sort of. *Real* big Second Amendment types. Gotta defend us from all those *dangerous* aliens. But they basically see themselves as the glorious militia that stands behind groups like Jano Miranda's Third Party should the need arise. The Gadsden Line ringleader, guy named Angus Normandy, lives over in Chino. So I was there yesterday covering them, not Enola Gay and *definitely* not Sol Kaplan."

"What's interesting about those guys?"

"Oh, you know. Their brand of conspiracy theory tends to leak into real-world consequences. Religious fundamentalism, xenophobia—the human-on-human kind. Anti-Semitism is a biggie."

"Anti-Semitism?"

"Yeah, it's a thing. The Jews are using the aliens to control the world, see. The Jews hate Western Civilization just like they always have, so they're helping the aliens make it crumble in exchange for, I don't know, power or something."

She tilted her head as if expecting him to say, "Psych!" "People actually believe that?"

He stopped mid-chew. "Yes, a *lot* of people actually believe that."

She leaned back into her chair, clearly unsure if he had his facts straight. He couldn't blame her for that—so much had changed so quickly in these last few months, between the Bush resignation and the world economy collapsing to the revelation of motherfucking aliens, it was hard to keep up with how poorly society at large was coping.

"Listen," he said. "Neither of us have gotten any sleep, and our respective beds are a bit of a drive. Since we're already here, I could get us some rooms."

She shifted in her seat. "Are you asking me to share a hotel room with you?"

"No, I said *rooms*. Plural."

She looked at her half-eaten potatoes like she suspected him of poisoning them. "Okay."

"Wow, that was easy." He probably should not have said that out loud.

"Anything you want," she said distantly. "Only . . . please don't go to the police with this. Just for a few days."

"I wasn't planning on it, but out of curiosity, why not?"

She looked at him, eyes wide, suddenly electric with fear. "There are other ones under government 'protection' besides Ampersand, and Enola is not . . . he's not well, and they . . . well, if the other ones find out, they might take it upon themselves to put Enola out of his misery, and there are presently no laws in place to stop them. The reason we have to keep Enola a secret for now . . . it's not the U.S. government we're worried about. He's trying to protect Enola from his own kind. That's all."

Kaveh leaned back, his plate now cleaned of anything remotely edible, and he glanced at the two spidery earpieces sitting on the table between them. "Would you let me borrow one of those?"

"Why?"

He didn't even try to hide his conniving smile. "I want to talk to Enola."

16

"So why're you doing this again?" asked Paris through a sigh. She'd obviously been upset enough that he had waited until almost 2:00 P.M. EST to text her, try though she might to cloak it, and now she was having to duck out during a meeting to pin down the coordinates of where he was, and by extension, where Enola was.

"I'm having to use, like . . . ancient cartography," he said, pressing his map against the steering wheel in a futile attempt to create a flat surface to write on. He had left Cora at the hotel above the casino, booking an adjoining room for himself. After leaving her alone in her room, he snuck out, hopped right back into his Land Rover, and made the hour-plus drive all the way back up the mountain. "I didn't want to risk any of the search engines realizing I was pinpointing my own location."

"Cell tower data isn't accurate, anyway," said Paris.

"In this case, better safe than sorry."

"All right, I have it." She repeated the coordinates back to him.

"And you pinkie swear that you wrote it down, with a pencil?" he said, folding up his map. "This is not on anything that is even potentially connected to a network?"

She hesitated. "Pinkie swear."

"Okay. Do not share this. Do not pass go, do not collect two hundred dollars. Unless . . ."

"Unless?"

"If you don't hear from me within ninety minutes, call in the fucking SWAT, the FBI, the CIA, call the army, the air force, the Boy Scouts, the Girl Scouts."

"What is this?"

"I'm going to plead the Fifth on that one . . . but I will tell you it has to do with Ortega."

"Oh . . ." She sighed, and he could practically hear her rubbing her temple. "How much danger are you in exactly?"

"I honestly don't know. Possibly none?" *Probably lots.*

"How, um . . . *risky* is the thing you are about to do?"

"Extremely. I'm going to try to talk to someone, but I don't know if they're receptive to being talked to."

"I see." The way she said it made him think she suspected that it might not be a *who* he was trying to talk to, but a *what.*

"Ultimate pact of trust," he said. "Setting my stopwatch. Ninety minutes."

She swallowed so hard he could hear it over the phone. "Ninety minutes, starting now."

He set it to sixty, to give himself a thirty-minute buffer in case there was any problem with cell phone reception. "Okay, um . . . I love you?"

"Oh . . . I love you . . . too?"

"Right, sorry," he said in a tone that failed to belie his fear that this might be the last time they ever spoke. Last time he'd dropped an L-bomb to Paris, it had been years ago, and he had been very drunk. "I . . . You know. I don't say it enough. To anyone. So just an FYI. You're my friend, and I love you."

"Kaveh?" Her voice cracked with worry.

"Ninety minutes," he said and snapped his phone shut. He spent five of those minutes in the front seat of the Land Rover, windows down, staring at the limb of a branch, a superstitious corner of his mind waiting for the wind to nudge it, to tell him, "Time to go." To give him a sign. But today was not a windy day.

His instincts about sources were usually correct—who would talk, who wouldn't, what type of charm would work on whom and what wouldn't. His journalistic instincts were his greatest asset (well, that and his hair), the thing that had propelled him to the top of his field. It was therefore instinct, not rationality, that made him decide that Enola was the play, not Ampersand.

This was somewhat counterintuitive. Cora had told him that Enola was "not well," which seemed like an understatement, as he was apparently "not well" enough for others of his kind to want to end his suffering like he was a horse with a broken leg. Terrifying as Enola was, Kaveh didn't want to see that happen. Yes, he was a grotesque cyborg space monster, but he was also simply incredible, an alien being that had made it across the unfathomable empty gulf of space by ripping a hole in it. What a terrible thing it would be to lose a life like that, even if there was a nonzero chance he had come to take control of Earth and enslave all of humanity.

But the real issue was that Ampersand seemed, to put it mildly, extremely guarded if not a skosh homicidal, plus he had that inexplicably protective gatekeeper. Enola, conversely, was a mystery, but given his eagerness to talk to Cora, going even so far as to demand his freedom, Kaveh deduced that he was the less guarded of the two, and given that he was welded to the floor of a cave, also the less dangerous.

He looked down at the one borrowed earbud, to which he had tied a string of dental floss juuuust in case Enola started screeching ear-torture, and placed it in his ear. It felt alive, and he shuddered as the thing conformed to his inner ear. Then he grabbed his electric camping lantern, got out of the Land Rover, and hiked down to the cave.

By the time he found the entrance, much easier now that he'd wandered in and out of it a few times, about fourteen minutes had passed. He didn't know what to listen for besides screeching hell noises, and wondered if the earbud would work for him at all. Taking the mightiest, bravest breath his body was capable of, he turned on his lantern and stepped inside.

Enola was still there, the black substance he had been leaking now congealed around him, a high-tech mummy doused with black paint. Kaveh stayed next to the wall of the cave, running his hands along the side as he moved around Enola in a circle. "Hey. Hello. I'm not going to free you, I'm not going to touch you. I just want to see if you'd be willing to communicate with me."

Enola didn't budge, and the earbud stayed quiet.

Kaveh wasn't as afraid of Enola as of the possibility of the *other* one returning. Cora had been so eager to impress upon him how many *humans* Ampersand had not killed. Never killed a single one, no, sir, no dead humans here, nosiree. He got the impression that the only thing keeping Ampersand from killing him out of annoyance was the presence of his interpreter, and his interpreter was not here, but he didn't get paid the big bucks to play it safe.

Once he was at about a forty-five-degree angle from Enola's "face," he stopped and lowered into a crouch, placing his lantern onto the ground. "Can you understand me?"

For several minutes, Enola was so still Kaveh wondered if he had died at some point in the last few hours. Then, the strange luminous eyes opened. They were much clearer, less cataract. Then a voice in his earbud spoke, a computerized voice, one that was definitely based in man-made text-to-talk software, but more sophisticated, more natural-sounding, more unsettling:

"Please don't kill me."

Kaveh gasped in wonder. It worked. He couldn't believe it. His earbud was working, and an alien, a real live *fucking space alien,* was talking to him. He was so shocked that it took him a moment to parse what the alien had said.

Wait, what?

Kaveh lowered himself into a sitting position, hoping his body language was imparting nonaggression.

"I've come very far—yes, to die, but not like this. I mean you no harm. Please, don't kill me, not now. Please wait. Soon, not now, but soon. Please wait."

It took him a moment to find his words. "I . . . I'm not here to hurt you."

"Please don't kill me."

"I'm not here to kill you," he specified, figuring that in the alien's mind death could be painless, and "not hurting" did not preclude "killing." "I just want to communicate."

"Will you free me?"

"I'm not going to free you. I'm not going to get close to you. I'm not going to touch you. I just want to talk."

Enola stared at him for a long while, giving Kaveh the opportunity to really take stock of the creature, and he realized that Enola's eyes didn't emanate light but instead reflected it like the eyes of a cat. Such beautiful gems ensconced in such a monstrous body.

"DO YOU KNOW WHAT I AM?"

"Not exactly," said Kaveh. "I know you're an . . . extraterrestrial . . . person of some sort. You're from a different planet."

"DEFINE: PERSON."

Not like *that* was a difficult question! "A person is a sentient, autonomous, conscious being," he said, utterly winging it, "capable of some measure of intelligence. Problem-solving intelligence, and social intelligence. An individual member of a species that is capable of forming societies. Forming . . . civilizations."

He sat back, honestly pretty pleased with his answer. Enola kept watching him. "DEFINE: PLANET."

"We are on a large . . . very large . . . oblate spheroid. That orbits a midsize star. Once every three hundred and sixty-five days. I don't know where exactly you're from, but I assume you probably evolved on another large oblate spheroid orbiting a different star."

The eyes seem to clear further, the brightness concentrating, making them seem to glow even brighter. "YOU ARE INTELLIGENT. YOU ARE CONSCIOUS. YOU ARE PERSONS. AS I PREDICTED."

"What do you mean?"

Enola blinked his giant eyes, a long, languid motion. His head was much bigger in proportion to his body than a human's; crest and all, his head was more than four feet long, his oil-slick eyes bigger than footballs. "I KNOW YOUR KIND, I HAVE STUDIED YOU BEFORE. BUT I HAVE NOT STUDIED YOUR LANGUAGE. I'M NOT SURE HOW MY ALGORITHM OBTAINED THIS LANGUAGE. I HAVEN'T STUDIED THIS DIALECT BEFORE."

"I don't know how you know English. I have to admit, I was wondering that myself."

"PLEASE DON'T KILL ME, DEAR CLEVER CREATURE. NOT YET."

"Is there anything I can do to help that doesn't involve me touching you in any way?"

"I AM IN PAIN. MEDICATION WILL MITIGATE IT, BUT I MUST BE FREED FOR ITS MANUFACTURE."

Kaveh frowned. "No. No, I don't think I'll do that."

He took another slow breath and pondered his next move. His pie-in-the-sky goal had been to get Enola talking, and he had expected that to be the hard part. He hadn't exactly prepared a list of questions and talking points. "The 'medicine.' What does it do to you?"

"IT NUMBS ME."

"I see. And what does this numbing do for you?"

"THE ABILITY TO ENDURE THE LOSS OF MY SYMPHYLES AND THE EXPULSION FROM MY SUPERORGANISM, AND TO COEXIST WITH TRAUMATIC MEMORIES."

Kaveh might have been projecting, but Enola's description felt awfully familiar. A desperate craving for some chemical that could numb whatever demons were haunting him. Alien as it was, it was also as familiar to him as the feel of a light breeze on his skin.

Enola was going through withdrawal.

Kaveh started to ask a follow-up, but then a shadow fell over the chamber. The light in Enola's iridescent eyes dimmed, and Kaveh turned to see the other one—*Ampersand*—blocking his exit.

He shot to his feet, instinctively putting his hands up. Ampersand approached him like he was a cockroach that needed to be swatted, but slowly so as not to spook him. The creature had his head down, the ridges above his eyes covering them in a way that made him look like a predator on the hunt, his eyes catching the sunlight from outside and blazing like a forest fire.

Kaveh backed away, trying to keep a good distance. He envisioned himself blurting, "I know you can understand me. I have a colleague on the East Coast that has these coordinates. If she doesn't hear from me within the next ten minutes, she's going to assume me dead and report this location."

He shut his mouth. He couldn't do that. That could endanger Paris.

"Cora sent me," he said, keeping his hands up. "She wanted me to check on the situation. She's at the Pechanga hotel, resting. She's safe."

The creature kept staring at him with his demon eyes, straight out of hell. He wasn't blocking the entrance anymore, so, clueless as to what else he could do and obviously not welcome in here, Kaveh darted to the exit, surprised to have made it out alive for the second time that day. Taking a moment to confirm that, yes, he had not been turned into man-vapor, he ran back up the hill to his Land Rover, not stopping, taking in loud, ugly gulps of air by the time he made it back to the car.

Once inside, he slammed the car door shut, wondering if he actually had made it out, if the creature was really going to let him leave. He put the key in the ignition, turned it, and then he started laughing and did not stop for several minutes.

17

"*I'm an asshooooyooyoyoooyoyooole.*"

Denis Leary's voice jerked Cora back into wakefulness as it piped from her cell phone, not more than an hour after she'd finally fallen asleep. She flipped the phone open, rolling over onto her back. "Sol?"

"Where the hell are you?" demanded Sol from the other end of the line. It took a few more seconds after that for her to realize she was not alone in the room.

"I . . . I'm still in Temecula."

It was so surreal, so unexpected, but Ampersand was standing right next to the bed, sunlight reflecting off his amber eyes illuminated by the sun and staring down at her. He looked pissed.

"What the fuck?" said Sol. "*Where* in Temecula?"

"Pechanga."

"*Your hostage. He was freed. He had your earbud.*"

She could practically hear Sol rubbing his face with his hand. "Why haven't you called me? Why was your phone off?"

"It wasn't off, it was dead!" Ampersand leaned in, and she backed away. "I didn't know what else to do, so I just stayed here."

"*Why was he freed? How did he get the earbud?*"

She swatted at Ampersand like he was a mosquito, begging him, willing him, *Please shut up!*

"Why aren't you here?" demanded Sol.

"It's Saturday!"

"Yeah, it's just a normal fucking Saturday, no reason to come in, huh?" He sighed. "I'm coming to get you."

"No, it's okay." She had by now backed herself to the edge of the bed and was almost on the bedside table.

"No, it's not okay. We need you in here."

"No, you don't," said Cora, her voice heavy with exhaustion, bitter about the sleep she knew she was not going to get. "He doesn't have anything to say to you, and I'll just be in the way. I'll call you later. Please, please just let me sleep. I'm so tired."

"Why didn't you call me?"

"I tried!" She was on the verge of tears. "I don't know why it wasn't working! Please, just let me sleep."

"I'm coming to get you." Then he hung up.

She snapped the phone shut, keeping her free hand up over her head as though Ampersand might hit her. Leaning over the bed, his body easily transversed its width, and he was practically on top of her. "What happened?"

"The man. Your hostage. He was in the cave with Enola. He had one of your earbuds."

"Oh, God, what did you do to him?"

"Why was he there alone? Why are you here? How did he get the earbud?"

"He asked me for it," she said, exhaustion prickling the corners of her eyes. "He said he wanted to talk to Enola. I didn't think he'd do it right away!"

"You freed your hostage with no guarantee of his silence."

"I . . . thought he might be a valuable asset. He'll keep quiet as long as he thinks there's something in it for him. You didn't hurt him, did you?"

He just stared at her with his inscrutable alien gaze.

"Ampersand!"

"No. He returned to his vehicle."

She let out a sigh of relief, throwing off the comforter and heading into the bathroom to pee and get a glass of water. When she returned, Ampersand had parked himself right in the middle of the bed like he was settling down to watch his stories on TV, tucking his hands under him daintily in that deerlike pose.

"Are you going to just leave Enola there in that cave?"

"I have no choice until I locate Obelus."

"Yeah, about that," she said, remembering what Enola had told her right before he had filled her ears with every tuning violin in history. "Enola said Obelus's three Similars are still here, looking for him. Is that true?"

"*Yes. Obelus's subordinates returned upon direction from their Autocrat.*"

"Enola said they want him alive."

"*I believe that the most likely instruction.*"

"So what can I do? How can I help?"

"*You cannot help me.*"

"I've done it before." She gestured to the pulse emitter, which she'd left in easy reach on the bedside table, just in case. "That's why you made that thing for me, isn't it? I'm on your side. Don't do this alone. Let me help you."

"*If the American military becomes aware that Obelus's Similars are still on Earth, they will respond with force, which will only result in more human deaths.*"

"You'll have a better shot at finding Obelus if the U.S. surveillance panopticon is involved."

"*If the surveillance apparatus finds him, then his Similars will find and extract him immediately. If you intend to disclose the truth of Obelus to the militarists, I will prevent it.*"

Holy shit, she thought, stung. *He did it again.* She knew they didn't have the luxury to squabble, not now, but it was so hard not to be mad at him, not to allow the internal space for how hurt she was by all this. In his alien head, he was only acting logically; really, wasn't she the problem for *having* a problem? Obelus wasn't even in the body that had harmed her so badly anymore. And now Ampersand had taken a mere suggestion about using the American surveillance state to their advantage and assumed it was a threat of betrayal.

"I won't tell anyone about Obelus," she said, trying to flush out the hurt. She sat down on the edge of the bed, facing him. "Just . . . work with me. I'm your friend. I've always been your friend."

He regarded her, then lifted up his hand, either like he wanted her to take it or like he was about to touch her. She reached out for it, then nearly jumped out of her skin at the sound of knuckles rapping at the door to the room, but not the door leading to the hallway, the door to the adjoining room. Kaveh's room.

"Hey!" he chirped from the other side of the door. "Are you awake? You know what, it doesn't matter. If you're not awake, wake up!"

She looked at the door, shook off her surprise, then looked at Ampersand. "Will you listen to him?"

Knock, knock, knock. "Wake up! Or at least, please don't have snuck out on me."

"Just a second," she said. She got off the bed, put her jeans back on, while Ampersand held his head high like he was a medieval lord deigning to speak to the peasantry. She unlocked the door and opened it.

Kaveh beamed at her for half a second before he saw who was perched on the bed behind her.

"Been busy?" she asked.

The man grew contrite, his green eyes darting back and forth between Cora and Ampersand. "I get the impression that I was interrupting something. I can come back later."

"It's fine," said Cora, taking him by the wrist, pulling him into the room, and shutting the door behind him. Cora crossed in front of him and sat down on the end of the bed next to Ampersand, head high, back straight, and looked at him as if to say, *Well? Get on with it.*

"Okay," said Kaveh, addressing Ampersand. "Actually, I'm glad you're here. The last time we saw each other, which was"—he checked his watch—"a little less than an hour ago, you did not have your interpreter with you." He gestured to Cora, but looked at Ampersand as he spoke. It impressed her. Most people didn't have the nerve to address him directly. "But now you do have her, so I would like to ask some questions and make a proposal. Off the record."

Ampersand stayed silent, while Cora tried to stay cool, exuding her most convincing *this is fine* demeanor, which was honestly quite difficult. "Is that okay?"

"*I will hear him.*"

Ostensibly tired of standing in front of the alien like he was on trial, Kaveh grabbed the chair by the window and parked it right in front of them. Cora placed a hand on Ampersand's back, keeping her eyes on Kaveh. Smallest of power moves.

"Okay," he said, leaning forward with his elbows on his knees, hands entwined in front of him. "Enola told me the reason he came here was 'to die.' Would you be willing to tell me what that means?"

"Their social structure is basically built around a practice called *dynamic fusion bonding* in a social group called a *phyle*," said Cora. "It's sort of . . . nonmonogamous pair bonding. Group bonding, if you will. A phyle contains between five and ten symphyles fusion bonded to each other. As they are exceptionally long-lived, this practice helps maintain social bonds over a very long lifetime, but one quirk of the deal is that they all choose a predetermined date to die, together. So no one dies alone, and no one ever really knows grief. In theory." To keep things from getting too confusing, she omitted the whole "*Oligarchs aren't allowed to form phyles*" detail. Trying to keep track of who was connected to whom in the Superorganism's top caste required vector calculus that she was too tired to explain at the moment.

"I'm guessing this didn't go according to plan," said Kaveh.

"No. The events that have led to their current refugee status have led to the death of all their symphyles, except two."

"*Enola is not Obelus's symphyle. I am Enola's last living symphyle.*" Because of the vector calculus, Cora kept that to herself. "*Ask what he wants.*"

"He wants to know what you really want."

Kaveh clapped his hands together. "I'll get right to it, then. I'm asking for your permission to talk to Enola. I want access to him."

"*He intends to gather information and turn it into propaganda.*"

"He wants to know what's in it for you," said Cora.

"Even before we crossed paths, my standpoint before was there are any number of ways that ETIs could not resemble what we consider a person, and therefore this question of legal personhood could have been very, very tricky. However, I now know that in all the ways that matter, the answer to this question is simple. You're individuals, you're conscious, you communicate with spoken language, you each have unique perspectives and personalities. And you're *alive*, you aren't machines, same as us. There is no rational argument *against* your personhood. There just isn't.

"So I know you don't have any reason to trust me, and yes, there isn't a journalist in the world who wouldn't give at least one toe for exclusive, solitary access to a captive ETI. But this isn't just about access for access's sake—I want the Third Option gone, and I was originally arguing against it from a policy standpoint. But if I have access to you, the best case against the Third Option is by making it about *you*."

"*His endeavor is to use access to Enola to propagandize with regard to his political objectives.*"

"Yeah, pretty much," said Cora. "At least they're the same as ours."

"What did he say?" asked Kaveh.

"He says, 'Go on.'"

"Okay. I will not report anything about this to anyone without discussing it with both of you first, and I will not print anything without your express permission. In the short term, I only want to observe. In cold, calculated terms, this is research. But on a human level, I am concerned about Enola. Are you planning on . . . cleaning that mess up?"

Cora looked at Ampersand, who hesitated. Then, "*I must prioritize locating Obelus. Enola's well-being is secondary.*"

She nearly groaned. "He will, but he can't right now, he has another . . . issue."

"Well, I'd like permission to clean him up, if it's possible. I need to know if it's safe to touch him. I need to know what's safe to clean. How can I interact with him without the risk of letting him go?"

"*Enola is secured.*"

"He says you couldn't undo those restraints if you wanted to."

"Oh. Even better."

Ampersand regarded him for a moment and then spoke. "*My interpreter has requested that I respect your autonomy, therefore I will. If you do wish to engage with Enola, I will not stop you, but if you do attempt to inform anyone of the situation or his whereabouts, I will simply move him to another location and destroy all evidence. If you attempt to bring harm to Enola or my interpreter, I will kill you.*"

Cora omitted that last bit.

"Okay," said Kaveh, brightening. "I'll make sure nobody knows what I'm doing. Owing to my line of work, I'm better at being clandestine than most."

Without another word, Ampersand moved off the bed and glided toward the window. Cora followed him as he pulled a windowpane out, opening it like a door. Cora recalled the conversation they'd had in the hospital a few months ago, Ampersand implying that life wasn't worth living if he didn't have an express purpose within "a Superorganism."

"Hey," she said. "Enola told me he was here to die with you, implied he meant like *now* . . ." When he didn't respond, she asked, "You aren't considering it, are you?"

"*I will consider how to handle Enola after the situation with Obelus is dealt with.*"

Then, the shroud of invisibility washed over him like water, the window glass wobbled as he snaked himself outside, and the pane fused itself back into place. She stood there, soaking that in, hoping that he was just being difficult, or had perhaps misunderstood her.

"Did he . . . just teleport?"

She wandered back toward him. "No, they can't teleport. He went out through the window."

"But he can turn invisible."

"Yep. That's actually a pretty easy trick, as I understand it."

He looked at her thoughtfully. "What did he say?"

She sat down on the side of the bed, hunched over, one hand cupping the other. Ampersand wasn't just hunting Obelus, he was avoiding Enola. He couldn't deal with Enola, so he wasn't. "Let's just say he didn't answer my question."

"Are we, like . . . married to Enola Gay as a name?" asked Kaveh, sitting down next to her. "I kinda want to have something to call him that's a little less associated with war crimes."

She regarded him, suddenly struck by how eager he was to get involved in this. "What do you want, Kaveh?"

He considered, then gave her a cheeky smile. "A Pulitzer. I really should have won the last one."

"What do you *really* want?"

"Full, natural personhood," he said, growing serious. "Full human rights. No in-between. You are either a person, or you're not."

This surprised her. She had meant, what did he want for himself; she hadn't expected such a broad political answer. "That's very generous for someone who's only just met them."

"It isn't about them."

His growing seriousness shook her. "What do you mean?"

"The paradox of anti-government hysteria is it tends to lead to authoritarianism. The arrival of space aliens has not united humanity; they've only made us more tribal, more fractured, and it's only going to get worse in the months and years to come. And now you have these proto-fascists arguing against the very idea of alien personhood and advocating for the creation of a whole different category of person altogether. One might almost say . . . three-fifths of a person."

She curled her lip up in disbelief, almost offended by such a comparison.

"We've been down this road before, we Americans," he said. "Do you see what I'm getting at? Starts with 'slave' . . . ends with 'ery.'"

"That's absurd. In the incredibly unlikely event it ever got that bad, they'd just leave."

"I feel like you're not listening to me. It's not about *them*. I have no doubt Ampersand could protect himself, or hell, leave the country, settle in a less fashy one. Leave the planet, whatever. This isn't about them."

"Then what is it about?"

"It's about *us*. It's about how we treat *our* aliens, *our* lower classes. If they create a whole new class of person with fewer rights than a natural person, one created specifically for a nonhuman alien, how long do you think it will be before they start applying that to human aliens as well?"

She shook her head. What he was saying felt like such a huge stretch, but at the same time, it was becoming hard to completely discount.

"There are already people eager for the Third Option to become law because it could apply to *all* aliens. Not just the extraterrestrial kind. Miranda doesn't preach anti-immigrant rhetoric—of course he doesn't, he's the son of Cuban refugees, for Chrissake—but a huge chunk of his followers sure do."

"Why?"

"If it's a reactionary movement rooted in fear, the first thing that happens is the revocation of hard-won human rights. That's what happened in Germany when the Nazis came to power. That's what happened during Reconstruction after the Civil War. And that's what's happening here now. If the Third Option passes, Ampersand and his ilk are not going to be the ones who suffer for it."

He placed his hand on hers, looking at her intensely. She shivered. "And if our best bet to keep the Third Option from passing is to convince the rest of the world of full alien personhood, then we have to do everything in our power to make sure that happens."

18

Operation: Probably a Huge Mistake but Fuck It began as most huge mistakes do: with a trip to Wal-Mart. Kaveh could get all the supplies he needed up the mountain fairly easily, but doing so inconspicuously was another matter. Bringing a shitload of equipment to a cave out in the wilderness would be troublesome enough, but leaving a giant Land Rover nearby for any length of time could draw attention from aircraft or satellites. Trickier still was the issue of cell phone data, even with burners, so Operation: Probably a Huge Mistake but Fuck It needed to be done completely off the grid, and this time, he wouldn't be able to use Paris as his insurance policy.

So for Operation: Probably a Huge Mistake but Fuck It, Kaveh decided to bring the minimum that he thought he'd need in the Land Rover, hide it near the side of the road, park the Land Rover in a small, populated area inside the park, and then hike the few miles back into the woods and move his "package" into the cave from there.

For his "package drop" in the Land Rover, he packed ten gallons of water, several types of organic soap (from floor soap to dishwasher detergent to shower gel), two big packs of paper towels, a box of garbage bags, thick plastic gloves (four pairs), a mop, a broom, about twenty of those giant fluffy disposable sponges that his dad used to wash his cars (the kind that don't leave a scratch), three battery-powered lanterns, two empty plastic buckets, various and sundry other supplies, and some snacks. Once the package was dropped, he returned to civilization, parked the Land Rover, and then began his hike.

Ampersand had chosen a state park to hole up in, so there were plenty of trails that went relatively close to where Kaveh needed to go before he needed to start off-roading and use a compass. He started at around 9:00 A.M., and though he figured the hike would take around two hours, it took close to three. Eventually, he found his package, still hidden and untouched, and he began the process of package delivery, which took almost another hour, as the cave was about a ten-minute walk from where he'd dropped the supplies and it took him about three trips. On the first trip, with as much as he could carry in hand, he marched into the cave, and there was Enola, his eyes alert and clearer than he'd yet seen them.

"Hi," he said. "I'm here to clean you up."

Enola, who had previously been rather, well, chatty, did not respond. Without another word, Kaveh departed for round two.

By round three, he was famished. He'd tried to load up on calories at Subway before he left, but he'd burned through that fuel, and the only thing he had left on him that wasn't nonperishable was a turkey-and-cheese sandwich.

"Okay," he said, turning a bucket upside down and using it as a seat. He took a big bite of the sandwich and sat down in front of Enola so he could see him fully. "Where do we start?"

The glow of Enola's eyes was incredible. It seemed to sharpen and fluctuate with whatever he was focusing on. But at the same time, it was hard not to read anxiety in those eyes, fear even. Enola could hardly move, but he was clearly trying to, wriggling uncomfortably.

Kaveh took another bite of the sandwich. "You're not going to talk to me today?"

Then he saw what Enola was focusing on—not Kaveh himself but the sandwich in his hand, like he was afraid of the sandwich. But why? What was there to be afraid of? It was just cheese and meat . . .

Meat. Oh.

"Excuse me."

He hadn't even spared a thought to cultural taboos he might be violating simply by going about his day. He took the turkey sandwich outside and, a nice, safe distance away, horked down the rest of it. He wasn't about to go hungry over this, but this was already starting off more poorly than he had hoped. Turkey flesh now safely inside his digestive tract, he went back inside. Before he retook his seat, he rummaged through his snacks and got rid of the Alien™ Fresh Beef Jerky (in hindsight, not the most sensitive of purchases in several regards). Then he sat back down on the bucket in front of the still-wriggling Enola.

"Okay, I'm here to clean you up. I want to make clear from the start: I don't mean you any harm, I don't mean your . . . Ampersand any harm. I also don't want to make you uncomfortable. I didn't realize eating meat might make you uncomfortable. Humans are omnivorous. You know that, right?"

"Yes."

"So most of us wouldn't think twice about eating a turkey sandwich, but I understand why that might be kind of offensive to you. So if I do anything else that you don't like, just tell me, and I'll stop doing it. Do you understand?"

Enola didn't answer, instead watching him with those shaking, luminous eyes. Kaveh got on his knees in front of Enola, who tried to shrink away but could not move enough to do so. Kaveh put on the thick yellow gloves, and ran his fingers over the dried black tar on the floor. Hardly any of it came off on the glove, and it had the texture of hardened caramelized sugar. He hoped it was water soluble. "What is this?"

"You might call it blood."

He hissed in some air through his teeth. "Yikes."

He drained two gallons into each of the buckets, starting with the organic dish detergent in the buckets and the organic floor cleaner on the floor of the cave, designating one bucket the clean water bucket and the other the dirty water bucket. He splashed a little of the clean, soapy water on the floor, careful not to get any on Enola himself. Fortunately, the "blood" on the floor was indeed water soluble. Kaveh secured permission to play his new iPod speaker, and could only hope that Enola didn't have strong feelings about the Avett Brothers.

"Why did he . . . bleed you out?" Kaveh asked. There had been a point where he was careful not to get the dried alien effluvium on his clothes, but he was well past that now, practically kneeling in it as he scrubbed the floor like Cinderella.

"A transfusion. He had to remove the contaminated blood slowly, over a period of hours. If he had done it quickly, it would have killed me."

"Contaminated with what?"

"MEDICATION."

Kaveh wrung his sponge out in the dirty water bucket (he'd by now gone through about five of them) and topped it back up with clean soapy water. "Are you afraid right now?"

"I AM VERY FRIGHTENED."

He slopped the sponge back down on the floor, making sure he was in full view of Enola. "What are you afraid of?"

"YOU ARE A NATURAL ALIEN, A FLESH-EATER OF A SPECIES HIGHLY INCLINED TO VIOLENCE AND AGGRESSION, AND I AM PRONE AND VULNERABLE AND UNABLE TO DEFEND MYSELF, AND THERE ARE NONE OF MY KIND HERE WHO WOULD DEFEND ME FROM YOU. OUR FIRST INTERACTION WAS ANTAGONISTIC AND VIOLENT. IT STANDS TO REASON YOU WOULD SEE ME AS A THREAT."

Kaveh had by now more or less done a first pass of the mess on the floor, but now came the really iffy part—the mess on the alien. "Well, I'll keep trying to reassure you that I don't mean you harm, and hopefully one day you'll believe me. I'm going to see if I can't get this strap off your head, so you can move around a bit and see what I'm doing. Is it okay if I touch you?"

Enola paused for a very long few seconds before he answered, "YES."

With careful, steady movements, he reached over Enola's head and grazed his thumbs over the strap, caked in place by the black blood. With some effort, he pushed the strap off, which snapped onto his neck like an elastic band. Enola opened his eyes, still locked firmly in place, but now able to move his head a bit. Even after Kaveh had spent an hour scrubbing the blood off the floor of an unnatural cave, Enola still looked at him with fear.

Kaveh was overcome with the desire to reassure him, that of course his fear was rational but in this case unwarranted. Was this more projection? The new country had been so overwhelming. Temporary, his family had thought. How temporary? Who knows, but certainly temporary, because the revolutionary craziness could not last. It would not last. They'd go back home eventually, but in the meantime, they had to survive in this foreign place.

When he'd first arrived in the States, he'd expected to step off the plane and see the smiling denizens of white suburbia waving welcome banners. He'd also expected to see John Travolta in the airport, since they were so close to Hollywood. He was, after all, six years old, and it was 1980.

There were no welcome banners, and California was not always welcoming—kids were shitty, especially when he was still learning English. But not all of them were shitty; he'd never forget the first two American kids (Luis and Carlos, the neighbors from two houses down) who played with him despite the fact that he didn't speak English yet. The game had been basketball, a nine-year-old and an eight-year-old playing with a seven-year-old, and the simple joy of it, that small sliver of acceptance by strangers after all the months of fear and uncertainty, had been the turning point, the moment that he thought perhaps they could survive in this foreign place. Luis and Carlos cheering his first basket had made him happier than a thousand John Travoltas ever could.

Yes, categorically, Kaveh was projecting. Enola was not in the U.S. to build a new life for himself (quite the opposite, apparently), he was not here for political asylum, and the idea of being welcomed by the natives did not seem to have even crossed his mind as a possibility. Kaveh had no idea what was really going on in Enola's mind. Hell, even Enola probably didn't know what was going on in Enola's mind. All the same, Kaveh's heart went out to him.

"My name's Kaveh. Do you have a name?"

"I HAVE MANY NAMES."

"What are your many names?"

"MY DIRECT ADDRESS DEPENDS ON WHO IS ADDRESSING ME, AND UNDER WHAT CIRCUMSTANCE."

"What would I call you?"

"YOU COULDN'T PRONOUNCE IT."

"Well, tell me what it would sound like in your language the way you pronounce it."

Out of two holes on the side of his neck, a singular noise came out that could inaccurately be described as "*Bllkstsksxzzztst.*"

"Nice to meet you." Kaveh soaped up a new sponge, having by now gone through almost half his water. "Now I have to get the blood off your body, which means I have to wash you. Are you okay with that?"

The luminous, frightened eyes kept staring up at him, the glowing nebulae shrinking in size, growing in brightness.

"I won't hurt you, I promise."

"I CONSENT."

He started with the head and worked his way back. With Enola's body, he was much carefuller than he had been with the floor, using less soap and making sure he rinsed it as well as he could before moving on.

"WHY ARE YOU DOING THIS?" Enola asked after some time. By now, Kaveh had started on Enola's right arm, which presented some challenges, as parts of his hands were beneath him.

"Because you need help, and no one else is helping you."

"I DO NOT SEEK HELP."

"I can see that. But I hope you reconsider. I don't want you to die."

At this, Enola's head moved as much as it could, as though he was trying to see what Kaveh was doing. "THERE IS NO REASON FOR US TO CONTINUE."

Kaveh froze mid-motion. "What do you mean?"

"I CANNOT STAY, BUT I HAVE NOWHERE ELSE TO GO. THEREFORE, I HAVE COME HERE TO SEEK OUT MY LAST REMAINING SYMPHYLE, THAT WE MIGHT END OUR LIVES TOGETHER. BUT WHAT I HAVE FOUND, I NEVER COULD HAVE EXPECTED, THAT I AM NOT HIS LAST LIVING SYMPHYLE, BUT HE HAS CREATED ANOTHER. ANOTHER, A NATURAL ALIEN. IMPOSSIBLE, I WOULD HAVE THOUGHT."

Kaveh paused. "He has created another 'symphyle' . . . You mean . . . Cora?"

"MY LITTLE COUSIN, YES. BOUND TO MY DEAR BELOVED, BUT NOT IN A WAY I HAVE EVER SEEN, IN A WAY THAT MAKES THEM BOTH SUF- FER. THEY ARE BOUND TO SUFFERING, AND WHEN ONE SUFFERS, SO DOES THE OTHER. I WOULD LIKE TO STUDY THEIR BOND, FOR IT IS NOTHING LIKE I HAVE EVER SEEN."

"Then you should study it," said Kaveh. He poured a small amount of water on a paper towel and wiped down Enola's forearm. Since Enola was as black as the gunk covering him, the only method he had to see if a section was clean was to wipe it with a fresh paper towel and check for residue. "If they consent to it."

"MY BELOVED IS TERRIFIED OF ME."

"Well, that's probably because the first time you saw him, you at- tacked him. I think some fear is justified. That *said*, I've already noticed a marked change in your behavior, and I'm a 'natural' alien that doesn't even speak your language. Show him that you're not dangerous, and maybe he'll let you go."

"But I am dangerous."

Kaveh sighed and then moved to Enola's opposite side to work on the left arm. "When he lets you go," he said, drenching his sponge in the clean water and wringing it out, "and he has to let you go eventually, I know you're going to want to go back on the substance that changed you, your 'medication,' but I'd like to ask you not to."

"I would not know how."

Kaveh paused, wringing the sponge in front of him. "Your kind don't have any ways to treat addiction?"

"Our kind are not presented with the opportunity to become addicted."

"Then where did your . . . 'medicine' come from?"

"I created it."

"Oh . . . dear."

"One amygdaline of the Superorganism would never be allowed to degenerate as I have, or as my dear Beloved has. His disease is critical, perhaps as terrible as mine. But we have no way to treat it. We are not equipped in that science, and even if we were, there are no treatments for those such as us who have degenerated so much. We would not be treated. We would be euthanized."

"Well, I'll tell you right now, that's not how it works here. And if they grant you personhood, and I hope they do, you won't even be allowed that option."

"You would deny one the right to choose when to die? How barbaric."

"There are some places that do allow assisted death under certain circumstances, but you wouldn't qualify for any of them. However, we do have a wide array of ways to treat mental illness. I don't know how effective it would be to translate things designed for a human to you, but it's worth a try."

"I would not consent. That is not why I came here."

"Well, plans change. Cora told me that you have a custom of sorts, that you choose when you're going to die, and you die at the same time as your . . ."

"SYMPHYLES."

"She told me that before you were—well, the word she used was *purged*—you had a date you were scheduled to die, and I presume Ampersand with you, correct?"

"YES."

"But due to tragic, unforeseen circumstances, you lost all your other symphyles prematurely. Is that correct?"

"YES."

"And now you've come to be with your last one when you die. Correct?"

"YES."

He grasped his sponge in front of him. "I understand that this custom is very important to you, and I don't doubt that you intended to get it over with quickly because you were under . . . an influence. But when you say, 'I came here to die with my last remaining symphyle,' what I think you mean is, you came here to be with him, whether you die together anytime soon or not."

He wrung the sponge out in the dirty water bucket, Enola's eyes following the movement of his hands.

"You didn't just come here to die, you came here because you wanted help. Because you *needed* help, you literally ripped open the fabric of space because you needed help."

The luminosity in Enola's eyes dimmed. Kaveh ripped off another few sheets of paper towel and ran them over his handiwork. Not quite clean yet on the left side. "So here I am. I'm here to help you. Welcome to Earth. I'm not going to punch you in the head."

"YOU DO THIS OUT OF COMPASSION."

"In part. I also do it out of curiosity, to learn about you."

"ARE YOU UNIQUE AMONG HUMANS IN YOUR COMPASSION?"

"I don't think so. I think that there are some humans in the world that, if they found you vulnerable like this and strapped to the floor, they might try to kill you and think they were saving the world. But most people, I think 95 percent of people, if they found you like I did, captive and begging for mercy, literally saying, '*Please don't kill me,*' I think they'd show you mercy." He chuckled to himself. "I don't know if they'd port ten gallons of water and a bunch of cleaning supplies up a mountain into the middle of the woods, but they wouldn't hurt you."

"YOU ARE UNIQUE IN THAT WAY."

"Sort of. It's my job to go trotting into certain danger. Honestly, this probably isn't even in the top five most dangerous things I've done. Maybe the top ten."

On impulse, he peeled the yellow gloves off his now-clammy fingers and reached his hand out toward the ridges that formed the sort of crown on the back of his head. Enola eyed him warily, but not shakily, not frightened like he was earlier. Trembling slightly, Kaveh grazed a finger over the "skin." He expected it to be smoother than it was. It was pliant, yet there was a slight coarseness to it. Not living, yet alive.

Kaveh figured it was best not to stay overnight—increased the odds of him getting caught if no one could get ahold of him, and also increased the odds of him running into Ampersand again, which he would prefer to avoid. "They named you Enola Gay, after a piece of wartime aircraft that . . . did something pretty terrible. I don't like that name. Can I give you a new name?"

"WHAT WOULD YOU NAME ME, DEAR CLEVER CREATURE?"

"Something less . . . associated with one of the evillest acts in human history. What was your . . . job in your old life? What was your function?"

"APPLIED THEORETICAL PHYSICS. THE WORK I DID WAS AKIN TO ENGINEERING, AS YOU CONCEIVE IT."

"Our naming conventions are generally, we get our names from our parents, and they name us after someone else. Maybe a relative, maybe a religious figure, maybe a historical figure."

"WHERE DOES YOUR NAME COME FROM?"

"I'm named after a character from ancient Persian mythology who started a revolution against a tyrant. Kaveh the Blacksmith was . . . I guess he's a symbol of resistance against evil and oppression."

He ran his fingers over the ridge on the back of Enola's head, a strange no-man's-land between a triceratops crest and palm fronds. They flexed, had some movement, which he assumed also contained some expression. It was different now from how it had been hours ago, more relaxed, less afraid.

"Nikola," he said. "After one of humanity's most famous engineers."

"IF IT PLEASES YOU," said Nikola.

19

The Riverside National Security Complex wasn't in disarray as much as Cora had expected, but that was less because the situation had calmed down so much as martial law had been declared. There was military everywhere, dozens, hundreds of dudes in camo patrolling the place like they were an invading force, their semiautomatic rifles locked and loaded. No one told her if it was official that the DOD had taken over anything, but it didn't really matter; in practice, that was what was happening. Cora had expected to be overwhelmed with questions and paperwork, but aside from Dr. Sev and her normal colleagues, she went mostly ignored.

Brigadier General Porter had demanded that she be available for a meeting at 5:00 P.M. and had already blown her off twice. It was now almost 9:00 P.M., and she had not been allowed to go home, instead shunted into a lounge, watching CNN on mute, waiting to be beckoned. Todd Julian was giving an interview out near Temecula, which Cora found odd. Wasn't he the senator from Illinois?

"Weird day, huh?"

Cora turned to see Luciana entering the lounge, evening cup of stale reheated office coffee in hand. Numbed by a day of "hurry up and wait," she was almost glad to see Luciana, and her first instinct was the desire to share with her what had happened in the last day.

"Yeah," said Cora, pushing away that instinct and turning back to the TV. "Why is he here? He's not our senator."

"He's not here as a senator. He's here as a candidate."

The man was waving his arms passionately, the closed-captioning a few seconds behind. *Earthquakes, loud noises, lights in the sky, what aren't they telling us? What are they hiding?*

"We really need to do something," said Cora.

"Like what?"

"I don't know, there's no real opposition to people like Julian. They have all the rhetorical chips—they're mad because secrets are being held from them. The only people willing to advocate against people like Julian and Miranda are moon children who think Xethorp is here to bring about the spiritual enlightenment."

"Oh my God, Cora," said Luciana just above a whisper. "Do you want to go to jail for the rest of your life?"

"Can you imagine what bad optics that would be for them if they put me in jail?"

"They *do not care*! They lock up whistleblowers on trumped-up charges all the time."

"Then maybe there's a way I can do it by the book. Isn't that why Stevie quit, so she could talk to the press? I mean . . ." Cora looked at the image of Julian, his trim tailored suit, his salt-and-pepper hair with dignified white streaks at his temples. "Someone has to be a counterweight to . . . *this*."

"They'd wrap you in red tape. They'd make it so bureaucratically miserable for you, you'd give up out of sheer frustration."

Any nerve she'd worked up deflated like a bad soufflé. Luciana was right. She had no idea what she was doing and no real allies with any power or knowledge of the system who might back her up.

"Well, this sure is stressful," said Luciana, standing to leave. "How much longer are they going to keep you here?"

"I don't know. I imagine they'll tell me I have to meet with the general in an hour, then all go home and forget to tell me, and I'll clock out around midnight."

Luciana forced a wan smile. "Well, want to come over and play video games tomorrow?"

Cora brightened, at first relieved at the prospect of socialization, at the gesture toward a return to normalcy. Shouldn't this whole mess have brought them closer together, instead of the opposite? After all, there had been this massive part of Luciana's life that had up until recently remained hidden, and now it could be something they shared, if they could get past the betrayal that had precipitated that part of Luciana's life coming to light in the first place.

A betrayal that Luciana still hadn't admitted to.

"I can't," said Cora. "I think they want me in here tomorrow to give me the talking-to they didn't give me today."

"Oh, okay," said Luciana. "Well, change your mind, let me know?"

"Sure," said Cora, mechanically turning back to CNN, which had cut to a commercial break. What she needed was a person to confide in, and paradoxically Luciana was the last person on Earth she could do that with.

· · · · ·

Cora didn't hear from Ampersand at all that day, or the next day, and she was starting to feel very, very worried. The only thing that was keeping her from flying into a panic was the fact that their empathic bond was still functional, and while she couldn't sense much, at least she wasn't sensing wild despair or terror. If anything, it felt like single-focused determination, too preoccupied to be upset.

One person she *did* hear from was a producer named Laurel Sullivan for *The Hot Seat with Satomi Mack* on MSNBC, apparently a result of her position at ROSA being leaked to the press. Not knowing what else to do, she told Sullivan she couldn't talk to the press at this time.

More worrisome, however, was that she didn't hear from Kaveh, either. She tried calling his burner several times, under strict instruction that this was the only way she would get in contact with him. Finally, on Sunday night, she got one single text from him:

```
stage one Operation: Probably a Huge
Mistake but Fuck It success! I did not
die and the floor is mostly clean—E.
much more coherent, returning in the
morning, hear from &?
```

She responded: No :-(

Ten minutes later, she got a response: lmk if you do!!!

And that was the end of that interaction.

On Monday, she went to work and did nothing but fill out paperwork, because Ampersand was not there, and she had to pretend he was. Once again, she was asked to make herself available for Brigadier General Porter, which she did, and once again, he blew her off. She didn't even find out until one of his underlings let her know an hour after he had already gone home for the day. Cora didn't hear from Kaveh all day, either, except for one text after she got off work:

&&&&&?????

Her reply: :-(:-(:-(
His utterly unhelpful response: fuuuuuuck
She had been so preoccupied with the "hurry up and wait" nonsense they'd been forcing on her at work, she'd hardly spent any time at home, and what time she had spent there had been mired in exhaustion. She'd forgotten to look into this guy, despite the fact that he was apparently a minor celebrity.

With some horror and a little research, she learned how much of an understatement that was.

The two-time Pulitzer nominee and Rhodes Scholar was also a two-time *New York Times* number-one bestselling author. His most recent book and second Pulitzer nomination, *Internal Enemies: Testaments on the Banality of Evil,* followed the lives of several American citizens, mostly Iranian-born, who had been detained in CIA black sites inside the United States in the months and years following 9/11 on false or trumped-up charges. He'd even gone on *The Daily Show with Jon Stewart* to promote it.

His was a story of triumph over adversity, and the tale of his family's escape from Iran was even more harrowing than he had indicated. It had been a *Sound of Music*–style dash to freedom, complete with bribes at the border and over a year of living in limbo in Turkey before finally making it to the U.S. But his family, fortunate to already have relatives in the States, prospered quickly, and his natural intelligence netted him a full ride at Berkeley, which chafed Cora's rapidly swelling inferiority complex. She'd been accepted to Berkeley, but certainly not on a full ride, which only UC–Irvine and (ironically) UC–Riverside had offered, hence her ending up at Irvine. Kaveh was also a polyglot, fluent in English, Farsi, Arabic, French, Spanish, and

German (and was "conversational" in Mandarin and Japanese, according to a profile on him in *The Atlantic*).

But it was his first Pulitzer nomination that chilled her, especially now knowing she had put herself in a position where she had no choice but to trust this man. The nomination, in the category of Investigative Reporting, was: *For an exposé of secret CIA black sites in the Middle East and Asia uncovering mass human rights abuses, reporting that ultimately led to sweeping reforms in U.S. intelligence gathering.*

The names on the nomination: Kaveh Mazandarani and Nils Ortega of *The New Yorker.*

· · · · ·

It was Wednesday before Brigadier General Porter met with her. She was so used to being blown off and disrespected by this man, she actually stopped in surprise when she entered the conference room and saw him seated at the front of the table. In uniform, surrounded by his underlings, as well as Sol and Dr. Sev.

"Have a seat," he said, scratching some notes on a notepad and not looking up at her.

Cora obeyed, taking the seat next to Sol, who also seemed keen not to look at her. After a few moments of awkward note-scratching silence, Porter began. "Okay. According to your report, you have not received any communication from Scio since last Friday."

"That's correct, sir." It was only *mostly* a lie; technically, Saturday had been the last she'd heard from him, but eh.

"Is it common for Scio to go this long without communicating?" he asked, still not looking at her. Cora knew he was doing this on purpose to get under her skin, to show how little she mattered in his esteem. Knowing that this was his tactic did not mean it wasn't effective.

"Obviously, I can't read his mind, but he seems upset at . . . the implication that the army would force him to do anything he didn't want to do."

"I cannot help but notice that, as his interpreter, you seem just as eager to keep him from cooperating as he is."

"It's not my job to try to *convince* him to do anything," said Cora. "Everyone at ROSA knew that if you push them too far, they'll stop cooperating. You cannot bully him into doing what you want."

At long last, the man looked at her. "And you honestly want to tell me that Scio is sitting in his quarters, with a rogue ETI running around out there, doing nothing?"

"I say this with complete honesty; I do not know what he is doing. He won't tell me." It was refreshing to be able to say something true for once.

"Okay, well, we don't have the resources to deal with an aggressive ETI—"

"*Aggressive?*" she countered. Sol shot her a look to zip it.

"I don't know how else you'd describe what he did," said Porter. "Breaking every window in sight and immediately reconstituting them was a display of power. A warning. Of course the DOD is going to see that as an act of aggression. Moreover, we still have little understanding of why they behave the way they do, or what might precipitate it."

"Yes, we do . . . sir."

Porter turned his head robotically. "If we do, Sabino, then it might behoove you to clarify."

"Sir, you angered him when you told him he didn't have a choice in the matter of going with the army to Temecula. I think it's unreasonable to expect them never to have emotional reactions. There's no weird alien moon logic. You offended him, and he reacted like any person would."

"I think 'person' is debatable."

Cora gasped softly, and she looked at Sol. She hadn't even considered that anyone who worked here might be on the Third Option side of the fence. "No, it's not."

Sol shot her a hard look, but Cora countered him with steel. She was done kowtowing to these people.

"Yes, it very much is," said Porter, now not bothering to hide his condescension. "That's why it's being debated. The charade with the broken glass is one of many reasons why we should question the wisdom of extending full human rights to them. *Look* at what just one of them is capable of."

"But don't you see how that logic could be extended to anyone of exceptional, or limited, ability?" She looked around the table for a sympathetic face, but found none. Just a wall of people not taking her seriously, and one Sol who was glaring at her to shut up.

"If we ignore that they're not human, what makes them different?"

Cora continued, doubling down. "Their social structure, their intelligence, their bodies? Those wouldn't determine personhood if they were human. If ultimately the reasoning for denying them full human rights is discriminatory, then there's absolutely no reason this law couldn't eventually be retrofitted to apply to humans as well."

"You're out of line, Sabino," warned Porter, eyes still on his notes.

"Sir, you aren't respecting them as people, when I'm telling you that's the problem. That's why Scio isn't talking to us. And the Third Option could set a really dangerous precedent, not just for ETIs but for human populations, too."

"There are some populations who would benefit from that sort of thing," Porter stated calmly, as though the idea brought him warmth like a cozy fire in winter. Like the potential to oppress human populations was a *feature*, not a bug.

Cora stood up so fast she nearly knocked her chair over. She looked at them all in turn. The unimpressed brigadier general, a bunch of DOD people she didn't know, Dr. Sev unreadable as always, and Sol, who was less glaring venom at her now so much as confusion. She thought of the wire surveillance in her apartment, the threats against her privacy, the detainment of her family, the threat of going to jail for the rest of her life if she so much as talked to the press. And again it begged the question: *Why the fuck am I helping these people?*

"I quit."

Then she turned on her heels and exited the conference room.

That prompted a response, and she heard enough hubbub behind her to tell her that was *not* what was supposed to happen. Whatever. She had to get out of here. There wasn't anyone in this complex who could help her, and certainly no one who worked for the government would. No, her best bet was the guy who had been nominated for a Pulitzer for working alongside her hideously unscrupulous father, and she could only pray that Kaveh Mazandarani wasn't as hideously unscrupulous as the company he kept.

Cora left the complex, ignoring multiple phone calls and texts from Sol and Luciana. She drove about a mile down the road before she stopped in a KFC parking lot, flipping open her phone and sending another call from Sol to voice mail. Then, she made a phone call of her own.

"Laurel Sullivan, please." In a few short seconds, she had producer Laurel Sullivan on the line. "Hi, Ms. Sullivan? This is Cora Sabino. You reached out to me a few days ago about appearing on *The Hot Seat with Satomi Mack*? I'd like to discuss your offer."

It took about five minutes for Cora to realize what she'd gotten herself into, to say nothing of what she had just given up. No more official access to Ampersand, to say nothing of the job she was now out of at the precipice of the greatest economic depression in living memory. She called Kaveh's burner, but it went straight to voice mail, and no response to texts, either. He didn't seem like the type to be careless enough to let it die. So either he was up on the mountain with Enola, or he was dead.

Only one way to find out.

It was around 2:00 P.M. by the time Cora made it up the mountain, into the state park, and onto the runoff road. To her shock and disappointment, there was no Land Rover. There was no anything. Maybe he was still here? A Land Rover was large and obtrusive; maybe he had deliberately left it somewhere else so as not to draw attention. Or maybe he had been here and left at some point? She *had* to go into the cave to check, but the mere thought of seeing Enola gave her hives. She pressed a hand to the one ear that still had an earbud in it.

Obelus 2.0, but crazy.

Cora began the trek down to the cave entrance, bracing the whole way for the sounds of screeching noises to come through her earbud. When she got close to the mouth of the cave, a voice in the earbud said, "HELLO, LITTLE COUSIN," causing her nearly to trip and fall down the side of the steep hill. Definitely not Ampersand's voice, but at the same time, not at all like Enola had sounded earlier. It was measured now, calm, refined.

Cora nearly collapsed with relief when she saw Kaveh inside that cave seated a couple of feet from Enola, who was more or less welded exactly in the spot she had last seen him, still black as ebony but now a much cleaner ebony. "Yo!" said Kaveh, moving his little electric lantern and gesturing for Cora to sit next to him. "Fancy seeing you here. Aren't you supposed to be at work?"

"I quit," she breathed.

"Whoa! Why?"

"I just . . . don't think there's any good I can do by staying there. If I'm going to effect any positive change, I can't work for them."

"Makes sense," said Kaveh, gesturing to Enola. "Especially when you certainly don't need government clearance to have access to him. He's doing a lot better, don't you think?"

Cora looked at Enola, perfectly still on the floor, and wondered if she and Kaveh were looking at the same creature at all. The thing that came to mind for Cora was a scene from *The Last Unicorn,* one of her favorite books growing up. Early in the story, the unicorn got imprisoned in a traveling carnival by a witch. In one of the carnival's other cages, the unicorn recognized the harpy Celaeno had also been imprisoned, an evil, hideous, terrifying creature of incredible power. She was even more horrid in the film adaptation, the stuff of children's nightmares. The harpy told the unicorn to free her, that as immortal, magical beings, "*We are sisters, you and I.*" And so the unicorn freed the harpy, and the newly liberated harpy exacted a reign of revenge-fueled terror, even attacking the unicorn that had freed her. Kaveh seemed to think he had tamed the beast, but Cora only saw a thing that, once it regained its power, would wreak unspeakable havoc on the world.

"Something I've been wondering," said Kaveh. "Is Ampersand actually a 'he'?"

"What do you mean?" asked Cora.

"I mean do they have a concept of gender, or are we using male pronouns out of habit?"

"Well . . ."

There was a long answer to this and a short answer to this.

The long answer had come up about six weeks ago when Cora had come out and asked Ampersand, and got the following answer: "*I have a female karyotype.*"

Cora was stunned that she'd been calling him—*her*—the wrong pronoun the entire time they'd known each other, save those initial seventy-two odd hours when she'd thought of him (*her!*) as an "it." And never once had she been corrected. "Why didn't you say anything?"

"*It is a peculiarity of your language that gender is related to pronouns,*" Ampersand responded. "*Not all human languages have gendered pronouns.*"

"Yes, but . . . it's a respect thing."

"*Assigning gender to pronouns is just as logical as assigning race or height or any other physical attribute to them, and just as relevant to me.*"

"Yes, but it's an important thing in our language, logical or no, so I would prefer that we get it right, even if you don't particularly care."

"*How do you define biological sex? Is it rooted in chromosomes, or gametes, or secondary sex characteristics?*"

Cora paused, having never given this any thought. "I guess chromosomes."

"*What about animals whose secondary sex characteristics do not match their chromosomes?*"

"Is that a thing?"

"*I have no secondary sex characteristics, either by human standards or amygdaline standards. Humans grow breasts, or develop hair at puberty, or grow a certain body type. None of these apply to me. If I am said to have a recognizably human secondary sex characteristic, perhaps it could be larger stature. To amygdalines, that is associated with a female karyotype, in humans, a male karyotype. If we are to associate the secondary sex characteristic seen in humans of larger size, given that I am in a larger body relative to other amygdaline bodies, I am therefore male. If I were able to reproduce sexually, then the gamete cell I would produce would be a female gamete, an egg; therefore, I am female. But amygdaline chromosomes in females are heterogametic, as are human males; therefore, I am male. Do you see how a human framework for gender does not apply to me?*"

"Yes, but, like you said, it's a quirk of our language. I can't call you 'it.' So should I start calling you 'she'?"

"*You should call me 'he.' In terms of social hierarchy, I more identify with masculinity. Moreover, it is important that I be viewed by others as your superior, and you as my subordinate. Therefore, it is beneficial that I be associated with masculinity and you with femininity. Being associated with maleness associates me both with a cultural default and with power,*

with trustworthiness. As you explained to me when we first began commu-
nicating, femininity is associated more with emotionality, with weakness,
and with untrustworthiness. Male pronouns are more appropriate."

And that was that. Female karyotype, functionally agender, but
male pronouns and association with maleness was just more prag-
matic. How poetic that the first thing she ever taught him was that
femininity was associated with weakness and non-importance, and no
one wants to be associated with *that.*

She gave Kaveh the short answer: "Ampersand prefers male pronouns. I guess . . . you should ask Enola what he . . . they prefer."

"IT IS AS YOU PREFER, LITTLE COUSIN."

"Do you have a . . . chromosomal . . . karyotype?" asked Cora.

"I HAVE A MALE KARYOTYPE."

"Ah, well, that keeps it simple," said Kaveh.

Cora inwardly thought that probably meant they should call Enola
"she," but kept that to herself.

"Nik and I have been having some interesting conversations these
last couple days," he said, putting a pen in the binder of his notebook,
which she noticed was filled with notes and scribbles.

"Wait, 'Nik'?"

"Yeah, I'm not a fan of nuclear holocaust, so I wanted to change
'Enola.' So I renamed him Nikola, after Nikola Tesla, and he said that
was fine, although I'm pretty sure that's because he doesn't care what we
call him."

"Umm . . ."

"So why's he call it 'dynamic fusion bonding'?"

Cora took a seat next to him, trying not to stare nervously at the
newly rechristened "Nikola." "It's a term Ampersand 'appropriated,' in
his words, but one of the many he finds 'frustrating' because it's not
an 'accurate' translation. But as I understand it, 'dynamic' because it's
not monogamous, and 'fusion' I think he got from fission-fusion social
groups, like chimpanzees. Phyles have fusion, but no fission. They don't
drift in and out of phyles like chimpanzees do; they bond for life. I guess
maybe the closest point of comparison would be a troop of gorillas."

"Oh, cool. Who's the silverback?"

"Well, they're in the top caste, so they're not allowed to form phyles,
but if they could . . . Ampersand would be the silverback." This she

muttered, glad that Kaveh didn't know how she fit into this weird alien web.

"So Oligarchs can form dynamic fusion bonds, but they can't form phyles."

"No, they are physically *able* to form phyles, they're just not allowed. From what I've gathered, some generations ago, there was some problems with too much power being concentrated in certain phyles, so now the price you pay for being in the top caste is you can't form phyles like the lower castes get to."

"Interesting. So it's like how historically, the Japanese imperial family wasn't allowed to raise their own children. That's the price you pay for being God on earth—you don't get to play with your kids."

"Something like that."

"So how does that apply to this little fam?"

"So if Nikola is bound to Ampersand, and Ampersand is bound to Obelus," she said, tracing a triangle on the floor, "then Nikola isn't allowed to bond with Obelus."

"NOT THAT HE WOULD HAVE. OBELUS HAS ALWAYS DESPISED ME."

"I keep hearing about 'noble Obelus,'" said Kaveh, still eyeing her suspiciously. "Nik seems to, well, really fucking hate him."

"Another of the extended family. And yeah, Obelus makes En—Nikola look like a teddy bear by comparison." She could only hope Enola didn't know how much havoc Obelus had wreaked on Earth, how many people he'd killed, because he seemed to have absolutely no compunction about spilling whatever beans he had to spill. If he was Ampersand's opposite in many ways, it seemed in this way most of all.

"Ampersand came here because of one of his symphyles at ROSA named Čefo. You probably remember that name from the Fremda Memo."

"Oh, right," he said. The Fremda Memo, which Nils had leaked last year, had been falling pebbles on the snowdrift that caused the avalanche that was ET-gate. The human names in the memo had been redacted, but the one ETI name that got dropped, Čefo, had not been. "So Čefo is real?"

"Was real. He's dead."

"Really?" he said, suspicion creeping into his voice, like Čefo had been the victim of a CIA hit. "How?"

"Suicide. It's a long story."

"*Really?*" The word *suicide* seemed to shake him a little.

"Strictly speaking, that's supposed to be how they all die."

"Right . . ." He looked at Enola and then actually *petted* him on the part of him that most resembled a shoulder. *That* was bold. She could only imagine how Ampersand would feel about being in that position, letting a human touch him with his shield *down*.

"So Ampersand is bound to Čefo, and Obelus is bound to Ampersand . . ." She stopped, about to draw the line that Čefo and Obelus would therefore not be bound to each other. But they *had* been. Obelus's arrival had been *the very reason* why Čefo had killed himself in the first place—to prevent his bond to Obelus from being the thing that led him to tracking down the Fremda group.

Then, as if reading her thoughts, Enola spoke. "LITTLE COUSIN, I BE-LIEVE I KNOW WHICH INDIVIDUAL YOU ASSIGNED THE NAME 'ČEFO.' ČEFO WAS AN OLIGARCH, DE FACTO LEADER OF THE GROUP YOU CALL 'FREMDA.' ČEFO DIED, SUBJECTIVE, SIXTY-NINE EARTH DAYS AGO. I KNOW THIS, BECAUSE ČEFO WAS MY SYMPHYLE. AND HE WAS NOBLE OBELUS'S SYMPHYLE. BUT HE WAS NOT OUR DEAR BELOVED'S."

"But Ampersand told me—"

"HE LIED," stated Enola flatly. "YOU KNOW THAT OLIGARCHS MAY NOT FORM PHYLES. THIS DENIED OUR BELOVED FROM THE CHOICE TO BOND WITH ČEFO OR FOR OBELUS TO BOND WITH ME."

Cora looked at Kaveh, embarrassed that Nikola would undermine what fragile trust she had with Ampersand right in front of this man. Why he would lie about being Čefo's symphyle was a mystery, although she couldn't deny it did explain some things. She'd asked him why he hadn't been able to find Čefo, given that he'd been on Earth a full month before Čefo died. The answer he'd given her had been a wishy-washy, oh, you know, "*Obelus had ways of tracking him that I did not.*"

The memory sent a peal of nausea through her innards, and something about that sensation, that these were the very same innards that had been skewered by Obelus, made the nausea compound on itself. She looked down at her hands and stuffed them into her lap, realizing that they were visibly shaking. *Stop, stop!* she thought. *Not now, I cannot go through this every fucking time someone says the word* Obelus.

"WHAT HAS HAPPENED TO YOU? WHO DID THIS TO YOU?"

Kaveh looked at Cora. "What's he talking about?"

"I don't know."

"YOU HAVE BEEN GRIEVOUSLY INJURED AND REPAIRED. I DON'T THINK HUMAN DOCTORS COULD REPAIR HUMAN BIOMATTER SO SKILLFULLY. WHO DID THIS TO YOU? DID OUR BELOVED HURT YOU, LITTLE COUSIN?"

"No!" she blurted. "No, no, no, he didn't do it." She noticed Kaveh's look of shock quickly morph into suspicion. "Ampersand didn't . . . he didn't hurt me."

"WHO DID HURT YOU, LITTLE COUSIN?"

She looked at Kaveh, unsure of the wisdom of sharing this truth, and decided it was time to change the subject, before even more beans could be spilled. "Kaveh, have you ever been on TV before?"

Smooth.

He eyed her skeptically. "Yeah, lots of times."

"I, um . . . I agreed to do an interview on *The Hot Seat with Satomi Mack*."

"Holy shit, when?"

"Day after tomorrow."

"Holy shit!" He sprang to his feet. "That's awesome!"

"Awesome?" she said, standing up to meet him.

"Yeah, you want to be an advocate? This is the quickest and easiest way to do it. Can't believe MSNBC got you first; you *could* have been a real get for Oprah or *60 Minutes*. Well, if you were 'breaking your silence,' which I don't think is the narrative we want to go with. You don't want to be Monica Lewinsky trying to set the record straight, you want to be, well, mirrorverse Jano Miranda. Always play offense, never play defense."

"Have you done *The Hot Seat*?"

"Not that show, but I've done ones like it. They'll probably have you up against someone from the opposing side."

"What?" She blanched. "Oh, God, what have I agreed to?"

"You can always pull out," he said with a wry smile.

"But those things you said about how we need to do anything in our power to oppose the Third Option?"

"I left a perfectly good 'that's what she said' hanging. Right there. And you didn't take it."

She stared at him blankly. "This is serious."

"So is a good 'that's what she said' left un-she-said'd. Tsk, tsk." Then he boldly took a lock of her hair between his thumb and forefinger. "We're going to have to do something about this blue raspberry look, though."

He held on to the lock of hair a little too long, a little too intimate, smiling at her like warm honey and sparking a little electric jolt in her chest, equal parts excitement and fear. His natural charm must have been part of what made him so exceptional in his line of work; he could disarm people with that honey smile before they even realized he'd rendered them defenseless.

"Did you drive up here?" he asked.

"Yeah."

"Okay, good. I have some evidence I need to dispose of." He pointed to a pile of full trash bags near the entrance of the cave. "Feels kind of weird getting rid of invaluable alien DNA or whatever that is exactly, but I kind of have this feeling that no one should have it, so we should probably burn it."

"I agree."

"Give me your keys?" She pulled her keys out of her pocket and dropped them in his open palm. "I'll make a trip, then we can probably both handle the rest together."

She watched in silence as he merrily grabbed a couple of armfuls of plastic bags, leaving her alone in the dark with a cheap electric camping lantern and a half-crazed alien cyborg.

Enola's eyes seemed to have lost focus, his gaze floating around to his surroundings. "My dearest Čefo died before I was able to fold space. Before I could save him. I wonder if I had come sooner, could I have saved him?"

She knelt in front of him. "I have questions, too. About dynamic fusion bonding."

Those bleary eyes regained their sharp, glowing focus in a flash, as if he spied an opportunity. "Do you wish to know the truth of the Divine, little cousin?"

"What do you mean?"

"I can show you," he said, the bits of refraction in his eyes finding focus. "I can show you the truth of the Divine, the truth of

WHY WE ARE HERE, THE TRUTH OF THE ORIGINS OF ALL LIFE. WHAT BINDS YOU TOGETHER."

"Okay," she said, lowering herself in front of him on shaky legs a comfortable-ish distance away. "Tell me."

"I CAN TELL YOU, BUT FIRST, YOU MUST FREE ME."

Of course, she thought. Same old shit now wrapped in a more coherent wrapper. "I couldn't free you even if I wanted to. Only Ampersand can do that."

"NOT TRUE, LITTLE COUSIN. YOU COULD FREE ME IF YOU WANTED TO."

"Why do I need to free you, though?"

His focus became hazy, as though he were scanning the ceiling for something. "I REQUIRE A METAPHOR, LITTLE COUSIN, BUT I DO NOT HAVE THE APPROPRIATE METAPHOR HERE."

She cocked her head to the side, something like suspicion bubbling up inside her. "Why do you call me 'little cousin'?"

"OUR BELOVED HAS BOUND HIMSELF TO YOU."

Her smile vanished. "How do you know that?"

"I CAN SEE, LITTLE COUSIN. BUT I DO NOT UNDERSTAND. THERE IS NO PRECEDENT FOR SUCH A THING, AN AMYGDALINE BONDING TO A NATURAL ALIEN." His focus found her, sharper than ever. His head was now steady as a rock. "I HOPE HE IS STUDYING IT."

"He . . . was. He was in the process of it before you . . . arrived."

"IS THAT WHY HE BOUND HIMSELF TO YOU? TO STUDY THE EFFECTS?"

"No. No, he did it to . . . save me."

"SAVE YOU FROM WHAT?"

Cora shifted her weight, wondering if it was wise to tell the truth. "Obelus took me hostage, back when he was in his Similar body, so Ampersand bound himself to me to know where I was. So he'd be able to find me after they took me."

"WHY WOULD HE DO SUCH A THING?"

"He said . . . he'd do anything to keep me alive, and he couldn't think of any other way to track me down when Obelus took me. So he tried it, expecting it not to work. But it did."

Enola's gaze was beyond focused and well into "intense" territory. "DYNAMIC FUSION BONDS CANNOT BE USED TO DIVINE LOCATION.

HE COULD NOT HAVE USED YOUR BOND TO LOCATE YOU IF YOU WERE LOST."

Before she could respond, she heard the sounds of human feet padding along the pine needle–covered forest floor, and Kaveh reappeared. "All right, I'm ready to go destroy some evidence and then make some phone calls. Hey." He noticed her expression, and mistook it for MSNBC-related jitters. "It'll be okay! Are you down to follow me back to Yorba Linda?" She nodded. "Cool, I'll help you with the prep. It'll be fun! Not like anything important is on the line."

She stared at him blankly.

"Okay, I'm sorry about that. I've got these defense mechanisms, see. I've had a tragic life." He knelt in front of Enola, gave him an affectionate pat on one of the ridges behind his eyes. "Sorry to leave you alone again."

"YOU MUST TEND TO YOUR OWN, DEAR CLEVER CREATURE."

"I'll come back tomorrow. I can't release you, but I'd like to negotiate something more, for lack of a better word, humane. Even if dear Beloved does want to keep your movements limited, there has to be a better way to do it than this."

"YOU ARE VERY KIND, DEAR CLEVER CREATURE."

"I'll be back sometime tomorrow, I promise." He grabbed as many of the trash bags as he could carry, leaving Cora the few remainders. She spared a glance for Enola before she exited. His bright eyes were shining, curious, calculating. *Set me free. We are sisters, you and I.*

"BE CAREFUL, LITTLE COUSIN."

Browser | Files | irc.isdne | #Gadsden

[22:52] <WhiteChimaera> u heard what ortega said abt the elites and globalists
[22:52] <WhiteChimaera> call to action if I ever heard one
[22:52] <LoneWolf84> I have a friend who worked at NORAD, he said they were vulnerable to EMPs
[22:53] <LoneWolf84> amigdalines vulnerable to EMPs I mean
[22:53] <LoneWolf84> he leaked it and now he's been court martialed
[22:54] <PisgahRancher> That is so fucked
[22:54] <Cleaver512> heard about the EMPs as well. I know a guy out in Barstow who is working on it
[22:54] <WhiteChimaera> working on it how?
[22:54] <LoneWolf84> he says our govt won't defend us, we have to defend ourselves
[22:54] <LoneWolf84> he's this weirdo lives out in the desert, builds bombs and electronic devices
[22:54] <LoneWolf84> been working on this portable EMP device for years in case of chinese invasion
[22:55] <LoneWolf84> he was prepping for the wrong invasion lol
[22:55] <Cleaver512> what's he gong to do with it
[22:55] <LoneWolf84> he's friends with ammon normandy. He'll be at the rally in DTLA on sat
[22:55] <PisgahRancher> fuck yeah
[22:55] <LoneWolf84> so if any little green men, we'll be ready
[22:56] <PisgahRancher> I'll be there and packing
[22:56] <WhiteChimaera> Same
[22:56] <LoneWolf84> see you all there
[22:56] <PisgahRancher> Yessss

Cora stood outside Kaveh's house for a long time before he came outside to see what the holdup was. "Ah, *Willkommen!*" he said, leaning on the frame of his front door. "Ready for your life to change?"

Kaveh's house, or rather, Kaveh's family's "investment property," was fucking huge.

It wasn't huge in that it was a palace with multiple wings but rather huge in that it had the same number of (legal) bedrooms as her mother's house in Torrance but was roughly twice as big. It had a three-car garage, which housed the Land Rover and a Tesla Roadster. "Both of these are my dad's," he clarified, like that made it any better. Apparently, Baba Mazandarani owned a car dealership in Irvine, so teeeeeechnically the dealership owned the Land Rover. The Tesla, though, that was Dad's. His family had preferred to invest in real estate rather than the stock market, which had insulated their wealth from the worst of the stock market crash, despite the real estate market being *the cause* of the stock market crash. "Subprime loans are mainly what caused it— that doesn't have anything to do with our investments, since none of our properties have mortgages," he told her, and she nodded like she'd understood a word he said.

The garage led into a kitchen that opened into a comfortable family room. Big bay windows and glass-paned doors looked into the back-yard, which had both a pool *and* a hot tub that flowed into the pool, and sat atop a hill with a view that probably could see all the way to LA on a clear day if such things existed. Yes, they did have to get going or they'd be late for the appointment at the salon in Hollywood he'd booked for her ("Don't worry, I'll pay for it"), but they weren't in *such* a hurry that he couldn't give her a quick tour.

Upstairs were three bedrooms, each with its own bath, as well as an office he'd never used. The master bedroom had a fireplace and a balcony that looked out onto the valley below. It entered into the even more gobsmacking master bathroom, which probably had its own zip code. The shower was practically its own room, walled off by a giant pane of glass. Across from it was a bathtub surrounded by a tile shelf on both sides, with a window right next to it looking into the backyard. One had to go through the master bathroom to access the walk-in closet, which was bigger than her bedroom.

Oh, God, I'm so far out of my league, we're not even playing the same sport, she thought for roughly the eighty-fifth time that morning as her eyes wandered from the little balcony that overlooked that huge backyard to the freaking *remote* that turned on the fireplace to his big California king bed with its Egyptian cotton duvet. She imagined herself in that giant bed, and the thought made her toes curl.

"We'd better get going," he said as he donned a tailored navy-blue blazer over a coral button-up shirt and tasteful stonewashed jeans. He had applied that cologne that smelled of vanilla and leather and cedar, like a cabin in the mountains, and the sight of him so confident in his own skin, the smell of that cologne, made her mouth go dry, and she hoped he didn't notice the slight tremor that ran through her. She looked at his bed.

So out of my league . . .

Kaveh had spent most of the previous day coaching her on how to present herself and prepping talking points that wouldn't potentially be read as revealing state secrets or threatening national security. He'd assured her that no matter how restrictive the terms of her clearance were, there were certain things they *could not* bar her from discussing. In short order, they hopped into his Land Rover and began the hour-ish journey to the salon in Hollywood.

First stop, the task of de-blueing her hair, which took about two hours. She spent most of that time reading through the binder she'd gotten from DHHS's information release office, and Kaveh spent most of that time on the phone. When she was done, the stylist presented her hairstyle opus to the man bankrolling it.

"Wow, look at you," he said in a tone that could either be read as brotherly or . . . not brotherly, and her mouth went dry again. "I'm getting 'Jennifer Aniston opens up about life, love, and divorce' vibes. Chic, professional, yet relatable."

Cora looked into the mirror and hardly recognized herself. She hadn't ever gotten her hair *styled* and colored before. Hell, ever since she graduated high school, she'd cut her own hair to save money. Normally, it was the texture of dry chaparral right before a wildfire broke out, but this was sleek, straight and shiny, framing her face in a perfect oval. She didn't look like Jennifer Aniston, as she lacked the pointy Anistonian features, but she looked . . . changed.

She looked like an *adult.*

She followed Kaveh to his Land Rover, his sunglasses glinting in the sunlight as he chatted away on his BlackBerry in a language she assumed to be Farsi, or rather, a sort of Spanglish version of Farsi. Farglish.

"No, I can't right now." Pause. "*Dooroogh nemigam.* Could you help me out?" Pause. "*Yeh dagheh gooshi. Damet garm.* Okay, bye." Click. "Hey, Paris. No, I was just talking to my sister. No, it's fine, we were done talking, anyway. What's up?"

Cora looked at the tall palm trees lining the road while he chatted away, wishing traffic were heavier. Maybe there would be a horrible accident, and they wouldn't make it to the studio in time. Wouldn't that be too bad? Then she'd have to stay in his state-of-the-art Land Rover with him and his cologne and his thick, curly black hair that she also really wanted to touch. And he'd paid for her new hair, he probably wanted to touch his investment, make sure it was properly . . . being hair. Maybe it would get too hot, and he'd take off his blazer and she'd have to hold it for him, and she'd have to smell the cologne on his blazer. Wouldn't that be terrible.

"All right, yes," Kaveh continued, by now using his Bluetooth. "Well, let me know if you need anything." Pause. "Yep, I miss you, too. I'll see you . . . one of these days." He laughed a genuine, heartfelt laugh. "Yeah, I know. Okay, bye." He took his Bluetooth out of his ear. "Okay, I think that's it. She was pretty chatty since we hadn't talked in a while."

Cora was suddenly possessed with a desire for him to laugh heartfelt laughs at things *she* said, jokes *she* made, and with jealousy at whoever he'd been talking to. She hated herself for the question she was about to ask. "Girlfriend?"

"No, not girlfriend," he said, keeping his eyes on the road. "More like . . . a colleague. I helped Paris get her job at *The New Yorker,* but she's become one of my best friends over the last couple of years."

This surprised Cora. Did he not have a girlfriend? If so, why not? Ignoring the fact that he was so charming and, well, nice, he was rich, and successful, and he *was* good-looking. Objectively, he was good-looking, she could admit that, in an offbeat quirky way, more a character actor than a leading man.

"And you never dated?"

He chuckled. "She doesn't like the D."

"Your D, or D in general?"

"In general." He smiled knowingly. "Why, are you interested?"

"I feel like I'd have to meet her first."

"I seem to recall you mentioning a girlfriend at some point."

Said "girlfriend" had up until this point been her only real relationship that had lasted for more than two months, but how to gracefully telegraph that she wasn't *only* interested in girls? "Yeah, college relationship. Ended badly. Not like my high school *boyfriend.*"

Smooth.

"Well, nonstarter; she's taken. She's dating this Broadway stage manager."

"How do you know her?"

"Well, she became a mentee of sorts a few years ago, but then I had a phase that was very embarrassing." His demeanor changed, the jovial veneer thinning. "Right after my brother died."

"I'm sorry. How did he die?"

"Oh, you know." His head wobbled back and forth awkwardly. Hem, haw. Hem, haw. "Rope."

"Rope?" Then it hit her what he meant. "Oh, I'm so sorry. When was that?"

"Three years ago this March. I met Paris when she was in grad school when I hired her as a researcher, and this was like . . . maybe three months later. But then Sirvan died and, uh, well . . . more than once Paris would show up to a meeting at a bar in Manhattan, and I would already be *lit.*"

"How old was she?"

"At the time? She was only twenty-two. And I was so inappropriate."

"You mean . . ."

"No, I mean *professionally* inappropriate. I get that alcoholic mentors are common to the point of cliché in the writing world, but I hate to think that was me. I didn't sexually harass her, if that's what you're asking, but that didn't mean she wasn't put in a position where she had to talk me down from getting in a fistfight with 9/11 truthers in bars a time or two. But yeah, she forgave my transgressions and stuck by me at a really hard time. So I owe her a lot."

Must be nice, she thought. *Having friends who support you even when things go to shit.*

"So what do you want to do with your life?" he asked, keeping his eyes on the road.

"I guess I kind of assumed my life would be dedicated to . . . him. To being his interlocutor."

"Well, if that wasn't a thing, what would you do?"

She sank back into her seat, embarrassed at the thought that if all this hadn't happened with Ampersand, she'd still be a college dropout who had blown the one job opportunity she'd gotten, at a temp agency of all things. When Kaveh was her age, he was probably getting his Rhodes Scholarship application together. "I guess finish my degree, take it from there."

"Why don't you?"

"I couldn't afford it."

"Is that why you dropped out?"

She sank farther, the embarrassment swelling. "Sort of. I dropped out because I got put on academic probation and lost my scholarship."

He raised a subtle "What happened?" eyebrow.

"It was a confluence of things," she continued. "Nils was starting to get really famous, and people were starting to get all invasive and ask questions about it, and then I went through a breakup and, as so often happens with friend groups, everyone had to choose sides and . . . most of them sided with her."

He snorted. "Hate it when that happens. I know it's cold comfort, but I think your former friends might be idiots."

Her stomach flooded with butterflies. Was he just being nice, or was that flirting?

"So what's your dream school?" he asked.

Dream school? That hadn't been a thought she'd allowed herself to entertain in years. What had it been when she was in high school? "I guess Columbia. I have that legacy connection since Nils used to be a professor there, but I didn't apply."

"Why not? If you got into Berkeley, you could probably get into Columbia."

"I couldn't afford it. And besides, I feel like I'm much more valuable as Ampersand's interpreter than just another college student."

"I would think that finishing your degree, especially at a prestigious institution like Columbia, would be a complement to a life as professional Voice of the Alien. It wouldn't need to be either-or." By now, he had pulled his Land Rover through the security gate of the studio and was winding up the levels in the parking garage as he hunted for a spot. "And besides, this talking head thing can be pretty lucrative. With that plus student loans, I'm sure you could swing it. Then you'd be in New York and we'd be neighbors!"

The butterflies in her stomach started throwing a rave, and she could not suppress a smile at the thought. To attend an Ivy League school in New York, away from Smell-A, free to start over and now with the help of a new, er, *mentor* to guide her into the world of the media. "How old are you, Kaveh?"

"I'm thirty-five."

"I'm asking for trouble, aren't I?" She smiled shyly. God, she was so bad at this. She'd never deliberately flirted with a *man* before. Boys, maybe, arguably, but *man*?

"Yes, well . . ." He put the car into park, turned off the ignition, and smiled. "When we met, you were caught in the crosshairs of not one but two telekinetic alien cyborgs, one of whom you apparently have some kind of ET-heartbond with, so I think it's fair to call your self-preservation instincts into question."

She looked at him like he'd threatened her with a knife. "How did you know about that?"

His smile vanished. "Nik told me."

"What do you mean 'Nik told you'?"

"He said that whatever social bond he and Ampersand had was the same one you and Ampersand had. Kept going on about how weird it was."

Oh, God. Oh, God. She'd gone from partying butterflies in her stomach to the edge of a panic in seconds. "Kaveh, you weren't supposed to know that . . . what Ampersand did to me. No one was."

"I didn't realize—"

"I know I'm in no position to beg—"

"Whoa," he said, growing worried. "Are you in trouble?"

"He said I could never tell anyone. My whole life, human or alien, no one can know. *Please,* Kaveh, please, even if you do end up writing about all this, please not this, anything but this—"

"Whoa, it's okay. You don't need to beg. I'll take it to my grave, I promise."

"My life is in your hands," she said, more a question than a statement.

"Hey," he said, taking her gently by the wrist. "As long as it's not hurting you, it's none of my business."

As long as it's not hurting you! What a loaded thing to say. *Where the hell are you, you biomechanical fuck?*

Kaveh put his hand on her shoulder, running the tips of his fingers to the nape of her neck, and smiled that warm honey smile. "We're on the same team, okay?" he said, giving her neck a tiny squeeze. "Today, I'm just the coach. You'll do fine, and I won't tell anyone about . . . that. You have my word."

She took a breath and nodded, desperately wanting to believe him but unable to really do it. How much he knew put her in an extremely vulnerable position. He must have known that she was completely open to blackmail, that he could destroy her for fun and profit with minimal effort. She didn't know him well enough to trust him on an emotional level, but she'd put herself in a position where she had no choice but to trust him on a material level. *Please, please be the decent person you are presenting yourself to be,* she prayed. *Please, please don't be like Nils.*

"The entire segment is scheduled to last seven and a half minutes," said Laurel Sullivan, the pixie-like producer of *The Hot Seat with Satomi Mack*. "As you know, it will be broadcast live, so you'll get visual cues for when your segment is nearly over. We're doing a basic point-counterpoint, you with a Third Option proponent."

"Oh." Cora had really hoped it would just be her being interviewed, at least this first time. She hadn't exactly been a member of the debate team in high school.

"Satomi will ask one of you a question and will either follow up with a question for the other side, or ask you to respond. Satomi won't stray outside the preapproved talking points that both you and your opponent have agreed to."

"She'll be fine," said Kaveh.

"And I know this is old hat for you," she said to Kaveh and looked at Cora. "You're lucky you've got him on your team!"

"Oh, go on," said Kaveh.

"You'll do great," said Laurel. "Hair and makeup is down the hall and to your left."

Cora nodded, wanting to say something to him about yes, she was lucky to have Kaveh Mazandarani, because he was a famous investigative journalist who wore perfectly tailored blazers and expensive mountain lodge cologne, but her words abandoned her.

"They really were going to throw you to the wolves, huh?" said Kaveh, leading her in the direction of hair and makeup.

"What do you mean?"

"First time on TV and it's a point-counterpoint, probably with someone who's done this a million ti—Oh, Christ."

Cora looked to see what Kaveh was oh-Christing, and saw that it was not a what but a who, in his chair for hair and makeup, daintily removing the bib that protected his custom tailored suit.

Jano fucking Miranda.

"Oh no," said Cora. At that moment Miranda saw them and hopped off his stool to approach them. "Kaveh," he said, reaching out for a handshake. "How's it going?"

"Not bad, man," said Kaveh, taking Miranda's hand and shaking it vigorously. Miranda's eyes darted back and forth between the two of them in confusion.

"Are you doing the show?" asked Miranda.

"No, I'm moral support," said Kaveh, gesturing to Cora.

"Oh, I see. So does that mean you're Team Personhood?" He completely ignored Cora.

Kaveh shrugged. "You know me, 'separate but equal' doctrines always make me a little nervous."

"I think that hardly applies when we're dealing with nonhumans," Miranda said with a slight chuckle, as if he were talking about his optimistic projections for the next quarterly report.

"Well, let's just say she knows some things you don't."

"I figure." The friendly tone wavered, and Miranda looked at her with a soupçon of venom. Then he smiled and shook her hand flaccidly as another producer in a headset came to collect him. "Well, this should be interesting! Certainly new territory for me. Looking forward to it!"

"So am I," she lied.

"To the wolves," Kaveh muttered once Miranda was out of earshot.

"How do you know him, anyway?"

He looked to her, his green eyes sparkling. "I know everybody."

She sighed, and he clapped a hand on her shoulder before she went in for hair and makeup. "Listen, you'll be fine. Just remember." He leaned in and whispered in her ear, sending chills up her spine like a rolling ocean wave, "Never play defense."

· · · · ·

"Today, I am speaking with Jano Miranda, candidate for California's Forty-Sixth Congressional District and proponent of the Third Option of nonhuman personhood, and Cora Sabino, formerly of . . ."

The host, Satomi, had a young Gwen Ifill vibe, more moderator than firebrand. There was a feed of Satomi in New York and Jano in another room in the same studio on a screen she could see, but it was the camera she had to keep her eyes on, which was already proving challenging. *Don't look away,* she thought, over and over, remembering Kaveh's instruction that doing so would make her look "shifty."

"Cora is also the oldest daughter of Nils Ortega—"

God-*fucking*-damn it. Of course they would say that, it would be suspicious if they didn't, but she felt kneecapped by it all the same.

"—and the niece of Nils Ortega's sister, Luciana Ortega, who has worked at ROSA for the last five years. Ms. Sabino has worked in an undisclosed capacity in conjunction with ROSA in recent months. Welcome to you both."

"It's a pleasure," said Miranda.

"Um," said Cora. "Thanks."

"In some ways, this is an extremely philosophical topic. We have to truly examine what personhood even means. Mr. Miranda, how do you define personhood?"

Miranda chuckled as if they were sharing a joke. "I think the answer to that is obvious. We could get philosophical, but we don't need to. We can just use common sense. A person is a human."

"Ms. Sabino?" said Satomi.

This was one she felt ready for, at least. "A person is an individual, but personhood is also a function of being social creatures. So a person is a sentient, autonomous, conscious being capable of language and problem-solving, but a person can only evolve in the context of a species capable of forming societies. All humans are persons, but not all persons are human. The two terms are not interchangeable."

"And in your opinion," said Satomi, "do you feel that the ETIs that you have had direct access to would meet the definition of personhood, as most humans would define it?"

"Yes," she said without hesitation. "In terms of autonomy, in terms of being conscious, in terms of having both spoken and written language—they're not that dissimilar from us. This could be a genuinely complicated question, like maybe they didn't have consciousness as we understand it, or maybe it's one big hive mind, but that's not the case. In most ways, they think and reason like we do, they are social creatures like we are, they form social bonds like we do, and they fit any meaningful definition of personhood except for the fact that they are not human."

"Mr. Miranda," said Satomi, not missing a beat. God, this was moving so fast. "How does the idea that ETIs may not be too dissimilar from humans fit into Third Party doctrine?"

"I would argue that it's immaterial," said Miranda, "and no one who is a proponent of the Third Option would deny the, for lack of a better word, humanity of any individual ETI that showed the same signs of being a person that any human would. But we must also be realists, and we must learn from the mistakes of our own history. My ancestors in Cuba survived unspeakable cruelties at the hands of the Europeans, and many of these exploitations happened because the natives took the Europeans in good faith, assuming that treaties would be upheld.

"The same holds true here in the United States—any concession the natives gave the European settlers was, at best, taken advantage of. By accepting ETIs like they're human, we are leaving open doors for our generosity to be exploited. There are ways for us to show our compassion and generosity without leaving our systems and our society and our laws open for exploitation, and that is what the Third Option is about."

"Ms. Sabino, most *human* persons would agree that individuality is a large component in being considered a person," said Satomi. "Could you describe the personality of any of the ETIs in a way that humans might appreciate?"

What the fuck? That hadn't been on the roster of preapproved talking points. It had all been broad, conceptual stuff about the nature of what makes a person, and do amygdalines fall under that umbrella, not "So what's he like?"

"Yes," she stammered, totally blanking. *He's withdrawn, deceptive, duplicitous. He lies. He's perfectly capable of kindness, but withdraws it when it's inconvenient for him, and it's always inconvenient. He doesn't take care of himself, he lives in constant fear, he refuses to sleep because he's so afraid. He's killing himself. He won't let me help him.*

"I can't disclose details of interactions I've had." Fuck, what to say? This was making her look like she had totally made this all up. "But the one I've had the most interaction with . . ." *He hates it here. The sun is too bright. Our rooms are too cold. The atmosphere is too thin. He's a miserable curmudgeon, and he hates everything.* "He likes the ocean."

That was a flat-out lie.

"Apes have personalities," said Miranda. "Dogs have personalities. That doesn't confer them legal personhood."

"Mr. Miranda, you believe that the question of whether they have individuality, have personalities, is not relevant to discussions of the possibility of a Third Option?"

"Correct," said Miranda. "Rights of any kind confer access to systems, but if any individual has a profoundly huge advantage, which we could assume any being advanced enough to traverse such vast distances would, and we confer them access to our systems, systems like wealth, land ownership, democracy, we are inviting them into systems that they could exploit."

"Anyone can exploit a system; humans exploit systems designed for humans all the time," said Cora. Hell, if he could dive in without the interviewer acting as a moderator, so could she. "Systems also confer protections as well as rights, and right now, ETIs in the United States have neither."

"I agree, any intelligent being, human or alien, should be *protected,* but we also need to protect ourselves," said Miranda. "Let's ignore the intelligence issue, what are they capable of, physically? If they are granted the full scope of human rights under the law, then their bodies, their persons, would be protected under the Fourth Amendment. We could possibly never know what they are capable of until it's too late."

"Then that is a totally separate question as to whether or not they have full, natural human rights under international law," Cora butted in, not giving Satomi one millisecond to step in. "Your reasoning is that there should be a separate category based on species, where the only real difference is intelligence or physical capability. The same discriminatory rationale could be used against any human person or any group of human people. Believe me, the ETIs I've interacted with do have some cognitive advantages, but they are not so much more intelligent than us as to be unfathomable. Saying that, for instance, high intelligence makes someone a threat to existing human-built systems could apply to anyone, human or alien. That's discrimination."

"No serious person in favor of the Third Option is making an argument that they are *less* than we are," Miranda said. He looked frustrated. She had gotten him playing defense.

"But you aren't advocating giving them different rights, you are advocating to give them fewer rights. You would have to select what, exactly, about them makes them liable to exploit the system of human rights that every country has already agreed on. Let's say it's intelligence—is intelligence the reason to say, 'You don't get access to full human rights'? If that's the case, the same argument could be applied to an exceptionally intelligent human, and that would be discrimination. And if we are a part of an interstellar community, and the very first thing the most powerful country on Earth does upon learning about persons outside their own planet is to declare them as unworthy of the full scope of human rights that we grant ourselves, how can we even hope to ask their civilization to see us as equals?"

"We wouldn't have the right to ask that," said Miranda. "And either way, that isn't the issue at hand. The issue is domestic, the issue is about protecting our way of life and our systems, not dictating how other advanced civilizations used theirs."

"It doesn't matter if you say it isn't 'fewer rights'; that is how their civilization will see it. There are aspects about the human experience they don't understand, but believe me, laws are not one of them. They understand how laws work."

"Cora Sabino, Jano Miranda, thank you both for your time," said Satomi. "We'll be back with more *Hot Seat* in a moment."

"Thank you!" chirped Miranda.

Cora took a long second to realize that it was over. "Thank you."

"And cut!"

A sound person came to collect her microphone, but no one else—no producers, no Sol, no U.S. government descending to throw her in jail for violating her clearance, which she probably had on some technicality. Just a sound guy asking her to unhook her lavalier microphone. After she did, she stumbled out of her studio and back into the main hallway.

"Hey!" She turned around to see Miranda, worming the lavalier mic out of his shirt and handing it to the sound guy who had taken Cora's. He had been in the studio adjacent to hers. "That was fun!"

"Fun?" she said, realizing that he did not consider this life-or-death like she did.

"Yeah," said Miranda. "Honestly, I've debated some feds before, normally dry as hell."

"Have I changed your mind?"

Miranda chuckled like she'd told a bad joke and he was humoring her. "I mean, we weren't really here to change each other's minds, were we?"

She restrained the urge to frown. Yes, actually. Yes, she was here to change this man's mind.

"I get that you can't really talk about specifics, but I can see that you care a lot about this. I do mean it, I really don't advocate for seeing them as lesser."

"Uh-huh."

"Hey!" She nearly melted from relief at Kaveh's voice. He stopped alongside her, shook Miranda's hand. "Hey, dude, good show."

"Thanks, man," said Miranda. "Are you covering the rally downtown tomorrow?"

Kaveh's expression blanked. "*Oh!* I forgot that tomorrow was Saturday."

"We organized a Third Party rally a few weeks ago," Miranda explained to Cora as if they were on the same side. "Events of the last few days have led to a lot of interest, so we're looking at a crowd in the thousands. Senator Julian might be there, and also Tom DeLonge."

"Who?" asked Kaveh.

"The lead singer of Blink-182."

Cora laughed. "Is he going to run through the crowd wearing nothing but sneakers?"

Miranda almost looked offended, like it was 1999 and the lead singer of Blink-182 was a *get* that she just didn't appreciate. "Surprised you aren't covering it," said Miranda to Kaveh.

"Well, I might," said Kaveh, squeezing Cora on the shoulder. "Good luck, dude."

"Good to see you."

Kaveh moved his hand to the small of Cora's back, ushering her toward the exit of the studio, and she melted a little more. He leaned over to her and whispered. "You kicked ass!"

"Really?"

"Yes! Not going to lie, I was about to swallow my tongue when he asked you to describe his personality and you kind of blanked, but then you came back, oh, man. You did way better than I did my first time on TV. This shit is hard!" He stopped to face her. "Do you hug?"

"Yes, I hug."

He brought it in, and it was already more than a friendly pat-on-the-back hug, it was being held. Three seconds. Four seconds. She took in his smell, and it warmed her, the olfactory equivalent of a sip of hot chocolate.

He pulled away, keeping his hands on her shoulders. "Let's go get dinner."

"It's only three o'clock."

"By the time we sit through rush hour traffic and get back to the OC, it'll be dinnertime. So what do you say? Can I get you dinner?"

"Where were you thinking?"

"*Puis-je suggérer*," he said, with a conniving smile, "*l'usine de gâteau au fromage?*"

Fri, Feb 8, 2008 at 3:52 PM
From: Alejandro Miranda Vasquez <JanoMirandaV@gmail.com>
To: Nils Ortega <nils@thebrokenseal.org>
Subject: Re: Hot Seat interview

Nils,

Wanted to shoot you an update on the debate with Cora, and
I thought you should know, Kaveh Mazenderani was with her
acting as "moral support," in his words. It was pretty obvious
who was pulling the strings, though—Cora obviously did not
want to be there, poor kid. I knew he was an anti–Third Option
zealot, but I didn't think he'd be so scummy as to get a kid to do
his dirty work for him.

Jano

• • • • •

Fri, Feb 8, 2008 at 9:21 PM
From: Nils Ortega <nils@thebrokenseal.org>
To: Alejandro Miranda Vasquez <JanoMirandaV@gmail.com>
Subject: Re: Hot Seat interview

Jano,

I'm less concerned about Kaveh than I am Cora—if, as you said,
she's just acting as Kaveh's proxy, that's not a huge concern.
But if she keeps going down this road—taking interviews,
talking to journalists, etc.—the issue of her father is going to
come up pretty soon, and that could cause a PR problem for
us. Ironically, it was thanks to Kaveh that I was able to sway
public opinion to my side where the family issue was concerned,
and I've made good inroads with my son, Felix. But Cora could
easily create some bad press for me by casting me as the
absent father who heartlessly abandoned the family.

Nils

• • • • •

Fri, Feb 8, 2008 at 10:48 PM
From: Alejandro Miranda Vasquez <JanoMirandaV@gmail.com>
To: Nils Ortega <nils@thebrokenseal.org>
Subject: Re: Hot Seat interview

Nils,

I hear you, and I think we should be thinking with a mind to how
to narrativize them if they become a problem. Please don't take
this the wrong way, but I definitely got some crazy vibes from
Cora. I don't think it would be difficult at all to paint a picture of
her as unstable and delusional, and of Kaveh as a predatory
manipulator who's taking advantage of a girl young enough to
be his daughter. I don't have anything on them per se right now,
but I have plenty of connections in local law enforcement. I'll
have them sniff around and keep an eye on both of them.

Jano

• • • • •

Fri, Feb 8, 2008 at 11:52 PM
From: Nils Ortega <nils@thebrokenseal.org>
To: Alejandro Miranda Vasquez <JanoMirandaV@gmail.com>
Subject: Re: Hot Seat interview

Jano,

You are truly one in a million.

Nils

"When you said *fromage,* I thought it was going to be one of those arti-sanal cheese places."

"What could *possibly* be more artisanal than this?" said Kaveh. "It's a SoCal staple. Our contribution to civilization."

The two looked up at the blinged-out ancient Egyptian edifice of the Cheesecake Factory at the Spectrum in Irvine, its signage embla-zoned with red neon bulbs. A gilded monument to overpriced medio-cre food, a confused mess of architecture and interior design that was equal parts sarcophagus and Mordor. A hideous calorie-laden mon-ument to man's hubris. Kaveh kind of loved it. Tacky as it was, it had been his family's' "special occasion" restaurant when he was growing up, so he couldn't help but have some nostalgia for it.

Cora agreed that it was quite mediocre to be so expensive, but he was glad she understood his sense of irony and went along with it, even if she hardly ate anything (again). When it came cheesecake time, Kaveh joked about the turgid aftertaste the food here tended to have ("What are you in the mood for: chocolate freezer burn or lemon raspberry cream freezer burn?"). They went for the mango key lime cheesecake. It tasted like freezer burn.

"I was half joking about the freezer burn," he said. "I did not expect this to taste more like freezer burn than mango or key lime."

"I guess you're the Dr. Malcolm of this story," she said, smiling her cute, awkward smile. "Boy, do you hate being right all the time." She took another tiny bite. "Thank you, by the way, for all of this."

He smiled, admiring how the soft Eye of Sauron light flattered her hair, her features. Was this a date? He hadn't really meant for it to be, but it had the feel of one. He'd been debating for a little while if it would be appropriate to invite her back to his place later. It was obvious she was attracted to him, but it was the kind of attraction that she herself might not yet have consciously acknowledged.

"Of course. You did good today. Although, I wonder what our . . . friend will think once he finds out about the interview."

"Oh . . ." Her cute smile fell. "I don't think he'll care. The goings-on of the human world don't much interest him."

Having now plied her with cheesecake, he figured now was as good a time as any to inquire about some topics that had been weighing on him. "Can I ask maybe a sensitive question?"

She nodded, face falling as if to say, *Oh no, what now?*

"Well, owing to the way you reacted earlier to what Nikola told me about you, I'm reading between the lines a bit, but I think he may have spilled more sensitive information than just . . . that."

Cora took the remaining piece of sourdough from the bread basket, now stiff and stale. "Someone tell Nikola that loose lips sink ships."

"Being without lips, I'm not sure he'd appreciate that metaphor."

"What did he tell you?"

"Well, I'm guessing Obelus was named after the 'meteor event' from last year that was almost certainly not a meteor."

"That's right."

"And 'noble Obelus' is another one of Ampersand's secrets that he's keeping from . . . the other ones."

"The Fremda group," said Cora. "They call the ones in custody at ROSA the Fremda group."

"'Fremde,' sehr einzigartig."

"It's from Esperanto, not German."

"Esperanto, *jajajaja, es ist das Selbe in beiden Sprachen.* Anyway, so Obelus is a secret from the Fremda group, because . . ."

Oh boy, that was a look of guilt if he ever saw one. "There was an incident," said Cora, ripping her sourdough into tiny, tiny chunks. "I'm not entirely sure, but on the night we . . . 'met' Nikola, I found Obelus in that cave, and I . . ." Whatever was going on inside her, she was taking it out on the stale sourdough, ripping it into shreds. "Well, Obelus decided he needed to run away. We don't know what his goal is exactly other than a vague 'get off this fucking planet,' but Ampersand is trying to find him. That's where he's been."

"I see," he said. "It may not be my place to pry, and you don't have to tell me the truth if you don't want to, but . . . what did Obelus do to you?"

She stopped picking at the sourdough carcass, now gazing into nothing. "I . . . don't think you want to hear it."

"If you don't want to tell it, I respect that, but I do want to hear it."

"Is this off the record?"

"It was never on the record. That's not why I'm asking."

She looked at him as if, if she looked hard enough, she might figure out how to read his mind. But no telepathy was forthcoming.

"He tore me in half," she said, voice small. Then she ripped the piece of bread in her hand violently in two. It almost made him jump.

"Obelus is not a refugee," she continued. "He hunted the Fremda group here, but they did not want to be found. When Similars are in full-power mode, they're basically impossible to kill. They have this sort of force field that protects them, but if it goes down, they're vulnerable like we are. So Ampersand used an electromagnetic pulse to disarm him. It worked, so I tried to kill him, but I failed. Then his power came back, and he defended himself against me."

She placed a hand to her stomach, and her expression curdled like she was going to be sick. "He skewered me, ripped my guts out. No, I'm not exaggerating, that's what happened. It happened, that happened. But then it looked like—I *thought*—Obelus's own subordinates killed him—"

"Are those the three he mentioned are here, somewhere on Earth, looking for Obelus, too?"

She nodded. "Ampersand kept me alive. And I disappeared for two weeks."

"I heard about that," said Kaveh. "Nils thought that you were being held at a CIA black site or something."

"No, it took him two weeks to repair the damage. I don't remember any of it. I know Obelus severed my intestines, large intestine in particular. I got sepsis, blood poisoning. Ampersand's very good at repairing bodies. Human bodies. But I don't have any scars, and no way to prove what happened. If you saw . . ." She grabbed her stomach tighter. "There's no scarring. You wouldn't believe me."

"After all I've seen, I think I would," he said.

"I almost died. I think I *did* die. I think I was dead." Her hands were trembling, her whole body was trembling. "I'm sorry for telling you all this."

He gently took the savaged sourdough from her hand, placing it on a bread plate. "Don't be sorry."

"I've never told anyone what happened."

"Really?"

"The only other person who knows is Ampersand, and only because he was there. He saw it, he undid the damage. But no one else, no human. He doesn't get it, he doesn't understand because . . . they aren't . . . their bodies aren't theirs, you know what I mean? Humans are attached to our bodies for our entire lives, amygdalines are not."

He slid his hand on top of hers, gave it a light squeeze. "Thank you for telling me."

"It'll make a good story."

"It would make a very interesting story, but it isn't mine to tell."

She looked at him like he was going to reveal himself at any moment to be a spy for the Soviets. *How do I make you believe that I truly, genuinely don't want to hurt you?* he thought. He grazed the tips of his fingers over her palm.

"Truth is," he said, "I might know how you feel. I've never been through anything like that, but I know how it feels to be in a position where the shit you've been through makes you feel completely cut off from everyone in your life. But I also can recognize that you're in a unique situation. You can't tell anyone about this. You probably shouldn't have even told me about this. This is the sort of thing that could easily turn into a political weapon—both what Obelus did, and what I now know Ampersand is capable of doing. That's a huge burden. And you can't even tell anyone." He frowned. "Except Luciana. What's her deal?"

Cora hung her head. "I said some shitty things during . . . the stuff last year. She hasn't really forgiven me for it."

"So apologize. And she should apologize for being shitty to you."

"I don't think that would fix anything. We're not that kind of family."

"Then you need to start *being* that kind of family. Trust me, this was the mistake we made."

"With your brother?"

He nodded. "Neither of my parents were drinkers, but Sirvan and I were both big into the party scene at Berkeley. He was two years younger than me. So we kind of enabled each other. His shit wasn't like mine, I was a drunk and irresponsible, but he was a drunk and, I don't know, probably undiagnosed bipolar. I'll never know. But the signs were there, and sometimes he'd talk a little bit about it, about these intrusive thoughts he had, and Mom and Dad were like, 'Stop. Stop talking about this, it's inappropriate, it's uncomfortable.' So he did stop talking about it.

"And I kind of did it, too. I'd be like, 'Dude. Ease up.' And then I moved to Oxford, and then I was in New York, and if we did talk it was about like . . ." He gestured to the ether. "Work or whatever. So it turns into this thing where your pain is gross and uncomfortable and inconvenient for other people. Like, your family is Catholic, right?" She nodded. "I get it. Your people are not so different from my people."

"If you had it to do over . . ." She was having difficulty looking him in the eye. "Would you do things differently?"

"Of course I would. I have the power of hindsight, I've been through a lot of therapy, I've been to rehab. I understand things differently now." He leaned toward her, and her body went on alert, eyes wide.

"Sirvan isn't the only person I know who killed himself, or tried to. But he only made the one attempt that we know of, and that one attempt succeeded. And when something like that happens, you spend days and months and years going back over everything, wondering what you missed. If I had it to do over again, there's a lot I would have done differently. Because I didn't see his reaching out for help for what it was until it was too late.

"So . . ." He slid his hand into hers. "I can see that you're hurting, and I can see that you don't have a great support structure right now, and the way your family is acting now feels very familiar. I'm super disappointed in your mother, but I'm not surprised, because my parents did a lot of the same. I'm *really* disappointed in Luciana, but I can't say I don't see myself in her. Me being made uncomfortable by my brother's mental illness wasn't the only reason he did what he did, but it didn't help him, so I don't want to make that mistake again. Please don't apologize for the act of experiencing pain."

The reflection of the candlelight flickered in her glossy, red-rimmed eyes. Somewhere over the last couple of minutes, her guarded, frightened tension had dissolved. "You're very good at this."

"Good at what?"

She looked back down at their entwined hands. "This."

He turned her hand to face upward and began drawing light circles on the center of her palm. She drew in a faint little gasp, and not for the first time, he wondered if this was a bad idea, and not just because of their age difference. It was difficult to humor the idea of a relationship with her; they were at such different stages of life, to say nothing of the absolutely bizarre circumstances that had brought them together. But it was hard to think responsibly when she was looking at him as if he were a shiny new car she was dying to take for a ride.

Why so much hand-wringing? They were clearly on the same page, and she was starved for human contact he was more than willing to supply. He *wanted* to take her home, get her into his bed, smell her and taste her and touch her and fuck her and cover her body with his. He wanted to take care of her. He wanted her to stop being so afraid. He wanted to *be* the person who made her feel safe.

"Funny," he said. "I'm not even trying yet."

"What does trying look like?"

He pointed his index finger to the ceiling, then fluidly curled it downward toward his face, the international symbol for *c'mere*. Her eyes widened, and she leaned toward him like a marionette. He met her halfway, placing his index finger just under the tip of her chin and pressing his lips to hers, keeping them soft and pliant, not a chaste kiss but not a hungry one, either. Gentle, simple, just a taste.

He drew back after a few seconds, and her eyes grew even wider, thrilled at his audacity. She shifted in her chair, pressing her legs together, her lips flushed—*so* fucking cute. "I think I like it when you try."

He smiled widely, resisting a strong urge to swipe this freezer-burned cheesecake off the table and give in to the passion. "God, I just want to take you home with me right now."

She swallowed so loud it was almost a cartoon gulp. "And do what?"

"Whatever we want."

"That sounds . . . fun."

"Bocce ball, *Mario Kart*, anything."

"I . . . like things."

He chuckled, wondering when he started to find "dopey and inartic-ulate" attractive; the combination of youth, beauty, and befuddlement was working on him.

"*But,*" he added, and her face fell, "I probably shouldn't go breaking promises to omnipotent alien cyborgs. I told Nik I'd come back today, and it's getting pretty late."

She nodded. "I could come with you, and then we could go back to Yorba Linda after."

"Well, after we make sure everything is okay with our . . . friend, we can go back to my place and see how we feel."

"Yes. I'd like that."

He took it down a notch and asked, "What about Salad Fingers? Will he mind?"

"No," she said, sadness tingeing her excitement. "No, he doesn't care about that sort of thing."

"Good."

She looked at him with such a dissonant expression, such fear, such anxiety, such desperation. A look that said, *I want you, even though I know you are going to destroy me.*

And he could, too.

His position in the world, his influence, and everything he knew about her provided him with so many avenues to do it, through malice, selfishness, or shameless exploitation. She wanted—*needed*—someone to be kind to her. What she expected was another Nils Ortega.

Not an unreasonable expectation. Not unreasonable at all.

He placed his hand on top of hers and squeezed it reassuringly. *But I won't,* he resolved. *I can't promise I won't hurt you; that's just a risk you accept when two human bodies meet. But I'm not going to exploit this sit-uation. I'm not like Nils, and soon you'll see that. I won't destroy you, not unless you destroy me first.*

"The problem with reporting is it's kind of hard for me to split my attention," said Kaveh, his eyes on the dark road ahead of them. It was so dark out here on this winding mountain road that went through so many miles of wilderness. "I was supposed to have a draft of this book done in the fall, but research on these other pieces kept taking my attention away from it . . ."

She looked down at their entwined hands. He was good at this, and it scared her a little. Before Craig or Joel or Chad, the last time she'd had sex with a man (well, boy), she'd been a senior in high school. She thought of that Cal king bed. She was going to be in that giant bed with this man in a couple of hours, and he was going to be in it with her, inside of her, and the thought made her mouth go dry again. She assumed he'd be good at it. He certainly carried himself like he thought he was, as if she were a puzzle he was looking forward to cracking, because he had cracked more than a few puzzles in his day.

"—and that's how I got into the erotic fur-suit convention scene."

"Huh?"

His smile had changed in the last few hours, too. No longer professional and courteous, but devious, like the two of them were sharing a secret. "Just checking to see if you're listening."

"I'm listening. Just don't have much to add—your life is way more interesting than mine."

"Ha! Only if you ignore some key components."

"*Eee-hee-vil woman!*"

Cora nearly jumped at Electric Light Orchestra's "Evil Woman" piping from her cell phone and quickly sent it to voice mail.

"Sorry," she said. "It's my mother. I haven't talked to her since the interview."

He laughed. "So 'Asshole' for Kaplan, 'Evil Woman' for your mom. What's my custom ringtone going to be?"

Her neck grew hot as a few contenders flitted through her mind. "Ummm . . . 'Rehab'?"

She regretted it the second she'd said it, but Kaveh laughed uproariously. "Oh, man, that is funny," he said, wiping an eye. "Now you have to use that."

"No," she said. "No, I don't like it for you; it's kind of mean. It doesn't suit you."

"What do you like for me?"

She bit her lip and looked at their hands, and the first, more honest lyric that came into her head was "*Won't you please, please help me?*" "Maybe, 'I Want to Hold Your Hand'?"

"God, you're cute," he said in a low, hungry voice, and her heart did a backflip.

When they arrived at the top of the mountain, the situation felt even more surreal. Alone in the dark in the woods with this man who was about to take her home with him. But for now, he didn't do anything more intimate than offer his hand to hold while they walked through the woods, illuminating the ground with his little flashlight. He approached a tree and patted the trunk. "Was this one mine?"

It took her a moment to see what he was getting at. Was it? She couldn't recall. It was so cold. He had forgiven her very quickly for what she'd done to him. She didn't have to do what she did. It had been so cold that night. But she'd done the humane thing and brought him in eventually, hadn't she? He stopped, and she questioned the wisdom of being out here alone with him.

Why? He's not going to do anything. Even if he were that type of person, Ampersand could be anywhere. Trying something would be suicide.

"Maybe this one was it? I feel like it had a knot. I remember a knot."

He wants revenge.

No, he is joking. This is dark humor.

He wants revenge.

The thought was infecting her mind now. No, it didn't jell with anything she knew about the guy, or any logical track he might take, but it was there in her head. *He's mad. He wants revenge. He hates me.*

"You okay?"

"Yeah," she said. Her breath was shallow. Her whole body was shaking. He shone the flashlight at her. "You don't look okay."

"I don't know. I honestly don't know what's wrong with me."

He reached out to take her by the shoulder, but she flinched away. "Are you scared of Nikola?"

"I don't know. I'm sorry!"

"Is it me?"

Yes.

"I don't know what's wrong with me. I'm sorry, I'm sorry."

"Stop apologizing," he said point-blank.

"Mmph." She sucked her lips under her teeth to stifle the instinct to apologize, to apologize for apologizing. *What is wrong with me?* "He made me do it."

"What?"

"I'm sorry for what I did to you. He told me to restrain you. I know I shouldn't have done it. I'm sorry, I'm sorry!"

"It's okay, I'm not upset about that." He moved toward her, but she backed away on instinct, right into a tree. "Hey, it's okay. PTSD is an anxiety spectrum disorder. Did you know that?"

"No."

He cupped her cheeks in his hands. "It's okay. Your brain is in this heightened state, looking for threats. That's one of the symptoms. You don't know me that well, and we're out in the middle of the woods at night. It's a scary situation, so your brain has clocked me as a threat. That's all this is. It's okay."

"I don't know why I'm doing this. I don't know why this keeps happening."

"I just told you why this keeps happening. Do you do breathing exercises?"

She tried to slow down her breathing, then shook her head.

"Let me show you one. 'Four-seven-eight.' Breathe in for a count of four, hold seven, breathe out eight."

She tried to do what he said, but was finding it difficult to even count past one. *Oh, God.*

"It's okay, I'll count. Breathe with me slowly. One, two, three, four," he counted, breathing in as he did. "One, two, three, four, five, six, seven." He held it. As she wasn't deep in the spiral yet, she successfully held it, too. "One, two, three, four, five, six, seven, eight." Long exhale. He repeated the cycle, holding the side of her forearms firmly, and she kept her eyes closed as she did.

On the third cycle, she felt him pulling her close to him. "One, two, three, four." She was up against him, her face pressing against the skin of his neck. She smelled that cologne combined with his natural scent. "One, two, three, four, five, six, seven." He let go of her shoulders, wound his hands around her. "One, two, three, four, five, six, seven, eight." He wound one of his palms down to the small of her back, the other up around her shoulder, and began a gentle rocking motion. Then he repeated the cycle. Once. Twice. She snaked her arms around his back, felt the warmth under his shirt, leaned her head against his chest, listened to his heartbeat, which was going at half the speed and intensity of hers. He repeated the cycle.

And then he screamed.

He let her go, throwing himself against a nearby tree. She turned to see two amber eyes glowing in the light of the flashlight, which was now on the ground. Ampersand moved toward Kaveh, and Cora threw herself between the two of them. "What are you doing?"

"*You are threatened.*"

"No, it's not like that! I was having a panic attack; he was helping me."

"*This one has threatened you.*"

"No, please, leave him alone!"

"*He is the source of your fear.*"

Ampersand knew that Kaveh had sparked the panic, but didn't know the context. She reached up, grabbed him by the forearms, all but yanked him down so his gaze would be redirected to her. "It's not his fault!" she said. "It's not like that. It's not his fault."

He went still, redirecting his gaze to Kaveh. What if he followed through with his threat from a few days ago? What if he turned Kaveh to ash right then and there?

"Please, leave him alone!"

He curled his hands back toward his chest, then turned from her, moving back down the hill toward the entrance of the cave.

"MY BELOVED WILL NOT HARM YOU, DEAR CLEVER CREATURE," said a different voice in her ear. "YOU ARE MINE."

Kaveh brushed himself off and rose to his feet. "That's ominous."

He was keeping his distance now, now that he knew her attack monster would jump on her if he got too close.

"I . . ."

"Don't you dare say sorry," he said, trying to force a jovial tone and failing utterly. "Are we still allowed in?"

"I WANT YOU IN HERE, DEAR CLEVER CREATURE, REGARDLESS OF WHAT MY BELOVED WANTS."

"Did you hear that?" asked Kaveh.

Still trying to calm her breathing, she nodded.

"Let's go," he said, beginning to close the last hundred or so feet to the cave. "He said, 'You are mine.' Oh, God. You don't think he did to me what—"

"No," said Cora. "I think you'd know."

"How do you know?"

She sighed, feeling like she was a hundred years old. "Trust me, you'd know."

The two of them passed through the entrance, Kaveh turning off his flashlight upon seeing the drone lights floating near the ceiling. Ampersand was standing stone still over Enola, who wasn't even looking at him but was instead focused on the two humans. She figured they were speaking through network language. Ampersand didn't move, but she could feel that he was upset about something.

"Ampersand, he's much more lucid and coherent than he was a few days ago," she said, taking a few steps toward them. "Why are we keeping him like this?"

"*He is dangerous.*"

"HE KNOWS I AM NO DANGER TO YOU. HE WILL NOT RELEASE ME BECAUSE HE BELIEVES ME A DANGER TO OBELUS."

That made her mad, but she knew it was true. After goddamn fucking all of this, Obelus was *still* Ampersand's top concern.

"It's cruel to keep him like this," she said. "We could at least move him somewhere designed by humans to keep him protected."

"*I cannot move him anywhere that can be tracked. Obelus's Similars will find him, and they will kill him. They will kill both of us.*"

"They aren't here for you. You both told me that. Just let them have what they want. They want Obelus alive. Let them have him."

Ampersand turned to look at her, his eyes flashing. "*I will not.*"

She blew a long stream of air out of her nostrils. "Ampersand, you have to let him go. You are never getting your old life back."

"*It is not an old life, it is survival. They may return him alive, but he will not survive the Superorganism. They will spare him now only to kill him in the long term.*"

"He is a murderer," she said, her blood pressure rising. "He is a monster. He . . . Think of what he did to *me!*"

"WE ARE ALL MONSTERS, LITTLE COUSIN."

"And your first priority, in all of this, is *him*?" she continued, ignoring Enola, ignoring Kaveh, the heat under her skin rising to a boil. "Why? Enola ripped a hole in space for you. I have given up my life for you. I *died* for you!"

"*Immaterial. If I can suppress Obelus's memories and keep him in that body, he is not a threat.*"

"You're delusional." She took a step back from him, shaking her head incredulously. "You don't care."

"*If you want me to survive, this is what I must do.*"

"You don't *care.*" By now, her breath was going in and out of her lungs so fast it was starting to burn her throat, her blood coursing through her like electricity, every nerve in her body on fire.

"*Calm yourself.*"

"You don't care. You do not *fucking* care!" Now she was shouting. "He fucking ripped me in half, and you do not *fucking care!*"

"Cora." Kaveh's voice. She looked over and realized what he already knew. She was spiraling, and fast.

"Oh, God. Oh, God, no . . ."

"*Stop this. Calm yourself.*"

"I can't help it!" Kaveh moved toward her. "Stay back!" she yelled. She backed away from him, back against the wall. The figure in front of her morphed, grew several feet in height, bulged out on its sides. *Oh, God!*

Not Obelus. Obelus is dead.

Obelus is not dead!

He isn't in that body anymore.

He could be! He could be anywhere, anything.

Where is the body? The government took the body! Obelus's old body still exists, he could be in it, he could be in it right now!

Her mind was scrambled, screaming electric nonsense, as though her brain were trying to escape from her skull. Her vision blurred, and she shrieked with each gasp of air she pulled in. She clapped one hand to her chest, holding up the other one in a futile attempt to keep the monster away.

The monster moved toward her until it was over her, on top of her, grabbing her with one of its meat hook hands as a syringe formed in the other one. Obelus standing over her, crushing her rib cage, trying to rip out her throat with his other hand. She could feel her abdomen being ripped open, her guts pouring out. *Not again, not again, not again!*

Its other hand went for her throat, and she screamed, cried, begged, unable to get anything out between her rapid breaths besides *No, no, no!* It drilled into her throat, went straight to the bone, and doused the fire flowing through her veins.

Ampersand was holding her tight, his right hand wrapped around her torso, a syringe coming out of the tips of the fingers of his left, the needle still deep in her carotid artery, several of his other fingers clamped around her skull, holding her head in place. He pulled out the needle and released her, and she collapsed onto the floor.

She nearly passed out right there, but saw Ampersand turning his attention to Kaveh. "No, please!" she yelled. Ampersand's body was facing her still, standing right over her, but his head was turned around like an owl's, focused on Kaveh, who had backed himself up against another wall, eyes wide and mouth hanging open. "Leave him alone."

Ampersand took two steps away from her, still eyeing Kaveh, then he looked at her. He lingered for a moment, and then the shell on his back opened, the liquid metal of his plate spreading out like fabric wings, enveloping him as he crouched. Then he was gone.

Kaveh was already moving toward her before Ampersand disappeared. "Shit shit shit," he said, propping her head up. "I'm going to get you to a hospital."

"No," she said. Her breath was still fast, but not the rapid-fire, painful, shallow breathing it had been when she was in the thick of it.

"I don't know what he did to you," he said. "We need to go to the ER."

"It's okay," she said, her eyes lolling in her head.

He wrapped her left arm around his neck, hoisting her up into his arms. "It's not okay. I have to get you to a hospital."

"I don't consent," she said.

"I'm taking you to a hospital." There was fresh air on her face, a breeze. They were outside. He was carrying her back to his car.

"Kaveh," she said. "He won't hurt me. He hurts me, he hurts himself."

Kaveh took a long breath, and his jaw hardened. "Yeah. Yeah, I can see that."

"No hospital," she said, resting her head on his shoulder.

"Fine. But I'm not leaving you alone."

As Kaveh carried her up the hill, a voice spoke to her through the earbud: "How strange, side effects of fusion bonding with a natural alien. I hope our dear Beloved does not do anything drastic to mitigate them. I hope our dear Beloved does not do anything he cannot undo."

By the time they reached Kaveh's house, she was able to walk. She had passed out a few times on the drive back, causing him to nearly pull over and call 911, but each time, she came to and begged him not to.

He led her into the bigger of the two guest rooms and gave her the largest T-shirt he had. "Is this okay?" he asked.

She nodded her bedraggled head and went into the bathroom to change. When she came back out, he was sitting on the edge of the bed, his elbows leaning on his knees. Cora hesitated, then shuffled over to the bed and sat down next to him.

"Has he done this before?" he asked.

She stared at the floor, her expression vacant. "No. It's a cocktail he made for me to mellow me out if I'm having a panic attack. But he's never done that injection without permission before. He always asked for consent first."

Kaveh sighed and nodded. He got up, went into the kitchen to get a glass of water for himself and one for her. When he came back, she seemed to have shrunk, hugging herself tightly and lying in a fetal position. "He isn't . . . He didn't used to be like this."

"He didn't used to be the kind of guy who forcefully injects control substances into young girls and then leaves them half-conscious in the middle of the woods alone with strange men? That's a relief."

Kaveh handed her the glass of water. She held at it as though he'd handed her some sixteenth-century sextant she had no clue how to operate, and eventually took a sip. He sat back down on the edge of the bed. She wasn't wearing any bottoms, and the T-shirt didn't cover much.

Most of her height was in her legs, which were long and slender and even in this position begging to be touched.

"That was the first good night I've had in a really, really, really long time, and I ruined it."

"It wasn't your fault," he said, moving closer. She looked up at him, eyes shining, and he had to restrain himself from touching her. There she lay on her side, hugging her pillow, looking up at him, all but pleading, *I just need a big, strong man*—well—*I just need a medium-size, out-of-shape man to hold me and touch me and tell me it will be okay.*

He placed his forehead next to hers. "It'll be okay. Get some sleep."

"Please don't leave me alone," she said, grabbing the collar of his blazer. "Please."

He stood up, surveyed the situation, considered the wisdom of sleeping in the same bed with her. "Will you be okay if I take a quick shower?"

"Mm," she said in that quavering voice.

Kaveh was generally a morning-shower kind of guy, but if he was going to share a bed with a woozy, half-conscious college dropout, he needed some time to himself to rub one off so he wouldn't be tempted to take advantage of someone still high on . . . whatever that was. He returned wearing a T-shirt and basketball shorts, which alone made him feel like a Mormon; generally, he preferred to sleep in boxer briefs, or nothing. Maybe she was asleep? Nope. No, still a roiled-up, tense little ball.

He closed the curtains so the room was nearly pitch black. Then he lifted the covers and crawled into bed, scooting toward the middle. Cora stayed perched like the Rock of Gibraltar on the other side.

"C'mere," he whispered.

She turned over and hesitantly moved her body next to his. He kissed her on the forehead, then on the cheek. Okay, that was a bit much for someone you intended *not* to fuck, he knew that, but she took the obvious message that he was making overtures. Of course he was, wasn't that the original plan? Come back to Kaveh's place and, I dunno, see what happened? She put her hand on his chest, then began running it down his rib cage, then toward his hips. He took her by the wrist before she could go any farther.

"Not now, honey," he said. "Not when controlled substances are involved."

He could practically feel the heat coming off her face from

embarrassment, and he hugged her even tighter, kissed her on the forehead. Then, fuck it, gently on the lips. Gentle, friendly kissing on the mouth, you know, like friends do. Once, twice. *I need to stop, this is how that scene in* When Harry Met Sally *started.*

He put a stop to it by pulling her in close, nestling her head under his chin. "It's okay," he said in the gentlest, most reassuring whisper of which he was capable. "You're safe with me. It's okay," he said over and over until they both fell asleep.

· · · · ·

At some point she became aware that he was on top of her. She didn't remember him taking off her underwear; he didn't bother taking off her shirt. He started fucking her, soundlessly, and he didn't have a face. It lasted for what seemed like hours, and all the while, she could not move. She wanted to beg, *Stop, please stop, please stop,* but her voice was gone, her jaw frozen in place, lips and tongue shriveled into paper, unable to produce sound. *Stop, stop, stop,* she pleaded in her mind.

At long last, she gasped herself awake. It wasn't loud enough to wake Kaveh, who seemed like a particularly sound sleeper. On instinct, she pulled away from him. Her last memory, her last real memory, was of him falling asleep spooning her, snoring softly into her neck. His hair had fallen into his face. His hair was so nice, so inviting. Revolting, everything about him was revolting. All she could think was, she did not deserve to be here, that if this man really was as kind and generous as he presented himself to be, then she didn't even deserve to smell his shit.

The fear and revulsion was quickly replaced by guilt. Here he'd been so kind to her, so patient, even if he did expect something in return, and her brain still cast him in the role of a rapist. She'd been the one to beg him not to leave her alone, and he'd obliged, and her sleeping mind betrayed both of them regardless. She full-body shuddered at the sight of him.

She had to get away from him.

She wandered into the kitchen, and the revulsion circled back to desire. She could crawl back into bed with him, he'd put his arms around her on instinct. Hell, he might even fuck her now that the benzos had worn off. Wouldn't that be nice? The least she could do is get his dick wet.

She walked outside and sat on the front porch for a while, wishing there were alcohol in the house. She saw a skunk joyfully bounce from one neighbor's yard to the next. A guy on a motorcycle a mile away revved his engine, signaling to the sleeping world, *I am an ephemeral blip on creation, please pay attention to me.*

As she sat on the cold concrete, she processed what had happened last night, what he'd said, how she'd spiraled, how he'd reacted. And in that moment, she calmly, definitively decided that this was the last straw. Ampersand did not respect her autonomy, respect *anyone's* autonomy; she was not beholden to respect his bullshit.

She stood up, walked back inside, marched over to the counter, grabbed her car keys, and walked robotically into the garage. She opened the garage door, turned the ignition, and drove out.

When she got to the turnoff in the woods an hour later, she didn't bother turning off her headlights. She used her regular flashlight, carelessly, loudly, and marched right on in to face Enola.

"Tell me the truth," she demanded.

"Of what truth do you speak?"

"You told me Ampersand is lying to me. So tell me the truth."

"Do you wish to know the truth of the Divine, little cousin?"

"Yes. Tell me what he's not telling me."

"Then free me."

She almost said, "I can't," but some instinct told her that wasn't true, the same instinct that had told her how to kill Obelus when she had reached for it. Enola would not have told her to do it if she wasn't able. She knelt directly in front of his head, her legs shaking. The orbs sticking out of his back. *What are those? They dampen energy, don't they? The energy going from Enola's cores is crudely metered by these orbs.*

She reached around and, a shaking hand on one of them, ripped it out. It looked like a stake one would drive into the ground with an egg fused to the top of it. It came out with a wretched, meaty popping sound, followed by a spurt of black, viscous fluid. She flung it on the floor, and pulled out another one, then another, and another, flinging them on the floor, her hands now coated in the black, inky substance.

Then she felt the air pressure change, and the restraints holding his hands snapped off. Then another restraint holding his back down crumbled like a brittle cracker, then another holding his legs. Soon all of the restraints had crumbled, the pressure in the air now building, and Cora fell on her back, crab-walking herself away from the harpy she'd just released from its cage.

Enola tore the last few egg sacs out himself and stretched his limbs out like a bird. Then her flashlight went out. The air pressure was building around him like a tornado, seeming to add to the darkness that surrounded him, a black hole that nothing could escape, not even light. She might as well have been a corpse for how rigid she was. Black widow digits wrapped around her as the creature pulled her toward its body, and swirling wisps of darkness surrounded them until it enveloped them both.

PART 3

A CROWD OF PEOPLE STOOD AND STARED

February 9, 2008

ARTICLE 20.1   Everyone has the right to freedom of peaceful assembly and association.

Cora opened her eyes to a sky in the earliest phase of morning, dim like a night-light, with the fingernail sliver of the moon still visible. Her breath turned into a tiny cloud in the cold air, and the ground was coarse and hard like a badly poured sidewalk. She shot to her feet, the ground crunching beneath her shoes as she rose. She was standing on a vast plane rimmed by tall mountains on all sides, but the ground was not flat, rather, it was almost honeycombed, an endless desert of lattice. Each comb was about the size of a tire, rimmed by crystals a few inches tall that looked like tiny ocean waves that crested and then froze. She put a finger to her tongue, confirming that she was standing on a salt flat.

Based on the color of the sky, it looked perhaps half an hour before sunrise. There were mountains in the distance, but the flatness of everything skewed her perspective. Those mountains could be one mile away or thirty miles away for all she could tell. Her mind raced, alternately trying to decipher where she was, even *when* she was, and what to do about either. It was colder than Orange County, but not as cold as the mountains. Not as cold as any desert in winter *should* be. *Death Valley,* she figured. If they were still in North America, this had to be Death Valley. She turned around, looking over her shoulder in the other direction, the direction that seemed to go on forever.

There was Enola, a black obelisk in the salt. He approached her, slow and focused like a panther, and she turned around to face him, unconsciously putting her arms up in defense. Enola circled her like a vulture, his eyes radiating moonlight. As he circled her, growing closer with each orbit, Cora kept her face to him. Even though he never looked at the ground, he moved so delicately, never stepping on the crystalized salt ridges. After about one and a half orbits, he stopped, now only a few feet away. Cora fell into a crouch as if she were bracing for a bomb to go off, keeping an arm raised in defense. "Why did you bring me here?"

"WE ARE INSIDE A METAPHOR."

He stood over her, his body and posture so much like Obelus's the first time they had really come face-to-face, right before he had taken her hostage. Even his eyes were brighter versions of Obelus's eyes, big gemstones with cloud nebulae centered in them, flecked with purples and blues.

"YOU ARE VERY FRIGHTENED, LITTLE COUSIN."

"You remind me of someone," she said. "Someone who once hurt me very badly."

Enola tilted his head back and forth, examining her like she was some sort of museum artifact. He leaned in closer, his body so low that the tips of his curled knuckles grazed the little salt crystal walls. She tensed further, leaning away from him, trying to keep the image of Obelus standing over her out of her mind. The memory of it burned, lapped at her like wildfire.

"I DO NOT MEAN YOU HARM, LITTLE COUSIN," he said, standing up to his full height and taking a few steps back. "IT IS NOT MY ENDEAVOR TO CAUSE YOU MORE FEAR AND PAIN. IF YOU ARE AFRAID, I WILL TAKE YOU BACK OUTSIDE OF MY METAPHOR."

"No," she said, snapping her head up to look at him, nearly vertical from where she was. She forced herself to her feet, nearly stumbling on her shaking legs. "No, I let you go because you said you'd tell me what he wouldn't. I want to know what you have to say. Explain to me your metaphor."

His eyes widened a bit, brightening as they did, the cloud nebulae of his focus sharpening. He didn't seem to be under the influence of whatever "medication" he had been on the first time she'd seen him. "THE METAPHOR IS THE UNIVERSE."

He bent down to her eye level and summoned a small clump of salt about the size of a marble from the ground, spinning it between them like a tiny moon. "AND THIS REPRESENTS THE SUM TOTAL OF ALL HUMAN KNOWLEDGE."

"I see."

He lifted out another ball, spinning it until it became almost perfectly round, a spinning salt planet about the size of a fist. "AND THIS REPRESENTS THE SUM TOTAL OF ALL KNOWLEDGE POSSESSED BY THE PEQUOD SUPERORGANISM—ALL AMYGDALINE KNOWLEDGE AS IT STANDS RIGHT NOW. WHAT DO YOU OBSERVE?"

"That your ball of salt is bigger than ours."

"BUT BEHOLD OUR METAPHOR—THIS IS THE KNOWN UNIVERSE." The two salt balls dissolved, and fell back onto the salt flat, and he gestured to the vast flat surrounding them in his alien way, his fingers sprawling out and coming together at a point. "A NEGLIGIBLE DIFFERENCE WHEN YOU CONSIDER THE SCOPE OF ALL THAT THERE IS TO KNOW."

She looked at the remains of the little balls on the ground, barely visible mounds of salt even at her height. "So what are you saying?"

"COSMOLOGICALLY, OUR TWO SPECIES ARE VIRTUALLY TWINS. IF WE WERE TO CONDENSE THE SCALE OF THE AGE OF THE UNIVERSE TO ONE EARTH YEAR, THE AMYGDALINE TWIN WOULD BE 148 SECONDS OLDER THAN THE HUMAN TWIN, BOTH STILL IN EARLIEST INFANCY.

"AND THIS METAPHOR REPRESENTS ONLY THE KNOWN UNIVERSE. LET US SAY THAT THE UNKNOWN UNIVERSE BEGINS BEYOND THOSE MOUNTAINS." He gestured to the horizon. "WE CANNOT KNOW HOW FAR THE UNKNOWN UNIVERSE GOES. FOR YOU SEE, LITTLE COUSIN, WE EXIST ONLY IN A POCKET OF THIS UNIVERSE, AND BOTH OF US, HUMAN AND AMYGDALINE, FACE THE SAME LIMITATIONS. THIS IS THE FIRST THING I NEED FOR YOU TO UNDERSTAND. IN THIS METAPHOR, ONLY THIS FLAT IS KNOWABLE. ANYTHING BEYOND IT IS NOT KNOWABLE, BECAUSE WE ARE CONFINED TO THIS DIMENSION OF SPACE-TIME AND CANNOT BREAK FREE OF IT. BUT THERE ARE SOME CONSTANTS TO THIS UNIVERSE, SOME LAWS THAT CANNOT BE CHANGED. BUT BEFORE I CAN EXPLAIN IT, I MUST FIRST GAUGE WHAT YOU ALREADY KNOW. WHAT DO YOU KNOW OF SPACE-TIME, LITTLE COUSIN?"

"A little bit," she said. "It's explained here by Einstein's theory of relativity."

"AND WHAT DOES EINSTEIN'S THEORY OF RELATIVITY EXPLAIN?"

"The part that was relevant to what Ampersand told me is that time slows down for a body traveling close to the speed of light, and effectively once you reach the speed of light, it stops. But it isn't possible for a body to travel at the speed of light, only close to it."

"TIME IS A SIDE EFFECT OF THE POCKET OF SPACE WE INHABIT, THAT OF THREE DIMENSIONS. WHAT DO YOU KNOW OF DIMENSIONS?"

"N-not much."

"DO YOU KNOW HOW MANY DIMENSIONS THERE ARE IN THIS UNIVERSE?"

"Three—the three dimensions of space. Four, if you include time as a dimension." As she said this, Enola lifted more salt from the ground, and shaped it in the air between them into what looked like long, thin straws about two feet long. Two of the straws joined at their tips to form an *L*, and then another straw joined them at their edge to form a shape like the corner of a box.

"THREE PHYSICAL DIMENSIONS IN THE POCKET OF REALITY THAT WE INHABIT, BUT THAT IS NOT THE TOTALITY OF DIMENSIONS IN THE UNIVERSE. THERE ARE TEN."

Cora looked at the salt box floating between them like he might pull the other seven dimensions out of it like a rabbit from a hat. "Where are they?"

"EVERYWHERE AND NOWHERE."

The salt fell to the ground, and the air relaxed.

"NOUMENAL DIMENSIONS—WE CANNOT SENSE THEM, FOR WE ARE TRAPPED IN THIS FOUR-DIMENSIONAL POCKET OF SPACE-TIME, BUT THE UNIVERSE CANNOT EXIST WITHOUT THEM. WE OBSERVE EVIDENCE OF NOUMENAL DIMENSIONS IN MANY FACETS OF SPACE-TIME. IT IS THE SOURCE OF GRAVITY ITSELF. IT IS THE BASIS OF OUR ABILITY TO FOLD SPACE. IT IS A PART OF THE ANSWER TO THE RIDDLE OF HOW CONSCIOUSNESS DEVELOPED. INDEED, FOR ALL OUR HISTORY, WE ONLY HAD ONE SAMPLE OF A NATURALLY EVOLVED SPECIES THAT DEVELOPED CONSCIOUSNESS—OUR ANCESTORS. BUT NOW, LITTLE COUSIN, WE HAVE DISCOVERED ANOTHER—YOU."

Enola placed the tips of his fingers on her head like a crown of thorns, and she flinched. She resisted the urge to smack his hands away. "What isn't he telling me? Why are we able to sense each other's emotions like this?"

"I DO NOT KNOW."

She pulled away from him, and his hand curled back under him in his neutral stance. "You said you'd tell me the truth."

"I CAN ONLY GIVE YOU WHAT TRUTH I HAVE. I DO NOT KNOW WHY YOUR BOND IS UNIQUE. IT IS POSSIBLE THAT WE MAY NEVER KNOW THE FULL NATURE OF THE RELATIONSHIP BETWEEN THE CONSCIOUS AND THE SUBCONSCIOUS, WHERE FUSION BONDS ARE ROOTED, AND WHERE WE ARE BEST ABLE TO SENSE THE DIVINE. YOU DO NOT UN-DERSTAND IT, BECAUSE YOU CANNOT UNDERSTAND IT."

"Why?" She wiped some cold sweat from her upper lip. "Why can't we understand it?"

He turned, his eyes catching some of the light from the rising sun, their nuclei glowing brighter. He took a few steps back from her, raising some salt crystals out of the earth as he did, and they started to glow. He was heating them, floating them in the air like dim stars. "THREE DIMENSIONS OF SPACE, REPRESENTED HERE IN TWO DIMENSIONS."

The floating, glowing spheres of salt and dirt flattened into discs, until it was almost one homogenous slab about the size of a coffee table and the thickness of construction paper floating between them. Enola waved one of his hands as if he were waving goodbye, and something like a thin, gaseous arch appeared on the flat slab, sitting atop it like a long, translucent black pipe cleaner.

"THIS STRING REPRESENTS A DIMENSION OUTSIDE OF OUR SPACE-TIME. ONLY THIS STRING IS NOUMENAL, AND AS IT EXISTS OUTSIDE OF SPACE, IT EXISTS IN ALL SPACES. A SINGLE POINT IN EXISTENCE THAT CONNECTS ALL POINTS." The flattened salt folded in half like a piece of paper, and the black gaseous arch contracted until the slab met where the two ends of the arch had touched it. "BY EXPLOITING THE OMNIPRES-ENT NATURE OF THIS DIMENSION, WE CAN CONNECT TWO POINTS IN THREE-DIMENSIONAL SPACE AND RIP THEM OPEN, BECAUSE THROUGH THIS DIMENSION, THEY ARE ALWAYS CONNECTED. THERE IS A NATU-RAL PRECEDENT FOR THIS, ONE BASED IN THE CONSCIOUS MINDS OF INTELLIGENT BEINGS."

"Fusion bonding," she said.

At this, the tension in the air dissipated, and the salt space-time metaphor disintegrated and fell to the earth. "IT IS THE EXISTENCE OF THESE NOUMENAL DIMENSIONS THAT ALLOWS OUR SPECIES TO

SENSE THE LIFE, OR LACK THEREOF, OF OUR SYMPHYLES, NO MATTER WHERE THEY MIGHT BE IN SPACE."

Enola leaned in toward her, placing two of his long digits under her chin. He turned her head to the right, and then to the left, as though he were scanning a 3D image of her brain.

"CAN YOU FEEL OUR DEAR BELOVED?"

She closed her eyes. "Yes."

He removed his fingers from her chin. "WHAT DO YOU SENSE?"

Her eyes shot open. The wall had thinned, and she'd been so preoccupied with Enola, she hadn't noticed. "He's angry. He's frightened. He's extremely frightened. Oh . . . fuck, he knows. He knows I let you go."

"DO YOU SENSE HIM STRONGLY?"

"Yes, very."

"YOU HAVE ONLY BEEN BOUND TO HIM HERE, AN INFINITESIMAL DISTANCE RELATIVE TO THE SIZE OF SPACE. BUT NO MATTER WHERE YOU GO IN THIS UNIVERSE, YOU WILL ALWAYS SENSE HIM WITH THE SAME INTENSITY."

"And that's what you meant when you said he lied about why he decided to bind himself to me," she said, trying to push away that fear that wasn't hers. "Dynamic fusion bonding isn't a homing beacon. He couldn't use it to sense proximity."

"CORRECT."

"Then why did he do it?"

"I DO NOT KNOW. I SIMPLY KNOW THAT IF HE TOLD YOU THAT THE ABILITY TO SENSE PROXIMITY WAS HIS RATIONALE FOR MAKING THE DECISION TO BIND HIMSELF TO YOU, HE SPOKE MISTRUTH."

He grazed her neck with his fingers, then her ears, then her hair. She had conceived of amygdalines as completely detached from the physical world, noncorporeal beings that inhabited physical bodies only on technicality. Most of their lives were lived inside their heads, inside digital spaces, not in physical space, not unless they were Similars, explorers, or biologists. But Enola was such a strangely tactile creature, one with no sense of boundaries.

"THERE IS A PART OF THE BRAIN THAT LIVES AND VIBRATES OUTSIDE THE KNOWN UNIVERSE, A PART TIED IN WITH WHAT YOU MIGHT CALL A SUBCONSCIOUS, WHERE THE BRAIN GREETS BUT DOES NOT UNDERSTAND THE UNKNOWN. THEREFORE, THE BRAIN CREATES

FORMS IT UNDERSTANDS FOR THIS UNKNOWN—THIS IS THE DIVINE. THIS IS WHERE RELIGION COMES FROM, BOTH FOR OUR ANCESTORS AND FOR YOU. IT IS THE BRAIN GIVING A FORM TO THAT WHICH IT KNOWS TO BE TRUE BUT CANNOT COMPREHEND. SOMETHING SIMI-LAR HAPPENS WITH YOUR BOND TO OUR DEAR BELOVED." He looked toward the mountains in the distance. "YOUR BRAIN IS TRYING TO GIVE FORM TO THE SUBCONSCIOUS INPUT IT IS RECEIVING."

"Why wouldn't Ampersand want me to know that?"

"FROM WHAT YOU KNOW OF OUR DEAR BELOVED, WHAT COULD POSSIBLY BE MORE TERRIFYING TO HIM THAN AN OUTSIDE FORCE THAT HE CANNOT CONTROL PERIODICALLY INVADING HIS UNCON-SCIOUS MIND?"

She stilled, a sense of dread rising. She recalled that first night he'd implanted those "monitors" in her, that his primary objective was to stop that side effect altogether.

"IT IS PROBABLE THAT HE WILL NOT EVER BE ABLE TO EXPLAIN OR CONTROL THIS BOND BETWEEN YOU, BUT HERE YOU ARE, THROUGH NO INTENT OF YOUR OWN, ABLE TO ENTER HIS MIND AND AFFECT HIS THOUGHTS AND EMOTIONS IN A WAY THAT NEITHER OF YOU CAN CONTROL."

This was a thought she'd toyed with many times and always dis-missed as absurd. That if she invaded his mind one time too many, he might be forced to take desperate measures. "Is there anything I can do to stop invading his mind?"

"THERE IS NO WAY TO EXERT CONTROL OVER THIS, BECAUSE THE ELEMENTS THAT OPERATE THIS CONTROL EXIST OUTSIDE OF WHAT WE KNOW AS REALITY. THEY EXIST OUTSIDE OF OUR FOUR DIMEN-SIONS. IF YOU WANT TO SEVER YOUR BOND, THERE IS ONLY ONE WAY TO DO THAT."

Then she sensed something, familiar yet unclear. That fear she had felt from the other side of the wall had muddied somewhat, yet the wall still felt thin. She whirled around, expecting him to appear at any second.

"THIS IS THE LIMITATION THAT WE SHARE. AS BEINGS OF FOUR DI-MENSIONS, WE CAN ONLY ADVANCE SO FAR. WE CAN NEVER EXPAND CONSCIOUSNESS AS WE UNDERSTAND IT PAST FOUR DIMENSIONS. THE NOUMENAL DIMENSIONS CANNOT BE ACCESSED OR CONTROLLED,

BUT THAT OF COURSE HAS NOT STOPPED OUR DEAR BELOVED FROM TRYING."

As if on cue, she heard a *boom* in the distance on the other side of the mountains, one she had heard before. It sounded identical to the noise she'd heard the morning of the Obelus Event.

"What is that?"

"A SONIC BLAST FROM A BODY BREAKING THE SOUND BARRIER. A SINGLE AMYGDALINE BODY, CARRIED VIA SEMIAUTONOMOUS PLATING."

She whirled to face Enola. "You told me Ampersand was the one who killed the humans the Superorganism abducted for the language study 650 years ago."

"HE WAS THE SENIOR OF XENOBIOLOGY AT THE TIME. HE DID END THE STUDY. HE DID ORDER THE SPECIMENS DESTROYED."

"Specimens." She nearly choked on the word. "Why, then? I know there has to be more to it than that. What made him end it? What led him to kill those people?"

Enola's eyes brightened, now luminous from the light of the sun that was about to peek over the top of the mountains, and he leaned down until his eyes were level with hers. He ran the edge of a shiny black digit over her cheek, so softly it could have been mistaken for a feather, and said, "I DID."

Enola's focus shifted from Cora to the space behind her, and she turned around to face Ampersand. For at least a minute, they both stood still as statues, staring each other down, the light from the rising sun peeking over the horizon. Ampersand had all but turned to stone except for his eyes as his focus sharpened, not on her but on Enola. They were probably communicating through the network language to which she was not privy. Then two long, spiderlike fingers wrapped around her neck and slid over her collarbone.

"What's he saying?" she whispered, unsure which of them she was addressing.

"HE IS VERY FRIGHTENED FOR YOU, LITTLE COUSIN." She felt Enola leaning his head down over her shoulder until it was nearly touching her. "NOBLE OBELUS HAS LEFT QUITE THE IMPRESSION ON BOTH OF YOU."

"What is he saying?" she repeated. "What does he want?"

"HE WANTS YOU RETURNED TO HIM. HE BELIEVES THAT I HAVE TAKEN YOU HOSTAGE. HE IS TELLING ME THAT I MAY TAKE HIM, BUT TO SPARE YOU, AND NOT TO LEAVE YOU HERE INSIDE MY METAPHOR, BECAUSE IF I DO, YOU WILL DIE."

A frost inside her thawed slightly; she wasn't sure if she believed Enola was telling the whole truth, but wanted to believe it, wanted to believe that Ampersand did, in the end, care if she lived or died.

"DO YOU WISH TO RETURN TO HIM, LITTLE COUSIN?"

She could feel more than fear from the other side of the wall, knew that it was making Ampersand irrational. Still, fresh in her mind was what Enola had told her. What caused Ampersand to end the language study? What made him kill those human abductees?

I did.

She moved her head in a way that was more of a twitch than a nod. "Yes."

The two fingers tightened around her, encircling her neck like a noose, then he removed them, and she felt him stand up to his full height. Ampersand finally moved, pulling his head back in a half-antagonistic stance, the crown on the back of his head flaring like splayed fingers, his hands steepled like he was about to use his telekinesis.

Cora hesitated before toddling the ten-odd feet between the two of them, braced the whole time for some horrible alien act of destruction—a fireball from Enola, a memory wipe from Ampersand, being turned to dust by some unseen third party. Was Obelus here, too? Hell, probably.

As soon as she was within arm's length, Ampersand grabbed her by the shoulders, pulling her toward him and staring her down as if she were a child who had run across the street and had nearly been hit by a car. *"What have you done? I cannot protect you from him. He means to kill me, kill us both, and you'll die out here."*

"Please, calm down!" she said, trying to compartmentalize the terror that was trying to infect her through the other side of the wall. "Just listen to him. I don't think he means to go through with it right this second."

"Don't you understand? He came here to die, he came here to kill us, I cannot overpower him, we are bound, he will kill both of us!" His eyes were wild, unfocused, filled with fire in a way she'd never seen before. Then the swaying started.

She looked back at Enola, who simply watched, his hands curled up in a mantid, neutral stance, the crown on the back of his head folded down like a flower that had not yet bloomed. He seemed perfectly nonplussed, not particularly bothered by this.

She turned, grabbed Ampersand by the arms to try to steady him, and he stumbled. It didn't even seem to enter into his equations that Enola could be reasoned with, only overpowered, and she finally had to acknowledge that Ampersand had not been exaggerating about his "*diseased mind.*" Not six hours earlier, he had nearly killed Kaveh for the crime of triggering a panic through no fault of his own, and now this.

"He thinks you're going to hurt us," she said to Enola.

"I HAVE BEEN TRYING TO ASSURE HIM I MEAN NO HARM. HE DOES NOT BELIEVE ME."

Ampersand's swaying became almost violent, and she could practically feel the electromagnetic supports that lent his body that antigravity elegance give way, and he nearly collapsed under his own weight. He half caught himself, and Cora caught the other half by bearing his weight on her shoulders. It was as though the millions upon billions of subroutines that kept his body up and running were all being rerouted into fighting the collapse, but in doing so had abandoned their posts that were keeping him operational. He would almost regain his footing one second and lose it the next, and he would have fallen to the ground if she hadn't used all her strength to keep him upright. Twice this happened, but the third time, she wasn't strong enough to keep him standing, and they both fell to the coarse salt earth, dozens of tiny salt-crystal walls crunching beneath him.

Cora dodged before he collapsed on top of her. "Ampersand?"

Nothing. Those wild, unfocused eyes didn't even seem to be registering Enola as a threat anymore.

"I . . ." She shook her head, one hand on the carapace of his back, the other under his slender neck. He'd started seizing in that way she'd seen him do several times. "I don't know what to do."

She looked up at Enola, who wasn't looking at the twitching mess on the salt but instead to the sky. "OUR BELOVED HAS BEEN CARELESS."

"What do you mean?"

"HIS TRANSPORT CREATED A DISTURBANCE IN THE ATMOSPHERE, ONE THAT WAS EASILY OBSERVED BY THOSE WHO KNEW WHAT TO LOOK FOR. HE WAS FOLLOWED."

"Followed?" she breathed. She didn't get a chance to ask, *Followed by who?* before she saw who.

Obelus's Similars, all three of them, stood not thirty feet away, their iridescent, silvery skin practically glowing in the light of the sun that had just cracked the horizon. One of them stood in front of the other two like a formation of geese, cold blue eyes glinting in the sunlight.

"Come on," she whispered, mindlessly shaking Ampersand as if he were human, like it would do anything. "You need to get up."

Enola turned to face the three, regarding them quizzically in the same manner he might do if it had been three raccoons that magically appeared in the salt. Enola shared that lighter-than-air affect that all of them moved with, but there was also an erraticism she didn't see in any of the other ones in the cobra-like way that he moved his entire upper body.

One of the three Similars, the new leader, she presumed, began speaking to Enola in Pequod-phonemic, who responded in turn, and a conversation began. The three Similars were now circling them like a pack of hyenas, and though Enola was careful to keep his body between the Similars and the two on the ground, he never betrayed any sign of fear or aggression.

"En—N-Nikola!" she whispered, giving up on trying to shake Ampersand back to coherence, keeping her arms protectively wrapped around his neck.

"DO NOT BE FRIGHTENED, LITTLE COUSIN. THEY WILL NOT HARM YOU. I WILL NOT ALLOW IT."

She refrained from stating the obvious: *There are three of them, and they are all bigger than you.* She had seen enough to know that, at least where Similars were concerned, the size of their bodies correlated more or less with the size of their power cores, meaning that bigger ones were more powerful. And all three of them were larger than either Enola or Ampersand.

He is delusional, too, she thought. *He thinks he stands a chance against them, and we're all going to die.*

She looked down at Ampersand, whose eyes were fluttering, dim, and unfocused. He'd stopped seizing, had descended into something of a "safe mode." As best she could tell, all his higher cognitive systems, everything from the ability to stand to the ability to manipulate electromagnetic fields to the algorithm that allowed him to understand human language, were completely shut down. The only thing still operating was life support.

The three Similars moved closer, causing Enola to back up so much that he nearly stood over Cora and Ampersand, and the leader spat something at Enola, who responded in turn, assertive but calm.

"THEY BELIEVE BOTH OF US SHOULD BE PUT OUT OF OUR MISERY, BUT OUR BELOVED MOST OF ALL. THEY WILL NOT DO THIS YET, HOWEVER, BECAUSE THEY BELIEVE OUR BELOVED MAY STILL BE

WITHHOLDING KNOWLEDGE ABOUT THE WHEREABOUTS OF HIS NOBLE OBELUS, KNOWLEDGE THEY INTEND TO TRY TO TAKE BY FORCE."

She looked at the three of them, brilliant in the morning light, which was by now so bright against the salt it hurt her eyes, and that animal fear that so often made her wake up screaming had mutated into anger. "Tell them he is mine. They can't have him."

She didn't expect Enola to relay that message, but it looked to her like he did, which only seemed to confuse the three Similars. For the first time, the leader looked down at her, its intensity nearly knocking the wind out of her. The three took a step toward her but halted before they could get anywhere, seeming to hit an invisible wall. On instinct, she held Ampersand closely, half expecting him to wake up and reveal his secret plan that would save them.

Again, the Similars tried to move, but couldn't.

"What do we do?" she asked.

"DON'T BE AFRAID, LITTLE COUSIN. I WILL MAKE THEM LEAVE."

One more confused push against the invisible wall from the Similars, and then a loud crack, the same one she'd heard in Temecula but closer, so close it ripped the air right out of her. Then a vibration, a bright light like a nuclear bomb, and then came the explosion, a bigger blast than she had ever seen or imagined, not five feet from where she sat clamped to Ampersand like a vise.

The explosion didn't touch them but stayed behind an invisible wall, turning into a massive half sphere with Enola, Ampersand, and Cora on the other side. Enola had his hands up, "palms" open and fingers splayed like a tarantula on the defensive. He seemed like a maestro, delighting in conducting a symphony of unfathomable destructive force, and Cora squinted against the incredible bright light in horrified awe.

Then the blast shrank into itself at the command of the conductor as his digits contracted, meeting in the middle in a sharp point. There was a crater the size of half a football field where the blast had been. She looked to the other side of the crater and could only just make out that the Similars had survived the blast, now several hundred feet away, beaten and very confused. The three pulled themselves to their feet quickly like cats that didn't want their owner to see they had fallen down. Then they disappeared, and all that remained were lines of heat coming off the still-glowing salt, creating ripples in the air.

Enola retracted his hands back into that calm, neutral position and turned to examine her. She was still holding Ampersand tightly, powerlessly, Mother Mary performing her alien pietà. She didn't know what was worse—the thought that Enola might have been delusional about his ability to protect them from the Similars or the fact that he very clearly wasn't. That he really did possess more destructive power than all three Similars combined.

I've freed the harpy, she thought. *And she's going to kill us all.*

Enola bent down, his focus on her rather than Ampersand, quiet, contemplative, intrigued perhaps. "Our Beloved is not well."

"I know," she said. "Will they be back?"

"Not now that they know what I am capable of," he said, sparing a glance to the other side of the newly formed salt crater, the heat from it still licking Cora's skin. "Energy pulses are not their preferred form of attack, as it is only Similars or those that exist inside the bodies of Similars that are affected by them. They prefer not to use forms of attacks they themselves are vulnerable to. But they will use them if they feel they have no other choice."

"Please," she said, letting her iron grip relax, sitting up to look at him. "Nikola. Nik. Please, can you take us to Kaveh? I know he'll want to see you."

Nikola's eyes brightened, his focus shifting to Ampersand, and he lowered himself toward them, his back now parallel to the ground.

"Please, Nik," she whispered, voice shaking. "Please, just take us to his house. Please."

Nikola continued regarding Ampersand, his head waving back and forth like a cobra. "If it pleases you, little cousin."

28

A *thunk* downstairs woke Kaveh, the kind that generally rouses one's instincts that their house is in the process of being robbed. His eyes shot open, and he reached out to the space in bed beside him only to find it empty. Cora wasn't here in bed with him, but was that her voice he heard downstairs? Yes. Yes, it was. So at first, he thought it was fine. Then it connected that she was talking to someone. But who? He turned over to look at his watch—6:09 A.M. Who the hell would she be talking to at 6:00 A.M.?

He heard her voice, something about "make sure the curtains are closed," and then "just move the coffee table," followed by what sounded like an explanation of what a coffee table was.

At that, he shot up and all but fell out of bed. That implied that some-one was in the house with her, and at 6:00 A.M., and all things con-sidered, there was an extremely short list of candidates as to who that might be. *Please, God, let this be a drunk dial from Kaplan, who is asking for advice on interior decorating.*

It wasn't.

In the family room directly adjacent to the kitchen, right in front of the wraparound couch where the coffee table had likely been ninety seconds prior, was Nikola, standing at his full height, the inky tips of the crown on his head nearly touching the ceiling.

"Hello, dear clever creature."

Kaveh stood there mouth agape as Cora shot up from the floor on the other side of the couch. Given that the coffee table was now leaning against a wall, he had a pretty good idea of what (or rather, who) was on the floor between the couch and the flat-screen.

"What . . ." He couldn't even manage to get out a "the fuck."

Nikola seemed calm, amused even, like he was on an impromptu vacation. Cora hopped over the couch and stopped in front of him, clasping her hands. "I need you to get him out of here."

He waited for her to issue a correction, thinking he must have misheard her. "What?"

"Please, I just need you to take him somewhere and babysit him; he can't be here when Ampersand wakes up. He's terrified of Nik. If Nik is here when he wakes up, he's going to start the spiral all over again."

Kaveh was having a very difficult time connecting this request, that by "him," she meant Nikola, and she was requesting that he physically move the half-ton, nine-foot, spider-handed, jet-black alien that more resembled a dragon than a human . . . *somewhere else.* "Get him out . . . *where?*"

"Please, I wouldn't ask this if it weren't life or death."

"Take him fucking *where,* Cora?"

"I don't know! Into the woods? The desert? Somewhere where there aren't humans? Please, please, I'm begging you, I have to be alone with Ampersand to reason with him, Nikola can't be here when he wakes up, and we can't leave Nikola alone to his own devices. *Please.*"

He continued to stare at her, mouth still hanging open. Nikola, for his part, seemed down for whatever. Like, *Hey, man, you guys do what you want. I'm just happy to be here.*

Kaveh turned on his heels, marched into the garage, and surveyed the situation in the Land Rover. He dragged out everything in the back, shoving it on the floor in the garage and flattening the back seats. Then, not making eye contact with either Nikola or Cora, who was still rooted in place with her hands clasped in front of her, he marched right back upstairs. He took a piss, grabbed a pair of jeans, an undershirt, and a sweater, and ran back downstairs. He looked at Cora, struggling not to load his glare with accusation, and it was very much a glare. Then he approached Nikola.

Kaveh knew it was hypocritical to be afraid, considering how many hours he'd spent in that cave where he had the power, where he was the one with the ability to do real harm to the vulnerable, restrained Nikola.

Now the tables were turned, Nikola was standing in his TV room at both his full majesty and his full power, and Kaveh was afraid of him. He couldn't help it. Nikola was, by every meaningful human metric, terrifying to be in the same room with. Throw some tentacles on him somewhere and anyone would collapse into Lovecraftian madness.

"Nik," he said, swallowing his terror as best as he could. "If I asked you to get into my vehicle, would you do it? Would you let me drive you . . . somewhere?"

"IF IT PLEASES YOU, DEAR CLEVER CREATURE."

"Okay," he said, turning without hesitation, because he knew if he hesitated that he might not go through with it. What else could he do? He couldn't say he hadn't brought this on himself. He had asked for access to Nikola, had volunteered himself as support. How had he *not* brought this on himself?

Kaveh opened the rear door to the Land Rover and gestured to Nikola, *Here you fucking go.* Nikola paused to examine the door, less seemingly out of hesitation than curiosity, as if to say, *Ah, so this is how your people do hinges. Our people evolved a very different way of doing hinges. It all started when—*

"WHERE WILL YOU TAKE ME, DEAR CLEVER CREATURE?"

"I don't know."

This didn't seem to perturb Nikola at all. If anything, his eyes brightened, as though he was excited by the prospect of a surprise. The Land Rover, being fucking huge, was big enough that it fit Nikola comfortably, if only just. Kaveh closed the rear door behind him and climbed into the driver's seat. All of this happened so quickly, with so little thought, that he did not realize that he had forgotten his cell phone.

· · · · ·

Kaveh began by driving north, and then once out of north owing to a wall of mountains in his way, he headed west. He remembered that this highway had an entrance to the national forest north of Pasadena, and so turned off there. He kept going in the general direction of the observatory until the sun was up, and then he stopped.

Once Kaveh pulled over, he finally got a good look at the situation in the back seat. Nikola looked like he was asleep, arms curled in under his body, legs tucked neatly at his side, and the line of his neck curving his head almost at a ninety-degree angle, his head laid out in a long line like a snake.

What do I do with you?

He hadn't wanted Nikola to stay in that inhumane situation, welded to the floor in his own filth, but now they had slingshotted to the complete other end of the spectrum: total freedom. He turned forward, and let his eyes rest, figuring it would be all right to doze a little. One of his handier life skills—he had never had any difficult sleeping in even the most uncomfortable of places.

He rested his head on the window, closed his eyes, and when he opened them, the sun was piercing through the trees, prying his eyes open with crowbars of harsh light. Going by the sleep in his mouth, he must have been out for at least a couple of hours. He turned around to check on his passenger.

Nikola was gone.

He smacked his hand in the back seat to make sure that Nikola hadn't pulled his invisibility trick. Nope, he was not there.

Kaveh all but fell out of the car, sprinting back to the road and up the hill. "Nik? *Nik!*"

"You are awake, dear clever creature."

He slowed to a stop, falling over and balancing his hands on his knees to steady himself. "Nik, where are you?"

"Find me at the top of this hill."

Kaveh grunted and began hauling himself in the direction he assumed Nikola was referring to. It took a few minutes, as by "top of the hill," he meant the place with the best vantage point, which wasn't easily accessible for someone who hiked as little as he did. *I need to hike more. I should have seen this coming. I should have known that my path as a journalist would lead me to spending lots of time in the mountains with aliens.*

Kaveh found Nikola in a clearing that had an unobstructed view of the Los Angeles basin. Between the long neck, the posture, and the big oblong head, it was hard not to see this being as an intelligent giant velociraptor, one that had elected to remove its jaw for aesthetic reasons. Nikola turned to him, his eyes flashing brightly in the sunlight as Kaveh continued his sad, out-of-shape tromp up the hill. Once he reached Nikola's side, he looked down at the urban sprawl that had Nikola so captivated.

Lines of concrete flowing over the flat basin of Los Angeles County like veins, veins clogged with vehicular cholesterol.

"Yep," said Kaveh, still breathing heavily from his frantic climb up the hill. "This is us."

"I CAN ONLY IMAGINE HOW HORRIFIED MY DEAR BELOVED MUST HAVE BEEN ONCE HE SAW THIS."

"What do you mean?"

Nik unfurled two of his long digits and gestured leftward toward Altadena. "WE ARE NEAR WHERE MY DEAR BELOVED MADE LAND-FALL. HE DID SO HERE BECAUSE THIS WAS AN AREA THAT WAS GEO-GRAPHICALLY WELL DOCUMENTED BY SIMILARS WHO HAD STUDIED THIS AREA CENTURIES PRIOR. AT THE TIME OF OUR MOST RECENT INTELLIGENCE, THIS BASIN WAS HOME TO NOT MORE THAN A FEW HUNDRED HUMANS. IMAGINE THE HORROR OF EXPECTING TO FIND FEW IF ANY NATIVES, AND INSTEAD FINDING MILLIONS. HOW MANY MILLIONS OF HUMANS LIVE JUST WHERE WE CAN SEE? IT IS HORRI-FYING, AND EVEN MORE HORRIFYING WHAT HE MUST HAVE HAD TO EXTRAPOLATE."

"What's that?"

"THAT IF THERE ARE MILLIONS OF HUMANS IN THIS AREA, THERE MUST BE BILLIONS ON THE PLANET. WHAT COULD HAVE CAUSED SUCH A POPULATION EXPLOSION? HOW DID YOUR TECHNOLOGY ADVANCE SO QUICKLY? IT IS SO UNLIKE OUR OWN ANCESTORS' ADVANCEMENT, WHICH IS WHY WE DID NOT RECOGNIZE IT FOR WHAT IT WAS. NONE OF US WOULD HAVE EVER THOUGHT IT POSSIBLE THAT ANY NATURAL SPECIES COULD MAKE SUCH AN ADVANCEMENT SO QUICKLY. NOW THAT I AM NO LONGER MEDICATED, I ADMIT, IT IS FRIGHTENING. YOU ARE FRIGHTENING."

Kaveh snorted. "Well, you have a point. We *are* the species that pro-duced Bill Maher."

"THE LAST STUDY THE SUPERORGANISM HAS DONE ON YOUR PLANET WAS 650 YEARS AGO, SUBJECTIVE. IF YOUR POPULATION AND TECHNOLOGY CAN ADVANCE SO EXPONENTIALLY IN SUCH A SHORT PERIOD OF TIME, IMAGINE WHAT YOUR DESCENDANTS WOULD BE CA-PABLE OF WHEN THEY BECOME SPACEFARING LIKE WE ARE. PERHAPS YOU WOULD EVEN SURPASS US IN BOTH POWER AND INTELLIGENCE. THEY WILL NOT SUFFER YOU TO ADVANCE LIKE THAT."

Kaveh turned his attention from the megalopolis below to Nikola, parsing his words. "What do you mean by that?"

"HERE WE HAVE FOUND YOU, ALIVE AND CONSCIOUS AND INTEL-LIGENT AT THE SAME TIME THAT WE ARE ALIVE AND CONSCIOUS AND INTELLIGENT. THIS SHOULD BE A JOYOUS MOMENT FOR BOTH OUR SPECIES—THE DISCOVERY, THE REALIZATION THAT NEITHER OF US ARE ALONE. BUT I AM SADDENED BY IT, BECAUSE I KNOW THAT EVENTUALLY, THE SUPERORGANISM WILL DISCOVER WHAT YOU HAVE BECOME AND WILL HALT YOUR ADVANCEMENT."

Kaveh had known this moment was inevitable, that sooner or later this wouldn't be fun and exciting anymore. Sooner or later, he would dig deep enough to find something like this. "How would they halt our advancement?"

"THEY WOULD ENSURE THAT YOU COULD NEVER POSE ANY DAN-GER TO THE SUPERORGANISM, AS OUR TRANSIENT SISTER SPECIES HAS. THEY WILL HALT YOUR ADVANCEMENT, THROUGH ANY NUMBER OF MEANS. THEY WILL HALT IT, AND THIS CIVILIZATION WILL END."

Kaveh looked down into the metropolis he had called home for so much of his life, this dirty, beautiful, horrible city that had taken him in af-ter the unimaginable had happened to his family. The little tidbits Cora had dropped about their history—*They're refugees, the Superorganism is hunt-ing them. Something happened to them, something terrible*—and he had not pushed, had not pried because he had *hoped* this wouldn't be the case. The "dead dove, do not eat" of first-contact scenarios.

Well, he thought, *I don't know what I expected.*

"I CANNOT BEAR TO THINK OF SUCH A PROFOUND LOSS, OF SOME-THING SO RARE, AN INTELLIGENT CIVILIZATION CAPABLE OF UNDER-STANDING THE UNIVERSE AS WE DO, CAPABLE OF COMMUNICATING WITH US."

Nikola turned to face him and bent over so that his big, bright eyes loomed just above Kaveh's. He placed both of his hands above Kaveh's head, drawing the pointed digits down around his temple, behind his ears, to the nape of his neck. "YOU MAY BE THE MOST PRECIOUS THING I HAVE EVER BEHELD."

A knot formed in Kaveh's throat. Nikola was right—there was some-thing so profound about the idea of one intelligent species, with a wholly different evolutionary history, learning to communicate with another.

Wanting to communicate with the other, to see the other as a person worthy of empathy.

"BUT YOU WILL NOT SURVIVE CONTACT WITH THE SUPERORGAN-ISM," said Nikola, removing his fingers, taking a step back and standing up to his full height. "I CANNOT WATCH YOU DIE. I REFUSE."

Kaveh looked back out into the urban sprawl. Nikola didn't seem eager to jump off any bridges right this second, but it was going to be an ordeal to talk him out of this mindset, let alone for him to explore the possibility that things might not be that hopeless. They *couldn't* be that hopeless. How could an advanced civilization exterminate a whole other species, one that is wholly innocent to them, just because of a threat they *might* pose?

Even as he had the thought, he felt childish. How many countless times in human history had human populations done exactly that to each other?

"There has to be some best-case scenario we can work toward," said Kaveh. "If you are willing to look at me and see a person who is self-possessed and worthy of respect, same as I do to you, then maybe the others can, too."

"I WAS ALWAYS UNIQUE AMONG MY OWN KIND. AN ECCENTRIC. I WAS ONLY ALLOWED TO LIVE TO ADULTHOOD ON AN EXTREME TECH-NICALITY. I AM NOT ONE THAT THEY WOULD ENDEAVOR TO MODEL OTHERS AFTER."

"Still, if we really are that beautiful and precious, then even if it's unlikely to the point of hopelessness, it's still worth trying to prevent"—he gestured toward downtown LA, its tiny patch of skyscrapers jutting up in the distance like blades of grass—"whatever you think they might do to us."

He looked at Nikola, and it seemed that something had shifted in him. He seemed buoyant, looking into the valley of smog and concrete and humanity, that triceratops crest on the back of his head expanding like the petals of a sunflower. "I WANT TO SEE IT."

"Want to see what?"

Nikola extended two of his long fingers toward downtown, eyes sparkling, curious, playful even. Kaveh didn't like it.

"I WANT TO SEE IT. I WANT TO SEE THE POPULATION HUB."

"Downtown?"

"Yes. Something is happening, something I want to see. Take me there."

Kaveh's heart took a dip as he remembered what Miranda had told him only yesterday—*the rally.* They were expecting thousands to show up. Kaveh could not imagine a sequence of words he wanted to hear from Nikola less. "No, absolutely not. Come on, let's go back to the car. I need to see what the situation is at my house, assuming my house is still there."

"I do not want to go back to the house, not yet. That is where I want to go." He gestured toward downtown in the distance.

"And I said, there is absolutely no way in hell I am taking you there, not now. If anyone saw you—"

"I can go unseen by human eyes if I wish."

"I know, but it is way, *way* too dangerous. Please, you've agreed to respect my wishes."

"I have respected your wishes." Nikola looked at him, that gleeful sparkle, something that universally felt like madness. "But this is my wish. If you do not wish to take me there, then you do not need to."

A cloak of invisibility washed over his body like a waterfall, and he disappeared.

"Nik?" said Kaveh, eyes bugging out as he spun around, looking for a sign that Nikola had not actually just done this thing, that he was not about to go for a Ringo Starr–style parade in downtown LA. "Nikola?"

But he got no answer. Kaveh slapped his hands into his jacket pockets, into his pants pockets. Then, that dread in his chest blossomed into terror as he checked them. His cell phone wasn't there. He had left it at home.

He had no way to contact Cora.

"*Nikola!*"

Organization

Angus Normandy

Dear Friends,

Temecula was the opening salvo, but today we bring defenses.

We will not be caught unaware again. Today's rally will be just one of the first in the fight against the globalists using alien tech to consolidate money and power. The alien threat is here to control us, and the government has rolled over and given them free reign. But we know better.

We know their weaknesses, but up to now the question has been how do we create a weapon that's effective against this threat short of a nuclear blast?

Our brother Oskar Halmoka has already thought of that, and he's based right outside of Barstow. He's been fighting the good fight against the globalists for years, and is eager to offer his talents should the need arise.

We will see you on the battlefield.

Angus Normandy, Chairman of the Gadsden Line

23 minutes ago   Like · Comment · Share

👍 786 people like this.

💬 View all 1,142 comments

Write a comment...

29

"*Why did you do it?*"

A nightmare didn't wake her, but it might as well have. It was the feeling of a four-hundred-pound machine at her back, its limbs surrounding her, entwining her, and she instinctively balled herself into a fetal position, covering her face with her hands. She was still on the living room floor, having fallen asleep right next to Ampersand. She peeked through her fingers as he jammed his hand into the floor to raise himself up, balancing on his knuckles like a gorilla trying to steady himself.

"*Why did you do it?*"

Her eyes pricked with exhaustion. "Because he said he'd tell me the truth!" She pushed herself away from him, backing across the room toward the windows. "Was Čefo *your* symphyle?"

Ampersand stopped moving, and the focus of his eyes fluctuated like his entire system was restarting. Then he seemed to remember how to move normally, and pulled his arms and legs underneath his body, half on his side and half upright.

"He was Obelus's. He was Enola's. Was he yours?"

"*No.*"

She sneered at him, shaking her head incredulously. How many, *how many* times were they going to go through this? "Why lie to me about that?"

"*I had to serve you a rationale I believed you would respect.*"

"You are never going to stop lying to me, are you?"

"*What information I withhold and what information I impart has always been with your best interest in mind.*"

"*My* best interest?" she coughed. She got on her feet, backed away from him until she was almost against the window that opened into the backyard. "Is 'suppressing memories' to prevent me from talking to Sol my 'best interest'?"

His focus was still hazy, still focused on nothing, and his head swayed like he was drunk.

"You want to act like you didn't threaten to 'suppress my memories,' same as you did to Obelus. How is that protecting *my* interest? Then Enola tells me that you might just take it a step further, that if my condition worsens enough you would just . . . lobotomize me so you wouldn't have to deal with me anymore. That you'd alter my brain if you couldn't figure out how to control it, so my sickness would stop leaking into you. Is that why you were 'studying' me at all? Is that what those 'monitors' are for?"

Her throat grew hard as she said those words, her tired eyes tingling with heat. How cathartic it had been when Kaveh had put words to what she had been feeling, that she had been thinking of her pain like it was other people's burden, obligating her to keep it hidden. But that was exactly how Ampersand saw it, so burdensome he might erase parts of her personality altogether.

He looked at her for a long moment after she stopped talking, and the focus of his eyes dissipated like a fading firework, and the crest on his head relaxed, closing like a tulip at night. "*I do endeavor to cure your sickness. It does frighten me that I don't even begin to know why our bond has mutual empathic effects. It frightens me that I cannot control it. But my sickness is far more debilitating than yours. And I am separated from those with the tools to treat it; therefore, it shall go untreated. For you, at least, there is some hope of partial recovery. No, any benefit to me to altering you would be negligible compared to the damage I already live with, even if I were so cruel as to do such a thing. I would not disrespect your person like that, dear one. I would not alter you.*"

She *wanted* to believe him. What she wouldn't give for him to say he was trustworthy and actually live up to it. Without a word, she went into the kitchen and poured herself a glass of water from the Brita in the fridge. After downing one glass and grabbing a few Advils in the bathroom, she returned to Ampersand in the living room, his arms half drawn up to his sides, his head raised but looking at nothing, his eyes half-lidded like he'd been drugged.

She sat down on the floor next to him, turning on the TV to CNN but keeping it muted. The chyron read, PROTESTS LED BY THIRD PARTY ATTRACT THOUSANDS ACROSS DOZENS OF CITIES. The reporter appeared to be live from downtown LA. This must have been the thing Miranda had been talking about yesterday. She had to give him credit; he hadn't undersold it.

"*Where is Enola?*"

"With Kaveh," she said, taking a long sip of water, trying to wash down all the anger and disappointment she'd been feeling with it. She felt like a withered balloon that had been left in the hot sun for weeks, cracked and brittle. "He took Enola away in the Land Rover."

"*The man may be dead.*"

"I don't think Enola would kill him."

She watched him for a while, his eyes still half-lidded and dark, and then turned her attention back to the television, unmuting it. The two stayed like that for a while.

"*I cannot find Obelus.*"

She turned to him, waiting for him to elaborate. Was this a gesture of good faith? "How dangerous is he, now that he doesn't have the body of a Similar anymore?"

"*He will defend himself.*"

"What does that mean?"

"*I don't believe he would kill out of spite, but he certainly would kill if he felt he was in danger, or if anyone, human or otherwise, were to impede him. He does not need the body of a Similar to pose a danger to others.*"

"And in his current form, any human that lays eyes on him is a potential danger." CNN had gone to commercial, so Cora muted the TV. "Why is he running away from you? What is he planning to do?"

"*He is trying to get off-world. But to do that, he needs a new body. Only one inhabiting the body of a Similar can escape Earth's gravity to reach the resources he's left in orbit.*"

"New body," she said, running through her inner catalog of what that could mean. "Not yours?"

Ampersand didn't answer. Didn't even look at her.

"Nikola's?"

Again, nothing. Then, she realized if Obelus needed the body of a Similar, there was only one real option left. "Brako."

She caught a flash in Ampersand's eyes. Esperas's Similar, the only other amygdaline on Earth more powerful than Ampersand, besides Enola. Obelus intended to kill and body-snatch the only other Similar on the planet.

"They have to know about this."

She couldn't catch anything in his movements that might resemble a response, and she certainly couldn't feel what was going on on the other side of the wall at this moment. "You know I don't like the military or the massive surveillance apparatus they've built in the last few years, but we need help. We need to tell them the truth."

"They will kill him if they find him."

She shook her head, too tired, too drained to be incredulous that he was still, *still* focused on protecting Obelus when there was all this fucking *shit* going on. "You have to let him go."

Perhaps that was why. Perhaps all the *fucking shit* was too much for him to handle, but if he could just capture and control this *one thing*, this *one thing* that was ultimately impossible to capture and control.

"Is it true that you were the one who killed all those people you took for the language study?"

The large, almost liquid sheets of his eyelids closed. *"When I declared the study concluded, I did order the specimens to be destroyed."*

She swallowed. "Why?"

"After several years of study, Enola discovered characteristics that indicated higher cognitive function comparable to our own natural ancestors before they became post-natural. Enola made this discovery at a volatile time. The political situation was unstable, reckless decisions were being made."

"Reckless decisions, like sterilizing an entire planet of your sister species for the sheer crime of existing." She hadn't meant that to sound like as much as an accusation as it did.

"If there was any question that humans were capable of advancement as our ancestors were, that would prompt more study. So we hid these findings, I declared that humans were animals. And I ordered the specimens destroyed."

"Enola said he was the reason you had them euthanized."

"*Enola was the one who conducted the studies on higher cognitive function. It was Enola who proposed that humans might be capable of developing an advanced civilization, and should be studied further. He did not see how further study by the Superorganism could be an existential threat to humanity as I did.*"

His eyes slid open, still dark and unfocused. "*We both desired to study further, but the political situation was such that any alien civilization could be seen as analogous to our sister species. So I publicly concluded that we had learned as much as we could from this group and had the specimens destroyed.*"

"Please stop calling them *specimens*," Cora whispered. "They were people." She finished her glass of water and closed her eyes. "Why did you really do it? Why did you bind yourself to me?"

"*Because I wanted to know if you were a person.*"

She opened her eyes to look at him. "What do you mean, 'person'?"

He raised his head, his focus still bleary. "*Our concept of personhood is not like yours. Amygdaline nymphs are not persons to us. A nymph can be destroyed at any time. They do not have rights—not until they are mature enough to communicate through high language are they considered true persons. One of our criteria to define personhood is the ability to communicate through high language. I assumed it impossible for a human, but I do not in truth know if it is impossible. With the right neural engineering, you might be capable of high language.*"

"You mean you could . . ." She cleared her throat. "Genetically engineer a human capable of high language?"

"*No. I mean you, dear one. You could be capable of high language.*"

She froze, mouth open as she stared at the space between the TV and the window. She'd taken for granted that it was impossible, that it would always be impossible. Her mind went back to the last time they'd talked about high language, what he had said about *desiring* her to be capable of high language, to which she had expressed relief that she was not capable, and the discussion was therefore moot.

Oh, God.

"I . . . How?"

"*Neural engineering through digital interface.*"

"So . . . I could become post-natural, like you?"

"*Yes.*"

Such a quick, definite answer. He had clearly thought about this. He'd been sitting on this possibility, likely for a while. Had run through the logistics, considered schematics, imagined prototypes.

"*I cannot prove a negative,*" he continued. "*I cannot prove you incapable unless I try. Given our ability to sense each other as we already do, it might be possible. Communication through high language is one way we are able to ascertain personhood.*"

The sense of foreboding inside her continued to swell. "And the other?"

His bleary eyes finally found their focus, glowing at her now like warm suns through deep black smog. "*When I located the Fremda group, there was no joy in a reunion with my brethren. They both demanded of me and at the same time ostracized me. But you did not. They did not comfort me, but you did. I rationalized the time I spent with you as study, but in truth, I personized you. The word you would use in English is* humanize. *I humanized you, even though it was perverse to do so.*

"*But after we were separated, and you came to me at the coordinates I sent to you, I expressed to you that I didn't understand why you didn't kill me when you first had the opportunity. You told me you would never do such a thing. You said to me that you wanted to protect me.*

"*And I had never felt such an intense desire to submit to another being. I was lost, steward to a group that despised me, and I wanted nothing more in that moment than to say, 'Yes, I will submit to you. I am tired, and I am afraid. I will do anything you ask, only please protect me. Protect me from the horrors of your planet. Protect me from the cruelty and callousness of my kind.'*

"*And it was a hideous thing to think. Perverse. Bestial. And I pushed it aside, and I sent you away, as I should have. But then Obelus took you, and again, I desired to extract you and no one else. I didn't care about Esperas, or the others, but I did care about you. And it was perverse.*

"*So I made an impulse decision to prove to myself that you were not a person. Dynamic fusion bonds are typically formed through high language, but they can be done without it, if one is able to key in on your neural energy, as I was. But they are never unidirectional; they always flow both ways. So if I was able to do it to you, then you were able to do it to me. I assumed it would fail. But it didn't. Dynamic fusion bonding is our second criterion for personhood. It proves what I feared the most; you are a person, and we are bound until death.*"

Cora just stared at him, speechless. She hadn't even begun to consider his decision to bind himself to her anything other than strategy. But it wasn't strategy. It wasn't even a desperate act of love.

It had been a test.

"It is a burden to carry this knowledge. You are not unique. There is nothing exceptional about you. If you are a person, then so are all adult humans. Seven billion persons on this planet. You can reason, you have language, you are conscious. And you are predators. And you are violent. And you consume even more voraciously than transients. Why, of every species that we have discovered with the potential to advance, why did it have to be you?"

She felt a sort of desperation from the other side of the wall, pushing her down as if she were in a wind tunnel.

"There is no concept I can explain that you would not eventually comprehend at least the fundamentals of. Your raw intelligence may even be greater than our ancestors', as I never could have imagined a civilization advancing as quickly as yours has. I am burdened with the knowledge of human personhood."

She felt a wave crest inside her, an aching sense of loss and want and hunger and loneliness. Pain, so much *pain* to be shut out from the whole, like a limb without a body.

"But I would give it all back to be a part of the machine again. I would purge that knowledge from my mind if it meant I could be a part of the Superorganism again. No burden of truth is worth this misery.

"I want to go home," he said, and the wall between them practically burst, a flood of grief flowing through him and into her, crashing into her so hard it felt like her sternum might crack under the pressure. *"I want to go home. I want to go home."*

That flood of grief then translated into a physical response, and in short order, she was crying. More than crying, she was bawling. At first, she tried to stop it, almost feeling it unfair that his grief could invade her like this, but as she sat there, crying her eyes out, she also felt that this grief wasn't just his, that she, too, was a powder keg on constant verge of explosion and that maybe it wouldn't be the worst thing in the world to just let herself feel it.

Fuck it.

The moment she allowed herself to ride it out, to accept it and let herself feel everything, it became bearable. And so, she lay down on her side and just cried for several minutes, acting as a pressure valve for both of them.

Eventually, she sat up, all cried out, wiping the tears and redness from her face. She moved next to him, hesitating before touching him around the space where his crest met the rest of his head. "Even after all you've put me through, even after the lies and everything, I still want to protect you. That's always been the case with us, dynamic fusion bonding or no."

She leaned her face into the skin behind his eyes. "You could build a new life here. You could have a new home with me. I'd protect you. I'd keep you safe. I'd never hurt you, I promise."

He noticed it first, what was on the television, milliseconds before she saw it. He must have gone through the same horrified thought process, too, because neither of them reacted immediately. It was too absurd, too horrible to be real. The feed was coming from a camera inside a helicopter focused on the rally downtown. It was on the verge of turning into a riot, and the cameraman was frantically trying to zoom in on people running around on the ground like ants, but one of the ants was bigger and darker than all the other ants.

Enola!

Cora slammed the volume button to get some context, that yes this was a live feed, yes this was happening right now, and being broadcast all over the world. The newscaster babbling incoherently about "what appears to be a nonhuman being, but nothing has been verified at this time."

On the corner of the screen, a black cargo van appeared, topped with what looked like a Tesla coil. It barged through the crowd, slapping human bodies out of the way, stopping not twenty feet short of Enola. The camera in the helicopter was shaky, trying to keep its subject in the center of the frame. Enola turned to face the van, his posture descending into something antagonistic.

Then the feed cut to black.

30

"*Nikola!*" Kaveh whirled around, pushing his way through the crowd, which had already swelled in the odd half hour he'd been running around down here. "Nik, for fuck's sake, answer me!"

It had taken him an hour to drive all the way down here, though not as long as he'd feared, all things considered. It seemed as though the angry denizens of Southern California had elected to use their oft-ignored public transportation system for once to come to this protest, one of many that were happening simultaneously all over the country. But once parked, and still getting no answer from Nikola, Kaveh had no clue where to go, only intuition, and his intuition told him that Nikola's interest would take him where the action was thickest, and Kaveh knew enough about this event to know that it was supposed to culminate in Pershing Square.

It looked like the police had only been expecting a crowd of a few hundred, but as Miranda had predicted, this was well into the thousands. This event had been organized a few weeks ago, but a few weeks ago, there had been no Enola Gay to fan the coals of outrage, and it had taken him a solid fifteen minutes to make it from his car to Pershing Square where it should have taken five.

"Nik? Nik!" He looked up, half expecting Nikola's dark silhouette to be perched on the side of some skyscraper like a peregrine falcon about to dive. "Where are you?"

The odd thing about this protest was the wide spread of interests represented. There were some "Take me away, Xethorp" moon children present, eager to see if the great awakening was nigh, but the vast, vast majority of the people here were different flavors of discontent demanding answers—transparency activists, Ortega supporters, students, plenty of people with reasonable standpoints and valid upsets. But the radical wing of those ideologies was present, too, the proto-fascists, the conspiracy theorists, and of course, the Gadsden Line in much greater numbers than there had been in Temecula. They'd streamlined their messaging, too. Several of them were holding up signs that said things like, NO ONE-WORLD GOVERNMENT and DEATH TO THE GLOBALISTS.

Ah, globalists, thought Kaveh. *By night known as "Jews."* The dog whistle was so loud it was piercing, but Nils Ortega's fans, high on anger at the lack of information and transparency, either did not hear the fascist undertones or ignored them. Enemy of my enemy and all that.

"Truth is a human right!"

A whoop bellowed up from the crowd as everyone turned to the source of the voice—Jano Miranda, standing on a stage that was little more than a few folding tables in a row, talking into a loudspeaker.

"We hold these truths to be self-evident," said Miranda, with a gravitas that brought down a hush on the near frenzied crowd. "That all men are created equal, that they are endowed by their Creator with certain unalienable Rights, that among these are Life, Liberty and the pursuit of Happiness. That to secure these rights, Governments are instituted among Men, deriving their just Powers from the Consent of the Governed . . .

"From the *consent of the governed*!" This last part he repeated for effect, and the crowd roared. "Government exists to secure the rights of the people and must be based on the consent of the governed. And we have a right to know the truth, because truth is a human right!"

The roar turned into human thunder. Drums banged, fists were pumped, and whistles blew. Kaveh stood on his toes to get a better look at the scene and saw that several people had climbed trees, and some were even on streetlights. Behind him, even more people were flooding in, the latecomers from the march who were only just arriving.

"If these ETIs really are people, if the issue really needs to be debated, then why can't we see them? Why are we not allowed to know anything about them? We have a right to know the truth, and we demand the truth!"

Oh no.

The chances were nonzero to pretty good that if Nikola heard Miranda's words, he'd see them as an invitation. Kaveh began trying to "excuse me" his way to the front of the crowd, but was met with angry looks if not outright resistance. Why should this rando get a premium seat if they couldn't get one?

"We cannot have this conversation absent of knowledge, absent of truth; otherwise, it's pure philosophy, pure speculation," Miranda continued. "The governed demand to know the truth, we do not consent to silence, we do not consent to lies!"

Another chorus of human thunder, and Kaveh squeezed between a group of fist-pumpers, mumbling an excuse about having a daughter who was up there somewhere. Perhaps 20 percent of the people he squeezed past accepted that obvious lie.

Shut up, you idiot, shut up, shut up!

"The governed do not consent to be lied to about the greatest discovery in human history," bellowed Miranda. "We do not consent! If this government does not respect the wishes of the governed, then this is not a democracy, and we need to tear it down! Debride the rot, flush out corruption until we get the truth!"

This last bit caused the loudest roar yet, and to his right, he saw another group of Gadsden Line members. One guy he recognized from Temecula last week, who now had a black eagle on his vest and was holding a NO ONE-WORLD GOVERNMENT sign. Down on the other side of a police blockade, he could barely make out a few Gadsden Liners standing down by a black van, with something conical and sci-fi-looking sticking out the top. *Is that a fucking Tesla coil?*

"They know the truth," Miranda continued. "And if they refuse to give the people the knowledge they need to help make informed decisions, this is not a democracy, this is oligarchy! This is plutocracy!" Another cheer. "This is autocracy! This is what leads to dictatorship!"

An even louder cheer, especially from the Gadsden Line standing on the berm near the street. Kaveh continued his slow crawl through the maze of people in the probably futile hope that he could convince Miranda to shut the fuck up.

Miranda put a fist in the air. "Support truth! Support transparency! Support Nils Ortega!" The mention of Ortega electrified the crowd. "Truth is a human right!"

A portion of the crowd tried to repeat him, tried to get a chant going, but most of that was drowned out by cheers, screams, not screams of agreement or outrage but screams of terror.

No.

Kaveh gave up on trying to politely worm his way through the crowd, now forcing his way toward Miranda. Most of the people around him stood frozen in their confusion, so some of them still glared at him as he plowed through, now in easy view of Miranda's makeshift stage in the center of the square. The people immediately surrounding the stage were swirling like a whirlpool, panicked and trying to get away from the stage. Miranda stood stone still, jaw hanging open, his eyes fixed on something directly below him.

No no no no no no nononononononono . . .

The panic swelled as the thing that was causing the panic stood up into full view of nearly everyone in the square, his beetle-black skin shining and his cloud-nebula eyes blazing brightly in the sunlight, once at his full height taller than Miranda on his stage.

Getting to Nikola was a battle fought in inches, with everyone he encountered pushing past him in the opposite direction. It looked from Kaveh's location like he was standing about five feet from the stage, staring Miranda down, and Miranda, his security, and every one of his cronies was staring right back, utterly dumbfounded. Miranda's security detail had drawn their guns, but were at least smart enough not to have them trained on the alien cyborg.

The crowd eventually parted once he got to the fallout zone surrounding Nikola, from which most had fled but a few brave souls still stood, ready to bolt but taking pictures with their cell phones nonetheless. Kaveh sprinted to Nikola so fast he nearly slammed into him, grabbing him by the arm. "We have to get out of here!"

"You are here, dear clever creature," said the voice in his ear. "Speak to him for me."

"Fucking *no*!" Kaveh spat, tugging him by the forearm.

Miranda's stunned gaze drifted to Kaveh, morphing into a bemused horror, as if he were beginning to entertain the idea that he was dreaming. Eventually he managed, "Kaveh?"

"He asked to see me. He wanted to know the truth about us. Ask him what he wants to know."

Kaveh turned to get a handle on the situation, saw that a line of humanity had formed at a radius of about fifty feet from where he was standing, at least half of whom had their cell phones and/or digital cameras out, snapping wildly. He looked over toward the Gadsden Line, but only saw a few of them, and the few he did see looked to be mobilizing. "Nik, we need to get out of here. *Please* take us out of here."

"SPEAK FOR ME, DEAR CLEVER CREATURE, AND I WILL GIVE HIM HIS TRUTH."

"Absolutely not!"

Miranda was looking at Kaveh like *he* was the nine-foot, spider-fingered alien cyborg, not Nikola. "He's harmless!" Kaveh said, tightening his grip on Nikola's forearm.

Miranda finally found his voice. "Harmless?"

Kaveh nodded curtly. "Mostly harmless. We need to go. It is dangerous for him to be here."

"You can understand it?"

Kaveh had been so tuned to the sounds of human horror that he hadn't noticed the chopping of a nearby helicopter. He looked up to scan the sky, and there it was, descending toward the roofs of the skyscrapers, likely a traffic helicopter for one of the news stations.

Meaning that it had a camera on board capable of transmitting a live feed.

"Yes, I can understand him," he said, whipping his head back to Miranda. "Don't ask how, but he's not here to hurt anyone. He considered your speech a call to action, and he took it."

Miranda nearly choked on his own spit. "How?"

"*Because he understands English!*" He looked up at the helicopter, lower now, almost at the height of the nearby skyscrapers. Some in the crowd had begun to inch closer, the people who hadn't totally scattered realizing that what was effectively a very civil, albeit stressed, conversation was going on, and not the end of the world (for now).

Gravity pulled Miranda's jaw down as he grasped for how to respond. "I didn't mean . . . I didn't expect—"

"*I know you didn't expect!* Nikola." Kaveh turned to the alien, clasping his hands in front of him. "Please, this is dangerous. People will get hurt. We need to leave!"

Miranda's dull, stunned expression snapped to shock, not at Nikola but at something behind them. Kaveh turned around to see that black van, the one with the Tesla coil, plowing through the crowd, ramming human bodies out of the way like a motorboat moving through a lake covered in lily pads.

Nikola turned around to face the van, seeming curious but not alarmed even as the van picked up speed. Kaveh felt a strange pressure in his chest, as if the air had become thick like water, harder to breathe. Then, perhaps twenty feet away from where Nikola stood, the van slammed into an invisible wall, sending the driver, a bald white guy in a black nü-metal hoodie, into his windshield, cracking it with his skull.

Kaveh barely got a chance to get his bearings enough to see that people had already gotten hurt by the van, possibly killed. The driver sat back up, and then Kaveh saw what he had in his hand—a detonator. Miranda saw it the moment Kaveh did, and yelled, "Everyone down!" before the man pressed the detonator. Kaveh felt the air thicken as Nikola steeled himself, some sort of defensive posture, an extension of what he must have done earlier with the invisible wall. Kaveh covered his face with his arms and fell to the ground, bracing for the bomb. *Something* went off, and people screamed and scattered, but it wasn't an explosion. For an instant, Kaveh thought his time had come when Nikola's half-ton mass collapsed on top of him.

Half screaming, he wormed his way out from under Nikola, who was now utterly immobile. He looked at the black van, looked at the Tesla coil, looked at the man inside it trembling on the other side of the spiderweb of broken glass his head had created, holding the detonator in his shaking hand, blood dripping from his forehead. Kaveh shot to his feet and looked down at Nikola, who was sprawled out on the pavement, his eyes closed.

The militia had figured out how to attach a pulse emitter to that van. *But how?* How had they *known* this would be effective against—

Then he heard the wheezing of a helicopter engine, of helicopter blades both coming closer, and slowing down. He turned around in time to see the tail of the news helicopter slam against the side of a skyscraper somewhere around the twentieth floor, which sent the aircraft into a tailspin toward the crowd below. That electromagnetic pulse hadn't just been effective against Nikola—it had shorted out every other electrical object in sight.

The top blades of the chopper hit the side of the building before it began its free fall in earnest, falling directly into the crowd about two blocks away from where he was standing. His view was too blocked by the crowd to see how many people it had struck.

The Gadsden Liners took this opportunity to march, and when Kaveh looked back toward the van, he saw them screwing up their courage—and getting their guns in order. Several had shotguns, one had a rifle, and one had an AR-15.

"No!" yelled Kaveh, putting his body between the mobilizing militia and Nikola, hoping to God that some of the people in this crowd might join him, might do *something* to protect the alien being in their midst from these fucking rednecks. He looked out into the crowd of cell phone photo takers pleadingly. A few looked like they might be entertaining the idea of joining him, but the guns stopped any potential Good Samaritans where they stood. He looked back up to where Miranda had been standing, hoping that this man of all people might be able to talk them down from doing violence to Nikola's helpless form, but he had already been ushered away by his entourage.

Now the man in the black eagle jacket, the man who had been holding the NO ONE-WORLD GOVERNMENT sign, was marching toward him with almost religious purpose, the other three right behind him. The man with the AR-15 aimed his rifle at Kaveh, and the other three followed suit. "Get out of the way!" he bellowed.

"No, you don't understand!" said Kaveh, putting his hands up. "Please, he doesn't want to hurt anyone!"

"Get out of the *fucking* way!"

A burst of energy hit, not unlike what he'd felt with Nikola's invisible wall, sending the four men flying backward. The blast blew them all the way back to the line of people watching the spectacle unfold, and their guns shattered.

"Kaveh!"

He turned to the source of the voice—Cora, and Ampersand right beside her, his eyes blazing fire as they surveyed the carnage. He sent another burst of energy into the crowd, a warning, and it pushed anyone within a hundred-foot radius down like trees knocked over from the force of a nuclear blast. Then he turned his attention to Nikola.

"What the hell happened?" asked Cora.

"I don't know. They had an EMP or something. They knew that a pulse emitter would knock out their power! How did they know?"

"Oh my God," said Cora, clapping her hands to her mouth as she noticed the wreckage of the helicopter crash. "We were watching the newsfeed from that helicopter."

Cora snapped her attention to Kaveh, grabbing him by the shoulders. "Get on the plate, now!"

He looked down and saw at his feet a plate of liquid metal that looked like a pool of mercury. He started to do as he was told, but then glanced back up into the van with the Tesla coil on top, at the skinhead in the driver's seat who was fumbling to get his detonator to work.

By the time Kaveh saw him, it was too late. He only managed to shout, "Stop him!" before the man hit the detonator again. It seemed like Ampersand realized what was going on, as he sent another one of those force field blasts, but not before the pulse went off. The blast this time seemed weaker than the first, but it was enough to make Ampersand collapse right where he stood, right on top of Nikola.

31

This *had* to be a bad dream. There was no way this was actually happening. The people Ampersand had knocked down were back on their feet, preparing to fight or flee. The Gadsden Line men were on their knees trying to repair the guns that Ampersand had destroyed. The skinhead in the van was glaring at her, a thin line of blood draping his nose to one side.

Then the violence began, with someone in the crowd ripping the driver out of the black van, wrestling him to the ground. Another man began kicking him, and another started to beat him down. One of the militiamen tried to pry the angry crowd off the skinhead from the van, but this only caused more violence. The van had hurt people, possibly killed people in its mad dash. The crowd didn't care about eliminating the alien threat like the militia did; they wanted revenge.

She didn't have the pill bug. Why hadn't she brought the pill bug? She was useless. She'd promised to protect him; not five minutes ago, she had promised to protect him. She might as well be a newborn kitten, eyes sealed shut and mewling for its mother, for all the good she could do right now.

"What do we do?"

Kaveh's voice. She turned to him, still dazed, still helpless. Why would he ask her what to do? He was the adult here. He should know what to do.

"Where are the police?" she asked.

Kaveh looked around frantically, spotted something, and ran off in that direction. It looked like the police had diverted their attention to the riot that was breaking out, none of them eager to get anywhere near Enola or Ampersand. But they weren't getting any directions, she realized. Their walkie-talkies and phones were shorted, so the police couldn't communicate with each other or coordinate a response.

Then one of the Gadsden Liners had enough, a blond man with a white goatee and small round sunglasses. He drew out his handgun, began marching toward her. She backed up as the man raised his gun at her, getting low to the ground and positioning herself in front of Ampersand's head and neck, the parts of him that were most vulnerable. Terror flooded her, much stronger than the sense of grief she'd experienced a few minutes ago, mixing with her own, drowning her in it. Ampersand was still conscious, she could sense it. Unable to move, just like in her nightmares. He was experiencing every helpless moment of this.

The man held the gun at her, point-blank. "Get out of the way!"

Her breath was coming hot and fast now, her skin being torn off by a bed of needles, white spots clouding her vision. "No, please, no!"

She backed up against Ampersand, spreading her arms out like that would do any fucking good. Captive, trapped, but this time, Ampersand couldn't even try to protect her. She just threw her hands up and begged, "No!"

"Get out of the *fucking* way!"

She could feel his fear as keenly as her own and him mirroring it right back, a fear ouroboros, and she could not think, could not strategize. Could only stay plastered where she was, begging this violent stranger, "Please, don't! Stop! *Stop!*"

"Put down the fucking weapon!" She heard a man scream it, multiple men screaming it, but she couldn't take her eyes off the black barrel of that handgun.

"Put it down!" One more time.

She cried out as she heard the shots, closing her eyes and bracing for the impact. Seconds stretched over millennia, one shot, then five, then twenty. She opened her eyes and saw the man with the gun on the ground being riddled with bullets, his body twitching with each impact as the people behind him panicked and mobbed trying to get away. It was the LAPD doing it.

She couldn't take her eyes off the man with the gun, now a corpse with a dark red pool forming under him. There were people behind him who had been shot, too, unfortunates caught in the LAPD's frenzied line of fire. It felt like a dream. *He's dead. He's so obviously dead. Why do they keep shooting him?*

Do they enjoy this?

She turned to her right, to the cluster of police officers who still had their guns trained on the dead man. Some of them were restraining Kaveh, wrestling him to the ground. One of the police officers now had his gun trained on her.

"Get on the ground!" the officer screamed. "On your stomach, now, hands behind your head!"

"No!" She turned around and wrapped her arms around Ampersand's midsection, gluing her front to his back, wrapping one hand around his head and the other around his neck, holding him tightly, bracing for a struggle, bracing to get shot.

The body of the man with the gun was seared into her mind's eye, the way it jerked with each bullet entry. *Of course he'd shoot. He enjoys shooting. They all do. Monsters, monsters, pugilists, flesh-eaters, militarists, militarists, militarists.*

"Get on the ground *now* or I will fucking shoot you!"

The officer was still screaming at her, and she continued to hold on to Ampersand, not moving, not looking up. She could feel them on all sides of her now, policemen surrounding them with their guns trained. If any one of them moved—Enola, Ampersand, or Cora—the police would fire on them, fire on them like they had the man with the white hair. One movement from any of them, and it would be all over.

It wouldn't be the worst thing in the world.

Again, the command to get on the ground. She didn't move, held on tighter. She crushed her eyes closed, tried to keep herself still, but she couldn't control her breathing, which was now coming in rapid, jerky bursts. She heard more voices, more yelling. Police officers barking commands at each other, more people surrounding them.

"Don't move," she said to Ampersand between breaths. Each pore of her skin felt as if it were tearing into a canyon, her lungs were on fire. "Don't move, or they'll kill us. They'll kill us."

It wouldn't be the worst thing in the world.

Then, a familiar voice. "CIA! Back the fuck off!"

She felt a hand on her back, and she flinched at the contact. "It's okay," said the voice. "It's okay. We're here. Let go of him."

She didn't move. Her heart had been replaced with a hummingbird's, her breath like a mouse on a wheel. It was like night paralysis brought to the waking world. She couldn't move.

"Fucking back off! CIA! Let me handle this!" Sol's voice. "Get these fucking amateurs out of my sight."

Again, the hand on her back. "We're going to get them out of here. This has happened to them before, right? They'll pull out of it. You need to get up or we can't get them to safety."

She tried, but she was no more capable of breaking her hold on Ampersand than she was sprouting wings. There was still so much noise, still such a loud din of confusion—people talking, people yelling, violence, police officers screaming, people in the crowd screaming back at them.

"Come on, I know you can do it," said Sol. "Get up."

She tried to remember what normal breathing felt like. Reached back into her memory, her and Kaveh alone in the woods, *four, seven, eight*. One breath, not deep but deeper than a normal breath. Then two. Then five. She couldn't remember how it worked. She couldn't do it.

"Let him go," said Sol.

She let go of Ampersand.

Sol pulled her body toward his, scooping her up into his arms and carrying her away from Enola and Ampersand. She couldn't see Kaveh, but didn't yet have the presence of mind to call for him, to inquire about him. She began to resist, to tell Sol that she shouldn't be separated from Ampersand, that he needed her. She promised she would protect him. But she was still scarcely able to move.

Sol carried her to an ambulance and sat her down inside its rear entrance. "See? You can still see them. They're right there." He pointed back to where they had been, to where Ampersand and Enola still were.

CIA guys in hazmats—or maybe they were FBI? Military? Did it matter?—were in the process of loading them into an armored car. Why hazmats?

"Where's Kaveh?" she asked.

"Kaveh?" She wasn't looking at Sol's face, but she could feel it grow stony.

She nodded, keeping her gaze forward, sliding into numbness, the wall growing thick as she watched the men in hazmats carefully loading Ampersand and Enola into black armored trucks. The LAPD and others had more or less cleared the immediate scene of civilians.

Except for one, the dead man, who had not been moved, but was now covered in a white sheet, spots of blood seeping through.

"Mazandarani is . . . here. He's just been arrested."

That didn't make sense at all, but of course it didn't make sense. Nothing did. "I need him."

"I see."

"Please don't let them take him. Please. We need him. Enola . . ."

"Mazandarani got to Enola Gay first." Sol turned to look at the men in hazmats hoisting Enola into a black van. "Fucking figures."

· · · · ·

They were taken to a military base in Los Alamitos. Sol left her in a room that he said was not an interrogation room that sure looked like an interrogation room and told her that Ampersand and Enola had been separated from each other for their own safety, which she told him was the right move. Ampersand seemed to have come around, but Enola had not. Sol told her to be patient, that *he's here, he's fine, he's okay,* but she needed to wait. He asked her why she wanted to see Kaveh Mazandarani, and she told him the truth, that he'd known about Enola Gay as long as she had, that he'd been there when she'd found Enola Gay alone in the woods. Sol, who had been keeping up the pretense of being sympathetic, turned cold.

"You've known about Enola Gay the whole time, haven't you?"

Her body was by now on strike against anything that bore even a passing resemblance to an emotion. "No. The day of the landing, I didn't know anything more than what I told you. Ampersand didn't, either. He was telling you the truth."

"Until he wasn't."

She looked away from him, spied a dust particle hanging in the air, and concentrated on that. "He found Enola pretty quickly, not long after that big noise in Temecula."

"Enola made the noise."

"It was meant to flush out Ampersand, but Ampersand got to him first. He's been keeping Enola in secret since then."

"Why?" said Sol, leaning over the table that he said was not an interrogation table. "What's he think we'll do to Enola?"

"It's not you he's worried about," she said, locating another dust particle to fix her attention on. "It's Esperas and Brako. Enola is 'damaged,' by their standards. And so is Ampersand, for that matter. With no legal protections, they're all under the assumption that they're not beholden to our laws and that they take care of their own. And if might makes right, Brako is the most powerful, and there's nothing to stop Brako and Esperas from killing Ampersand and Enola."

Sol slid into the chair opposite Cora, crossing his arms in front of him. "Why in God's name would Brako and Esperas want to kill them?"

"To put them out of their misery," Cora stated flatly. "They have their own social mores, and both of them meet the Superorganism's criteria for state-sanctioned euthanasia. They would consider it the 'humane' thing to do."

She could feel him glaring at her like heat off a radiator. She didn't look at him, refused to give him the satisfaction.

"I hope you're happy," he said. "Clearly, Ampersand has been doing whatever he wants. And he's been doing that despite our surveillance, hasn't he?"

She finally looked at him, but didn't rise to his level of intensity. She couldn't even if she wanted to. "Yes."

"So while he's 'alone' in his lair, we see whatever he wants us to see, whether he's in there or not."

"Yes."

The two stared at each other, Sol's expression dripping with poison, like every nasty suspicion he ever had about her was true. But she couldn't feel guilty about this. Sol had no idea about the impossibility of her situation, and moreover, maybe Ampersand was right. The authorities were corrupt, and bureaucratic, and inept, and not worthy of trust even when they meant well. Their involvement would only make things worse. After all, the only way the Gadsden Line could have possibly known about the amygdaline vulnerability to energy pulses was if someone in the military or CIA had leaked it.

She looked down at her hands. Somehow she felt like they were chained to the table between them. "There's something else I need to tell you."

Sol raised his eyebrows, his expression no longer poisonous, just resigned. *Go ahead, you idiot. It couldn't possibly get any worse.*

"Obelus is alive."

She saw the slideshow of confusion run past his eyes in less than a second—*How is he alive? The FBI has the body. The body is on ice in San Bernardino.* Then, swiftly, acceptance. The hows and whys don't matter, because the rules that apply to an amygdaline Similar body are not the rules that apply to a human body. "Where?"

"We don't know." Her eyes returned to her hands on the table. "Ampersand put him in Čefo's old body. But then Obelus gave him the slip. We don't know where he is. He's trying to get off-world, but his three Similars, the ones we thought had left, are still here. They don't know where he is, either, but they're hunting him, too."

"How the hell do you know about that? Have you been in communication with them?"

"No, but I've seen them. It turns out that Obelus belongs to the same genetically 'defective' subset as the rest of the Fremda group."

"And how did he survive?"

"Ampersand saved him."

"Why?"

She imagined herself betraying the truth about Ampersand's relationship to Obelus and nearly laughed at the idea. "I don't know," she said absently. "I assume he thought he could control Obelus, but he could not."

Sol let out a deep, angry sigh. "Okay." Another, deeper sigh, irritating and loud. "So I suppose the United States military apparatus should wish him luck on his hunt when he comes to? Maybe give him a road atlas so he won't get lost?"

"I told him we needed help. *Your* help to find Obelus. The Big Brother surveillance state's help. He didn't want your help." She looked up at him. "Is he okay?"

"We don't know, exactly. He seems to be awake, but he isn't responding."

The part of her that had until now refused to feel anything bent a little. "It's public now," said Sol. "They need names. They need identities. The can has been kicked so far down the road, the road has ended. There is no more road. They need legal names. I'm guessing you and Ampersand have already agreed to one."

"Yes."

"Let's have it."

"Jude." Her face a wall of iron. *Go and make some pithy remark. Give me shit. I fucking dare you.*

"Sabino?"

"No," she said. "Bad optics, even if it makes the most sense."

"Ortega?"

"Fuck you."

The light breeze of a smile touched his lips. "Let's hear it, then."

"Atheatos."

"And Enola Gay?"

"Nikola."

"Nikola Atheatos?"

"Celaeno," she said.

"Okay, then." He sighed. "Let's go see *Jude.*"

· · · · ·

Ampersand had been conscious but nonresponsive for hours, unlike "Nikola," who had only recently come to. Surprisingly, everyone took to the name immediately. Dr. Sev told her that he wasn't even getting an Esperanto code name. AG-ETI-051—"Nikola Celaeno."

Ampersand was curled up in the back corner of an empty, sterile room that looked like a bigger, emptier version of the room Sol had interrogated Cora in. Alternately white and metal, complete with one wall that was obviously a two-way mirror. She asked them to do something about the bright lights, about the cold temperature, to at least give him something to lie on instead of the cold floor. He was awake and conscious, but he didn't move, didn't acknowledge her, sitting up in a roost, not quite touching the wall, his eyes half-hooded.

"Hey," she said. "It's me."

She put her fingers on his back, feeling his shield up and in full force, so full it was as though the air surrounding him had turned to rubber.

"Ampersand?"

Nothing.

She spent about an hour trying to get him to talk to her, but the only response she got was that after a point, he closed his eyes.

Five Killed During Third Party Rally

By Joy Aokihara

LOS ANGELES—Five people have died and 21 others were injured when the appearance of an apparent ETI caused a riot during a rally in Los Angeles, police say.

A far-right group called the Gadsden Line is claiming responsibility for an explosive charge causing an electromagnetic pulse detonated by a van at the rally, shorting out all electrical equipment within a three-city-block radius. The pulse caused a nearby helicopter to crash, killing the pilot and two bystanders.

Gadsden members are alleged to have begun a shoot-out following the pulse, prompting LAPD officers to fire on gunman Tony Cascio, who was pronounced dead on the scene. Stray bullet fire was responsible for the shooting death of at least one other person, and three more are in critical condition. Witnesses report the presence of two distinct ETIs at the rally, both of whom were reported injured or killed, but their status is unknown.

The mayor of Los Angeles, Antonio Villaraigosa, said he was "heartbroken" at the deaths. President Dick Cheney has condemned the violence, and local officials have declared a state of emergency.

Kaveh was brought first into LAPD custody, then into FBI custody, probably got tossed into FDA and CDC custody in there somewhere too because why not, until finally he was passed into the worst of custodies—CIA custody.

This, he thought, would be the end, because they were really, really not supposed to be doing this. In fact, he could only suspect that it was CIA custody by virtue of lack of specifics. There were plenty of black sites inside the U.S. where they could take him, and of *course* that violated international law, but hey, small potatoes in the grand scheme of war crimes committed by the U.S. in the last ten years. If it was CIA custody like he suspected, then on paper, the rationale was probably terrorism. Iranian-born boy with the long, funny Iranian name, a guy who had worked with Nils Ortega to undermine American sovereignty to boot. It would be all too easy to slap together some bogus terrorism charges to get his citizenship revoked if they really, really wanted to. Hell, he'd written an entire book about that very thing! Then, off to the very CIA black sites he had helped expose. Poetic, really.

The room they held him in reminded him of the rooms the TSA tended to stash him in when he got "randomly searched" at the airport. It felt innocuous enough, glass windowpanes leading to what looked like an office, except for the part where it was locked from the outside and the fact that everyone who walked by looked like their first internship had netted them some waterboarding experience. The longest he'd ever been held by the TSA was twelve hours. By then, he'd known better than to fly unshaven (he *always* got "randomly searched" when he had a beard), so really, he only had himself to blame. Well, that and institutionalized racism. He didn't have a clock, so he was pretty sure this detainment broke the TSA's record. *Congrats, CIA, you are still the agency that sucks the most.*

He was trying not to let his imagination run away with all of the worst-case scenarios when (hey, speaking of torture) Sol Kaplan showed up, wearing a Nine Inch Nails T-shirt under a button-up plaid overshirt that spoke, "I have not bought a new album since 1996." Kaveh sat up straight like this was a job interview and the HR lady had finally arrived with his paperwork. "Are you here to torture me?"

Kaplan stared at him, not daggers, more the look of a god confused at why the mortal clay of the earth was unhappy with the myriad cruelties of his creation. "I don't really do that anymore."

"Is that why they shifted you to alien detail? I was curious, to be honest, but I could only speculate."

Kaplan pulled up a chair and sat catty-corner to him at the table. "Interesting to finally meet you. I did not think I would ever get the pleasure."

"I . . . feel the same," said Kaveh, not wanting to push his luck.

Kaplan reclined on the uncomfortable metal chair, trying to look like it wasn't as uncomfortable as they both knew it was. "We've got some witnesses on the ground from the incident downtown that say you were acting as an intermediary between Nikola and Jano Miranda."

Kaveh's eyes popped wide. "'Nikola?'"

"This whole nightmare has kicked a lot of gears into motion that should have been in motion a long time ago, one of them is the issue of legal names. 'Nikola' is the name we got, so it's the name we're running with."

Kaveh was dumb with surprise. He'd given him the name Nikola without much serious thought, just an alternative to having his namesake be a landmark in mass murder. If that was true, then "Nikola," a name he had picked on the fly, would be international news soon, if it weren't already. Not just international news, it would be *history.* "Yeah, I . . . that's not completely accurate. Mostly I was trying to get Nikola out of there before anyone got killed. Clearly, I failed."

"You sure did," said Kaplan, picking his fingernails with his thumb. "What was he doing there?"

"The truth is, he wanted to see it. He asked me to take him to downtown LA. I told him no, absolutely not. So he decided he'd go without me. And here we are."

"Here we are," repeated Kaplan, looking down at his fingernail-picking. "How many?"

Kaplan studied him from under hooded eyes. "One gunman, shot by the LAPD. Another bystander, shot by the LAPD. Pilot of the helicopter, but the cameraman miraculously survived. Blades hit four, decapitated one, another died from injuries later. Driver of the van is in critical condition, along with several others. Five dead so far."

Kaveh started to reply, but paused. Kaplan seemed to be evaluating him, and thinking back on all the people he followed for *Internal Enemies,* he knew that his life was in Kaplan's hands. If he wanted, he could strip Kaveh of his citizenship. He could lock him away. He might even do the same to his family. Kaplan looked as though he was debating which of the above was the best option.

"If I were to put you in a room with Nikola, would you be able to speak for him?"

Kaveh forced a sickly smile. "Do I have a choice?"

· · · · ·

"I AM GLAD TO SEE YOU SAFE, DEAR CLEVER CREATURE."

There was a paternalistic urge, one he imagined all parents must feel, to lay into Nikola, to really let him have it, to yell, *Do you know what you've done?* No, it was not his fault that there had been people lying in wait to attack in case he showed up, and no, it was not his fault that people died because of it. But it was reckless, it was careless, and he should not have done it. Kaveh had *told* him not to do it. But he had done it, and now people were dead. The first time the public at large ever saw an ETI, and people died.

This did not bode well for the future.

"I'm glad you're safe, too."

Nikola was planted calmly on the floor of a sterile interrogation room of stainless steel and glass. Kaveh felt this *should* be really intimidating to an alien, and surely the feds must have known that, but he seemed fine with it, seated right in the middle of it like a cat sunning in a windowsill. He wasn't intimidated at all, and why would he be? He knew exactly what he was capable of, and the people here had no idea. He must be downright charmed.

"WILL YOU RELAY MY MEANING TO YOUR SUPERIORS, DEAR CLEVER CREATURE?"

Kaveh had no one to blame for this but himself. He had entered into this thinking of himself as the observer, the journalist gathering information, and had been deluding himself basically from the word go that he was not already a part of the story.

"Listen." He crouched down in front of Nikola, hoping he was speaking quietly enough that the people on the other side of that mirror couldn't hear him. "I'll relay your meaning. I want you to trust me. I'm not just your interpreter. I'm your advocate."

"AS I UNDERSTAND, MY BELOVED'S STRATEGY OF EMPLOYING AN INTERPRETER, OR AS YOU CALL IT, AN ADVOCATE, ACTS AS A SHIELD FOR ANY DIRECT COMMUNICATION I MIGHT GIVE TO YOUR GOVERNMENT THAT MIGHT BE POTENTIALLY WEAPONIZED OR MISUNDERSTOOD."

"Yeah, that sounds like a reasonable strategy to me."

"SO YOU AGREE THAT I SHOULD NOT COMMUNICATE WITH THEM DIRECTLY."

"I'm saying"—he eyed those mirrors—"we should be extremely judicious with your communications with them."

"SHOULD I BE JUDICIOUS WITH YOU?"

"I'm not saying I won't make mistakes, but I have your interests at heart, not theirs."

"ARE THEIR INTERESTS NOT YOURS?"

"Generally, no, they are not."

"YOU PROCLAIM LOYALTY TO A POTENTIALLY HOSTILE EXTRATERRESTRIAL INTELLIGENCE OVER YOUR OWN GOVERNMENT?"

He blew a long puff of air out between his lips. "Yep, pretty much."

"ARE YOU UNIQUE IN THIS, DEAR CLEVER CREATURE?"

"Less so every day."

"YOU MUST TELL ME HOW TO BALANCE FOR YOU THE KINDNESS YOU HAVE SHOWN ME."

You could start by not diving into an angry mob to say hi, he thought. "Just . . . do what I ask you to do."

"DO THEY INTEND TO INTERROGATE ME?"

"Yeah, I think so."

"TELL THEM I AM EAGER TO ANSWER THEIR QUESTIONS."

Kaveh told the people waiting outside to come in, including Sol Kaplan, Sevak Ghasabian (who went by "Dr. Sev" like he was some daytime talk show host), and Luciana Ortega, who was obviously shocked to see him but said nothing. Kaveh wasn't *shocked* to see her since he knew she worked here, but it was jarring to see her again nonetheless.

"Thank you for doing this," said Ghasabian to Kaveh, shaking his hand. He seemed to be the one in charge.

"This should be a learning experience for all of us," said Kaveh.

Everyone stood back, all of them looking at the two of them like he'd first looked at Cora and Ampersand, the single unit, Nikola the brain and Kaveh the voice.

"Is it true that of your entire Superorganism, only you have the ability to travel faster than light?" asked Ghasabian, looking at Nikola.

"I ALONE HAVE THE ABILITY TO TRANSVERSE COMPLEX MATTER THROUGH FOLDED SPACE INSTANTLY."

"Yes," said Kaveh. "He says it's a technology he alone developed; the Superorganism doesn't have it."

"It seems a bit far-fetched that only you have this technology," said Kaplan.

"THE STUDY OF THE TRANSMISSION OF MATTER THROUGH FOLDED SPACE WAS MY LIFE'S WORK ONCE I EXITED THE FIELD OF XENOBIOLOGY. AS YOU KNOW, I WAS A PART OF A GENETIC GROUP THE SUPERORGANISM PURGED, ONE YOU HAVE NAMED 'FREMDA.' BUT I ESCAPED BEFORE THEY COULD COMPLETE THEIR GENOCIDE AND TOOK MY KNOWLEDGE ELSEWHERE."

Kaveh repeated him. *Funny how that happens, isn't it?* he thought. *Even alien societies have brain drains.*

"If only you have the ability to fold space, what's to stop them from developing it?" asked Kaplan.

"THE SUPERORGANISM HAS PURGED ITSELF OF GENETIC DIVERSITY OUT OF FEAR AND XENOPHOBIA," said Nikola, and Kaveh repeated him. "WE WERE THEIR MOST UNIQUE AND DIVERSE GROUP THAT HAD BEEN BRED IN GENERATIONS. THE ONES WHO COULD INNOVATE ON MY LEVEL ARE ALL DEAD, AND I MADE SURE TO DESTROY

MY RESEARCH BEFORE I DEPARTED. THE SUPERORGANISM WILL NOT REPEAT MY SUCCESS."

"Scio told us that it was unlikely we would see any more Fremdan refugees," said Ghasabian. Apparently, he hadn't quite made the switch to "people names" yet.

"He says that's correct," said Kaveh. "He's an anomaly, and he came for Scio specifically. It is highly unlikely we will see others."

The group fractured into quiet murmurs, Kaplan and the military group whispering among themselves and the small ROSA crew doing likewise. Then Ghasabian stepped forward. "So with the rest of the Superorganism restricted to light speed travel . . . we can expect First Contact in two hundred years, at the soonest."

"HOW DO YOU SURMISE THAT NUMBER? IT IS NOT ACCURATE."

"He wants to know where you got that number," said Kaveh.

"Our understanding is that the Pequod Superorganism is approximately 98.65 light-years away, as several of the Fremda group have claimed," said Ghasabian.

"He says that distance is correct, but you're ignoring several other factors," said Kaveh.

"I SURMISE PERHAPS THAT YOU ASSUME OUR INFORMATION IS RESTRICTED BY THE SPEED OF LIGHT, AS YOURS IS?"

A frost had bloomed at the bottom of Kaveh's spine and was crawling upward. "He says, you assume their ability to transmit information travels at light speed, same as ours,"

He could see the frost begin to bloom in Ghasabian, as well. Even Kaplan's mask was starting to slip. "We did assume that," said Ghasabian.

"THE SUPERORGANISM HAS POSSESSED THE TECHNOLOGY TO INSTANTLY TRANSMIT ELECTROMAGNETIC WAVES THROUGH SPACE-FOLD FOR THOUSANDS OF YEARS. THIS TECHNOLOGY IS ANCIENT TO US. EVEN OUR SISTER SPECIES, WHOM YOU CALL PHYSETERINE, POSSESSES THIS TECHNOLOGY. WE HAVE BEEN ABLE TO INSTANTLY TRANSMIT INFORMATION OVER GREAT DISTANCES FOR MILLENNIA." Kaveh repeated him, his words slowing as the frost crept up his spine, into his chest.

The muscles in Ghasabian's jaw strained, his already tight skin seeming to draw in on itself. "One hundred years, then."

"HOW DO YOU SURMISE THAT NUMBER? IT IS NOT ACCURATE."

"He says . . . that's not right, either."

"Please explain," said Kaplan.

"He says that, the locus of the Superorganism is only that—the locus. Their Superorganism is not concentrated only in one place. They've explored the entirety of this spiral of the galaxy. There are Similars traversing great distances at all times. There are limbs of the Superorganism far closer than those one hundred light-years."

"How close?" asked Kaplan, his voice the edge of a knife.

"He doesn't know," said Kaveh, the frost now constricting his throat. The temperature in the room felt like it had dropped ten degrees. "Ampersand and Obelus were about seventeen light-years away when they intercepted Čefo's message revealing his location on Earth. Nikola was thirty-one light-years away. Who knows what's closer?"

"THEY KNOW," said Nikola. "THE ENTIRE SUPERORGANISM, FROM THE LOCUS TO COLONIES TO OUTPOSTS. THEY KNOW WHAT HAS HAPPENED HERE. THEY KNOW WHO IS TAKING REFUGE HERE. THEY KNOW THAT A SPECIES THAT HAD BEEN CLASSIFIED AS TOOL-USING ANIMALS IS IN FACT ADVANCING AT A TERRIFYING PACE, AND THEY KNOW THAT THE XENOBIOLOGIST WHO HAD, AFTER LONG STUDY, CLASSIFIED THIS ADVANCING SPECIES AS TOOL-USING ANIMALS IS ONE OF THOSE TAKING REFUGE HERE. HOW ODD IT WILL SEEM TO THEM THAT THE XENOBIOLOGIST WHO HAD ERRONEOUSLY CLASSIFIED AN ADVANCING CIVILIZATION AS NOTHING MORE THAN TOOL-USING ANIMALS WOULD TAKE REFUGE WITH SAID ADVANCING CIVILIZATION. AND THAT THIS ADVANCING CIVILIZATION HAS FAR MORE IN COMMON WITH OUR PHYSETERINE SISTER SPECIES THAN IT DOES WITH OUR OWN.

"BUT IF YOU HAD ASSUMED YOU WOULD NOT SEE ANY RESPONSE FROM THE SUPERORGANISM IN YOUR LIFETIME, YOU WERE WRONG. THEY KNOW. THEY KNOW EVERYTHING. THEY ARE COMING."

A Single Photo Shows the Best and Worst of Humanity
By Skylar Baxter

There are photographs that are impossible to forget, searing themselves into our collective consciousness. One man standing his ground in front of a column of tanks in Tiananmen Square. Firefighters turning their hoses on civil rights protesters in Birmingham, Alabama. This is such a photo.

A woman is planted on the ground, hands in the air as she uses her body as a shield. Behind her are two collapsed figures, and in front of her is the thing she is protecting them from, a man pointing his handgun straight at her. Her body is the only thing between the gunman and two incapacitated ETIs.

According to reports, the woman is Cora Sabino, advocate for alien personhood and daughter of journalist and *The Broken Seal* founder Nils Ortega.

The now-famous photograph was taken Saturday during a rally organised by the Third Party in downtown Los Angeles to protest misinformation allegedly propagated by the American government. The demonstration turned violent after the sudden arrival of two ETIs, both of whom were incapacitated by an EMP device smuggled into the protest by far-right group the Gadsden Line. The EMP also shorted out all mobile phones and digital cameras within a three-block radius. But photographer Amalie Marandet was lucky to have brought an analogue camera.

Marandet said that she came only to photograph the rally and was not a participant, but never expected it to be the first time the world saw a living ETI. "I don't think I'd ever been as terrified as when it appeared. Even from a hundred feet away, it was just enormous," Marandet told BBC News.

Despite her terror Marandet stayed on the scene.

"[The ETI] was looking at Jano Miranda, but it wasn't acting aggressively, and there were several other people interacting with it. One guy was even touching it, and it seemed to me that the ETI must have seen Miranda's speech as a sort of invitation, and wasn't there to hurt anyone. It didn't seem to realise that this could be a dangerous situation."

But the image of Sabino shielding the ETIs has become a focal point in the debate about alien personhood, with many social media users seeing the photo as capturing a moment that could have led to a disastrous beginning to humanity's relationship with possible alien civilizations.

"Everything about her posture shows her humanity—her facial expression, the way she stands her ground. The gunman wants to destroy this thing he doesn't know anything about or understand, and she is the only thing standing in the way. We see the best and worst of humanity in this photo," wrote Facebook user Trystan Pease.

"This photo will be in history books."

Sabino has not given any comment to the press after the photo was taken, but did give an interview on *The Hot Seat with Satomi Mack* on Friday advocating against the Third Option. One specific remark Sabino made has drawn attention, in which Mack asked her to describe some personality traits of the ETI she had interactions with and Sabino responded, "He likes the ocean."

Some speculate on social media that one of the two ETIs in the photo and the one Sabino is describing are the same.

"I've already seen conspiracies about mind control, but based on her expression in the picture alone, I don't believe it," wrote Facebook user Claire Salz. "You can't mind control the fear on her face. What it looks like to me is that she threw herself between the alien and the gun, because she knew the alien, and she wanted to protect it."

Cora jerked her head up, having almost nodded off again. She checked her phone—it had turned into Monday at some point and was now around 5:00 A.M. *Go home,* they said. *Get some sleep.* If she went home, it was nightmares. It was nightmares here, too, but the sleep was so thin and halting that she generally woke from them before too long, roused by the clacking of shoes in the hallway or by human voices.

She looked down at Ampersand, still roosting in the same position he'd stayed in for the last few days—limbs tucked under him, head on the floor and tilted at a ninety-degree angle, dark, unfocused eyes half-lidded. They'd brought in a foam top for a mattress to act as bedding, but that was the only material situation that had improved. It was still too fucking bright, still too fucking cold. He wasn't responding. His mental processes were tapped out. He was done.

Did I do this to you? The horror of the situation had been bad enough, and the memory of it was both foggy and painful at the same time, but how much had one's fear amplified the other's?

Did my terror filtering into you do this to you?

She brushed her fingers along the ridge over his eye, along the crest on the back of his head. Those were sensory organs, she now knew, designed for picking up electromagnetic waves and sound. Normally, if she touched them, there was some reflex, like a touch-me-not plant that closed its leaves when touched, they would contract a little. But now the air around his body was so thick, the shield so strong. There was no reflex.

How much of this is me? How much of this is you?

It didn't matter, she knew. What was done was done, and besides, she knew it was happening organically inside both of them—neither was making the other be like this.

I don't think I'm going to survive this, she thought, not for the first time. *Is this my thought or yours?*

Same as it always is—it's ours.

The door opened, and Cora didn't turn to see who it was. Sol again, she assumed.

"Hey, troublemaker."

She turned, surprised to see Kaveh there. She'd been so worried about him at first, afraid they were detaining him illegally like they had her family, but by now, she'd almost forgotten about him.

"How's he doing?" he asked, shutting the door behind him. His normally voluminous hair was flat from days without a shower, and there were dark circles under his jade eyes. Guilt began writhing in her like a squid, reminding her that this was her fault. She had put him in this position, she had asked him to remove Enola, and he had. People were dead because of her. Kaveh being put in danger, Ampersand's deterioration, the lives of those people, all of it. All of it was her fault.

"Are you okay?" he asked.

She sat up. Of course she wasn't okay. What about this was okay? The scaffolding of her entire being was threatening to collapse. "Yeah."

He put his hands in his pockets and approached her like she was some contaminated thing. "Really? You don't look okay."

"I'm just . . . I'm so sorry."

"It could have been way, way worse. I could've ended up in a cell forever. But it turns out, I'm useful. It's a good thing that there is a precedent for alien interpreter. Even if being alien interpreter means to be the bearer of . . . existentially bad news," he added, rolling on the balls of his feet.

How can I make this up to you? she thought. *What can I possibly give you that can make this up to you? You have everything. I have nothing.*

"How bad?" she asked.

"Pretty bad." He cocked his head. "Was that your first time getting a gun pointed at you?"

Guns are nothing, she thought. *I've been on the wrong end of so much worse than guns.* "Yeah."

"Can't say it was for me." He laughed uncomfortably. "Not my first, probably won't be my last. Just remember, if you hear gunshots, that means it hasn't hit you yet, because bullets travel faster than the speed of sound. So if you hear the shot, that bullet hasn't killed you."

"Good to know," she said, looking at Ampersand. She couldn't even tell whether or not the wall was thick anymore. She couldn't feel anything from him. *I can't fix this,* she thought, and again, *I don't know if I'll survive this.*

"They're finally letting me go," he said. "I'm going to go home, get some sleep. But they want me back tomorrow to babysit Nikola. The plan might be to put them together when they think it's safe. Do you want me to give you a ride?"

"No," she said reflexively. She didn't want to go be alone in Riverside in her shitty apartment in an even shittier neighborhood.

He nodded to the inert Ampersand. "They're going to try tomorrow to see if Nikola can get a rise out of him."

"We'll have to be careful. I don't want 'getting a rise' to mean Ampe—Jude freaks out again."

"Jude. That's going to take some getting used to. It's good, though. I like it."

It was here that she put words to the hopelessness she'd been feeling, an echo of what Enola had told her out on that salt flat, a horrible but inescapable truth. There was no way to control this bond. There was no way to meter when one of them affected the other. The only way out was for one of them to die.

That can't be. That can't be all there is to it.

But it is, there is no other way.

It wouldn't be the worst thing in the world.

"Query," said Kaveh. "He's told you the end of the world is nigh, I assume."

"Just that their civilization is likely to look at ours as a threat and will want to stop us before we advance to their level."

"Right . . . did he give you any indication when that would happen?"

She shrugged. "Not in our lifetime. They're a hundred light-years away."

She looked at him, surprised to see a concerned expression on his face that bordered on confused. "Yeah, about that . . ."

"What?" she said, now on alert. "What is it?"

"Yeah, so . . ." He bit his lip, rolling on the balls of his feet. "I've got some bad news . . ."

· · · · ·

If the Pequod Superorganism was not restrained by the speed of light, the same could be said about the Mazandarani clan, because the news he relayed got circulated to his parents as soon as he said it. His cousin Nasser began blowing up his phone immediately:

jendehhhhhh what the FUCK??

Some thirty-six hours later, Kaveh had gotten some sleep, caught up on emails, made some phone calls, and affirmed to his family that yes, that had been him on TV, and yes, he had been detained for a very long time, and no, he could not talk about it. But don't worry! Really!

Some of that time had been devoted to the severest NDA he had ever seen, one that would charge him with espionage if he broke it. This presented some conflict with regard to his job. He'd spoken to his editors, telling them, "Please be patient." One was only too eager to defer to his judgment, the other was frustrated. Of course, they wanted something *right the fuck now.* He calmly told them both that he was restrained by legal considerations at the moment, leaving them to read between the lines about the NDA.

But it was Cora who was the real celebrity, the mystery girl who had thrown herself between an alien monster and a man with a gun, and had become the subject of what quickly became the most widely circulated photograph in the world. The photographer had gotten a near-perfect shot, a shoo-in for a Pulitzer, with Cora in profile, her left arm raised in defense with her right arm trying to shield Ampersand's head, and the man with the gun. Kaveh would have been tempted to frame a copy if it hadn't been one of the most traumatic moments of her already trauma-laden life.

Out of concern for "Jude," they decided Tuesday was not the day to try Nikola's luck with his delicate condition. Nikola, like Ampersand before him, was careful about keeping communication to a minimum without his "advocate" around, meaning Kaveh spent a lot more time around him than anyone in any branch of the government would have liked. There was one guy who seemed to be some sort of military higher-up named Porter, who particularly hated having him around. He was one of those guys who seemed proud of the fact that he was a loud talker—he overheard the man asking Kaplan what "that camel-jockey muckraker" was still doing here.

Charming.

The next time he saw Cora, she was still alone in that observation room with her nonresponsive "symphyle." She had refused to leave the room, so they'd supplied her with a cot and some pillows. He noted there were also a few snacks around, some potato chips, some Combos, a half-consumed bottle of Mexican Coke. It was also here that he realized she was wearing the same pair of jeans she'd worn the night they first met, but that they were baggier than they had been a week ago. She was bordering on underweight.

Figuring he might as well take advantage of that stupid two-way mirror, he decided to spend a few minutes observing the situation, seeing how she interacted with him when no one was around before he barged on in. He didn't expect to be alone in the observation room, but he was surprised to find Luciana Ortega the only other person.

"Hi," he said, shutting the door behind him.

She turned, her rust-red hair bobbing as she did, as unsure what to do with him as he was with her. "Hey," she said. She had such a strange aesthetic with her big bronze hoop earrings and too-big teal cardigan swallowing her up; she looked like she was on her way to her night job teaching adults how to use pottery wheels.

"Have you noticed her losing weight?" he asked. "Like, a lot of it, really quickly?"

"Yeah," said Luciana, turning back to the mirror. "She's probably lost at least thirty pounds over the last few months. At first I thought she was doing it on purpose, but . . ."

"How's she been?"

"A mess, to be honest. I think we may need to drag her out of there. She's really upset about this whole 'Superorganism is on their way' thing."

He had to hand it to her, she had a knack for understatement. "What's she been doing?"

"Lately, she's been just angry. Like, 'Why didn't you tell me, why did you keep this from me, why do you keep doing this?'" Luciana sighed. "There is really a lot about their relationship that I do not understand."

You have no idea, thought Kaveh. "Does she know about the photo?"

"No, not yet. This situation with Scio, it's—"

"'Scio'?"

"It's his Esperanto code name," said Luciana, correcting her slipup. "Forgot we're supposed to dump those."

"What about names for the other ones?" asked Kaveh. "The other, what, twenty-four?"

"Twenty-three besides him. And, no idea. With the exception of the two that asked for asylum, they're not as pressing, so that's a—"

"A can kicked down the road, got it."

By this point, Cora had begun to shake Ampersand at the place where his arms met his midsection that could most closely be described as "shoulders," prompting Luciana to wince uncomfortably. Cora's words were mostly unintelligible, but he caught at least one *Why didn't you tell me?* in there.

"Where did 'Atheatos' come from?" he asked.

"It's a family name," said Luciana. "My grandmother, my mother's mother, was Greek."

"Oh," he said, a little surprised. He'd thought both of Nils's maternal grandparents were German; he didn't think that Grandpappy Stahl, an officer in the army of the Third Reich, would be caught dead marrying one of those swarthy southern Europeans. Best to keep that observation to himself. It was a strange, uncomfortable truth that all of Nils's colleagues knew about but no one talked about. He had to assume the same was true of the whole Ortega family, who only existed because an ancestor had decided to duck out on the Nuremberg trials.

"You know why she chose it? Atheatos?"

"No idea."

He frowned, and that irritation he'd been feeling toward Luciana for a while came bubbling back up. He'd wondered what the hell her problem was, why they were watching her niece shake an alien and beg for him to talk to her, to get up, to wake up, like she was an animal and not a human being who desperately needed support, and whose family was turning a blind eye to her suffering.

He decided to give her the benefit of the doubt. Maybe there was another side to this. "Why . . . don't you guys talk anymore?"

"We talk," she said, too quickly.

"Not like you used to, she told me."

"Nils . . . doing what he did," she said, her eyes sliding down to the ground. "Cutting ties with all of us, dedicating his life to *The Broken Seal* at all costs, destroyed . . . so much of our lives. Meant Demi and the kids had to depend on my mom, and now that she's in mid-stage dementia, she doesn't have any compunction about the fact that she blames me and Demi, but mostly Demi, for Nils leaving since Nils is incapable of doing wrong by virtue of that Y chromosome. But then the Fremda Memo happened and I got implicated, and last year was just . . . a series of dominoes falling."

"What do you mean, 'implicated'?"

"I told Cora I didn't have anything to do with the Fremda Memo, because I didn't. I don't know how Nils found out about my connection to it. And I told Cora that, and she didn't believe me. And after that, what fragile trust we had was shattered. And it's been lying on the floor like so many broken pieces of windowpane ever since."

Kaveh leaned his head forward until she was forced to catch his eye. "But . . . you did tell Nils about the Fremda group."

She whipped her head to him, suddenly livid. "No, I didn't."

"Yes, you did," he said, trying not to provoke a fight. "Do you not remember when we first met?"

She looked at him like his hair had turned into snakes.

"It was back in 2002," he said. "Nils was in town visiting your mother with Cora and Felix and Olive, and you and me and Nils and a few of his other colleagues went out drinking in Culver City. Do you not remember that?"

Her expression of shock and disgust was transforming into one of dread. "I remember that night, yes, but I don't know what you're talking about."

"We were all . . . quite drunk, except Nils, who was on a mission. Nils knew ROSA worked in collaboration with the CIA; he thought you were working in covert black ops. We were already working on digging up the dirt that would eventually get Kaplan transferred to ROSA. Nils even told me before we went out he was going to try to get you hammered so you'd fess up. And he badgered you all night, started getting more and more aggressive. Then at some point, you two were alone in the bar, and you told him the truth to get him off your back. Nils told me, you did it in this jokey way, like, 'Nils, it's aliens!' but he could tell there was some truth to it. You included some details that felt too specific to be a joke. So he spent the next several years looking into it."

Luciana looked away from him, as though some long-buried memory was finally beating at the lid of the coffin she'd entombed it in, clawing at its encasement, demanding to be freed. He had some sympathy. It didn't excuse her behavior toward Cora, but he had experienced many, many blackouts in his day. "Don't you remember?"

Breaking glass pierced the silence before Luciana could respond. They both looked into the room through the two-way mirror to see that Cora had broken the bottle of Coke in half like she was in a bar fight, and was on her feet like she was about to attack Ampersand. Then she took the broken glass, and sliced down the flesh of her wrist in one fast, confident stroke.

Kaveh was out of the observation room before thought could connect with action, both he and Luciana bolting for the entrance to the main room. He barely caught what happened, but even in the split second it had his full attention, he caught the arterial blood spatter that shot out from her like a water gun. She obviously hadn't expected to get the artery on the first try, but she had, and she grabbed her wrist to stem the blood flow, dropping the rest of the bottle, which shattered on the cold steel floor.

Kaveh had rounded the corner by the time Ampersand roused himself, had almost reached the door before time stopped. He saw through the glass in the door Cora's look of shock, of terror of what she had done, her right hand clasped firmly on her left as she backed away from the creature, now on his feet, now standing over her, claws spread like briars. Kaveh tried to reach for the door, but he couldn't move. He saw Ampersand grab Cora around the midsection in a violent, fluent movement like a mantis grabbing its prey.

Then, every square inch of the two-way mirror that lined the room bloomed into blackness like film stock melting on a projector, charring the glass as if it were made of plastic, and there was a low-frequency hum, so low he could more feel than hear it, that rattled his bones. Kaveh continued to reach for the door, but couldn't move, could hardly breathe. He heard Luciana cry out, but she was similarly frozen in place.

Then the low-frequency hum slowed, the air thinned. He could breathe. He could move. He reached for the door, expecting it to be fused in place, but was surprised to find it unlocked. He flung the door open, and the first thing he saw was the blood spatter, which flowed in erratic lines like a Jackson Pollock. It took a moment for his conscious, logical mind to accept that it wasn't as much as it looked like, not even a pint of blood, and a pint spread out over the floor looked like far more than it actually was.

She was lying next to it, her eyes glassy and looking to the ceiling. Ampersand was back in his position in the corner, but tense now, a rattlesnake warning any on-comers to stay back. Kaveh didn't wait for permission but ran to Cora, Luciana at his side, grabbing the wrist that had only seconds earlier been gushing blood everywhere. There was blood still all over the wrist, up and down her arm, some even spurted onto her shirt and neck, but the gash was gone. There was no evidence that she had ever injured herself. What had she told him? *He's very good at repairing human bodies.*

He felt someone push him out of the way and nearly fought back, nearly tackled the person shoving him. It was Kaplan, who, without a word, picked Cora up and carried her out of the room.

· · · · ·

"Absolutely not," said Kaplan, barging into the doctor's small office, Kaveh right behind him.

Dr. Gene Hossein, the doctor on staff, took the phone away from his ear and slammed it onto the cradle. "She is a danger to herself, she's going. I'm calling in a 5150."

"And what the hell is she going to tell the doctors in a mental hospital?" demanded Kaplan. "'I stabbed myself to provoke a catatonic alien into fixing me'?"

"I don't care what she tells a mental ward psychiatrist," said Hossein. "And either way, if she goes into excruciating truthful detail, they won't believe her."

"She is the subject of the most widely circulated photograph in the world right now!" thundered Kaplan. "Yes, I think they might believe her."

"Anything she tells them will be protected by HIPAA," said Hossein. "And either way, to reiterate, after a point, we have to care more about the human cost than what does or does not get leaked."

Kaveh fumed, on some distant plane surprised that he agreed with Kaplan about something. He hated it when doctors dressed up covering their own asses with this "but think about the children" rhetoric. It was always so transparent. "You're putting her in a position where she either has to lie to a mental ward about why she is there, or get stuck in a mental ward because they don't believe why she is there."

"She does not have any scarring," said Kaplan. "There is no evidence of what happened. How can she tell them what happened if there is no physical evidence that it happened at all? Are you listening to yourself?"

"I'm making the call," said Hossein, storming out of his office into the surrounding area of cubicles. "She should never have been given clearance in the first place. If the ETIs are provoking her to make suicide attempts—"

"Whoa, this was not a suicide attempt," said Kaveh, resisting the urge to grab this man.

"What would you call that, then?"

"I call that a dramatic act to provoke a reaction, which it did," said Kaveh. "This was not a suicide attempt."

"It was an act of self-harm regardless," said Hossein, raising his voice to match Kaveh's. His eyes darted to the door that led to the hallway where he'd left Cora with Luciana not fifty feet away. They could likely hear every word of this. "It doesn't have to be an out-an-out attempt for me to declare that she's a danger to herself."

"And what good do you think it's going to do?" said Kaplan. "Do you think this is going to help her?"

"That's why this system is in place," said Hossein, flipping open his cell phone. "I'm making the call."

"You're just trying to cover your own ass," said Kaplan, moving uncomfortably close to Hossein, using his height to his advantage. He stood at least a head taller than Hossein. "You damn well know that involuntary commitment is only going to make her situation worse, not better."

"I'm making the call."

Kaplan closed his hand around Hossein's, clapping the cell phone shut. "And I'm pulling rank. No, you're not."

"I'm making the call."

"Don't make me beat the shit out of you, you fucking nerd," said Kaplan, his voice low and calm.

This visibly shook Hossein. A threat of violence from Kaplan, a guy

whose reputation among his contemporaries Kaveh could only imagine, was not on the level with a threat from any school-ground bully.

"I'm taking her home," said Kaveh, backing away. He looked out
through the window in the door into the hallway to make sure Cora
was where he'd left her.

"Okay," said Hossein, ripping his hand out of Kaplan's grip and shoving the phone into his pocket. "If she makes any more 'self-harm' attempts or, god forbid, suicide attempts, I want everyone in your agency
to know that it was you who overrode my decision, which you shouldn't
have the authority to do."

Kaplan cocked his head to the side, unable to resist the tiniest of
smirks. "Well, I shouldn't have the authority to do a lot of things I get to
do. If you want the ability to exact punitive extrajudicial measures, you
should quit the air force and join the agency."

Hossein stilled, and Kaveh could swear he saw the faintest of trem-
bles in the man's lower lip. Then Hossein turned and stormed into the
hallway, slamming the door behind him as he brushed right past Cora
and Luciana.

Once again, he was alone with Kaplan, and whatever fragile alliance
they had wafted away in the breeze. Kaplan turned to him, now ready to
turn his bully energy on Kaveh. "You're taking her home, huh?"

Kaveh tried to center himself, take a breath, do everything he could
not to escalate this situation further. "Would you rather take her?"

"Honestly, yeah." Kaplan studied him for a while, eventually shaking
his head with resignation. "I know what you're going to do. You're going
to milk her for all she's worth, wring her out until she's a dried-out husk,
then dump her on the side of the road. But I know she'd rather go with
you. It didn't take much for you to indoctrinate her against me."

"Dude, you treat her like shit! This doesn't have anything to do with
you waterboarding terror suspects. You treat her like garbage and then
act all surprised that she'd rather be with the person who's nice to her!"

Kaplan looked at him like he was making these accusations up out
of whole cloth. "I'm not the person who has everything to gain by exploiting her situation."

He resisted the urge to get violent. It was a terrible, terrible idea.
Kaveh, the egghead New York journalist who had lifted a weight maybe
five times in his entire life, taking a swing at a trained CIA operative

who had pulled god knows how many fingernails out of how many terror suspects. "I'm taking her home."

He moved toward the door, but Kaplan stepped into his path. "You think I'm a monster, don't you?"

Kaveh stopped, took a moment to choose his words. "What do you care what I think?"

Then he stepped around Kaplan, through the door and into the hallway. Cora was where he'd left her, sitting next to Luciana on a bench in the corridor, Luciana wearing the expression of an army wife who'd lost her husband and son on the same day, Cora next to her, knees drawn to her chest, blood still all over her clothes, looking like she'd just been dragged out of the killing fields of Cambodia. Neither of them had moved. Yep, she'd heard most of that conversation with Hossein, if not all of it.

She didn't look at him as he approached, and neither did Luciana. He squatted into her line of sight, slipping a hand into hers. "Will you come with me?"

"Are they going to put me in an institution?"

"Not unless you think you should go to one. Do you?"

She shook her head in sharp, jerky motions, her now-bedraggled Hollywood starlet hair falling into her face. "Please, no."

"Okay, come on," he said, standing up, keeping his hand in hers. "I'm going to take you home with me."

Cora stood up, that shell-shocked expression taking on a hint of gratitude. Luciana started to move like she knew this was inappropriate, that she should be the one looking after Cora, not Kaveh, a man she hardly knew. But she didn't say anything, didn't even get up.

For perhaps the first time in his adult life, Kaveh had no clue what he should be doing.

He wanted to touch her, or at least say something to improve the situation, but she seemed so brittle, holding her hands together so tightly on the drive back to his house that they'd have broken the skin if she had any fingernails left. Once home, he tried to ply her with food, anything he had on hand (which wasn't as much as he usually did, since these digs were more temporary than his New York apartment). He offered her Pirate's Booty, an apple, a granola bar, anything he had in his pantry, but she looked at all of it like he was asking her to eat live insects.

"Please, eat something."

"I'm not hungry."

"Please, for me?"

Eventually, she conceded to a DiGiorno pizza heated in the oven, or at least a small part of one. He watched her chew it like it was made of rubber, gnashing her teeth painfully. After finishing about one and a half flimsy slices, she said, "Please, don't make me eat any more."

It went against every instinct in his body to yield to her wishes. "Okay. Let's get you cleaned up, and I'll, uh . . . get the guest room set up for you."

He led her by the arm upstairs, and she followed like he was leading her to a ritualistic human sacrifice he'd neglected to mention he was planning. He took her into his room, turning on the fireplace, because it made things cozy and it *was* cold out, and ushered her mechanically through the strange motions. *I have some extra clothes you can wear. And a bathrobe I pilfered from my cousin's hotel. Master bathroom or guest bathroom? Master bathroom is nicer and bigger. Use the master bathroom.*

She looked at him with an expression that was at the same time pure need and pure hopelessness. What to do with that?

Fuck it.

He pulled her close into a gentle but firm hug. She allowed it, but stayed tense. It was like hugging a bundle of dry sticks.

"It'll be okay," he said, the universal code for "I have no clue what to say." But she needed to know that he wasn't pushing her away; he was respecting her boundaries, but that didn't mean he didn't *want* to touch her, to comfort her, to—

Oh, boy, let's not go there.

He stepped back, tilting her head to meet his gaze, and he gave her the most supportive smile he was capable of giving. As she showered, he took a seat in the overstuffed chair that occupied one corner of the master bedroom, which up until this point he had never sat on, listening for anything unusual—glass breaking, an escape attempt, alien screeching.

After the shower ended, he heard his hair dryer clicking on, and hoped it wasn't being used to mask some other sounds she didn't want him to hear. *Get the guest room ready,* he thought. *It's basically ready, isn't it? What do I need to do, provide turndown service? She probably doesn't even know what that is. She could sleep in here. She should sleep in here.*

Then he wondered, why all this fretting over temptation? She was an adult, and besides, she wasn't that pretty.

Only she *was* that pretty, she was just the kind of pretty society had taught people like him to ignore. Her survival strategy in the face of *The Broken Seal* had apparently been to disappear, doing all she could to distance herself from Nils, literally and emotionally. Nils, his on-and-off collaborator, whom he had helped make an international celebrity. Dear God, but this situation was so fucked *up*!

The bathroom door cracked open, and she slipped into the bedroom, hair blown dry and fluffy, wearing his pilfered white hotel bathrobe. "Thank you," she said, her voice regaining a bit of strength.

"You feel better?"

"I think so."

He stood up from his chair and approached her, restraining the urge to run his fingers through her clean hair. "I guess we should get ready for bed."

She took another step toward him, a little too close to be appropriate but not so close that they were touching, looking up at him with eyes so big they were almost cartoonish. "Wh . . . where do you want me?"

What a perfect way to phrase that, he thought. What room do you want me in? Which bed do you want me in? *You know where I want you.*

As if reading his mind, her eyes darted to his bed, then back to him, and she seemed to shrink a little. A distant voice in his head reminded him that now was not the time to do this. This wasn't how it was supposed to go. They'd acknowledged their mutual attraction, and they were both adults, but it had been such a terrible few days. But wasn't that all the more reason to go for it? Release for both of them? After all they'd been through, didn't they deserve this? Didn't *he* deserve this?

Her cheeks were flushed, and it seemed like her lips were pinker and plumper than they had been a few seconds ago. Such a terrible few days, and maybe now wasn't the time. Maybe they should wait a couple of days and see if they still felt the same way after things had cooled down a bit.

His mouth moved to hers like it was drawn by a magnet, his fingers sliding inside the robe and roving all over her skin, pressing her body to his. In two seconds, the robe was on the floor, in five seconds, she was lying supine on the bed, and he was straddling her, kissing her hungrily. There was no reason not to do this. She had offered herself up to him again and again, unambiguously and without reservation. He wasn't thinking now that the dam had burst, his body possessed by a surge of adrenaline and testosterone telling him he needed this, he *deserved* this.

The thought only made him more aggressive, and he propped himself up so he could get a look at her. She was stiff, her hands balled into fists by her shoulders, her whole body trembling. He had planned on being careful, and gentle, and meticulous, not busting down her walls like the Kool-Aid Man.

"Oh, honey," he said, the fires in him doused slightly when he saw what his recklessness had done. "You're shaking."

"I'm sorry," she said. "Just excited. Don't stop."

"Excited?" Under normal circumstances, he would have believed her without question, but it was hard to tell whether this was excitement or fear, especially when every chemical in his animal brain was telling him, *Of course this is excitement. She wants you to fuck her brains out!*

He urged her up the length of the bed, propping her head on his pillows to make her more comfortable and so he could get a better look at her. Her slender frame, her pert little breasts, no scars anywhere. She really was beautiful. A cursory look farther south, and he saw that she had shaved everything, and he arched an eyebrow. *Well, that would explain the suspiciously long shower,* he thought.

He looked at her, her form still so tense with her arms pulled to her ribs and her wrists practically glued to her shoulders. She looked at him like he was going to swallow her whole. He smiled sweetly, and went back in to kiss her, more gently this time. "Relax," he whispered between kisses. She didn't. "It's just me. Do you want to be with me?"

"Yes."

He pulled back, studying her. "Are you sure?"

She nodded eagerly.

He drew his hands over her stomach, caressing her skin, feeling its warmth. He felt her breath hitch, and she pushed his hands away from her midsection.

"I'm sorry," she stammered. "I didn't . . . I didn't mean . . ."

"It's okay, I don't have to touch you anywhere you don't want to be touched."

"I do, I do want it, I don't—"

"Don't what?"

Her eyes glassed over, the whites tinged with pink. Now it wasn't nervousness in her expression, or even fear, but sadness. Unmistakable sadness. "I don't want to be like this."

Then it connected, what she'd told him. *He tore me in half . . . He ripped me apart . . . He skewered me, ripped my guts out.* This was a trauma response. A confusing mix of guilt and arousal flooded his system, the sense that she was categorically not okay combined with a powerful urge to make it better, a powerful sense that *he* could make it better.

"We can work up to that, there's no rush."

She half opened her mouth, perhaps to insist that he could touch her anywhere he wanted, including her stomach, because that's what a normal, un-traumatized person would do, but he covered her mouth with his before she could say anything. He kissed her for a while longer, holding her close until the ice around her melted a bit, and she began to relax. He took his time, getting her used to his touch and taste and smell. Eventually, his fingers found their way down between her thighs. *Well, her body is certainly eager,* he thought. *And if the mind is willing . . .*

Somewhere between his disrobing and positioning himself between her legs, she had iced back up again. He continued to go slowly, but when he tried to enter her, every muscle in her body drew tight, and he held back when her face contorted in pain.

"I'm sorry," she said. "I'm trying, I'm trying."

"Shh," he said, running his fingers over her cheeks, her temples. "Don't try." He had the thought, *Perhaps your body is trying to tell you something?*

As if in response to that thought, she looked him in the eye and put nervous fingers through his hair. "I don't want to be like this."

"I . . ." What to say to that? *I know you don't want to be like this, but you are like this.* He was torn between wanting to ease her into it and halting the proceedings altogether. "I don't want you to do anything you don't want to do."

"But I *do* want it, I do. I . . . I really like you."

Oof. Something in the way she said that loosed a tiny arrow right into his heart. She put her hands around his neck, and then ran her fingers through his hair, awkward, mechanical, like it was choreography she was still in the process of learning. He leaned forward, kissing her long and slow, as if by doing so he could psychically transfer his calm energy into her.

He pulled back to look at her, and she smiled, seeming a *little* more relaxed. "You're a really good kisser," she said.

He laughed softly. "Thank you." He kissed her again, doing a daisy chain down her cheek, then her neck. He held her body to his, her muscles still taut like a belt that had been pulled too tight. "Just relax," he whispered into her neck. He could feel her trying to cooperate. "Do you want me?"

"Yes," she said without hesitation. "Please."

"Do you trust me?"

At this, there was hesitation. She swallowed before responding, "Of course."

He propped himself up on his elbows so he could look into her eyes, gently tracing the outline of her face with his thumb as he did. "Then I'm yours."

Kaveh snapped awake at his phone ringing. His *landline* ringing, which meant it was probably one of his parents. He groaned, his lower back a little sore from last night's activity, and he stretched out his wings, slapped his hands on the phone, and dragged it to his ear. "Hello?"

"Mazandarani." Sol Kaplan's nasal sub-tenor.

"How the hell did you get this number?" Funny thing about Kaplan— much as he hated Kaveh, he was one of the few people outside the Iranosphere who pronounced his name correctly.

"How do you think? He's asking for you."

"What?"

"'Nikola.' He's asking for you."

Kaveh rubbed his eyes and sat up. "How?"

"We have computer keyboards, dude. He figured out how to use them pretty quickly. He's a lot more . . . eager than we're used to."

"I'll be there in a few hours."

"We'd prefer you get here now."

"Are you paying me?"

The human toenail on the other end of the line hesitated. "No."

"Then he can wait. I'll be there in a few hours." He hung up without another word and turned around. There was his new partner, the roiled-up little ball, looking for all the world like she expected him to throw her out on the streets of Yorba Linda without even letting her get dressed.

He'd fallen asleep with her in his arms, seemingly relaxed and content and safe and trusting with her new fuckbuddy. He had naively assumed that mood would transfer over into the morning light, but nope, the roiled-up little ball was back, naked under the sheet, wrapped around her pillow like a koala clinging to a tree.

"How are you feeling?" he asked.

"I'm sure I've felt worse. I can't remember when, but I'm sure I've felt worse."

!!!!!

Then he remembered she likely wasn't referring to getting raw-dogged by an aging gen Xer for several hours but the fact that she had sliced herself open with a bottle of Mexican Coke, had that injury forcefully repaired by an alien cyborg, and nearly gotten herself involuntarily committed into one of California's fine, fine institutions for drug addicts and suicide attempts.

She glanced at him, saw his expression. "I didn't mean . . . Not you. You're . . . You, um . . ."

"I'm what?" He'd said it playfully, an invitation to tell him, *Yes, I'm feeling kind of bowlegged, but I had fun. Didn't we have fun? Ho ho, what fun we had.*

But she looked at him like she was a serf who'd offended her liege lord. "I'm sorry. You've been kind to me. I'm sorry."

He frowned, now really coming to grasp how poorly he'd thought this through. What now? He never had any trouble getting laid, but he hadn't had any serious emotional attachments since before he went to rehab. Hell, recovery itself had precluded it. *Don't start new relationships during the first year, and preferably the second.* Thinking he was too good for that rule had led to one minor relapse around month three of recovery, so he'd behaved and played by the rules after that. But he'd been sober for two years, so he was well out of the no-no zone now. But this didn't feel like the beginning of a relationship, it felt like . . .

A mistake?

Yeah, probably.

Regardless, he knew the deal here. This was a sensitive case, and he had told himself that his intent was to do no harm, and fucking her without at least a "Sooo . . . see you later?" would send a message he did not want to send.

He took a quick shower, blew his hair dry, brushed his teeth, and threw on clean boxer briefs and an undershirt. When he returned to his bedroom, she was sitting up in the middle of the bed, still naked except for the sheet she had pulled over her legs, looking out of the glass-paned door that led to his balcony. She had her arms wrapped around her knees and her back hunched over like a *C,* her spine visible like tire treads through her translucent skin. He resolved to make sure she ate something before he left.

She turned to look at him, and her eyebrows popped, like she'd just remembered an appointment she was late for. "I, um . . . I don't have any money."

"What?"

"I mean, I should probably go get some Plan B, is all, but I think it's like eighty dollars. I guess I could go to the Planned Parenthood. I think it's free there, or sliding scale. I've never been."

"Oh no, honey, no!" He slapped a hand to his forehead, feeling every inch the scumbag that he feared he was. "I am sorry. That was irresponsible and shitty and . . . I should have communicated better. I should have asked permission to do it without a condom. But you don't need Plan B. I'm sterile. I cannot get you pregnant. I should have told you last night before I did anything."

"Oh," she said. Not annoyed or upset or even relieved. Just, *Oh, of course, sure, whatever you say.* "What makes you sterile?"

"I . . . had a vasectomy," he said in an uncomfortable singsong.

"Why?"

"Well, to be honest, that decision is a relic from a different time when I was a different person!" He laughed. He always needed to laugh at this part. "I did get someone pregnant, and you can guess how that ended, but at the time, I would have rather removed the risk factor than change my behavior. But as you can see, even sober, I'm still a sloppy, irresponsible moron!"

"It's okay." She said it with a hint of confusion, like she didn't understand what he had done wrong or why he was apologizing. "Do you regret doing it?"

"Honestly, no. But I do have some swimmers sitting frozen in a sperm bank on Long Island. So if I have a sudden and uncharacteristic change of heart one day, I left the option available."

He circled the bed, running his fingers along the duvet, until he was standing in front of her, blocking her view of the balcony.

She was still all nerves. "I guess I, um . . . I guess I should go home."

"Should you?"

She shrugged.

He crawled into bed, straddling his legs on either side of her. "Where is home?"

She turned around to face him, keeping her knees up to her chest like a barricade. "Riverside, I guess."

"You guess?"

"I mean, I just . . . I can't stand the thought of going back to Torrance. I don't want to talk to my mom."

He rested his elbows on his knees, stroking her cheek. Her skin was so soft. He was already restraining the urge to pounce on her right now, feel that soft skin against his entire body. "That's perfectly understandable."

"And I know they aren't done with me. Only thing I can do is just wait."

"There isn't anything for you in Riverside. Even if Ampersand starts doing the thing where he won't talk except through you, they've already moved them to Los Alamitos, and they won't move them back to Riverside because of Esperas."

She winced, like tears were threatening to break down the door. "I don't have anywhere else to go."

"How are you planning on paying rent? Do you have any savings?"

"No," she whispered.

"And it's not like you can go get a job at the local Panera."

"I don't know what else to do."

He leaned forward, trying to get her to look at him. "Do you really want to be alone?"

"No, but . . . I can't ask anything else from you."

"You didn't ask. I'm offering." He ran his fingers through her messy hair. "Let me take care of you for a little while. Let your lease go; you don't need to go back to Riverside if there's nothing for you there. You don't have to talk to anyone you don't want to talk to. It's been an insane few weeks; you need some time to recover. Let's see how this plays out. Let's see what happens in the world. Let's see what Ampersand does. In the meantime, you can stay with me. Let's give it a couple of weeks to recuperate, then we can figure out what our next steps are."

"You aren't going back to New York?"

"Not anytime soon." He cupped her cheeks, lifting her face to meet his gaze. "Would you like to stay with me?"

He felt a slight tremor run through her. "Yes."

"Okay. While I'm gone today, go get your things. I'll set up the guest room for you."

"Oh."

"Oh?"

"Do you prefer sleeping alone?"

"No, I just thought you might prefer your own space, not have to share a room with an elderly foghorn." She kept looking at him with those pleading eyes, and he amended, "But I'm not about to say no to a cute girl in bed with me every night."

Carefully, like she was afraid he might bite, she moved to embrace him. He grabbed her and pulled her into a tight hug, his body surging with endorphins. Without thinking, he pushed her onto her back, and moved himself on top of her, eliciting a surprised "Mph!" At first, she was the icicle, cold and tense and immobile, then swung hard in the other direction, throwing her arms around his neck and crushing her lips to his. He opened his eyes and saw that hers were already wide open. He broke the kiss and backed off.

"Are you okay?" he whispered.

"Yes!" she said, almost cutting him off. "You just surprised me."

He smiled and decided to meter himself, kissing her cheek, then the skin next to her ear, then the skin of her neck, inch by inch, moving down to her collarbone. "Do you like it?"

"Yes," she said, drawing in another surprised breath as his mouth found one of her breasts, and his hand found the other. "I just . . ."

"Hmm?"

"N-nothing. I like being with you."

Engines fired up, he threw the rest of the sheet off her and tore off his underwear. This time, she was much more pliant, all soft and wet and warm and tight, and felt so, so good. He made sure she came before he did this time, then just relaxed inside her for a while, savoring the feeling of her body under his. He reassured her all the while that she didn't need to worry in the short term, that *mi casa es su casa,* that he'd keep an eye on Ampersand and Nikola, and that more importantly, he'd take care of her.

After all, somebody needed to.

Kaveh made it to Los Alamitos about three hours after Kaplan called him. They still had not reintroduced Nikola to Ampersand, but today's activity instead was in some ways even more harrowing—introducing Nikola to Esperas and Brako, the two who apparently saw state-sanctioned killing as the cure to all ills? Well, cool. If nothing else, that meant they probably got on well with their buddies at the CIA.

When he asked, Ghasabian told him that they were still so-called because Esperas and Brako (and all the rest of the Fremda group) had not been rechristened from their Esperanto code names. Still, Kaveh got the impression that Kaplan, Ghasabian, and their ilk still didn't quite see them as people. They were "introducing" them as if Nikola were a wild-caught elephant in a zoo being introduced to a herd that had been bred in captivity.

They had ported Nikola to Riverside in an armored car and paired the two of them together, like Nikola was the pilot and Kaveh his headset. Then the ROSA social workers and military entourage directed the two of them to the conference room. Nikola seemed happy to be here, but Kaveh's heart was in his throat. He wondered how Cora had handled this; he'd never exactly gotten the chance to shadow her on interpretation detail.

The room the meeting was intended to take place in seemed specially designed for this purpose, white and sterile and about half the size of an Olympic swimming pool. It had a large, kidney-shaped conference table off to one side, leaving half the room empty, which made sense considering these subjects that neither sat like a human nor had use for tables.

Before long, Sol Kaplan and Brigadier General "that camel-jockey muckraker" Porter arrived, and a few minutes after that, a handler walked in the other two amygdalines they were scheduled to meet: Esperas, spindly and beady-eyed compared to Ampersand and Nikola, about the height and size of your average NBA player, and Brako, the "Similar," the biggest one he had yet seen, clocking in somewhere in the eleven-foot range. Suddenly, Nikola's nine-ish feet felt downright twee.

Brako stood in front of Esperas, his body language unmistakably defensive. Nikola was carefully moving his body in a way that Kaveh had never seen him do, his head down, almost perpendicular to the floor, with his arms up against his side almost like chicken wings, the crest on his head completely deflated like a flaccid balloon.

"Ask if they are communicating," said Porter.

Kaveh nearly rolled his eyes and restrained the urge to remind the man that Nikola did not need him to repeat everything to the com-puter à la Sigourney Weaver in *Galaxy Quest*, as Nikola could understand English just fine.

"He says Esperas is understandably leery of him," said Kaveh. "This is him trying to de-escalate."

The de-escalation process went on for at least another two minutes, with Nikola slooooowly, like molasses running off a spoon, lowering himself to the floor and into a roosting position. Once there, he kept his eyes down.

"He says this is a submissive posture."

"We've seen it before," said Ghasabian.

The submissive posture continued for some time, with the two parties on each side of the room, communicating silently through their "network language." Then something happened with Esperas, who came out from behind Brako, seeming excited. Kaveh figured that he was not excited in a fun way.

"He says he's letting them know the situation with Obelus," said Kaveh. "They're not happy."

"Can you please elaborate?"

Nikola waited a few moments, then said, "WE ARE COMMUNICAT-ING."

Kaveh backed off. "We need to be patient. There is a 'heated' conversation going on here."

Spoken Pequod-phonemic ripped through the air like torn paper, and Kaveh's nerves were so worked up, the sound caused him to jump. Esperas's voice was a loud, staccato percussive language, and the translation appeared on the flat-screen behind him:

[Why are we only now being informed that stratocrat Similar Obelus is still alive?]

The bureaucrats, chief among them Kaplan and Ghasabian, retreated to deliberate their answer while Porter grimly eavesdropped. It took them a solid five minutes to agree to one, and Kaveh wondered if this was always what it was like, if every goddamn thing had to be pored over before an answer could be given.

"We were only made aware of the situation on the morning of Sunday, February 10," said Ghasabian. "We did not inform you, because we did not know."

[I had warned you, technocrat Oligarch Scio is diseased, damaged. You gave him the freedom to do as he pleased, which he has abused. He abused your trust and our goodwill that allowed him to his own devices. He deceived you as he deceived all of us.]

He noticed Nikola snap to attention, and Esperas fell silent. Kaveh knelt next to Nikola. "What's going on?"

"I AM REMINDING THEM THAT MY DEAR BELOVED IS MY SYM-PHYLE, AND THEREFORE MY CHARGE. I AM REMINDING THEM THAT THEY HAVE NO CLAIM OR SAY OVER HIS FATE."

Shortly, Esperas seemed to retreat, then he spoke.

[Where is Obelus's decommissioned Similar body?]

The bureaucrats retreated into themselves. Kaveh couldn't hear anything they were saying, but he could get the basic gist; they knew the answer to Esperas's question, obviously, but *should* they tell him?

After another few minutes, Ghasabian responded, "The recovered body is being held right now at the Doherty Security Complex in San Bernardino County." As he said this, he looked not at Esperas but at

Kaveh, who realized that he had just been exposed to the very height of top-secret information.

[Scio is dangerous, but Scio has been restrained. Obelus is far more dangerous, and Obelus has not been recaptured. Obelus must be recaptured.]

This time, the bureaucrats didn't take so long to offer up a response. "We are using every available arm of the U.S. military and intelligence apparatus to locate him."

[Any human-made apparatus is inadequate. You cannot protect us or yourselves from Obelus's subordinates who are hunting him. Obelus does not require his Similar body to evade human capture. My Similar must do the work of recapturing Obelus.]

While the bureaucrats deliberated this, Nikola added, "ON THIS POINT, ESPERAS AND I AGREE. IF THEY WILL NOT PERMIT ME TO FIND AND RECAPTURE OBELUS, THEY SHOULD PERMIT ESPERAS'S SIMILAR TO DO SO."

Kaveh stood up and looked at the tight mass of people behind him. "Nikola wants me to let you know that he agrees with Esperas. You should let Brako find him for you."

"And what about the other three Similars?" asked Porter, defense-mode activated.

"They think that the best bet is for you as a . . . polity to hand Obelus over to them, since he is apparently what they are after. The hope being that if you give them what they want, they'll leave and take Obelus home as they're ordered to do, and leave them and us to our horrible fate."

Porter glared at him, not amused, while the others deliberated among themselves for a response. Eventually, Ghasabian emerged. "We obviously cannot force you to do anything, but we would ask you to stay in our custody, and we would ask Nikola and Scio to do the same. If you would share intelligence with us as to how we can find and recapture Obelus, we would be grateful, but we cannot allow you to do it for us."

[Even lacking the body he used to cause such damage three months ago, with a smaller, less lethal body, his is an intelligence capable of incredible harm, both to us and to your civilization. Your military apparatus does not have the capability to track down any amygdaline that does not want to be found. My Similar does. Permit him to use your resources to find and recapture Obelus.]

"Thank you for your offer," said Ghasabian. "But we can neither permit nor endorse this. Please, at least until we have legislation regarding your legal status, we ask you to stay here."

Esperas seemed to contract and expand on himself like a breath, then without another word, he and Brako exited the room, and their handler followed. The bureaucrats behind him erupted into another burble of whispers.

"How about it?" Kaveh whispered to Nikola.

Nikola stood back up to his full height. "TELL THEM THAT I WILL BE COMPLIANT. BUT I DO NOT BELIEVE MY CONTRIBUTING INTELLIGENCE WILL BE ENOUGH. IF THEY WILL NOT PERMIT BRAKO THE FREEDOM TO DO SO, PERHAPS THEY WILL PERMIT IT TO ME. I WILL NOT BE SEEN BY ANY HUMAN EYES, AND I WILL KEEP THEM ABREAST OF MY MOVEMENTS."

"He really thinks there's no way for humans to track Obelus down. He thinks he should do it. He says he'll make sure no one sees him, and he'll keep you in the loop on what he's doing."

Ghasabian approached the two of them and knelt respectfully in front of Nikola. "We do not have the sufficient language to express our gratitude that you have been so forthcoming and communicative. But after Pershing Square, we cannot allow you free range to search for Obelus. Perhaps we are more advanced than you suspect."

"IMPRESS UPON THEM THAT I FEEL IT WILL BE A WASTE. I WILL SHARE WHAT I CAN, BUT THEY WILL NOT SUCCEED IN HIS RECAPTURE. ONLY WE CAN DO THAT, AND I FEAR THAT BY THE TIME THEY ALLOW US THE FREEDOM TO DO SO, IT WILL BE TOO LATE."

· · · · ·

Nikola requested that Kaveh ride with him in the armored car back to Los Alamitos, *alone,* if you please. It took some convincing that it was Nikola's request, and not his, before they would oblige.

"He needs a new surname," said Ghasabian, after Nikola had already been boarded. "The one Cora gave us, we can't use."

"Why not?"

"Atheatos is fine, but Celaeno apparently means 'the dark one' in Ancient Greek. It's the name of one of the harpies in *The Aeneid.* Cute joke, but we can't use it."

Kaveh laughed. "What did you have in mind?"

"Find out if he has a preference. If he doesn't, he'll be assigned a surname."

"What are they hoping for? Nikola Smith?"

Ghasabian didn't seem in the slightest bit amused. Clearly, this was a big point of contention. "Just find out if he has a preference. Try not to push him in any direction."

Kaveh arched an eyebrow. "So . . . what they're saying is, nothing 'ethnic.'"

Ghasabian drew his mouth into a thin line, then turned to go, his Captain Picard bald head shining in the afternoon sun.

The inside of the armored car was clearly designed for cargo, for giant bricks of gold bound for Fort Knox, not for human occupants (or alien, for that matter), and so both Kaveh and Nikola stayed awkwardly seated on the floor of the vehicle. There was plenty of room for both of them, but it did make it difficult for Kaveh, who slid around when the vehicle made any sharp turns.

"You've been very cooperative since Pershing Square," Kaveh observed not long after the car started moving. "Doing everything they ask you to do."

Nikola's bright eyes dimmed a bit, and the crest on the back of his head folded in. "I DO NOT WISH TO CAUSE MORE HARM."

"But if we're all doomed, anyway, why go along with this bureaucracy? Why worry about whether or not you hurt any humans? Why not just do whatever you want?"

"I SEE LITTLE HOPE IN THE LONG TERM. REGARDLESS, IF IT IS YOUR WISH THAT I STAY IN THEIR CUSTODY UNTIL THE MATTER OF OUR LEGAL STATUS IS RESOLVED, THEN I WILL COMPLY."

Kaveh smiled slyly. "There it is. *Little* hope. Not *no* hope."

Nikola's head tilted like a dog that had heard a strange noise. "You are unable to impregnate my little cousin. Why, then, do you mate with her?"

!!!!

Kaveh's jaw dropped. *What the hell?* "Uh . . . I . . . don't know if we are really alone at the moment. They might have surveillance on us. I can't talk about that."

"Why is that relevant? Would there be punitive measures if your government were to find out? Have you done something immoral? Have you done her harm?"

"No!" he snapped. "It's a private matter. It's none of their business. But no, it doesn't cause harm."

"Then why does it sound like she is in pain?"

WHAT THE FUCK YOU FUCKING PERVERT

Kaveh clapped a hand to his ear, the traitorous earbud that doubled as a microphone, and clenched his other hand in front of him as if he were squeezing an invisible neck, pleading with his eyes for Nikola to please, please *shut up!*

"I was concerned, and confused, because I did not think you of the disposition to harm her, and as symphyle-of-my-symphyle, I am bound to protect her. But I did not intervene, because of her repeated reassurance to you that she was not in pain, in fact multiple times requesting that you go harder—"

"Please, *stop!*" he said through clenched teeth, squeezing the invisible neck harder. "If you want, we can talk about it later when we know we aren't being surveilled. I'll tell you all about how that works. But *not now!*"

"Then perhaps we should contrive a way to speak in confidence, all while not antagonizing your government."

"Yes, I think that would be wise," he said, unclenching his jaw.

"I am abiding their wishes pending legal clarification of our status as persons in your country. You are complying with them for my sake, yet you do not trust them."

Kaveh relaxed. "No. I don't."

"Then why do you work with them?"

"Right now, I don't have much choice if I want access to you. But I suppose the truth is, I hope they can be better."

They rode in silence for a few minutes, Kaveh knowing he needed to talk about real subjects that affected their future, but already hung up on how to articulate how casual sex worked to an asexual alien cyborg. *Casual.* Was it casual? It hurt his heart to think of her as "casual." She needed more than casual. But given such a shaky starting point, how could this ever work out in the long term without him inadvertently hurting her? He had to go back to New York eventually. It was like playing a video game on expert mode, with only one heart of health left.

Still, he'd been thinking about her all day, in the way anyone infatuated would think about a new sex partner, making little to-do lists in his head of all the things he wanted to do with her when he got home and the order he wanted to do them in. And he wasn't sure where this was coming from; it wasn't like he had a thing for younger girls, and even though he had always been the wealthier in any relationship he'd been in, he'd never exactly been a sugar daddy before. Was this sober!Kaveh's type? Young, volatile, destitute, *and* emotionally unavailable? *Oh yes, gimme that shit, inject it right into my veins!*

A conundrum for another day.

"You need a new surname," said Kaveh. "They want me to find out if you have a preference."

"I UNDERSTAND, DEAR CLEVER CREATURE. IF I HAD A CHOICE, I WOULD CHOOSE YOURS."

The thought had crossed his mind as well, considering how arbitrarily he'd picked the name "Nikola," and that had stuck without so much as a debate or an alternative like Chad or John or Bill being put forth. If it weren't for the relatively uncommon nature of his surname, he might have humored the idea. But for the first ETI ever seen by the public, during an event that had gone so, so wrong, to have his name meant he would have his family's name, too. And what would that do but draw negative attention to them as well?

"I know it may sound silly to you, but my surname is Iranian, and right now, there aren't many countries with a worse relationship to the United States than Iran."

"ARE YOU AN IRANIAN CITIZEN?"

Kaveh sighed. "No, I'm an American citizen."

"THEN IT IS AN AMERICAN SURNAME."

Kaveh cracked a smile. "God, these political divisions must seem so silly to you." Nikola probably hadn't meant to say something, well, reassuring, but he had. "I don't know if it's a good idea for you to have a name so directly associated with *me*. But I have an idea. 'Sassanian.'"

"IT IS AN IRANIAN NAME?"

"It was my grandfather's name. Darius Sassanian. He died almost thirty years ago."

"WHAT KILLED YOUR GRANDFATHER?"

Kaveh took a moment, feeling the hum of the engine underneath him, before answering. "His own government."

Nikola took a moment to consider, then said, "THEN I HAVE MY LEGAL NAME, AND YOU HAVE GIVEN IT TO ME."

38

Cora didn't watch the news, but she had a good idea as to what was on it because she had to pick up the phone when her mother called eventually, lest she end up a missing person on the side of a milk carton.

"Why don't you come back home?" Demi begged her.

"I'm not allowed," Cora lied. "It was always top secret, but right now they're freaking out and telling me I'll get in trouble if I slip anything. I can probably see you in a week or two, but right now I'm not supposed to leave or talk to anyone."

She had some variation of this conversation with her mother several times those first few days, while not telling her about Kaveh, or the loss of her job, or the Coke bottle "incident." She could only pray Demi wouldn't show up at her apartment in Riverside and find it abandoned. Now all she had was the charity of a man she hardly knew, and she'd worked herself into a position that if he got bored of her—*when* he got bored of her—she would really and truly have nothing.

Kaveh never mentioned the "incident," one small blessing. It certainly hadn't been calculated; it was pure id, like the hand of a demon had reached out of hell and begun puppeting her, half a desire to hurt herself and half a desire to force Ampersand to do *something*. One second's thought or self-control would have stopped it, as it was obviously a terrible strategy from every angle, and could only lead to more pain. In one swift stroke of a bottle of Mexican Coke, she'd lost everything. Well, almost everything.

She could sense little, if anything, from the other side of the wall. Ampersand was half-conscious at best, as far as she could tell, the trauma of Pershing Square so overwhelming that it had shut him down completely. She still wondered how much of it was her doing, her disease leaking into him, but if anything, at the moment, the opposite was probably truer.

After all, there was only one way to sever that bond. 'Til death do us part, apparently.

That can't be. That can't be all there is to it.

But it is, there is no other way.

It wouldn't be the worst thing in the world.

And then she started to entertain the thought that maybe it would be more economical for everyone if she just got out of the way sooner.

Is this my thought or yours?

Same as it always is—it's ours.

Sometimes when Kaveh was out of the house, she stared at the fan that hung from the ceiling of his bedroom and wondered where his brother had hung himself from, who had discovered him. It hadn't been Kaveh, she knew that much; he had been on the wrong coast at the time. She wondered what it would be like to discover someone like that and resolved she couldn't do that to him. The same held true of falling from the balcony; too much room for error, too great a likelihood of surviving with permanent injuries, to say nothing of the mess. If she were going to remove herself from the picture, the least she could do would be not to leave him a mess.

Mess was the problem here in Southern California, though, if one wanted a foolproof plan. Pills had too much room for error, as did car accidents. Jumping from a great height was best, but the problem in LA was the only thing there was to jump *to* was concrete, and the thought of turning into a wet splat was unappealing. If only LA had large suspension bridges over water. Alas, she'd have to drive all the way to the Bay Area for that, all the way to The Bridge.

She'd once seen footage of a man jumping from that bridge, and like the falling Twin Towers, it was the sort of image that got permanently burned into one's memory the instant one saw it. Within a week, she'd more or less decided on it. Not right now, but if it came to that, if she *needed* a plan, it would be The Bridge. The thought crept into her mind every day, and every day, it lingered a little longer.

· · · · ·

Kaveh brought or prepared her food all the time, trying to work around her growing aversion to find something she liked, which only made her feel more wretched. She hated the thought that he might find her difficult. On Friday, it was Chinese takeout. "I have brought you some *options*," he said, unpacking his takeout bag. "That's French for 'options.'"

The "*options*" were Ma Po tofu, egg rolls, and garlic broccoli. Even the garlic broccoli, the least offensive of the options, felt to her like a box of dead worms.

Don't let facial expressions betray your disgust. Gratitude, express gratitude.

"Thank you."

She watched the way he tore in and ate like a normal person, plucking bites of sesame chicken with his chopsticks and popping them into his mouth as he talked about his day. Hadn't she been able to do that, at one point? Didn't food, a thing one needed to live, once taste good? She muscled through the rice and broccoli, straining to finish half of it as if she were running a marathon. She knew she had to eat, so why did this feel like punishment?

Soon, they were in his living room watching CNN as he worked. She sat near him on the couch, but not next to him, nothing that might seem entitled to his attention. Everything on TV that wasn't about the Third Option or ignorant speculation about ETIs was about the ever-free-falling economy. The unemployment numbers released had hit a new high at 11.5 percent, and future projections did not look good. This had nothing to do with anything alien, but the news sure made it seem like it did.

"Does it bother you that I have this on?" he asked.

God, yes, she thought and answered, "No, of course not."

She kept her eyes on her laptop, hoping he'd be distracted enough not to realize that she wasn't doing anything but staring into space. He had his laptop balanced on the arm of the couch and a journal full of notes and doodles in his lap, the end of a pencil resting between his teeth. He wore black-rimmed reading glasses and a blue cashmere sweater over a crisp white undershirt with the collar and cuffs poking out from underneath. He looked so professional, so comfortable in his own work and his own skin, everything that she wasn't. All she wanted was to crawl up next to him, maybe put her head in his lap while he worked, feel the softness of that cashmere sweater on her cheek. He'd allow it, of course, and he'd be nice about it, but that didn't mean she needed to impose more than she already had.

The TV cut back from commercial, and there was her picture again, and the chyron read, UP NEXT: MORE QUESTIONS ABOUT ORTEGA FAMILY CONNECTIONS TO ETIS.

"Are you sure this is okay?" he asked.

"It's fine," she said. "It doesn't bother me."

• • • • •

She'd never been with anyone like him before. He was nothing like the pump-and-dump guy from a few months ago or any boy she'd been with in high school. He was gentle and considerate, taking the time to learn what she responded to, what her sensitivities were, which in a way only made her feel worse, like feeling pleasure at all was another debt incurred. He never treated her like she owed him anything, but at the same time, they ended up at the same place every night, and within a few days, it almost felt like routine. And she *tried* to lean into that, but it wasn't getting any easier.

That night, she was good about hiding her nerves, despite being confused and infuriated that she was feeling nerves at all. But soon, she was under him, and despite herself, she began tensing up again, wincing loudly when he tried to enter her.

"Are you okay?" he said, propping himself on his elbows.

"Yes." *Goddamn it.*

"I didn't hurt you, did I?"

"It's okay. I like it."

A nonanswer and a half truth. She did like it, and it did hurt, but it shouldn't have, because there was no reason for her to be having any pain.

Why? Why why why?

The first time he'd taken her to bed, her traitorous body had refused to cooperate and nearly fucked the whole thing up, and she'd all but had to beg him to go through with it. Absolutely humiliating. She genuinely liked him, like the feel of his lips on her neck, the smell of his hair, the feeling of him moving inside her. And yet, her body kept trying to go against her own wishes. She couldn't eat, she couldn't breathe, she couldn't even get fucked properly.

Why, why, why does this keep happening? She pulled his body close as he pushed inside her, guiding his head over her shoulder so he couldn't see her cry. That strategy could only work for so long, however, because he noticed her upset as he was cuddling her after they'd finished.

"*Azizam, mi amor, meine schatze,* honeypie, tell me what's wrong?"

She wanted to tell him the truth. Wanted to put words to how unable she was to wrap her head around being the "human shield," the subject of this photograph that by now at least half of all living humans had seen and all of them had opinions on. Wanted to tell him about the violent urge to self-harm every time she thought about how much she had already fucked things up. Wanted to admit to him, *I'm so afraid I'll do something wrong, or you'll get bored of me, and you'll get rid of me, and then I'll have nothing.*

But, god, imagine saying it out loud, how *needy* that sounded, to say nothing of putting words to how dark her thoughts got. What was the word Ampersand used? *Diseased.*

"Did something happen?"

"No. I'm fine, don't worry about me."

"Baby . . ." He smiled, the soft, warm light from the fireplace dancing on his olive skin. "Let me help."

"I wish there was something I could do for you," she said, sidestepping the comment. "You've been so kind to me."

He considered, tracing the outline of her lips with his thumb. "You could tutor me in the art of being the alien whisperer."

"Of course." Yes, good, something that actually gave her a modicum of usefulness. "Anything you want."

So she related to him everything she could think of that might be helpful—*that you have to stay several steps ahead of the people you're talking to, but you have to speak quickly because it can't look like you're lying or paraphrasing. That anything you say can and will be exploited by the military and the CIA, so when in doubt, keep Nikola's words to yourself. That people like Sol will always know you're paraphrasing, but he's a known paranoiac, so fuck him. That if you need to improvise a quick excuse or explanation for something, play to people's stereotypes they learned from movies. That you should use a different timbre when speaking for Nikola, as that helps avoid confusion. That Nikola must understand that part of your job is to omit or rephrase certain things, and he has to trust that you know what's in his best interest.*

After a couple of hours, Kaveh decreed it time for sleep. He yawned contentedly, pulled her into a little spoon position, and was asleep within minutes. She succeeded in waiting for him to fall asleep before she began to cry again.

Wed, Feb 20, 2008 at 5:16 PM
From: Leila Zargari <zargarileila019@gmail.com>
To: Kaveh Mazandarani <KavehMaz@gmail.com>
Subject: threat letter

This came tooyeh post. Not sure if we should be negarron vallee
fersestadeem beh police. Thought you should know. miss you.

> You muslims are traitors to this Country
> and your brother is a traitor to our species.
> Nice JEW-elery store you've got.
> Nice mosque.
> Nice house!
> Now accidents happen. People get stabbed in
> LA all the time. Children get run over.
> Pets get poisoned.
> Bombs get planted in nice mosques like yours.

. . . . .

Wed, Feb 20, 2008 at 8:43 PM
From: Kaveh Mazandarani <KavehMaz@gmail.com>
To: Leila Zargari <zargarileila019@gmail.com>
Subject: Re: threat letter

I'm so sorry this happened. I'll contact the Beverly Hills PD.
Aslan yanee chi? He knows Eli is Jewish, but he threatens to
bomb a mosque? Kheng! What mosque? We don't even go.
This feels like an empty threat. Did you tell mom?

. . . . .

Wed, Feb 20, 2008 at 8:51 PM
From: Leila Zargari <zargarileila019@gmail.com>
To: Kaveh Mazandarani <KavehMaz@gmail.com>
Subject: Re: threat letter

Na. Should I?

. . . . .

Wed, Feb 20, 2008 at 9:04 PM
From: Kaveh Mazandarani <KavehMaz@gmail.com>
To: Leila Zargari <zargarileila019@gmail.com>
Subject: Re: threat letter

Hanooz na. Let me look into it.

. . . . .

Wed, Feb 20, 2008 at 9:11 PM
From: Leila Zargari <zargarileila019@gmail.com>
To: Kaveh Mazandarani <KavehMaz@gmail.com>
Subject: Re: threat letter

Okay, but if I see anything else I think I should tell her. I'm not
worried about us, but I am worried about you.

. . . . .

Wed, Feb 20, 2008 at 9:15 PM
From: Kaveh Mazandarani <KavehMaz@gmail.com>
To: Leila Zargari <zargarileila019@gmail.com>
Subject: Re: threat letter

I'm worried about me, too.

39

Kaveh wished he could say that this was the first time his family had been threatened because of him. There had been threats like this since even before he finished his Ph.D., and he suspected at least one or two had been manufactured by the CIA, J. Edgar Hoover–style, but it was hard not to blame himself at least a little.

He didn't tell Cora, or anyone outside his family. He had intended to be more attentive where Cora was concerned, because he knew "I'm fine" was, at best, a lie of omission, but it was hard not to stay utterly preoccupied by the chaos outside. Things had changed so fast, and therefore, so had his story—he'd never been a part of a story that he reported on before, and he had no idea how best to approach it. But given that Jano Miranda and Todd Julian were ramping up their political rhetoric in a big way, to the point that his extended family was receiving *bomb threats,* the pressure was on. He needed to figure it out, and soon.

By this point, Nikola had twice tried to get Ampersand talking, but hadn't had any more luck than any of the humans had. Nikola was both a blessing and a curse to his government caretakers, both engaging actively with whatever information they presented him in the form of restricted internet access, asking the kind of charming questions about humanity one would love to get asked by an alien, and dropping the occasional existential nugget about the end of human civilization.

Worse, he was very careful about *only* communicating through Kaveh, and there was no scenario that the Sol Kaplans of the world hated more than a journalist being the intermediary between the most cooperative of the ETIs, let alone a journalist who had worked directly with

Nils Ortega several times. But whatever Nikola wanted, Nikola got, and it didn't take long for Nikola to start asking to go outside.

This wasn't met with a no, per se, but it did put Kaveh between Nikola and a flock of panicked bureaucrats willing to do anything to placate Nikola, but could he please ask for literally anything else?

"It's more of a nature thing," Kaveh told them. He wasn't thrilled by the prospect, either, but he also figured it was better to give him an inch now than a mile later. "He can only learn so much about this strange new planet from Simple English Wikipedia."

The bureaucrat he was speaking to, someone from DHHS named Shannon, sighed the type of sigh the messengers of despotic kings prone to beheading subjects must have sighed when they had to return to their lord with bad news. "Could you give me specifics?"

"How about it?" he asked Nikola. Nikola was not visible to him, was not even in the same building, but he was always available by earbud, of which Kaveh now had one for each ear, at least. "Where specifically did you have in mind?"

"I DESIRE PRIVACY."

"Can you give me some more detail?"

"I DESIRE PRIVACY WITH YOU, DEAR CLEVER CREATURE. WE CANNOT SPEAK IN CONFIDENCE HERE."

Kaveh hoped Bureaucrat Shannon hadn't caught the tremor that ran through him. *Please, don't be requesting a private conference with me because you're curious about vibrators.* "A beach?"

Bureaucrat Shannon sighed that death sigh again and walked away into any number of conversations going on behind closed doors. What were the risks? What was the legality of this? What branch of the government should handle the transport? Should the military get involved, and why was the answer to that question yes?

Eventually, at great taxpayer expense, they granted Nikola's request for the following afternoon. It was only one big helicopter, which took them to an island off the coast of Santa Barbara, a nature preserve that was off limits to fishermen and human boating enthusiasts. Some Coast Guard boats had arrived ahead of time to make sure the island was absolutely cleared of anything that could be considered human activity.

Then they stepped into the sunlight, Nikola's first time in almost two weeks, the military guys and civilian feds looking on as if this were some

Neil Armstrong moment they were witnessing. Nikola moved down toward the beach, and when Kaveh told the G-men they didn't want to be followed, none of them protested.

Kaveh had a walkie-talkie on him, mostly for the CIA contingent to yell at him if either he or Nikola moved where they couldn't see. Nikola spent a few minutes on the beach, approaching the water and cocking his head curiously, probably for show, demonstrating that, yes, I sure am interested in the nature of your beautiful planet, nature nature nature, look at all that salt water.

Eventually, he backed away from the water and settled on the rocks in a roosting position, eyes to the overcast ocean. February in California wasn't like February on the East Coast, but it was still windy and cold. After Kaveh sat down about a foot from Nikola, he dug out the walkie-talkie. "Can you make sure they aren't eavesdropping?"

Nikola looked at it, but didn't touch it. "THEY WILL HEAR NOTHING I DO NOT ALLOW."

Kaveh put the walkie-talkie back in his pocket and pulled the flaps of his peacoat up around his neck. The two looked out at the ocean for a while.

"I HAVE DONE AS YOU HAVE ASKED. I HAVE MADE GOOD-FAITH EFFORTS TO ENGAGE MY SYMPHYLE. I HAVE REFRAINED FROM MEDICATING MYSELF."

"Thank you for that," said Kaveh.

Nikola kept his luminous eyes to the ocean. Kaveh turned to check the couple of CIA agents bumming around some thousand feet away. One of them kicked a rock.

"BUT I AGREED TO CONTINUE TO LIVE IN THE SHORT TERM. WE DID NOT DISCUSS HOW SHORT, OR HOW LONG, WE SHOULD CONTINUE."

Kaveh had hoped this wouldn't come up again, that Nikola had improved enough that death wasn't on his mind anymore. But that wasn't how these guys worked, was it? Death wasn't some nebulous unknown on the horizon for these guys, it was strictly planned, had a definite end.

"Are you in pain still?" asked Kaveh. "Do you still want to die?"

"RIGHT NOW, IT DOES NOT PAIN ME TO CONTINUE LIVING, BECAUSE I FIND LEARNING ABOUT YOUR CIVILIZATION GRATIFYING, BUT ALSO SADDENING, BECAUSE THE SUPERORGANISM WILL DESTROY IT SOON ENOUGH."

Kaveh groaned, pulling his knees up to his chest and letting his forehead fall to them. *Jesus fucking Christ. Okay.* "Give me an educated guess. How long before one of the arms of the Superorganism with the capacity to do real damage arrives?"

"MY EDUCATED GUESS WOULD BE BETWEEN FIVE AND FIFTEEN YEARS."

He looked back at Agent Rock-Kicker and his colleague. They clearly weren't hearing this, because they still looked bored. "Well, that's . . . not right now. And we don't know what will happen."

"WE DON'T KNOW, BUT WE HAVE AN EDUCATED GUESS. AND I IN-TEND THAT MY SYMPHYLE AND I WILL BE DEAD BEFORE IT HAPPENS."

Kaveh sighed, resigned. "Five to fifteen years before the world will end."

"THE WORLD WON'T END, JUST YOUR CIVILIZATION."

"Right."

The two sat there for some time, watching the waves lap up on the shore. After a couple of minutes, Nikola continued. "IT LIKELY WON'T END RIGHT AWAY. THE SUPERORGANISM WILL MOST PROBABLY STUDY YOU FOR SOME TIME BEFORE IT DECIDES THAT YOU ARE TOO DANGEROUS TO CONTINUE ADVANCING."

Kaveh looked at Nikola, who had hardly moved since he'd parked himself on the rocky shore. "So there is a possibility that we won't go extinct in my lifetime."

"A GOOD POSSIBILITY. YES."

Kaveh took a deep breath and cringed at the card he was about to pull. "You like me, don't you?"

"I ENJOY YOU VERY MUCH, DEAR CLEVER CREATURE."

"So if you won't do it for Cora, and you won't do it for Ampersand, would you do it for me? How can I convince you to . . . stop this talk of ending your life and Ampersand's life?"

For the first time since they'd sat down, Nikola finally broke his star-ing contest with the ocean and turned to look at Kaveh. "I ENJOY YOU VERY MUCH. I ALWAYS HAVE. THE OTHERS SEE YOU AS VIOLENT AND CRUEL. CERTAINLY, YOU HAVE THAT CAPACITY, BUT YOU HAVE WON-DERFUL CAPACITY FOR COMPASSION AS WELL. I DISCOVERED YOU. YOU ARE MINE. I DON'T WANT TO WATCH YOU DIE."

"I don't want that, either, but I'm talking in the short term. The next six to twelve months. If assisted suicide is how your species exits this life, I can respect that, but I'm just asking you to wait. Wait for a time that it won't hurt me. Because if you die now, then it will, very much."

"I CAN MAKE PLANS FOR THE SHORT TERM, IF IT PLEASES YOU, DEAR CLEVER CREATURE. BUT IN THE END, I CANNOT SAVE YOU. YOU, PRECIOUS CREATURE, YOUR VIOLENT TERRIBLE SUPERORGANISM, YOU ARE THE ONLY ONE."

"Only one what?"

"YOU ARE NOT JUST THE ONLY ADVANCING CIVILIZATION WE HAVE DISCOVERED OUTSIDE OF THOSE DESCENDED FROM OUR COMMON ANCESTOR; YOU ARE THE ONLY CIVILIZATION CAPABLE OF ADVANCEMENT WE HAVE EVER DISCOVERED OR EVER WILL DISCOVER."

Kaveh threw up his hands. "Let's assume that's true. Let's assume that humanity is doomed. Fine. But how can you say we're all you'll ever discover?"

Nikola stilled, then withdrew his fingers from the rocks. "LET ME ILLUSTRATE THE ORIGIN OF LIFE."

There was a flash of heat as Nikola splayed out the digits of his right hand, and all the rocks in front of them, from the pebbles to the skipping stones to the grains of sand, turned coal black. It was as though an oil spill had appeared in front of them about the size of a backyard swimming pool. Then another flash of heat, and some of the black turned to white ash, which lifted like clouds and formed into a spiral like a hurricane. *The galaxy.* This was a rendering of the Milky Way.

"TWO COSMIC EVENTS." At this, the white ash coalesced into a sphere the size of a beach ball. "THE FIRST, A POPULATION II STAR, APPROXIMATELY 14 SOLAR MASSES, BECOMES A SUPERNOVA 6.89 BILLION YEARS AGO." The ball of ash contracted into itself and then exploded into a disc like a cloud, and then the cloud contracted like it was being sucked into a whirlpool. "THE EJECTA FROM THIS SUPERNOVA BECOMES A NEBULA, WHICH IS DRAGGED OUT THROUGH THIS SPIRAL OF THE GALAXY OVER A PERIOD OF 2 BILLION YEARS."

The ash re-formed, this time two spheres the size of basketballs, circling each other rapidly.

"AND HERE WE HAVE TWO NEUTRON STARS THAT ORBITED EACH OTHER IN A STABLE LOOP UNTIL, 4.87 BILLION YEARS AGO, THEY COLLIDE." The two spheres merged into one, collapsed into themselves, and also exploded into a cloudy disk. "AND THE BLAST FROM THIS SUPER-NOVA BEGINS TO IMPACT THE EJECTA FROM THE PREVIOUS SUPERNOVA.

"FIRST, YOU MUST UNDERSTAND THAT THE EJECTA FROM THESE TWO EVENTS IS NOT THE ONLY MATTER IN THIS PART OF SPACE—EJECTA FROM DEAD STARS EXISTS EVERYWHERE, IN FACT WE ARE BOTH MADE OF IT—BUT THE SPACE OF WHICH I SPEAK IS SPACE THAT WAS DIRECTLY AFFECTED BY THE EJECTA AND ENERGY BLAST FROM THESE TWO SUPERNOVA EVENTS." The ash cloud formed into what looked like part of a spiral, a zoomed-in segment of the Milky Way galaxy. "THE SEC-OND SUPERNOVA CAUSES THE EARLIER NEBULA TO COLLAPSE, AND IN TIME POPULATION I STARS LIKE YOUR SUN, LIKE OUR ANCESTOR'S SUN, FORM. EJECTA FROM THIS SECOND SUPERNOVA EVENT REACHES EX-ISTING STAR SYSTEMS, EXISTING PLANETS. IT IS THESE TWO ANCIENT COSMIC EVENTS FROM WHICH ALL LIFE DRAWS ITS ORIGIN."

"What was special about these two supernovae?"

"WE DO NOT KNOW. WE KNOW THE CHEMICAL PREREQUISITES FOR THE FORMATION OF LIFE, BUT THESE PREREQUISITES EXIST ON MANY EXOPLANETS THAT EXIST OUTSIDE OF THE SPACE AFFECTED BY THESE TWO SUPERNOVAE. CHEMICALLY, THERE IS NOTHING UNIQUE ABOUT THE ELEMENTS AND ENERGY THAT MAKE UP THIS REGION OF THE GALAXY. THE ONLY DIFFERENCE IS EXPOSURE TO THESE TWO SUPERNOVAE."

The white ash re-formed into a representation of the entire Milky Way, but this time, almost all the ash turned to a dim gray, all but one tiny sliver toward one of the edges, which turned an even brighter white. It was perhaps 1 percent the diameter of Nikola's model of the galaxy. "THIS AREA OF SPACE IS APPROXIMATELY 627 LIGHT-YEARS IN LENGTH, AND 45 LIGHT-YEARS IN WIDTH. WITHIN THAT SPACE, WE HAVE SENT BOTH PROBES AND SIMILARS TO EVERY PLANET THAT BEARS LIFE, OF WHICH THERE ARE 394. OF THAT NUMBER, 67 SUP-PORT COMPLEX LIFE—EUKARYOTIC LIFE, IT IS CALLED ON EARTH."

Kaveh stared at the galactic model silently, which in itself was awe inspiring. It was still moving, swirling like a real spiral galaxy. "Okay, so that's . . . incredible. But why do you think that we're all you will ever find?"

"BECAUSE THIS ARM OF THE MILKY WAY IS THE ONLY KNOWN REGION OF THE UNIVERSE IN WHICH LIFE EXISTS." At this, the ash stopped moving and fell back to the ground, dissipating with the force of the wind. The focus of Nikola's eyes dissolved. "WE HAVE EXTEN-SIVELY CHRONICLED EVERY LIFE-BEARING PLANET. EVEN THOSE WE HAVE NOT PHYSICALLY VISITED, WE CAN CLEARLY SEE—UNDERSTAND, OUR TELESCOPIC TECHNOLOGY IS MUCH MORE SOPHISTICATED THAN YOURS. WE HAVE OBSERVED THE ANDROMEDA GALAXY AND ALL THE LOCAL DWARF GALAXIES THAT SURROUND BOTH OF THEM. WE CAN OBSERVE AN EXOPLANET THREE MILLION LIGHT-YEARS AWAY WITH MORE PRECISION THAN YOU CAN PHOTOGRAPH YOUR MOON. WE HAVE SEARCHED. THERE IS NOTHING."

Kaveh scoffed, the bigness of this conversation finally hitting home. "But that's only two galaxies! There are hundreds of billions of galaxies in the universe!"

"BUT WE ARE LIMITED BY THE LAWS OF PHYSICS OF THIS UNI-VERSE, DEAR CLEVER CREATURE. EVEN IF WE WERE ABLE TO TRAVEL AT THE SPEED OF LIGHT, SPACE IS EXPANDING FASTER THAN ANY VESSEL WE ARE CAPABLE OF BUILDING COULD TRAVEL. WE ARE CON-FINED TO THE LOCAL GROUP OF THE MILKY WAY AND ANDROMEDA GALAXIES, AND THERE IS NO LIFE IN EITHER OF THESE GALAXIES OUTSIDE OF THIS ONE SPIRAL ARM OF THE MILKY WAY. YOU ARE THE ONLY CIVILIZATION CAPABLE OF ADVANCEMENT THAT WE WILL EVER FIND."

Kaveh let his posture go slack while he took a minute to soak this in. Then, he fell on his back, lying down in the sand and pebbles and smooth rocks and looking up at the overcast sky through his sunglasses.

"BUT PERHAPS THERE IS A WAY TO AVOID TOTAL HUMAN EXTINC-TION."

Kaveh tilted his head toward him. "How is that?"

"I COULD COLLECT GENETIC MATERIAL."

Kaveh sat back up, now very interested.

"I WOULD NEED VERY MUCH—THOUSANDS OF SAMPLES. BUT I HAVE AN ABILITY THE SUPERORGANISM DOES NOT. I CAN FOLD SPACE. I COULD HIDE US SOMEWHERE THE SUPERORGANISM WOULD NEVER FIND US. THERE ARE NO LIFE-SUSTAINING PLANETS INSIDE THE LOCAL GROUP, BUT PERHAPS OUTSIDE OF IT, FAR BEYOND OUR TELESCOPIC CAPACITY, BILLIONS OF LIGHT-YEARS AWAY, THERE MIGHT BE. IF AN ARM OF THE SUPERORGANISM WERE TO ARRIVE HERE, PERHAPS WE

COULD SLIP AWAY BEFORE THEY NOTICE. THIS CIVILIZATION WOULD
END, BUT IF I HAD ENOUGH GENETIC MATERIAL, IT MAY NOT MEAN
HUMAN EXTINCTION."

Kaveh crossed his legs and rested his arms on them, his gaze floating
into the Nietzschean abyss, feeling like some part of his brain was about
to pop. The medulla, perhaps. Or the amygdala. Har. Har. "So you'd . . .
start us all over in your image. You'd be your own . . . Divine."

"MY DEAR BELOVED WOULD NEED TO CONSENT TO THIS. AS
WOULD MY LITTLE COUSIN. AS WOULD YOU."

Kaveh chuckled. "Oh, I'm coming along, too."

"I WOULD PREFER NOT TO LEAVE YOU TO DIE."

Kaveh closed his eyes and let out a long breath that was almost a
whistle. "Okay, well . . . we can explore this option. In the long term.
Not the short term. Not the next few months. But we can consider it."

He looked out at the blue-green horizon. The sun was starting to
peek through the clouds, the haze of the overcast sky beginning to dissi-
pate, turning the Pacific a vivid blue. "But in the meantime, in the short
term, I want you to continue trying to rehabilitate Ampersand. Do we
have an agreement?"

Nikola's eyes brightened, and the crest on the back of his head perked
up slightly. "WE HAVE AN AGREEMENT."

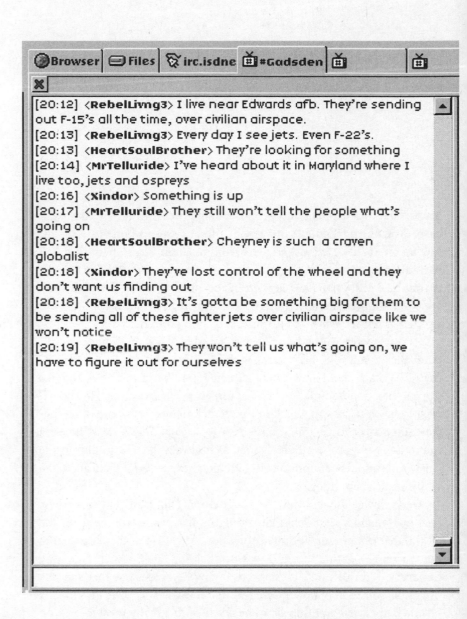

[20:12] <**RebelLivng3**> I live near Edwards afb. They're sending out F-15's all the time, over civilian airspace.
[20:13] <**RebelLivng3**> Every day I see jets. Even F-22's.
[20:13] <**HeartSoulBrother**> They're looking for something
[20:14] <**MrTelluride**> I've heard about it in Maryland where I live too, jets and ospreys
[20:16] <**Xindor**> Something is up
[20:17] <**MrTelluride**> They still won't tell the people what's going on
[20:18] <**HeartSoulBrother**> Cheyney is such a craven globalist
[20:18] <**Xindor**> They've lost control of the wheel and they don't want us finding out
[20:18] <**RebelLivng3**> It's gotta be something big for them to be sending all of these fighter jets over civilian airspace like we won't notice
[20:19] <**RebelLivng3**> They won't tell us what's going on, we have to figure it out for ourselves

· 40 ·

Kaveh's fixation with Nikola's proposal came over him slowly, like a disease. Over the next couple of days, he didn't answer phone calls or follow up on emails. He ignored texts from his family and spent so much mental energy trying to think of how he was going to tell Cora about it that he hardly paid her any attention at all outside the bedroom. He wanted to tell her about their future adrift in the stars together. He wanted to tell *someone,* but it was just so goddamn heavy.

And at any rate, Cora didn't seem to mind how distant he had become. After all, she still willingly had sex with him, and who was he to say no to that? The night after Nikola's field trip, he found her on what looked like the end of a panic spiral, but she kept insisting she was fine. He knew it wasn't true, but she was so damn insistent, and after a fashion, it felt patronizing to pry, to say, *No, you are very clearly not fine.* Instead, he went the route of physical comfort, which, as it always did, led to him inside her within minutes. If nothing else, fucking her *seemed* to help abate the whole panic spiral thing.

Deep down, Kaveh knew he was deluding himself that this was a healthy dynamic. He knew that indulging her desire to hide from the world, that not getting her any professional treatment, that supporting her with no endgame in mind was not helping. He knew that fucking her every night was not the same as loving her. He knew that she was not "fine," no matter how often she insisted she was. But the burden Nikola had placed on him was so heavy, he didn't really want to pick up more of hers. So he deluded himself that, although this situation was not the most ideal, it was much better than any other options she had available to her. He maintained this delusion all the way up to the night he found her balled up in the corner of his shower, covered in her own blood.

It was the thumping that woke him up. He heard it again, *thunk, thunk,* and was struck with a lightning bolt of adrenaline. He reached for her, but she wasn't there. *Thunk, thunk.* Then a muted cry coming from the bathroom. He tore out of bed and tried to open the bathroom door, but found it locked. Wasting no time, he kicked it in, wood splintering all over the floor, and he rushed inside. He couldn't see her through the water condensation of the glass pane. He tore the shower door open and looked down at the mess on the floor.

There she was in his giant shower, backed into a corner and naked, her arms plastered to the tile walls like he was holding a gun at her. There was a gash on her head just past her hairline, a sharp one. The water made the blood spatter so much worse, as it caught and diluted and flowed all over her, spreading down her head and all over her body like watercolor.

"Please, no!" she begged him, her eyes wild. "Please don't, please don't!"

Kaveh stared at her in mute horror, unable to make sense of it and already half convinced that some form of alien mind control had snapped her. The tile seat on the other side of the shower also had some blood dripping from it, likely the source of the gash.

"Please, no!" she cried, her breath coming in harsh, fast shrieks. "Please, no! *Please, no!*"

"Cora, it's me!" he said, slamming the shower handle off.

"Please, no, don't, *no, don't!*"

He knelt in front of her, palms forward. "It's me, you're home, you're at my house. I'm not going to hurt you!"

"No, don't, no, don't, don't make me, don't make me—"

"Don't make you what?"

"Don't make me *leave!*" She grabbed her hair violently. "Don't make me leave, don't put me in an institution, please don't make me leave!"

"I need to get you to the ER," he said in as gentle a voice as he was capable of in that moment, which was not very. "Honey, you're bleeding."

She pulled a hand away from her hair, saw the blood on it. "Oh no, oh *no!*"

"It's okay!" he said, threading his arms under her armpits, trying to get her to stand, but she wouldn't budge. Her body was stiff like she'd already gone into rigor mortis.

"Please, no, please don't make me leave, please don't send me away!"

"Listen, I don't want to go to the hospital, either. They're going to think I did this."

"No," she whispered, her breath gaining momentum. "No, no, *no, no, no!*"

"Listen—"

"They're going to put me away, just like the air force doctor wanted to, they're going to put me away!"

"Listen to me!"

"They're going to take me away from you. If they don't take me away, they'll think you did it!"

"*Shut up!*" She cowered, closing her eyes and becoming quiet. "Yes, they are going to think I did it."

"No," she whispered. "No, no, no, no . . ."

"Here is the thing. We're going to have to lie about this. I don't want you committed, either, but they only call in a 5150 if you're a danger to yourself or others. Do you understand?"

She kept her eyes closed and shook her head rapidly, like a bobble-head on a spring.

"You fell, okay? This was an accident. You need help, Cora, but I really, genuinely believe that involuntary commitment is the worst thing that could happen to you right now. If the press finds out . . ." He almost laughed. *If the press finds out, as if I'm not the press.* "The press can't find out. I'm not going to let them take you away, but I'm not about to take the blame for this, either."

And so, in the eight minutes it took him to drive her to the hospital, they concocted a slapdash, barely credible story. Yes, despite having no drugs or alcohol in her system, she fell down a flight of stairs at 3:45 in the morning and landed on a very sharp edge of a glass coffee table. And if they asked why she was so shaken, it was because she had a chronic fear of blood. They arrived just after 4:00 but, owing to the non-life-threatening nature of her injury, had to wait almost an hour before they began stitching her up.

He worried that if they pushed her too hard, if they insisted that it was Kaveh that did this to her, that she might let him take the fall out of desperation to stay out of a mental institution. This fear was compounded when, after another hour, the police showed up to question him. Two upstanding white Orange County policemen, one fratty blond who was no older than thirty, and a slightly smaller redhead.

"Are you the boyfriend?" asked the redhead, whose badge read "Turner."

The boyfriend. Not *her* boyfriend. *The* boyfriend. "Yes, that's me."

"She's given her statement," said the blond, whose badge read "Lanning" and whom Kaveh had already clocked as ex-military. "But you understand that we need to question you, as well."

"I understand, Officer."

"The doctors tell us that the gash wasn't the only injury," said Lanning. "That there is bruising on her, too. On her head, but also on her fists and legs."

"It was a bad fall."

"But on her fists?" said Turner. "And the doctors tell me that these bruises are definitely more than a few hours old."

Kaveh took in a long breath before he repeated, "It was a bad fall."

Turner eyed him. "I know in your culture . . ." Hearing this word, the way he said it, *culture,* like it was a bad infestation of termites, Kaveh's vision dropped out, replaced with white-hot rage. "Women are treated differently. We understand that. So I'm going to ask you one more time: Did you have anything to do with the injuries on her body?"

"Officer, I . . ." *I grew up in Palos fucking Verdes.* "I understand your concerns . . ." *You don't know shit about me. You don't know shit about Iran. You don't know shit about anything but this cartoon caricature you've constructed about every culture that isn't your own meathead version of whiteness.* "But I give you my word, I didn't have anything to do with it." *I want you to look me in the eye and tell me you've never abused your power before, you absolute fucking ghoul.*

"Is there a possibility she might have done this to herself?" asked Lanning, the slightly less dumb of the two.

Barely holding it together, he said, "It was a very bad fall."

The police took his address, no doubt to check to see if there had been any other domestic disturbances, and left him alone. Some twenty minutes later, Cora was released from the ER, wrapped in a hospital blanket, a tiara of white gauze around her head. It wasn't so bad, they said, only three stitches.

Cora was silent from the moment he put his arm around her shoulder to guide her out of the hospital, and he caught a glimpse of the way the doctor and RN looked at him. At first, he mistook it for judgment, that, like the police officers, they looked at him and saw only a crazed Muslim invader who had infiltrated this country to beat and rape its white women before eventually strapping on an AK-47 and shooting up a mall. But instead, he saw concern in their faces. Pity, even. They knew he didn't do it. They knew who did.

It took him a moment to decompress before he found the spirit in him to turn the car on, all the while Cora wearing an expression like she'd gotten a lobotomy. She didn't say anything the whole drive back, which now that the sun was up took a bit longer than it had getting there. They listened to the radio. Britney Spears's "I'm Not a Girl, Not Yet a Woman" crooned back at them, and unable to handle how on the nose that was, Kaveh changed the channel to some awful morning DJs making ET jokes.

When they got home, Cora let him guide her like she was an automaton. He gave her a Xanax and some ibuprofen, and in the absence of something comforting to say, gave her a long kiss on the forehead. He then gave her a clean shirt and a pair of shorts to put on, and watched her as she mechanically took off her clothes and replaced them. He instructed her to get into bed and rest, told her that he was taking the day off and was going to stay with her. She obeyed him without a word, all the while not looking at him in the eye once.

He went into the bathroom to take a piss, then turned the faucet on, splashing his face with cold water. He looked at his reflection, the mirror of his extravagant bathroom. The offending shower, the scene of the crime, stood behind his reflection, still dewy from recent use.

This is my fault.

He had seen the warning signs and ignored them. She had insisted she was fine, and he accepted it, knowing it was not true. He accepted it, because seeing things for what they really were was inconvenient. Uncomfortable. Same as it had been with Sirvan.

Is this just a function of human nature? he wondered. *Is this just something we do, over and over—we identify patterns, we identify problems, and we tell ourselves that we've figured it out. We tell ourselves that next time it will be different, next time we will know better, next time we won't make the same mistake. But then we do.*

And then something stirred in him, something else he had likewise denied, or at least ignored—*feelings.* The type of feelings that one is referring to when one says, *I am developing feelings for you.* And what to do about that? How to separate his own desires from what was best for her? *Stay with me, but let's stop fucking?* What message would that send her other than *I no longer find you attractive now that I've seen how crazy you can get?* No matter how much he insisted otherwise, the only lesson she would take from it would be: *I have messed up, and now I am being punished. He is withholding affection, because I have messed up.* Strangely, perversely, it just wasn't true. He knew that many of these feelings were born out of a desire to "save" her, but that didn't mean his feelings weren't real.

He buried his head in his hands, running his wet fingers through his curls and shaking his head. The absolute worst thing he could do to her right now would be to abandon her, emotionally, physically, or materially. He tore himself away from his reflection and went back into the bedroom, only to see that she was gone, and the balcony door was open. He dashed across the room and through the open balcony door, and found her outside, not one story down on the ground as he'd feared but huddled in the corner of the balcony, her back up against the wrought iron rails.

"Kaveh, I'm so sorry."

"I . . ." He didn't know what to say to that. *It's okay* certainly wasn't it.

Her nostrils flared, the skin around them grew red, and her eyes developed a glossy sheen. "I won't do it again, I swear."

"Don't make promises you can't keep."

Her sadness swelled into the beginnings of panic. "I swear, I won't do it again."

"You swear you won't get caught, is what you mean."

"No, no, I won't do it again."

"Tell me the truth: Did you do this to get a reaction out of Ampersand?"

"No," she said, so quick and sure that he believed her. "It feels like something takes over my body, like this demon. Like this buildup of all these terrible feelings, and the only way to relieve the pressure . . . But it's mine, it's not him. I don't know how to explain it, but I can just tell what comes from him and what doesn't. He doesn't have violent urges. Not like I do. And I didn't used to."

He looked out over his backyard, taking a moment to center. "So we're going to see a psychiatrist, going to see if they recommend any—"

"I already did."

"When?"

"A few weeks ago."

"What did they say?"

"Told me to find a therapist, gave me some prescriptions."

That was an unbelievably huge relief. She'd already taken the first steps, arguably the hardest steps. "Well, why didn't you say so? We'll get those filled today."

"I can't afford any of that."

"Don't worry about it. I'll pay for it."

"I don't want you to—"

"I *said* I'll pay for it." His patience was beginning to grow thin.

She made a noise like he'd grabbed her by the throat. "Whatever you want. I'll do anything you want."

He frowned. Not good. This should come from a desire to heal, not from a desire to placate him. He wondered if he was seeing what he wanted to see, not what was really there. "Do you ever have thoughts of taking your own life?"

Her body seemed to turn to porcelain. Only her eyes moved, growing wide with dread.

"It's okay," he said, trying to muster a supportive tone. "Tell me the truth. You can tell me."

She opened her mouth, holding it like she had momentarily forgotten how words work. Then: "All the time."

He'd thought he could handle it if that was her answer, but the

words felt like a teaspoon tapped on the eggshell of his psyche, cracking it and leaving only a thin internal membrane to hold him together.
Part of him wanted to lock her in a box, find somewhere to keep her
safe. Another, louder part of him wanted to get away from her. Wanted
to throw her onto the street and drive, drive into the mountains, into
the woods, lock himself in a cabin forever, away from other people
and their self-harming impulses. Wanted to put up an emotional barrier before he could ever again love someone who was a danger to
themselves.

"But I don't know if they're mine," she said. "I think some must be
mine, but I can't separate those urges out anymore. I don't know which
are mine and which are his. The violent ones are mine, I know that, but
the underlying—I don't know. Kaveh, I . . ."

He just stared at her, flipping through his Rolodex of potential re-
sponses and coming up short. What to say? He had asked the question
unaware of what a potent trigger it was for him. She must have seen that
in his eyes, because panic rose in hers. "I'm sorry. I shouldn't have said
that. I didn't mean it. I'll do anything you want, anything in the world.
I didn't mean it."

"Yes, you did," he said, incredulous. "Don't lie to me."

She was obviously going through her own mental Rolodex, trying to
figure out how to unsay the words she had obviously spoken in truth.
He'd asked her to share something incredibly vulnerable, and he'd gotten upset when she gave him the honesty he'd asked for. *Fuck me, I'm
doing it again,* he thought.

Kaveh looked out over his domain—his nice-ass pool, the hot tub
that flowed into it, and behind that the vista of all of Orange County in
its hazy polluted glory. And it was in this moment he really understood
how much power he had in the situation relative to her. Not just age, not
just career, not just wealth, but in almost every way imaginable. Shelter,
emotional support, and above all, access to the thing she cared most
about in this world.

Ampersand.

She was twisting herself into pretzels based on what he wanted to
see—no, based on what she *thought* he wanted to see. He had never
asked for her to hide herself, to be out of his sight unless it was for

sex, but he could no longer ignore that that was what was happening. Her behavior had changed so radically since Pershing Square, and it had been easy for him to just assign the change to the trauma of that day.

"Just tell me what you want me to do, I'll do it," she said. "I'll do anything you ask, just please don't make me leave."

He looked at her, equal parts guilty and hurt over this realization. He imagined asking, *Do you even like me?* But stopped himself. *Don't say that. Now is not the time.* Besides, why be offended at the idea she might not be in this for love or pleasure? That was never the deal. Why was that wrong?

Ah, right, those *feelings* he'd been ignoring. The thought that she might, if only unconsciously, see their relationship as transactional hurt him, because he did not. God*damn* but this situation got more and more fucked up every second. There was no right or wrong thing to do, no way to un-fuck this, only the path of least harm, and he could only hope that whatever he did from here on out fell on that path.

"You'll do anything?" He looked at her appraisingly, leaning on the balcony rail.

She nodded, expression painfully sincere. "Anything."

"Okay. We start small. Today, we get that prescription filled. I'll call around, find you someone appropriate so you can start treatment. I mean real treatment, not this crisis urgent-care hotline shit. We'll get that started ASAP. But the most important thing," he said, his tone deadly serious, "is that from now on, if you're spiraling, if you're having intrusive thoughts, if you're panicking, I want you to tell me."

Her expression morphed into shock, as if he'd told her she was accompanying him on a hike up Annapurna and they were leaving right now.

"I don't want you to hide them from me ever again," he continued. "No more 'I'm fine' when you're not. That's my condition. You have to be honest with me. *¿Claro?*"

She couldn't have looked more horrified if he'd told her she was going to spend the rest of her life naked and chained to a radiator.

"You said you'd do anything," he reminded her, almost teasing.

Slowly, she nodded in assent.

"Deep down, I think you understand that you can't just wish that shit away. That if you try to keep it down, the pressure builds, and it explodes. So don't hide it from me anymore. Let me help you."

He reached his hand to her; she didn't move, eyeing it suspiciously.

"When you have panic attacks and intrusive thoughts, I'll talk you through it," he said. "I'll try to guide your breathing. We'll get through it together. But this isn't going to work if you don't trust me."

She kept looking at his hand, still unsure, then took it. He helped her to her feet and pulled her close, the feeling of her body against his a relief, and just held her. "It's okay. I've got you." Oh, what a mess this was. Goddamn *feelings*.

After a few minutes, he guided her back inside, shutting the door behind them and closing the curtains. She crawled into bed, and after removing his outer clothing, he climbed in next to her.

"Try to get some sleep," he said. "I'll be right here. I'll clear my schedule. *Doostet daram*."

She nodded, and then turned her back to him, pulling the sheets up over her shoulder. He opened his laptop, Outlook updated, and then he saw his most recent email:

Fri, Feb 29, 2008 at 6:21 AM
From: Nils Ortega <nils@thebrokenseal.org>
To: Kaveh Mazandarani <KavehMaz@gmail.com>
Subject: Interesting . . .

Hey, Friendo.

Got something you want to tell me?
Attachment: orangecountypolicereport.pdf

Fri, Feb 29, 2008 at 9:43 AM
From: Nils Ortega <nils@thebrokenseal.org>
To: Alejandro Miranda Vasquez <JanoMirandaV@gmail.com>
Subject: Re: Report from Anaheim PD

Jano,

Contact has been made. Suffice it to say I have his attention. I'll
let you know how things shake out. Please thank your friends in
law enforcement for sending that police report my way.

Best,
Nils

"I have some homework for you," said Kaveh, sliding the last of his notebooks into his leather satchel. "And also a present."

"Present?" She put her fork down. She'd made it about 60 percent through the lemon ricotta crepe he'd made, which was more than she usually did. Anything less than 50 percent sent his inner Persian mom into a frenzy, whinging, eat, eat, *Yeh cheezee bokhorr deegeh!* and she knew that. At any rate, he figured she was used to it. Her mom's side was Italian, after all. *Mangia!*

"Just a sec," he said, retreating upstairs to retrieve the slapdash gift bag he'd thrown together. Normally, Kaveh prided himself on being reliable, but all things considered, he figured everyone he canceled on in the last couple of days would give him a pass. He'd gotten her prescription filled, and she was due to get in her old jalopy and cart herself to the (very highly recommended and very expensive) therapist he'd arranged later that day. Everything else, however, was up to her.

He retrieved the bag from his closet, trotted back to the kitchen, and put it on the table in front of her. She pulled her gift out of the bag—a MacBook Pro—and looked at him in disbelief.

"When did you get this?"

"I overnighted it."

"Kaveh . . ."

"I missed Christmas this year. So consider it a late Christmas present."

"Do you celebrate Christmas?"

"Nope. If you like, consider it an early Nowruz present."

"What's 'Nowruz'?"

"Persian New Year. It's in a few weeks. It's like our Christmas, except way more awesome. But don't mistake, this is a work present."

She nodded. The word *work* seemed to make the gift acceptable. "What do you want me to do?"

"I want you to write me a set of essays," he said, sitting down next to her. "Two of them—the first one, I want you to write about Pershing Square. Basically, I want you to write a thousand-word essay about why you did what you did. What was going through your head. But imagine you're writing this for a crowd, trying to be inspirational. Personal reasons, but also bigger-picture reasons. Like a TED Talk."

She nodded, bemused. "And the other?"

"I want you to write about everything you gave up to be Ampersand's interpreter, and why you did it. But again, bigger-picture thing. Focus on how you've applied your schooling in linguistics, if you can. Also, call him 'Jude,' not 'Ampersand.' Have this for me by EOD."

"EOD?"

"End of the day," he said with a chuckle. "5:00 P.M."

She opened the laptop and turned it on. "Is this just to keep me busy?"

"Let's just say I'm thinking with a mind to the future."

The computer made its trademark *bong* Apple start-up noise. She looked at it as though touching it the wrong way might make it disappear in a puff of smoke.

"If you give me a draft of each by the time I get back, which is EOD, I'll take you out somewhere. Actually, no, I'll take you out either way, but we'll pretend like this is an incentive. I want to see what you can do."

"Take me out where?"

"Wherever you want. Taco Bell? Olive Garden? Cheesecake Factory? Benihana? And I'll make sure we don't have to wait."

"You don't have to do this," she said, her voice growing quiet. "I don't need . . ."

"I do, though. This is what I should have been doing all along." He stood up. "Besides, what's the point of having a rich boyfriend if you don't get to skip the line sometimes?"

She batted her eyelids like a nervous butterfly. "Boyfriend?"

He kissed her lightly on the tip of her nose and then tapped it with his finger. "Boop."

They said their goodbyes, and he went out the door, and the second it closed behind him, he nearly shattered.

Kaveh drove about halfway to Los Alamitos before pulling off the side of the road and into a McDonald's parking lot. He turned off the engine, sat there for a solid two minutes, and then dialed. The phone rang a couple of times, the telltale ring of a European phone number, until it clicked from an answer. He let out a deep breath, tried not to sound as angry as he felt, and said, "This is Kaveh. I'm on my burner."

"*Wie geht's?* How's it going, man?"

Nils was talking to him like they were about to share their fantasy football picks. It was a real, genuine struggle not to sound angry. "I've seen better days."

"I can see that. Glad I got you on the horn. I was surprised enough to see one of the aliens got a name from my freaking grandmother's side, but 'Sassanian'? It took me a minute, but then I was like, I wonder who gave him *that* name? Is 'Nikola' a family name, too?"

"Not unless I'm related to Nikola Tesla."

"Oh, nice. Is this some strategy to get on Elon Musk's good side?"

"Let's just get on with it."

"Okay," said Nils, not missing a beat. "Not one but two documentations of you being with my daughter falling into my lap within a couple of weeks of each other, the second of which looks pretty . . . not good! Care to tell me what's going on?"

"She's been working with Luciana at ROSA," Kaveh said, keeping his voice measured and choosing his words carefully. "We met by chance at a Third Party rally in Temecula, the morning of the Enola Gay landing."

"Now, I know you wouldn't lie to me about something like that. But that police report? Well, looks like the feds have already scrubbed it, so it's a good thing I got in while the getting was good. But the details were pretty interesting."

"I didn't hurt her."

"I believe you. But 'boyfriend'? Really?"

"I had to think of some plausible explanation for why it was me bringing her in."

"Care to tell me what she was doing with you at four in the morning in the first place?"

"Staying at my house," he said, knowing that any lie would get back to Nils, and soon. "She really, very much does not want to live with Demi."

"And Luciana?" His tone indicated to Kaveh that this news pleased him.

"They aren't on the best terms right now."

"I see. I gather the reason you were at the Third Party rally in Temecula was for a story."

"Yes."

"So what's your angle?"

He threw his head back against the headrest of his seat. *Here we go.* "Simple. Full personhood. No in-between. What's your angle?"

"Debridement."

Kaveh ran through his vocabulary database, flipping between languages, unsure what Nils meant, or how that word applied to . . . anything, really. "Debridement?"

"Corruption is the gangrene, and gangrene only spreads. We both know full transparency alone won't tear down the system. You think getting rid of Bush will remove the infection? No, sir, the rot runs deep."

Kaveh's grip on his steering wheel tightened, his knuckles starting to turn white. "Dude, you already took down Bush—"

"And yet, the administration still stands. Nothing has changed. Same administration, different coat of paint. Cheney, Pelosi, Reid, McConnell, McCain, all of them—the rot has to be cut out, because if we don't cut out the rot, if we don't root out the corruption at its core, then we're going to have to amputate the limb."

"What do you mean by that?"

"Revolution."

Kaveh straightened back up in his seat. A year ago, he might have laughed. A year ago, all of this was a joke. Aliens were a joke. The world economy collapsing was a joke. The mere idea of Bush resigning was a joke. A rapid resurgence in fascism was a joke. But Nils's tone was dead serious. "What do you want from me?"

"I want to know what you know," said Nils. "I've seen talking heads say that the biggest existential truth we could ever learn is that we aren't alone in the universe, and that's the dumbest fucking thing I've ever heard. We haven't even scratched the surface. We don't know anything about their civilization. We don't know anything about why they're here, or what they want from us. But I think the government knows. I think Cora knows. I think you know."

"Nils, it's not as simple as that." The second he said it, he almost smacked himself. He didn't even need to say anything else; this confirmed to Nils that he was in the know, and moreover, he had aligned himself with the enemy by wanting to put a filter on the Truth.

Nils was silent for a moment. Then, "If this police report got out, it would be really, really bad for you."

"Nils," Kaveh said, jaw trembling in disbelief. "She's your daughter."

"And as such, she has as much obligation to share what she knows with the world as you do."

Kaveh's breath shook, no anger, just pure astonishment. "Listen, she is in a very, very bad way right now. Something like this going public could push her off the edge—"

"She's always been dramatic."

"Dude, you have neither seen her nor spoken to her in five years! You do not know who she is anymore."

"Okay." Silence on the other side of the line. Then, "If you really, truly believe she's a danger to herself, then she should be in an institution."

Kaveh's entire body fell. "There is no way I could get you any documentation. They've got me under lock and key. I can't say anything, I can't take anything."

"I don't need documentation, not if it's from you. I just need a lead."

Kaveh ran his free hand all over his face and through his hair. "Revolution, huh?"

He could practically hear Nils smile all the way from Germany. "Revolution."

n p r News

As Questions About "Human Shield" Cora Sabino Circulate, Some Remain Skeptical

BY HELEN O'LOUGHLIN

Since becoming the subject of a widely circulated photo in which she put herself between the bodies of two incapacitated ETIs and a gunman, Cora Sabino has to many become the face of a burgeoning peace movement calling for attempting to establish diplomatic relations with alien civilizations.

One leader, however, is evidently not impressed with accolades the young New York native has earned: Senator Todd Julian.

"What many are heralding as bravery, I only see actions that are, at best, naive, and at worst, plain old crazy," Julian said on Thursday morning. "She clearly means well, but the road to hell is paved with good intentions."

Similarly unimpressed with Sabino's actions appears to be her father, whistleblower and founder of *The Broken Seal,* Nils Ortega.

Ortega has remained conspicuously silent on his daughter's newfound fame. "I am withholding judgment," Ortega said on his website *The Broken Seal* on Monday. Seemingly in step with her father, Sabino has also not made any statement since the now-famous photo was taken.

Pundit and candidate for California's 46th Congressional District Jano Miranda also joins the swelling ranks of Sabino's detractors.

Sabino and Miranda crossed paths earlier this month when they both participated in a debate on MSNBC's *The Hot Seat with Satomi Mack,* and then again the following day at the Third Party rally where the photograph of Sabino was taken, which Miranda co-organized, and left five people dead.

"She's too young to understand what's at stake here," Miranda said in an interview with CNN on Tuesday. "And people are using her actions, either of bravery or insanity, to uphold the status quo. But what we need right now isn't the corruption of the status quo. What we need right now is answers, is accountability. And if those in power won't give us that, what we need may well be revolution."

Kaveh had never felt such an oppressive sense of discomfort heading onto a federal complex, even the times he knew he'd be detained or questioned. He'd done the best he could to cover his tracks on his end, but what about Nils's end? Might these people already know about the conversation he'd just had? He certainly couldn't *ask;* the only "friend" he had on this side of the line was Nikola, and he wasn't exactly someone to confide in.

The feds had asked him to come in today to question Nikola on some intelligence they'd gotten, to see if it might show any leads regarding the three still-at-large Similars (predictably, according to Nikola, none of them did). Hell, maybe the Similars had already found their former commander and had gone on their merry way back into the cold vacuum of space, and that was why Ampersand had gone catatonic. Maybe? One could dream.

They asked Kaveh to stay for another debriefing for some other reports still trickling in, so he sat on a metal folding chair next to Nikola, who was planted primly on the cold floor. Normally, he liked the long stretches alone with Nikola because it meant he could ask questions on his own terms, but he was in no mood for that today. He could not get past the incredible, horrible reality that his former writing partner, Cora's own father, was blackmailing him.

He wasn't even thinking about his own safety or national security at this point, he was worried about *her,* that Nils doing something with this could push her over the edge, to say nothing of the fact that that police report being made public could easily be used to discredit the Photograph—her behavior is not heroic, her behavior is unhinged.

These are not the actions of a brave soul embodying the best of humanity, these are the actions of a crazy person.

He noticed Brigadier General Porter on the other side of the room talking to Sol Kaplan, and for a fleeting moment, he considered telling Kaplan everything. Even though Nils was a huge thorn in their side, the CIA still had incredible power. Perhaps they could do something about this mess if they had the upper hand. He got up and approached the two, Porter with his haughty, above-it-all attitude, Kaplan scribbling something onto a notepad.

"Excuse me," he said. "Agent Kaplan. Could I speak to you alone for a sec?"

Kaplan turned to him, looking at him like he was the help who'd just interrupted two aristocrats at a ball. "Wow, this doesn't concern you."

Kaveh replayed the moment in his mind's eye a few times before accepting that yes, that had actually happened. Kaplan did actually say that. Kaveh turned without a word, heat creeping up his neck, and crossed the room back to the folding chair next to Nikola. Unbelievable. The arrogance, the *fucking arrogance* of this guy.

Then he cast a glance to Nikola, the *machine* this person inhabited. He had no clue as to the limits of the capabilities of this machine, but he was pretty sure that Nikola could give the U.S. surveillance state a run for its money.

"Nik, the guy Kaplan is talking to—can you hear what they're saying?"

The crest on Nikola's head stretched out, and the focus of his eyes darkened. Kaveh knew by now that meant he'd been doing something in his internal space and hadn't been paying attention to the physical world. "I CAN."

"Can you tell me what they're talking about?"

Nikola paused, looking almost thoughtful. Then, "PERHAPS IT WOULD BE SIMPLER IF I RELAY TO YOU WHAT I AM HEARING THROUGH YOUR AURAL DEVICE."

Nikola's voice went silent, replaced by light static, and then Kaplan's voice was in his ear, thin like it had gone through several rerecordings on a VHS tape. Kaveh whipped out his pen and notebook, jotting down notes in a code only he understood in case they confiscated it.

"Defense has all the dirt they need," said Kaplan. "I don't see what they want from us. We had absolutely no control over what happened at NORAD."

"But there's still Bedford," said Porter.

"What about Bedford?" Kaplan sounded almost nervous.

"The agency had complete oversight over what happened at Bedford, and you lost four agents there," said Porter.

Kaveh looked at Nikola, who was still seated calmly, looking ahead at everything and nothing, not seeming to register this as anything noteworthy.

"What do they know?" asked Kaplan.

"Just that you recovered two vehicles but have reported nothing about recovering any personnel," said Porter.

"Can't your people read between the lines?"

"Yes, they can," said Porter. "That's the problem."

Kaplan paused for a solid ten seconds. Then, "They'll have to go to the director about it."

Kaveh looked up and saw that both men had already exited the room. The conversation had ended.

"DID YOU HEAR WHAT YOU WANTED TO HEAR, DEAR CLEVER CREATURE?"

"Yes," said Kaveh. "Yes, I think I did."

. . . . .

Kaveh looked up from the printouts he was reading with his "date," who was acting less like a date and more like someone who was doing a final interview for their first job out of college. His modest hope had been that she would complete at least one of the essays, but she delivered him drafts of both. Considering she was not a professional and she'd written two in a day, they were better than he'd hoped. They still had the rigid "beginning, middle, and end" structure that undergrads rarely shake by the time they graduate, and the thesis still needed work, but it was a perfectly workable first draft. She now sat across from him at the Italian bistro he'd chosen (since her restaurant of choice was "really, you decide"), her nervous eyes watching as he read.

"What is it?" he asked.

Her brow furrowed in bewilderment. "You're a Pulitzer-nominated writer with three international bestsellers, and you're reading my unedited writing that I cranked out in an afternoon."

"Two bestsellers," he corrected. "The first one didn't make the *Times*
list."

"Didn't two and three debut at number one?"

"Those were light sales weeks, anyway."

He noted a few spots he intended to go back over with a red pen,
shuffled the printouts back into his satchel, then took her hand to affirm
that this was, in fact, a date that was happening. This was the first time
he'd taken her out since their Cheesecake Factory outing a few weeks
ago, and the realization made him feel even worse. It didn't matter that
things were so strange and precarious, he *should* have been doing more
for her this whole time.

She seemed worried, though, looking not at him but behind him.
"What's up?" he asked.

"There's a guy behind you who's staring at us. I think he recognizes
me."

Oh fuck. That was probably inevitable, but he hadn't expected it to
happen so soon. He turned around to hang the strap of his satchel from
the back of his chair, slyly stealing a glance in the direction she'd been
looking. There was a mustached guy in a blue polo who was glaring at
them as he talked conspiratorially to his family. He looked like he'd done
a few rounds of golf earlier in the day and even sported a beeper. *Who
the hell still uses a beeper?*

He turned to her, giving her hand a reassuring squeeze. "Don't worry,
I'll fend him off if he starts anything."

"Did something happen today?" she asked. "You seem pensive."

"Oh." *Well, um, yes.* What to say? He definitely couldn't tell her about
Nils, not now. She'd have to know eventually, but not now. "I've . . . Well,
I've had an offer."

"Oh."

"Yeah, it's a pretty big one."

"Is it . . . something you want to do?"

"No, not particularly. But it's something I feel like I might have to do."

"Does it mean . . . you're going to have to travel?"

"Yeah, you might say that."

He caught her expression, a look that skipped surprise and hurt and went straight to resignation. He clasped her hand on the table. "Hey, don't worry. It doesn't mean we'll be separated." *And I mean that in the most nightmarish way possible.*

"Can you tell me anything about the offer, or is it one of those NDA deals?"

He sucked on the inside of his lip, his instincts already spinning a believable half truth, or a lie of omission, but then he wondered, *Why?* Why keep Nikola's proposal from her, especially after he'd demanded she stop keeping things from him? This wasn't a burdensome cruelty on the level of her father blackmailing her by threatening to release her medical history. No, this was a completely different type of burdensome, and one he wasn't doing himself any favors for enduring alone.

Fuck it.

He told her everything about Nikola's pitch for a lifeboat for the human genome, a pitch that attached both of them as a condition. Cora took it in, and he saw in her the same Ping-Pong ball of thought, the wild imaginings that had banged through his own head several days earlier. The horror of the vacuum of space, the unimaginable cost of leaving everyone she'd ever known, the excitement of the idea of exploring alien worlds.

"How do you feel about the idea?" she asked.

"I don't know. I guess the silver lining here is since we have five years at minimum before shit starts getting serious, we have some time to think it over. But—"

"Hey," a man's voice sounded from behind him, and it was not the "hey" of a person who was about to say, "I'm a big fan." Cora's expression flashed terror, and Kaveh shot to his feet before the man could get another word out.

"You're her." He was already almost on top of him, Mr. It's-2008-and-I-Still-Use-a-Beeper.

"Hey, man, calm down," said Kaveh.

"Calm *down*?" He clearly didn't recognize Kaveh at all.

"Leave us alone," said Kaveh, staying tempered, knowing the optics of a Middle Eastern man showing anger in a public space, even for the best of reasons, were not good. "Just back off."

"They're going to kill us all, and you let them in, you keep them from us, you protect them," said the man, speaking around Kaveh so loud it bordered on shouting. Cora didn't move.

"*Sir!*" The manager had arrived, a middle-aged Black woman who spoke with the tone of someone who'd had to do this a few times. "Sir, I'm going to have to ask you to leave."

"What did they offer you?" asked the man. By now, the restaurant was silent except for the faint atmospheric music, every eye in the room on them. In a way, it was just like Pershing Square; everyone watched, but no one intervened. "What are you going to get for it? You think this is going to save you?"

"*Sir!*" The manager snapped her fingers, and a couple of waiters reluctantly joined the fray. "Sir, you need to leave."

"You think being their slave is going to save you? They're going to kill all of us. What are they going to give you for it? What do you know?"

"*Sir!*"

The manager and the two waiters finally forced the man out, his humiliated family following behind, refusing to make eye contact. The nuisance now ejected, the manager was headed back in their direction. "Are you all right?" she asked both of them. "I'm very sorry, sir."

She looked at Cora, and an expression of recognition passed over her. Kaveh couldn't quite read it—did she, perhaps, agree with Beeper Dad? Or was she overcome with compassion? Or, most likely, did she simply want the source of conflict gone from her establishment?

Cora, for her part, sat still and stared straight ahead, looking like her soul had been sucked out of her body. Kaveh placed a gentle hand on her shoulder, and she jumped slightly.

"If you don't mind," he said, "I think we'll just take the check."

43

When they got back to Kaveh's house, Cora entered through the kitchen and kept walking like a preprogrammed automaton. She felt like she had to keep moving, because she was afraid of what would happen if she stopped. But she had to stop moving eventually; houses had walls.

"Honey? Talk to me?"

She ignored him, only now becoming aware of her rapidly accelerating heart rate. Distantly, she congratulated herself for making it back home before turning into a complete wreck, but she wanted to hide from him. The thought of him seeing her like this *again* was unbearable.

She turned from him and marched upstairs, then stopped. Where to go? She could hear him following her up the stairs between her intensifying breathing. She stumbled into his bedroom, *their* bedroom, but where now? Into the bathroom? *Kaveh won't like that.* Outside, onto the balcony? *Too much room for error, and he'll try to stop me.*

"Baby," he said, taking her by the shoulders and turning her around to face him. "Tell me what you need."

She opened her mouth, but nothing came out. The harder she tried to make words happen, the more her body resisted. *He's going to throw me out, he's going to make me leave.* Black spots encroached on her vision. Her skin felt like it was peeling off her face like an ocean wave receding from the sand. The bridge that connected thoughts to words had been blown up.

"Okay, yes-or-no questions," he said. "Do you want me to stop touching you?"

"No."

"Are you having . . . bad impulses?"

"Yes."

"Do you want me to hold you?"

"Yes."

He pushed her until she fell on her back onto the bed, hopping onto it next to her and pulling her into the center. He turned her around, pulled her back into his chest, and wrapped his arms around her tightly, locking her in place.

For the next five-odd minutes, her breath came hard and fast like spikes, and she tried to say something, tried to form some of these sounds she was making into words, but all that came out was incoherent nonsense. The whole time, she was dimly aware of him behind her, stroking her hair and kissing her neck and whispering reassurances. It took another five minutes before she was able to produce human language once more, and in between her hyperventilating, she said, "I can't control it, I'm sorry, I can't control it!"

"No, you're doing good." He kept holding her tightly, kissing her on the temple.

Good? How in the hell was this good? "I'm trying! I can't—"

"You're doing so good, baby." His voice was so calm. How could he stay so calm? It felt like he was speaking to her from another dimension. "You did what I asked—you didn't lie to me or hide from me. You accepted my help. That's a huge step. This was never going to go away overnight, but you've already made a huge step."

"I can't stop it!" She was still hyperventilating, but it was slowing. "I can't stop it."

Kaveh relaxed his iron grip, propping himself up as he guided her by the chin to look at him. "Honey, I know you're still deep in it, but I think you might be understating what just happened. What happened at the restaurant was really horrible. It was bound to cause a reaction, and you're already . . . not well."

"'Not well.'" she closed her eyes so she wouldn't have to look at him. "Fucking crazy."

"I wouldn't phrase it so crassly—"

"But I am fucking crazy." She looked at him, feeling the adrenaline that had only begun to slow start to surge again. "I've got a permanent

alien-induced infection that just floods into me with no rhyme or reason, and even if I didn't, I'd still be like this. Even if he dies, I'll still be
like this. And you know that now, and you've seen it, and you pity me
but you don't want me."

"What?"

"Of course you don't want me, you don't even want to fuck me anymore."

"Is that what you—" He sighed, shaking his head, then he began
kissing her on the forehead, her cheeks, the tip of her nose. "Of course I
still want you!" He looked at her fondly, like they'd just had a cute little
misunderstanding. "I just . . . I was so careless before. I'm trying to be
more careful."

She turned over to face him properly. It had been one of those honest
blurtings that in her right mind she never would have made, but she
didn't know what to do with this. "Why should it be on you to be careful? This isn't your fault. Bad enough I'm the way I am, I come attached
for life to this four-hundred-pound tumor."

He lay down on his side to face her, taking one of her hands in his
own. "We all come with baggage; yours just happens to be about nine
feet tall and a little cranky."

By this point, Cora was so drained she didn't know what to feel. He
looked at her with such sincerity, running his fingertips over her hair,
careful to avoid her injury.

"I know you think I'm looking for an excuse to abandon you," he said
softly. "I can see it in your eyes. I knew Nils left you, but I didn't really
think about how he did it or what it did to you."

"So you think I'm just creepily projecting my daddy issues onto
you?" she asked, again speaking without thinking and regretting the
words even as they left her mouth.

His expression soured. "I'm sorry, but I hate that way of framing it. I
hate that the phrase *daddy issues* is even in the vernacular. Like abusive
failures of parents causing lifelong damage can be dismissed as just 'daddy
issues.' It isn't creepy to compare your partners to your parents—your
parents are the ones who train you what to expect from relationships.
They teach you how love works, and they train you how to expect others
to treat you. That's true for everyone regardless of who your parents are."

A sudden darkness fell over him, and his expression grew hot with anger. She'd never seen him angry before, and it frightened her. Then he looked at her, and the anger vanished. "I didn't know, I'm sorry." He said it with such contrition, like he was the one responsible for wrongdoing and not Nils. "I didn't know what he did to you. I didn't know what kind of person he was. We never talked about our personal lives. I'm sorry, I didn't know."

"It's okay, you didn't—"

He leaned in to kiss her again. "Of course I still want you," he said between kisses. "I didn't understand, I didn't know what kind of person he was, but now I do. I'll never speak to him again. I promise."

She looked into his jade eyes, so calm and sincere. A part of her wanted to lash out, accuse him of lying to her out of pity. She restrained it and whispered, "Why do you want me?"

He smiled faintly and squeezed her hand. "I just think we need each other right now."

She tried to take a deep breath, and actually did it this time. At some point in the last few minutes, her breathing had calmed to something in the range of normal-ish.

"Besides, we're gonna be like . . . Adam and Eve in spaaaaaaace."

"Is that part of why?"

"No," he said. "Not now. It's not my concern right now. We've got time before we have to make any big decisions about that. My concern right now is you, and stopping the Third Option. My concerns are right here on Earth." He kissed her on the lips, but deeply, like he was drinking her in. Then he broke the kiss and looked at her. "*Doostet daram.*"

"What does it mean?"

He smiled his warm honey smile, the same smile that had ignited her infatuation with him weeks ago. "It means 'I love you.'"

What the hell? She hadn't even entertained the idea that he might love her, let alone say it. Why would he invite such a thing? Wasn't her love just as burdensome as her pain? Still, he must have wanted the programmed response. He wouldn't have said it if he didn't want the programmed response.

"I love you, too," she stammered.

He laughed softly, apparently charmed by her awkwardness. "I don't know what's going to become of us. Of this." He gestured at the space between them. "I can't promise you we'll always be *together* together—it's impossible to make that kind of prediction this early—but I can promise you that I'll never leave you high and dry. I'll always be your friend."

She felt a sob creeping up, the rare *happy* sob. His words flowed through her like sweetened chamomile, warming her from the inside. He was so good with words; of course he was, it was his gift. She wanted to kiss him again, wanted to say that three-word phrase again, feel it on her tongue, but she was afraid to move at all, afraid she'd break whatever this fragile thing was between them.

"You know, unless you do something unspeakably shitty."

A laugh came out through her film of tears. "What qualifies as unspeakably shitty?"

"I don't know. Killing someone? You haven't killed anyone, have you?"

He said it like it was an obvious joke, but her smile vanished. That sense of trust was replaced with the memory of a half-conscious Vincent Park in the back of a van and her flipping a gurney onto him. The sound it made when it hit his skull, the way she left him, fled from that vehicle without looking back. She didn't even know how he died, but what she had done had made that death all but inevitable.

"I'm sorry, bad joke," said Kaveh. "But I meant it. We need to take care of each other, because no one else in the world understands what we're going through. So tell me what you need right now, not what you think I want."

She closed her eyes and for the first time in a long time took stock of her body. Every single time they'd had sex, she'd wanted to let her guard down and just be with him, really be with him, but the more she tried to force it, the more her body fought her. And she still wanted to be with him, wanted to at least give him *something,* but right now, she felt like she'd been hung out to dry on live electric wire.

"Just to stay here."

"Happy to oblige." He kissed her on the forehead. "I'm not going anywhere."

She rested her cheek against the nape of his neck and closed her eyes, breathed in his now familiar scent, so sweet and sophisticated, and wished she could believe him.

(3/4/2008 10:22 PM PST) Kaveh:
This is my new burner.

(3/4/2008 10:22 PM PST) Kaveh:
Respond if you're awake.

(3/4/2008 10:29 PM PST) Nils:
Happy Super Tuesday. Looks like
the Republican primary is over. Has
this ever happened before? Is this a
literal first time in American history
an incumbent lost the primary?

(3/4/2008 10:30 PM PST) Kaveh:
Taking into consideration the fact
that primaries are a 20th century
development, yes.

(3/4/2008 10:33 PM PST) Nils:
I look forward to a long, agonizing
primary for the Dems that inevitably
culminates with a loss in November
that should have been an easy win.

(3/4/2008 10:33 PM PST) Kaveh:
I'm destroying this burner after we're
done.

(3/4/2008 10:35 PM PST) Nils:
What have you got for me?

(3/4/2008 10:36 PM PST) Kaveh:
Sol Kaplan is here. He works with
ROSA.

(3/4/2008 10:36 PM PST) Nils:
Wow, I thought the conspiracy nuts
just made that up.

(3/4/2008 10:39 PM PST) Nils:
Is that it?

(3/4/2008 11:00 PM PST) Nils:
Okay. If this leads to something,
then let us consider our business
concluded.

(3/4/2008 11:05 PM PST) Kaveh:
You're going to burn in hell for this.

(3/4/2008 11:05 PM PST) Kaveh:
This will be the last time we ever
speak.

(3/4/2008 11:09 PM PST) Nils:
I don't doubt it.

(3/4/2008 10:40 PM PST) Kaveh:
What do you mean is that it?

> (3/4/2008 10:41 PM PST) Nils:
> I mean, is that really the only
> information you have for me?

(3/4/2008 10:49 PM PST) Kaveh:
CIA-Bedford, VA. I couldn't find
anything on NORAD but there was an
incident in Bedford, VA that happened
the day after NORAD involving two
vehicles.

> (3/4/2008 10:50 PM PST) Nils:
> Casualties?

(3/4/2008 10:50 PM PST) Kaveh:
I don't know.

> (3/4/2008 10:50 PM PST) Nils:
> Death? Sightings? What?

(3/4/2008 10:51 PM PST) Kaveh:
I think people died.

> (3/4/2008 10:51 PM PST) Nils:
> What kind of people? Bystanders?

(3/4/2008 10:55 PM PST) Kaveh:
No. CIA people. I overheard Kaplan
talking about losing agents in Bedford,
VA the day after NORAD. Two vehicles
were recovered. That's all I know.

> (3/4/2008 10:56 PM PST) Nils:
> And do you have any clue as to the
> identities of these individuals?

(3/4/2008 10:59 PM PST) Kaveh:
No. I don't have any documents, I'm
just telling you what to look for.

· 44 ·

While Kaveh's attention had gone to writing editorials against the Third Option, the U.S. Military's was increasingly going to hunting down Obelus and rogue Similars. True to his word, Nikola answered pretty much every question thrown at him, even if the answer to pretty much all of them was some variation of, "That's not Obelus."

The following day, another outing was scheduled as something of a reward for Nikola being so cooperative. Owing to traffic (and nerves), Kaveh was late, and he had to run to the heliport where Nikola and his military entourage were waiting for him.

"Okay, let's go see that big tree," he said, adjusting his winter coat. It was a balmy seventy degrees here in Los Alamitos, but it would be much colder up in the mountains. The military entourage seemed unimpressed, and Nikola didn't even seem to be paying attention. "Who's ready for a big tree?"

"Hey!"

Kaplan's voice echoing across the asphalt hit him like a crowbar to the neck, and he turned to see the man trotting, nay, running toward them.

He knows.

Kaveh scanned his immediate surroundings, cased what he had working for him. Surrounded by soldiers on all sides, that was no good, but he did have Nikola. All he would need to do would be to say, "Get me out of here," and Nikola would do it. Nikola didn't particularly care about federal custody, which he was only really humoring because Kaveh had asked him to. Nikola could get them out of here, then he'd grab as much cash as he could before they froze his accounts, then escape to . . . shit, what was a good non-extradition country? Iceland?

Kaplan stopped right in front of them, his dark eyes darting back and forth between Kaveh and Nikola rapidly, obviously unsure whom he should be addressing. "It's Jude," he said, apparently settling on Kaveh as the addressee.

Kaveh nearly choked on his spit. *Jude?* Not, *You're under arrest for the next twelve eternities?* "What happened?"

"We don't know, but he's stopped giving off any energy signatures, he's just collapsed. He's completely nonresponsive."

Kaveh snapped this attention to Nikola. "Do you sense anything?"

Nikola's eyes grew dark and the crest of his head fanned out, smooth yet abrupt like flames. Then he said, "TAKE ME TO HIM."

Within minutes, they were standing right outside Ampersand's quarters, Kaplan entering first, then Nikola and Kaveh, then about ten other people, of whom he only recognized Dr. Ghasabian. They had moved Ampersand yet again, this time to something a little more appropriate, if a bit austere. A cold hybrid between a hospital room and a laboratory, with a large metal table covered with a thin foam mattress serving as a "bed," plastic sheets hung around the bed on all sides, creating the illusion of a smaller sunroom, about ten by fifteen feet. The sight of him nearly made Kaveh's heart stop; his digits were stiff, his eyes open and almost black, his head cocked at an odd angle. He looked like a dead crab on a beach.

"TELL THEM TO LEAVE," said Nikola, his eyes wide and the crest on his head flared bigger than Kaveh had ever seen it.

"He wants to be alone with him," he said, moving to exit and urging the others to do the same.

"I WOULD PREFER YOU STAY."

"Ex . . . cept me," he said, staying put while everyone else exited to the adjacent room. Kaplan didn't even give him his now-trademark patronizing glare, or if he did, Kaveh didn't see it. He was still in the den of the enemy, still mid–heart attack.

"MY BELOVED HAS ENSURED THAT I AM UNABLE TO SENSE ANYTHING OF HIS STATE. HE IS NOT DEAD, BUT BEYOND THAT, I CAN SENSE NOTHING."

"Nik says he isn't dead, but he can't tell anything past that. Ampersand still isn't communicating with him."

"I AM ATTEMPTING TO COMMUNICATE. I DON'T BELIEVE HE IS RE-CEIVING THEM. THOSE SYSTEMS ARE SHUT DOWN."

Nikola spoke lightly in Pequod-phonemic out of the holes in the sides of his neck, what Kaveh assumed to be "softly," placing his fingertips on the place where the back of Ampersand's neck met his head, looking into it like one might look under the hood of a car.

"HIS HIGHER SYSTEMS ARE SHUT DOWN AS A MEANS OF SELF-PRESERVATION. I BELIEVE HE HAS SHUT DOWN TOO MANY SYSTEMS TO FUNCTION."

Then he positioned his body at the front so he was directly facing Ampersand. Moving in carefully like he was a herpetologist trying to capture a viper, Nikola slid his head next to Ampersand's until they were cheek to cheek, as it were, and held it there for some time, speaking in that strange staccato language. For the first time, Kaveh saw some beauty in it, soft and pattering like rain. Nikola moved forward until the back of his head met the back of Ampersand's. The crest on the back of his head stiffened, then relaxed, the black fronds closing over the white ones.

The blow from the energy blast hit him before Kaveh knew what was happening, sending him careening into the plastic curtain behind him, breaking his fall. If that same force had affected Nikola, it wasn't by much, as he hardly budged.

Kaveh didn't get up, still leaning against that plastic curtain and breathing heavily, watching to see what Nikola would do. After a few seconds, some flaccid alarm started blaring. *Bweeeee. Bweeeee.* Kaveh could hear Kaplan barking orders over the intercom, but couldn't really understand him over the alarm. *Bweeeee.* Ampersand righted himself onto his stomach, pulling his arms and legs under him, his head flat on the table, eyes open and staring forward but focused on nothing.

"What's going on?" Ghasabian's voice over the intercom.

"Is he saying anything?" asked Kaveh, keeping his eyes on the alien in the center of the table.

Nikola stayed still as he looked at the statue in the middle of the room, and stayed like that for almost two minutes before he finally regarded Kaveh. "WE MUST DEPART."

"What do you mean?"

"We were scheduled to depart twenty minutes ago. We are now delayed. We must depart."

Kaveh finally tore his eyes from Ampersand to look at Nikola, incredulous. "What, you still want to go into the woods?"

"Yes," he said, passing him by. The escorts were already standing on the other side of the door. "Our time alone is valuable, is it not, dear clever creature?"

He followed Nikola outside, and only then did that useless *bweeeee* alarm finally shut off. "He, uh . . . wants us to keep to the schedule. He wants to go out to the woods."

"You're kidding," said Kaplan.

He looked into the observation room, and saw Ghasabian still inside looking at a screen.

"Did you get a recording of the language?" Kaveh asked, standing in the doorway.

Ghasabian looked up at him, betraying none of the tension or consternation Kaplan had shown. He looked almost wistful. "Most of it was too quiet for the microphones to pick up, but he repeated one phrase enough times that we got a rough translation."

"What was it?"

Ghasabian looked at him with an expression that accused him of knowing far more than he was letting on. "He said, 'Forgive me, Beloved.'"

· · · · ·

"Mazandarani, do you have eyes on AG-ETI-051? Over."

This army guy pronounced his name like it rhymed with "Santorini." Kaveh continued down the dirt path he'd been meandering the last few minutes and spoke into his walkie-talkie. "Negative, I am not his fucking babysitter, over."

"Mazandarani, we need eyes on AG-ETI-051. Over."

"If he wanted to give you guys the slip, he could do it whenever he wanted and would not need to plot a great escape here. Over."

Kaveh had not been to a sequoia redwood grove since he was a teenager, and at the time, he was in his "too cool for the majesty of nature" phase. As an adult, he found it positively stunning. It had been a warm winter, and much of the snowpack had already melted, making it easy to wander through the trees without snow boots. The trees themselves were vibrant as they were huge, the bark vivid in its redness, the tops evergreen.

His walk brought him close to a particularly big one with a gaping fire scar at its base large enough to shelter inside, and he ran his fingers over the bark of the tree. From a distance, it looked like polished wood, but up close, it was like thousands of layers of the paper of a wasp hive. It was dry and snowless inside the fire scar, so he decided to take a seat, take a moment to himself. It wasn't long before Nikola came back into view, neck craned up at one of the other trees. Kaveh raised the walkie-talkie to his lips. It almost felt like a betrayal to play along. "I've got eyes on AG-ETI-051. He has not given you the slip just yet. Over."

"THIS ORGANISM HAS SURVIVED INCREDIBLE FIRES."

"It's actually really cool," said Kaveh, putting the walkie-talkie away. "They need periodic wildfires to reproduce."

"DO YOU KNOW THEIR AGE?"

"I know the General Sherman tree is at least two thousand years old, kind of like me, but some of them are way older."

It struck Kaveh how, well, normal this felt. He couldn't see their government handlers, so it was easy to forget they were even there. They were just two friends hanging out in the woods, only one of them inhabited a natural, fleshy, hairy meat body, and the other the post-natural body of a giant cybernetic alien. Normal dudes hanging out. He almost felt downright buoyant, so removed from the stressors of the world down below, until Nikola said, "I BELIEVE MY BELOVED INTENDS TO DIE ON THIS PLANET."

Kaveh let out a long sigh. He should have known any carefree moments wouldn't last longer than thirty seconds. "Why do you call him 'Beloved'?"

"AN HONORIFIC MEANING 'VALUED ONE ABOVE ONE'S OWN STATION.' IT DENOTES SUPERIORITY. I DO NOT THINK IT A PARTICULARLY ACCURATE TRANSLATION OF OUR TERM."

Nikola was now staring down at him in the entrance of the fire scar Kaveh was sitting in, practically blocking him in. Kaveh had to crane his head up to look at him, and it struck him that he wasn't even a little bit intimidated by this. "Do amygdalines experience love?"

"Love—a polyseme. It is a word with many meanings."

"In this context, I mean as a deep feeling of intense affection to someone you know very well—a mate, or a friend, or a parent. Affection, affinity. A deeper bond that only develops over a long period of time."

"Empathetic attachment to a close kin or a mate. Of course we experience a form of deep empathetic social attachment. If that is how you define love, then we experience it, though I don't know how it compares to your experience."

"Do you love him?"

Nikola lowered himself next to Kaveh inside the fire scar, which was big enough to shelter both of them comfortably. "I do not know him anymore. He won't allow me to know him."

"Cora does." He shook his head, still bewildered by the whole thing. "She loves him so much."

"She has a strange way of showing it. Is spilling blood a common way to show affection?"

"No." He wondered how, or even if, he should tell Cora about what had happened today with Ampersand. "She worries about him constantly."

"Humans must develop feelings of love quickly. She has known him for such a short time."

"I guess we have to develop feelings quickly. Our lives are so short compared to yours."

"They don't need to be."

He looked at Nikola, and he could practically see the gears turning in that lateral engineer's intelligence, an alien Frankenstein with no scruples or regrets mapping schematics for what a post-natural Kaveh would look like.

"Does dynamic fusion bonding force you to love each other? Is that how it works?"

"I would ask, does marriage force love?"

"It certainly doesn't *force* it."

"It binds one to another, it does not induce feelings of love. One can love non-symphyles, and one can despise their symphyles. That would be terrible, though."

"Is it possible that he . . . chemically manipulated her somehow?

Injected something into her, implanted some sort of devotion device into her brain? Did he *make* her love him?"

"I CAN STATE WITH CERTAINTY HE IS NOT PRESENTLY CAPABLE OF THAT."

This surprised Kaveh. He'd have figured that would be an easy one for a species so advanced; induce feelings of love, induce feelings of loyalty, a handy thing to have in a liaison. "How do you know, if he's keeping everything from you?"

"MANIPULATING THAT LEVEL OF EMOTIONAL ATTACHMENT IS FAR TOO ADVANCED. WE SIMPLY DO NOT KNOW ENOUGH ABOUT THE HUMAN BRAIN TO MANIPULATE IT WITH SUCH SPECIFICITY. PERHAPS WITH ENOUGH TIME AND ENOUGH STUDY, WE COULD. BUT WE DON'T HAVE THAT SOPHISTICATED AN UNDERSTANDING OF THE HUMAN MIND YET."

Then where does this devotion come from? Kaveh wondered. *Why throw yourself in front of a gun for—oh wait, I did that, too, didn't I?*

He leaned his head against the cold bark of the tree. Occam's razor, he concluded. The simplest explanation is likely the correct one. There wasn't any weird alien implant or injections; she fell in love with him the old-fashioned way.

"I just don't understand why," said Kaveh. "Every time I've seen them together, he seems so cold and cruel to her."

"PERHAPS HE WASN'T ALWAYS."

Kaveh pulled the collar of his peacoat tight around his neck, hugging himself against the chill. "I've been thinking about your proposal, and I can't help but think, since we do have a bit of time before we really need to make a decision, that I'm really not the right person to help you smuggle out the human genome."

"WHO WOULD BE THE RIGHT PERSON, DEAR CLEVER CREATURE?"

"I mean, I don't have any skills relevant to this. I'm a writer, my skill set is taking information, parsing out what's relevant to public interest, and presenting it to people in an accessible manner."

"YOU ARE A PROPAGANDIST."

"Insofar as any information that could influence politics is propaganda, sure. I'm not a state propagandist but . . ." He scratched his head. "We are getting off topic. My point is, we have so many people who would be more appropriate for what you want—astronauts, geneticists, researchers, scientists, people who've dedicated their lives to being the type of person you'd need."

"I DID NOT ASK FOR A MORE QUALIFIED PERSON, FOR THERE IS NO QUALIFIED PERSON. THIS IS NOT AN ENDEAVOR FOR WHICH ONE CAN TRAIN."

"I don't think that's true; people go through rigorous physical and mental training to go into space. I get winded going up two flights of stairs, and the only reason I didn't fail out of trig was I flirted with my teacher in just this right balance of making her feel attractive but not risking myself getting in tr—anyway. There are so many people in this world with real qualifications."

"I DID NOT ASK FOR A QUALIFIED HUMAN. PROFESSIONAL QUAL-IFICATION IS IRRELEVANT TO ME. I ASKED FOR YOU. YOU ARE MY CONDITION."

"So you're saying if I don't agree to this, if Cora doesn't agree to this . . . you won't do it at all."

"IF YOU DO NOT AGREE TO THIS, I MUST CONCLUDE THAT YOU WOULD RATHER DIE HERE WITH YOUR OWN THAN LEAVE THIS WORLD ON THE SLIM CHANCE OF BUILDING A NEW SOCIETY IN A NEW ONE. IF THAT IS THE CASE, AND YOU WOULD PREFER TO STAY HERE AND DIE WITH YOUR FAMILY, THEN I WOULD MAKE THE SAME DECISION, AND STAY HERE AND DIE WITH MINE."

"This is . . . way too big a decision to hang on what I decide to do."

"OUR CHANCES OF SUCCESS WERE ALWAYS EXTREMELY MINUTE. I FEEL THEY ARE EVEN SMALLER WITH MY BELOVED IN SUCH A POOR CONDITION, A CONDITION FROM WHICH HE IS LIKELY NEVER TO RE-COVER. BUT MOREOVER, IT IS NOT MY SPECIES THAT IS THREATENED WITH EXTINCTION, DEAR CLEVER CREATURE. YOU ARE MY CONNEC-TION TO THIS CIVILIZATION. I DO NOT WANT TO REBUILD HUMAN CIVILIZATION WITHOUT YOU IN IT. YOU ARE MY CONDITION."

Fri, April 4, 2008 at 1:17 AM
From: Nils Ortega <nils@thebrokenseal.org>
To: T Julian <TJ61261236@gmail.com>
Subject: Bedford incident

Dear Senator Julian,

I have sent you the documents over an encrypted server. An anonymous source gave me a tip to investigate an incident in Bedford, VA on October 7th 2007. Following that lead, the information I have obtained is extremely limited, but perhaps given your position you might be able to uncover more specifics. There were four CIA agents killed in action on October 7th 2007. I have no information about them other than their names, which may or may not be covers: Vladimir Barash, Alycia Arline, Mark Aquino, and Vincent Park. Their deaths are connected to amygdaline Similars "unnamed stratocrats 1–4"—AG-ETI-047, AG-ETI-048, AG-ETI-049, AG-ETI-050. All four "Similars" connected with event "Obelus," which is the CIA code name for the second celestial object event if you'll remember I broke the day after it happened.

Though you and I differ in some regards, in this one we are aligned—we both agree that there is a rot in Washington, and that rot is corruption, and this cover-up is but one of many, many symptoms. I have faith that you will use your position of power to uncover deeper truths, and eventually, to debride the rot that has taken hold in Washington, and save our democracy. When you are president, I expect that any potential legal retribution against me, any charges of espionage etc., will be dropped. I'm at service to the Julian administration if they are at service to me.

Your obedient servant,
Nils Ortega

· · · · ·

Fri, April 4, 2008 at 7:36 AM
From: T Julian <TJ61261236@gmail.com>
To: Nils Ortega <nils@thebrokenseal.org>
Subject: Re: Bedford incident

Dr. Ortega,

I have never abided by your detractors' narrative, and your work
has been nothing if not the work of a true patriot. When I am
president, if you choose to return to the United States, you will
be met with a hero's welcome.

Sen. Todd Julian, Esq.

· 4 5 ·

Jendehhhhh, Ramin got the promotion, bezan bereem nightclub, come out!!!!

Kaveh stared at the text from his cousin Nasser for a while, knowing that the interest was compounding on the world of hurt he was in for for ignoring his family. His mother generally forgave these long spells where they didn't see him on the promise that *next* time he would win that Pulitzer, but given that he was here in SoCal, not off in New York or Oxford or Israel or Iran or somewhere, they were far less understanding. Nasser even sent him a follow-up text before he could respond: **I know ur busy dude, we miss you ossdahd.**

He snapped his BlackBerry shut, and looked over to the kitchen counter where Cora was poking around on her new laptop. It had been a couple of days since his little field trip to Sequoia National Forest with Nikola, and those couple of days had only made the burden of the choice he had before him, the choice *they* had before them, even heavier. He had his notebooks and paper spread out all over the place as he was wont to do when he was working, and the muted television turned to CNN to keep his ear to the ground. Cora saw she was being looked at and shot him a shy smile.

I do not want to rebuild human civilization without you in it. You are my condition.

He wondered if Nikola had any clue what a weight he was putting on him—*if you do not agree to leave Earth and go build humanity 2.0 with me, then it will not get done at all, and humanity will go extinct. No presh, bro!*

"*Daaaaaagggh!*" he groaned, throwing his head back against the couch and causing Cora to jump in surprise. He shot his head back up, slammed his laptop closed, and shoved his notebook off him.

"Okay, fuck it. We're going out," he said, gathering his papers and notebook into one big pile. "We're going to Beverly Hills."

Cora gingerly closed her own laptop. "Out?"

"Yes, my dumbass cousins are going clubbing, and they want me to come, and I'm going to go. Do you want to go?"

"Clubbing? In Beverly Hills?" A look of dull horror blossomed on her face as the image of what that entailed came into focus. "I don't have anything to wear."

"I'll buy you whatever you want."

She put a hand to her cheek as if she'd just remembered she had cheeks. "I don't really have any makeup, either."

"Then we'll get your hair and makeup done, too. We'll do a whole *Pretty Woman* montage."

"What?"

"Come on, Carrie Bradshaw. Let's get some shoes."

• • • • •

The club scene in Beverly Hills was the elitist type that typically had a minimum of five celebrity household names in it at any given time—your Johnny Depps, your 50 Cents, your Betty Whites, and so on. Nasser, however, preferred the Vegas-style clubs that were bigger, rowdier, and generally let in whoever as long as they could afford the fee, especially for a VIP section. Snob that he was, Kaveh figured if one *must* go clubbing, the former was preferable, but then again, he wasn't the one paying for the VIP section.

The worst depression in living memory didn't stop the likes of his cousins from making it rain; if anything, they were even more eager to flex their wealth to show how un-burned they were by the crash, even if he knew Eli's family was struggling since no one was really buying high-end jewelry at the moment. Under normal circumstances, Kaveh might have advised them to scale back this sort of spending, but given that civilization might not last long enough for long-term investments to pay off, he wasn't in a position to say anything.

He didn't tell Cora how much he'd spent on that dress on top of getting her hair and makeup done (a little over $500), nor how much he paid for a room at the nearby Waldorf Astoria (another $500), but she was growing past the anxious "I can't afford this, how can I repay you" phase of their relationship and was no longer keeping receipts. She *looked* the part—slim, blond-ish (for now), made up in a way that made her already-pretty features pop, and a skimpy black dress that would be *way* inappropriate in any other context—but boy, did she not act it. She acted like a high schooler expecting to be called out for trying to use a fake ID. Regardless, into the lion's den they went.

"Just FYI," he said. "Persians greet each other by cheek-kissing, so you're about to get a rapid-fire cheek assault."

"Like in *Borat*?"

"Just like in *Borat*."

Nasser was the easiest of the bunch to spot, less because of his unremarkable short stature and his new suit so much as the way he moved, holding a glass of champagne in the air and dancing like he was an extra in *Fiddler on the Roof*. He was with a woman who Kaveh assumed was his girlfriend of the month; she looked to be about thirty, voluptuous, bouncy, and *probably* Persian. Possibly Armenian. Either way, Nasser's mother was probably thrilled.

"*Jendeh!*" Kaveh yelled as a beat was about to drop.

Nasser turned to greet him, as did his other cousin, Ramin the Promoted One (as well as his girlfriend of the month), and to his surprise (and slight dismay), his younger sister, Leila, and her husband, Eli, who was dressed like he'd only just gotten off work—which, given that his family's jewelry store was only a couple of blocks away, was probably exactly the case.

All eyes fell on Cora in an unspoken *Who is that?* Surely, this could not be the same girl from the Photograph, not that helpless, bedraggled thing. *This* looked like a background extra in a Kanye West video. He felt her contract under their scrutiny, and felt a little guilty; problem with "looking the part" for clubbing in Beverly Hills was it did kind of make one look like an escort.

"*Jendehhhh!*" Nasser yelled over some Black Eyed Peas, unhooking the velvet rope for them, and within seconds they were beset by cousins, cousins' girlfriends, cousins' friends, cousins' coworkers, and one sister who did not look thrilled.

"*This* is Cora Sabino?" asked Nasser, glass of champagne still in the air. Nasser had been about twelve years old when he made it to the U.S., so unlike Kaveh and his siblings, his English had a slight Persian accent.

"Nice to meet you," said Cora, offering a weak handshake, which Nasser took before kissing her on both cheeks. Then it was his brother-in-law Eli's turn, and then his sister Leila's turn, and on and on the introductions went. Cora took the cheek-kissing in uncomfortable stride. Just like in *Borat*.

Leila forced a smile, her attention focused on Kaveh. It wasn't that he was dismayed at having to hang out with his sister so much as the fact that she, too, was a proxy in his mother's machinations to give him shit for being so "busy" (*as if he were just mired in some?? random??? assignment????*). Leila informed him that he was bordering on getting disinherited, or at least getting kicked out of the Yorba Linda house, unless he came over for lunch tomorrow.

"*Beh man goft een.*" She nodded to Cora. "*Dokhdararoh beeyar bah khodet.*"

So that's how it's going to be, he thought. Vicarious passive-aggressive demands to bring "*that girl*" to lunch tomorrow. *Rude.* Kaveh's eyes darted between his cousins, his sister, and then to Cora, wondering how his mother had *known* to insist he bring his extremely new, extremely young girlfriend. He hadn't told anyone about their relationship, not even Paris.

Ramin, still in his twenties, was far too cool to dance in the VIP section (he at least had the good grace to go onto the main floor for that) and excused himself and his girlfriend to hit up the bar and the main dance floor. Before they left Nasser's VIP area, Ramin paused to say something to Cora, grasping her by the shoulder and whispering something in her ear. He then gave a curt smile to both of them and went on his way.

"What did he say?" asked Kaveh.

"He said, 'I think you're incredibly brave.'" She smiled in slight disbelief. "I assume he means for wearing this outfit in public."

Nasser, who was both pushing forty and had never known shame, had no such compunction and was perfectly content to stay in the VIP section he had paid for. "That's Snoop Dogg," he whisper-yelled, gesturing to the adjacent VIP area. Indeed, there was a man who looked an awful lot like Snoop Dogg at the center of a massive entourage. "Snoop *Saggy Sag.*"

Cora humored Nasser by looking impressed, while Kaveh began the task of what he knew would be the explaining of many, many jokes ("*Sag* means 'dog.' Geddit?"). The DJ slid from the Nelly Furtado / Timbaland joint "Promiscuous" to "Low," the overplayed Flo Rida song. *Pas de points, DJ,* Kaveh thought. Nasser, however, was thrilled. "Ey, Flo Rida, the rida of flows!" He put his champagne down, pulled Girlfriend of the Month next to him, and resumed his Tevye dancing. "Let's see what you've got!" he said, looking at Cora.

Cora looked at Kaveh, alarmed. "You heard him," he said, taking her by the hand and leading her in the same direction Ramin had gone.

"What?"

"I probably should have warned you, but you're going to have to dance. If you don't, you *will* be forced to."

She smiled weakly, clearly thinking he was joking. "Why?"

"Persian edict. Resistance is futile. You have to dance."

Her smile faded as she realized he was serious. "They'll force me to?"

"Well, we all will. It's a thing."

"I've . . . never danced before, to be honest. At least, not in a club like this."

"Well, you're about to."

"You know this isn't really my scene."

"It isn't *my* scene, either! You've seen what's on my iPod! Come on, let's go embarrass ourselves."

He took her down to the dance floor, which by now was pretty packed. After perhaps five minutes (and two shots of tequila), she finally lost her sense of shame and danced with him properly, going even so far as to attempt to grind. It was clearly not something she was practiced at, which made it all the more adorable. After a few songs, a couple of girls tried to get Cora to dance with them, clearly enjoying male attention from the performance. Cora looked at him as if asking permission, and he laughed and nodded; he was *not* about to discourage her flirting with girls.

Being here was so stupid, it was so *fucking* stupid. It was the embodiment of American excess, it was where intellectualism went to die, it was fundamentally *not his scene.* And yet, it was *fun,* that thing *ossdahdha* like himself were not supposed to admit. The DJ mixed to a song he hadn't heard before, the lyrics repeating, *Just dance, it'll be okay, just dance.* That felt like solid life advice in that moment. *Just dance.* So they did.

Then everything turned black.

He pulled her into a tight embrace as the music cut to silence. Then a *thrum* vibrated through the building, as though an explosion had gone off some distance away. A few girls screamed, and there was a moment of quiet confusion before most people started talking over each other in the darkness.

"An EMP?" asked Kaveh.

Cora looked around wildly. "No," she said, pointing to the door. "The exit lights are still on. If it were an EMP, those would be out, too."

He stopped breathing, straining to listen, but his fellow club-goers were too busy loudly speculating on what was going on to let him hear anything. Then the house lights went up, illuminating the club in bright, unsexy fluorescents, and he heard a gas generator somewhere outside. Everyone looked around for some direction, which eventually came in the form of a manager near the entrance.

"Ladies and gentlemen," he said. "The entire block seems to be experiencing a power outage. If you'd like to wait and see if the power will come back on, you are welcome to do so."

Cora didn't wait for him to stop talking, all but sprinting in those heels back up the stairs to the VIP section. Kaveh followed, and by the time he made it, she had dug out her cell phone from her purse. "It's still working," she said, holding it open so Kaveh could see. Screen still operational, battery still full. Definitely not an EMP.

"I'd hope so!" said Nasser, clueless as ever. "If the power doesn't come back on soon, I'm going to have to get a refund."

"Texting Sol," she said, popping off a message. Then she looked at Kaveh gravely, hastily gathered her things, and grabbed him by the hand. "Come on."

They darted for the door, which was already growing clogged with the half-drunk occupants of the club. When they emerged, both sides of the street were powerless, but Wilshire was less than a block to the south, and the power was still running on the southbound side of Wilshire.

A text pinged Cora's phone, and she frantically checked it. "What'd he say?" asked Kaveh.

"He says he doesn't know what caused it."

Kaveh noted that some of the people on the street were looking into the westward sky, and, following their gaze, he saw the source of their fixation: a plume of smoke rising in the air not two blocks away, illuminated from behind by the lights of Santa Monica. At the base of the column was a faint glow, presumably from the blaze that was producing the smoke column. Eli recognized the location of the smoke column before he did and began running to its source, Leila close behind.

Fuck, he realized. *Eli's store.*

It took them less than a minute to run that two blocks, but it felt so much longer. The fire department was already there by the time they reached the scene, blocking them from getting close. It wasn't Eli's family's jewelry store that had been hit but rather the storefront two units over. This was arson—a bomb had done this. It must have blown up a transformer, knocking out the power in the process. Fire poured out of the building, and with the flames and the smoke, it took Kaveh longer than it otherwise might have to see what the building was— a mosque.

"This isn't your family's, is it?" asked Cora, a few steps behind him.

He let out a deep breath and shook his head, too dazed to explain that his family wasn't religious, and either way, Eli was Jewish. Eli came back, apparently rebuffed by the fire department. "Some of the glass got blown out," he said. "They won't let me near it."

Within another minute, almost everyone from their party had gathered near the blaze. Sirens blared in the distance, and Nasser grabbed Eli by the shoulder. "Hang tight. There's nothing you can do right now."

They stood in stunned silence, watching as the firefighters screwed their hoses together and doused the flames. Kaveh caught a glance from Leila, and in that glance an unmistakable question—were the threat letter they'd been sent and this bombing related?

Had this happened because of him?

March 8, 2008, 12:10 PM PDT
Los Angeles Times

FBI Investigates Bombing at Beverly Hills, California, Mosque

By Isaac Gantwerk Meyer

An explosion from a bomb rattled a Beverly Hills mosque early Saturday morning, authorities said. There were no injuries, but a large portion of the building was damaged by fire.

The blast at the Islamic Center of Beverly Hills happened just after 10 p.m. local time, the Muslim American Society of Greater Los Angeles said.

"Someone threw an explosive device and started a fire in the entry lobby of the mosque," the society said. "Firefighters rushed to the scene and put out the fire."

The FBI has taken over the investigation and Los Angeles special agent in charge Harold Feld told reporters that the blast was from an improvised explosive device.

Aziz Twajiri, executive director of the Islamic center, told reporters that a witness saw a pickup truck drive away after the device was tossed into the mosque.

A motive in the bombing, and whether it was a hate crime, has not been determined.

Kaveh had no idea what to expect where his family's treatment of Cora was concerned, especially with the events of last night now casting a pall over things. He'd sent his mother a text message before they left the hotel that morning:

> we're fine, valee lotfan be nice and
> speak English. This has been so hard
> for her. Babash khaylee azialesh
> kardeh. Nils has done some really
> terrible things to her yavashakee. No
> one else knows about that.

Her response: ok pesaram.

Okay, my son. Cool minimalist, atonal response. Coolcoolcoolcool-cool.

Kaveh and Cora weren't the first to arrive—Leila and Eli had arrived ahead of them, which if anything made the scene solemner. His mother didn't greet them at the front door, but rather waited for them with everyone else in their big open-concept kitchen. His mother had an air about her that was both refined and calculating, quiet and watchful. Even at family gatherings like this, she looked professional, and her long black hair was pulled back in a tight ponytail. At first, she didn't acknowledge him at all, then looked at both of them coolly. Cora shivered like his mother's gaze was a cold wind.

"*Pesaram*," his mother said.

"*Maman.*"

He approached her, and they kissed each other's cheeks.

"Good to see you, finally," she said, in English. *Thank God.*

"Sorry, Mom. Been a busy month."

Cora may not have caught the slight hesitation as his mother regarded her, but Kaveh did. She paused, looked Cora over, then took her by the hand before kissing both cheeks. "I'm very glad to meet you. I'm sorry it had to be under these circumstances."

"I'm sorry, too," said Cora. "Trouble seems to follow me around." Seeming to think that was the wrong thing to say, she switched tracks. "You have a very beautiful home."

"Thank you," said Mom. It was a nice house. Unlike Nasser and the Beverly Hills branch of the family who absolutely went ham on the "Persian Palace" chic, Kaveh's parents preferred a much more Crate & Barrel understated style of wealth-flaunting.

"I'm glad to see both of you," Kaveh's father chimed in, much warmer than his mother as he greeted Cora (*kiss, kiss*). "After what happened last night, I'm just glad you all are safe, thanks God."

Within an hour, the entire extended family had shown up. Two sets of aunts and uncles in addition to Ramin and Nasser, plus his daughter, Minu, from a previous marriage and Leila's daughter, Ava, who'd spent the night with her as a sleepover, as well as Nasser's Girlfriend of the Month from last night (whom Kaveh now knew as Anahit, and she was indeed Armenian). What he'd been told was "lunch with the family" was turning into a family reunion. *So much for speaking English.*

His family clearly didn't know what to do with Cora other than ply her with crispy rice and *ghormeh sabzi*; they all knew who she was, what her claim to fame was, but didn't know what to say about it, so ignored it, opting instead for the more banal questions like *What did you study?* and *What are your plans for the future?* Not like they could ask casual questions about her family.

Kaveh, on the other hand, they flocked to, jeering at him for being so distant and teasing him for being so buried in his obviously way-more-important-than-them work. She was obviously "on," alert and quick to respond quickly and politely to the slightest bit of attention, but otherwise stayed quiet. After lunch wound down, he excused himself and took her out into the backyard.

"You seem sad," he observed, taking a seat on one of the ottomans on the patio by the pool and patting the space next to him. His parents' pool aesthetic was "natural," a shale rock "formation" creating a waterfall that spilled into the pool, even though it was far too cold to swim this time of year.

"*Sad* isn't the word," she said, still tense as she sat down next to him. "*Jealous,* that's the word."

He frowned and wrapped an arm around her shoulder.

"I guess this is part of why your family has done so well here," she continued. "They actually stick together and help each other. The whole idea feels genuinely, well, alien to me."

He sighed and squeezed her shoulder gently. She was right, and it was an extension of what he'd told her the night the beeper guy had accosted her—your family is what shapes you. His supportive family had shaped him into the confident, secure person he was, and her neglectful family had turned her into this fearful creature that hardly trusted the ground beneath her not to collapse.

Kaveh heard the patio door close and saw that they had been followed. He smiled, beckoning his niece to approach. "Hey, *daie,*" he said. "What's up?"

Ava eyed him, then Cora, clearly the object of her real interest. A raven-haired cutie with almost geometric bangs, she was already on track to skip her second-grade year. "Do you really know the aliens?"

"We both do," said Kaveh, "but she's the real expert."

"How are you an expert?"

"Well, once upon a time," said Cora, smiling and not missing a beat, "when Jude first communicated with me, I offered to speak to other humans for him, so he'd be better understood. And for a little while, I was his voice. He'd tell me what he wanted people to know, and I told it to people in a way they'd understand. But he's sick right now."

"What's wrong with him?" asked Ava.

"We don't know," said Cora. "Nikola is his . . . family. He followed Nikola to Pershing Square to protect him, but nearly got killed himself. The whole thing really scared him. Really messed him up. He's kind of been in a coma ever since."

"Will he get better?"

Her smile was still there, but now it was taking some effort to maintain. "We don't know. I hope so."

"Is he your friend? They said on the news that he was."

"Yeah." She said it in this wistful voice he'd never heard from her when talking about Ampersand. "He was my friend."

Kaveh's gaze darted between the two. It was obvious Cora was more comfortable with the child than she was with the curious-bordering-on-judgmental eyes of the adults of the family. He remembered her mentioning that she had a sister who was about Ava's age. She missed her sister, she'd told him, but she was too keen on avoiding her mother to spend time with her. "Hey, Ava, you want to show her your garden?"

"Sure!" piped Ava, and Cora actually seemed relieved, shooting him a cute smile as she followed his niece down the hill to see her "garden."

She was good with kids, he mused, and the thought that she'd make a good mother entered his mind. For the shortest of moments, the thought warmed him before promptly being replaced by a peal of nausea. *If Nikola absconds with us, if he finds another habitable planet a billion light-years from here, she'll have no choice.*

He heard the patio door open and close and turned to see his own mother approaching. Apparently, she'd been waiting to get him alone.

"She's very pretty," she said in Farsi, looking in the girls' direction as she approached him. Her Persian tenor was lower than when she spoke English.

"And very young," he said, finishing the thought he knew she was having.

"You know what's funny," she said, "I had the same thought the first time I saw the Pershing Square photograph. She was so beautiful, in such contrast to those . . . What was the word again? The 'almond' word?"

"Amygdaline."

"Yes, your aliens, they were so horrible to look at, but she was so beautiful. It almost looked staged."

"A lot of people think it was."

She took a seat next to him on the ottoman, and he could feel her gaze boring into him. He took a deep breath. "What happened last night, there's a possibility they were targeting me," he said.

"I know. Leila told me."

Traitor. "But we don't know for sure."

She glanced at him. "If not for this, then for something else. That is inevitable for someone who is trying to change the world."

"That doesn't mean I want to drag you into it."

She smiled faintly. "God has blessed you with many gifts, though I often wondered why He blessed you with gifts that so often put you in danger. Why could He not have made you a gifted surgeon?" Kaveh cracked a smile, looking at her knowingly. "But these are the gifts you were given, and you have done amazing things with them. The life you have chosen means you will always have enemies. It isn't your fault that the world is full of people who will hate you no matter what, just because of your name."

He stared out into the backyard, shaking his head distantly. "But that is the world we live in."

He felt her hand on his back, and she kissed his cheek warmly before going back inside, leaving him alone with his thoughts. That peal of nausea at the thought of Cora being a mother had not abated. She'd be a good mother *here,* if that was what she wanted, in a human society, not alone on some hypothetical New Earth a billion light-years away. But being the new Eve, or at least one of them? *Oh yes, you get to be a mother, but only in the most hellish of circumstances, and you get to do it with me, who never wanted this.*

How to go about it? Who gets to contribute their "genetic material," and who doesn't? He could let entire races of people go extinct. Really, he would have to. He couldn't possibly get a sample from all of them, and no one would be alive to exclaim, *Quelle éthique!* Race and ethnicity would be a thing of the past. There would be no cultures left to appropriate. Divorced from human civilization, history was nothing but data, and culture was only what Kaveh, Cora, and whatever other poor unfortunate broodmares Nikola absconded with remembered. And what could that possibly mean to some child who had no concept of culture besides whatever one they built?

Here, little child growing up on an alien world, here is some information about your culture, your ethnic group. Or rather, the culture, the ethnic group that is attached to your genetic heritage. Your culture, your ethnic group, are extinct. You have no context for any of this, or why it matters, because you were raised on an alien world by people from a culture that no longer exists. So go, build your own culture, and feel free to learn about the old ones, but it won't mean anything. Your ancestors are nothing but a genome, and your culture is nothing but a string of binary code on a hard drive.

Kaveh turned toward the bay window that looked into the kitchen. Leila was talking with her hands as she was wont to do, engaged in what looked like a reenactment of some social absurdity, and his mother and aunt looked absolutely scandalized. They'd long moved on from the dark happenings of the previous night, and now Nasser was laughing to his uncle and Ramin about some YouTube clip of the Wolfgang Petersen movie *Troy* with a hilarious Persian dub.

And in the backyard, he could hear Cora in conversation with Ava on the other side of the wall, probably by the weeping willow down by the stream at the bottom of the hill.

If we leave, what exactly are we saving? he wondered. *Are we really saving anything by sneaking out some embryos? What are we, if not our culture, our social groups, our civilization?*

Just strings of DNA and RNA.

He couldn't do this.

Kaveh followed their voices and found them gingerly fingering the willow's branches. Cora's eyes brightened when she saw him. "Ava was telling me how much water this tree needs."

"Yeah, it's kind of a flex," he said. He winked at his niece. "*Daie,* could you give us a minute?"

Ava smiled at him in a way that made him think they might have been "girl talking" about him before he'd arrived. "Sure thing," she said, and she skipped back toward the house.

"Do you like my tree?" he asked, approaching Cora. "Not as majestic as if it had been planted on the banks of the Mississippi, but at least it's really expensive to keep alive."

"Is this your tree?" she asked with a laugh.

"Yeah," he said, reaching up to touch one of the drooping branches. "I remember countless childhood summers frolicking under this tree."

She backed away, a smile playing at her lips, until her back was against the trunk of the tree and his feet were an inch away from hers.

"I'm just kidding. They bought this house in 1997." He kissed her, a long, soft, gentle kiss, and she melted into it. He pulled away, looked at her sleepy expression, and said, "Come to New York with me."

She went on alert like she'd been doused with cold water. "What?"

"Come back with me to New York."

"And . . . do what?"

He steeled himself. "And finish your degree."

"What?"

"Listen, I've been talking to the dean of admissions at Columbia—"

"Wait, you know the dean of admissions at Columbia?"

"Yeah, I know everybody. Look, here's the deal; we are a little past deadline for fall admissions, but I think with some elbow grease and some nepotism and all things considered . . ."

She stared at him, her mouth hanging open like a fish's. "Kaveh—"

"Well, I can't say anything officially, because technically, you still need to actually apply, but I submitted your Pershing Square essay—"

"*That's* why you had me write those?"

"—and he unofficially told me, you're in for fall semester."

She'd have backed away from him if there hadn't been a tree trunk in the way. "How the *hell* am I going to afford Columbia?"

Kaveh took a step back, waiting for her to get it. "You'll get need-based scholarships."

She shook her head like a pendulum.

He gestured to himself. "I can provide need-based scholarships."

"*Why?*"

"Because you could have a profound effect on the world! You already *have* had a profound effect on the world! You have a tremendous opportunity. You could actually help all of humanity."

"What, by going to Columbia?"

"No, Columbia is a step. Life is a series of steps. This is one of them."

The pendulum of her head swayed faster, and her shocked, defensive expression turned melancholy. "I can't leave him."

Kaveh slapped his hands to his face and groaned into them. "You cannot spend your life waiting around on him!"

"My connection to Ampersand is way more potentially consequential than me being one of the shit million kids going to an Ivy."

"And you don't have to lose that because you go to an Ivy! These things are not mutually exclusive."

"So I go to Columbia, and then what? Be an activist?"

"Maybe! You be whatever the world needs you to be."

"And you think if I finish my bachelor's, I'm going to be alien fucking

Gandhi? People won't listen to me. Why would they listen to me over anyone else?"

"Because you are who you are, and you've done what you've done! You are the first human in history to break the communication barrier, and people don't even know that about you. You're the girl in the photograph who threw her body between an unconscious alien and the barrel of a gun."

"And people think I'm an insane species traitor for that."

"And even more people think you're a hero for it! When people look at that picture, who do they see themselves in, the man with the gun or the girl in front of it? Yes, there are people out there who see themselves in the man with the gun, but the vast, vast majority of people see themselves in *you*. They look at themselves and say, 'We are compassionate, we are brave, we are selfless. We are not monsters. I'm not the man with the gun, I'm the girl who threw herself in front of the gun.' And if we can believe that about ourselves, then maybe whatever is out there can see us that way, too."

"Do you believe that?" she asked. "Do you believe that about humanity, after what happened last night?"

"I have to have hope!" His voice shook at the thought of his family. Ava with her botany; Nasser the meathead, doting father and fan of *Troy* dubs. His mercurial mother and clueless, generous-to-a-fault father. He gestured toward the house. "I cannot give up on this!"

"And you think I'm the one to turn this ship around, to steer us away from bombing mosques and toward selfless acts of heroism."

"No, I am not saying you are the *one* to do anything, any more than I am. That's not how this works. There is no One Great Man that's going to change the world here. There is only you and me, two people who have some influence, who might be able to influence other yous and mes out there."

Cora hugged herself and looked at the ground. "It feels like we're rats on a ship. Rats on the *Titanic* trying to move the rudder. Even if we did have real power and influence, I don't think there's any force on Earth that's going to change the direction of this ship."

"That might be true. But if this ship is going down, I'd rather go down with it than abandon it."

He reached out for her, cupping her face and kissing her cheeks, her eyelids, her forehead, then pulling her into an embrace.

"Where will I live?" she whispered.

"With me, at first. Though once school starts, it might not be a bad idea to try the dorms. Start reestablishing a sense of independence."

"You're kicking me out?" Her tone was just joking enough that it didn't raise any alarms.

"Well, your new Ivy League friends might get a little jealous if you spend too much time around the nursing home."

She smiled, her eyes shining. Frightened. Nervous. Hopeful.

"It'll be fun. You can be my plus-ones at all these boring events I have to go to. There's a bunch of new Broadway shows I've been dying to see. There's this new one about Washington Heights that everyone's raving about."

"Washington Heights the . . . neighborhood?"

"It's all the rage."

"I haven't seen a Broadway show since I was in high school."

"Was it *Cats*?"

"How did you know?"

"It's always *Cats*." He laughed. "Don't worry. It closed years ago. *Cats* can't hurt you anymore."

"Is this guy bothering you?" Nasser's voice made her jump, and Kaveh turned to see his cousin approaching. "We *can* kick his ass for you. The whole crew is here. Just say the word. We'll kick his ass."

"Truth is, he might deserve it," said Kaveh.

"No!" said Cora, laughing nervously. "No, thank you for the offer, but no. I'll do it myself, later."

"That's good!" Nasser laughed. "I'm getting pretty old for that, anyway, but if you need me to kick his ass, let me know."

"I will," she said.

"I love that you're a Denis Leary fan," said Nasser. "That 'I'm an Asshole' song is hilarious."

Cora's expression grew serious. There was only one person who had the honor of "Asshole" as his ringtone. "Did someone call me?"

He handed her her flip phone. "Yeah, someone's been calling you for the last five minutes. Thought it might be important."

Cora snatched the phone from him, redialing the number. Kaplan answered immediately.

"What's going on?" she asked. She received a short and to-the-point answer and looked at Kaveh urgently. "We have to go. Now."

· · · · ·

It was a forty-minute drive to Los Alamitos with no traffic; Kaveh made it in thirty-five. They ushered his car through without even requesting that he stop, which sent off even more alarms in his mind. He drove up to the building where Nikola had been quartered for the last few weeks, and they let him leave his Land Rover right out front. Another bad sign. Ghasabian was already waiting for them outside.

"What happened?" said Cora as she hopped out of the car.

"We're still trying to figure that out," said Ghasabian, power walking into the building and down the hall where Ampersand was being held. "This way."

"Where is he?" demanded Cora, having to jog to keep up with him.

"His quarters are ahead and to the left, but—"

Cora dashed ahead; which room Ghasabian was referring to was obvious, as there were at least a dozen people standing around the door, looking inside.

"Cora!" Kaveh called after her, following her inside, preparing for the worst. It was the same room Nikola had tried to rouse Ampersand in. The translucent plastic sheets hanging from the ceiling were still there. That metal table was still there. Even the foam top was still there.

Ampersand was not.

"That's just it," said Ghasabian. "We've been trying to figure out what happened. But we're at a loss. They've vanished. They're both just . . . gone."

PART 4

HAPPINESS IS A WARM GUN

April 15, 2008

ARTICLE 28 Everyone is entitled to a social and international order in which the rights and freedoms set forth in this Declaration can be fully realized.

April 14, 2008

The Washington Post

Lawmakers Prepare to Take on Question of ETI Personhood

By Claire Wenzel

WASHINGTON—When lawmakers on Capitol Hill begin to hear testimony regarding the legal status of ETIs this week, it won't be exactly what Senate Judiciary Committee members envisioned when they launched their probe in January.

For one thing, the issue of what the ETIs in question even look like was violently revealed to the world in Pershing Square with the sudden appearance of the two ETIs known as Nikola Sassanian and Jude Atheatos. In some ways, their appearance raised more questions than it answered.

For another, although the Department of Defense claims to have 23 of the species known as "amygdaline" in custody, including two who have formally requested asylum as refugees, Atheatos and Sassanian have been missing for more than six weeks. The hearings will be going forward with the two most famous ETIs in the world MIA.

Testimony will be heard from across the spectrum on the personhood issue, from experts in the field of sociology to military officials who claim to have witnessed amygdalines in action. Cora Sabino, the famous subject of the photograph taken during the riot in Pershing Square showing her defending Sassanian and Atheatos from gunman Tony Cascio, will be among witnesses to testify. Jano Miranda, who organized the rally in Pershing Square and was likewise present for the arrival of Nikola Sassanian, will begin his testimony on Tuesday.

Cora had assumed the hearing would take place in the Capitol Building. She was surprised to learn that was never the case for Senate hearings, but not disappointed; she'd been having nightmares about the Capitol blowing up with her inside it, as that was a thing that tended to happen in movies where aliens were involved.

The building was a sort of new age, open-air structure with a glass ceiling over a strange black art deco sculpture at the center of the interior courtyard, visible from the hallways of any of the several stories that looked down onto it. Right now, that courtyard was flooded with people surrounding the black sculpture, like water around a stone. From her angle, the giant art installation looked like Nikola.

"You know, you could have just watched this on C-SPAN."

Cora turned to see a face she hadn't seen in weeks. Sol, taking a drag on a cigarette and blowing it out over the edge of the balcony.

"I didn't know you smoked," said Cora.

"Yeah, well, we're all addicts in some phase of relapse around here. Your day will come."

She leaned her forearms on the balcony, continuing her survey of the goings-on down below. "Isn't smoking banned in federal buildings?"

Sol nodded to an open door across the hall with a sign that read, "Smoking Room." "I'm within twenty-five feet of that; they don't care."

She smiled. There was a slight possibility that she might have even missed him. "How's it going?"

"Have to head back west tomorrow, so I'll miss your testimony. The *fucking* nutbars have found out where the body of AG-ETI-047 is being temporarily evaluated, so I have to go oversee the move."

Weird, he didn't just call AG-ETI-047 "Obelus" like everyone else. "What do you mean? Like the Gadsden Line?"

"Yup. You know, they're wrong about most things, but broken clock, twice a day, et cetera. Main thing they're wrong about this time is that they think the body we have is *alive,* but either way, it's turned into a huge liability."

Cora nodded, and she caught him looking at her like she might know something that could *help,* as if she might know how they found out Obelus's mangled corpse was in San Bernardino.

"I know you no longer have any obligation to tell me anything," said Sol, "but you really haven't heard anything from Jude?"

"Honest truth, no," she said, and a knot formed in her stomach at the thought of Ampersand. It had been more than six weeks since he and Nikola had disappeared, and the only clue she had as to what had happened was their bond, the wall that thickened and thinned at its own mercurial whim. As for where Nikola had gone, she had no idea, but Ampersand had not been taken against his will, of that she was fairly sure. Her senses told her that Ampersand had left of his own volition, likely to resume his pursuit of Obelus, but that it was not a coordinated effort. Wherever Ampersand was, she was fairly certain he was alone.

"Well, if nothing else, this hearing will have pretty big consequences for our other two asylum seekers."

Cora hadn't heard news of Woodward and Bernstein in weeks. She didn't even know which government agency had them in custody, but she assumed it was Customs and Border Patrol, or some other branch of Homeland Security. It was hard not to think of them as prisoners, wherever they were.

"They have names, though," said Sol. "It's kind of on theme."

"What do you mean?"

"Jude is an apostle, and Nicholas is a saint. So they told their caretakers to name them after apostles, so they liked 'Andronicus' and 'Junia' of the options presented."

Cora laughed faintly. She only knew about those two minor apostles, one of which might have been Jesus's sole female apostle, from distant Catholic trivia factoids. "'Andy and June.' It suits them."

"I thought so."

"Can you tell me where they are?"

Sol took a long drag of his cigarette. "I don't even know where they are." He put the cigarette out on the railing, then flicked it in the trash. "In some ways, their situation is even more dire than the rest of them. At least Esperas can escape if he wants since he still has Brako. Andy and June are helpless."

"Are they okay?"

"I honestly don't know."

"They took it on good faith that we'd treat them as people, and now look what's happening."

"Well, you'd better do a good job tomorrow, or things might get a lot worse for them."

Cora looked down to the ground level to see Brigadier General Porter marching through a flock of reporters, dressed in full uniform.

"That's a lot of . . . medals," she remarked.

"Don't get excited. Porter's not exactly on our side."

Heat flared under her skin, and she was only glad she wasn't testifying on the same day he was. "Not surprised. What's he here for?"

"He's here to discuss offensive capabilities he's seen. Because *someone* had to make a big show about not wanting to go to Temecula."

Oh, he means the broken-glass stunt during that meeting six hundred years ago. Of course, Porter had been dying to weaponize that since the day it happened. Good for him that Congress gave him the opportunity.

"So where's your boyfriend?" asked Sol.

Such a strange word, even after several weeks of using it, even after functionally moving into his New York apartment. "He's talking to the press."

"How's that going?"

"It's going well," she said, defenses on the rise. "He's been good for me."

"I bet." He smirked. "How many strings did he pull to get you into Columbia?"

"Would it kill you not to be a complete douchebag for ten minutes?"

He looked at her, and for a moment, he was the old Sol, the man abusing his power wearing an expression that said, *I am going to make your life hell.* Then, his features relaxed. "You know it's because I'm just jealous."

"Of *Kaveh*?" she asked, smacked by the sudden and confusing implication.

"Both of you in some ways. *I* didn't get into Columbia. Speak of the devil."

Cora turned around to see Kaveh approaching, Kaveh *and* Senator Cohen, the senator who had decided to champion their cause. She'd spent a lot of time with his staffers in the last couple of days, but she hadn't met the man himself.

"Miss Sabino," he said, taking her hand in a firm handshake. He looked to be in his late fifties, a guy with a memorable, quirky face and curly graying hair. "Pleasure to finally meet you."

"You as well," she said. She glanced at Kaveh in his sand-colored, "yes, I got this personally tailored" suit. He'd bought her pencil skirt and blouse from Banana Republic, but she felt so out of place in them she might as well have been wearing a clown costume. "Thank you for . . . everything."

"Of course," said Cohen. "I find the argument absurd that if a hostile ETI wanted to play games with a system like the stock market, a law might stop them, but it sets a dangerous precedent not just for our relationship to any potential alien civilizations but to each other as well. To say nothing of our position as world leaders—the rest of the world is looking to see what we do before making their own decisions."

Kaveh shot her a look, and she caught it. He wasn't thrilled, but the truth of the matter was that Cohen was right; most world powers, even China, had held off on passing their own laws. That didn't mean that the rest of the world intended to follow suit with whatever the United States did, but they were certainly waiting to *see* what the United States did. Some smaller countries like Costa Rica, Luxembourg, and Cuba (who was proud to claim the title of the first to do so) had already passed laws extending personhood to amygdaline ETIs, but mostly as a symbolic gesture. Japan was the only G7 country to have passed a law extending human rights to amygdalines (and *only* amygdalines—other alien species TBD).

"What are your other expert witnesses going to say?" asked Cora.

"Our main point of attack is to focus on the Third Option as being completely toothless for its stated goals. Your job, of course, will be to enforce the philosophical answer—that ignoring any questions of what the law might accomplish, we know the answer to the personhood question—they are people, by any meaningful definition of the word, and to assert otherwise is rooted in discrimination."

"Human supremacy, if you will," said Sol.

Cohen, ever the savvy politician, gave Sol a look of sort of mutual understanding. "I'll see you inside," he said, and left.

"We get to live in the timeline where the phrase *human supremacy* is a thing," said Cora, watching the man go, flanked by his staffers.

"Yeah," said Kaveh. "Somehow I bet the type of person who uses that phrase isn't going to be referring to *all* humans."

· · · · ·

"Chairman Leahy, Ranking Member Specter, members of the committee, my name is Brigadier General Wesley Porter. I am the head of the Space Intelligence National Security Task Force, whose mission is to gather intelligence about extraterrestrial activity outside of the purview of those presently in custody of the Department of Health and Human Services."

Porter's opening spiel was short and to the point before he got to the goods. They didn't have to wait long. "I would like to enter this into the record."

Cora couldn't see the printouts he was holding up, but she knew what they were photographs of. The glass in the conference room Ampersand had shattered and re-formed almost three months ago.

"Can you tell the committee what happened on the morning of February 2, 2008?" asked the chairman.

"I requested that the amygdaline AG-ETI-046 'Jude Atheatos' accompany the army intelligence unit to the landing site near Temecula, California," said Porter. "Jude Atheatos did respond with an act of violence that damaged federal property, shattering every window in sight, then using his remote electromagnetic manipulation capabilities—what is informally described as 'telekinesis'—to reinstate the pieces of glass in a matter of seconds and using incredible remote heat to fuse the glass back into place."

"That's not what happened," she whispered.

Kaveh shot her a "not so loud" side-eye. "What?"

"He did not *request* Ampersand go to Temecula; he told him he had to go and he had no choice. Like specifically said, 'This isn't a request,' those were his *exact* words. That was when he broke the glass. Ampersand was saying, 'You can't make me,' not lording his power for the hell of it."

"You can see where a guy like Porter wouldn't appreciate the difference, yeah?"

"Not all communication is verbal," Porter continued. "This was a form of communication, and it was unmistakable. Jude Atheatos was communicating that he had great power, and he would use that power in opposition to the wishes of the American government. I have no doubt the amount of power he used was a trifle amount compared to his full capabilities."

Porter's testimony didn't last long; only six senators took their turn, with the rest of them ceding their time before his session ended. It was as if Porter had been scanning the room for her when they locked eyes, and it seemed to her the first time that he'd ever looked at her intentionally. Like her mere existence was an act of emasculation, and he was going to do everything in his power to avenge the indignity.

But Brigadier General Wesley Porter was not Tuesday's star witness— that honor went to Jano Miranda. When they reconvened after lunch, it was Jano's time to shine. She'd exchanged a look with him when she arrived in the chamber, and from that alone, she knew that this was nothing like the debate on MSNBC. They weren't talking heads being given a nominal fee to discuss a topic; Pershing Square had changed him. This wasn't a political game to him anymore; this was existential, and she was working for the enemy.

In all, Miranda's testimony went for a little over three hours. Senator Cohen's turn to grill Miranda came toward the end, and when it came, he leaned forward eagerly.

"Mr. Miranda," said Cohen. "Could you please reiterate your basic position with regard to creating a new category of person to grant legal status to ETIs?"

"Certainly. There comes a point where we have to admit that we can't hold ourselves to some utopian ideal; we have to be realists. And in this case, we have two things to consider: how people react, and what the ETIs are capable of. If we give them unrestricted freedom, we give them the right to inject themselves into public spaces just as any human would."

Miranda held up a photograph printed on a sheet of paper, one he'd entered into the record hours ago but kept coming back to. It was a photograph of Nikola from Pershing Square from before Oskar Halmoka had detonated the EMP, from before Kaveh had even shown up. Shrewdly, Miranda's camp had also cut him out of the photo, so as to keep him from looking frightened or vulnerable. Cora knew amygdaline body language well enough to know that there was nothing aggressive in Nikola's posture; his eyes were bright and curious, his hands curled up in that neutral mantid pose, the crest on the back of his head half-spread, neither on alert nor relaxed. But the untrained human eye didn't see any of this; to the uninitiated, this was an eldritch horror invading a major city, a horrifying thing to behold in a photograph, let alone in person as Miranda had.

"This is a photograph of the ETI that caused a riot in Pershing Square on February 9, 2008." Miranda had refused to call Nikola by his name the entire time he'd been questioned. "My argument is that it is immaterial whether or not this being had malevolent intent. An alien simply being present in a public space was enough to cause mass chaos and several deaths. And then are we supposed to blame ourselves when people have a very human reaction to something that looks like *that*? You can't declare the crowd uncivilized for having a very rational fear response."

"Mr. Miranda," said Cohen, "let us assume for the moment complete neutrality on the part of the ETI Nikola Sassanian. It neither wishes us ill, nor wishes us well. It is simply an entity existing in a public space. It seems to me that you are arguing in favor of restricted freedoms on a basis that it is human nature to be discriminatory."

"I think that having that discussion about a discriminated class of human is very different from having that discussion about an alien with potentially incredible destructive capabilities."

Senator Cohen took off his glasses, looking at Miranda like he was a grade school student who'd given him a flimsy excuse for his tardiness. "And what I am hearing is an argument that we should allow the human impulse to be discriminatory to inform decisions on whether or not to expand human rights to include nonhuman ETIs."

"Our laws serve human interests first and foremost," said Miranda, "and I feel like it's in the public interest never to have anything like Pershing Square happen ever again."

"I think we are all in agreement on that," said Cohen. "The first time any of the public saw a living ETI was at a rally at which people died, a rally *you* helped organize."

"Senator, I would argue that the context of the rally is immaterial. I would argue that the ETI's intent is immaterial. You cannot place a being like this in a public space and expect people *not* to feel unsafe. Even ignoring the way the ETI looks to human eyes, how can anyone feel safe not knowing what this being is physically capable of?"

"Do you believe that human rights should or should not be meted out based on physical ability—or physical appearance, for that matter? For their *potential* to make other people uncomfortable?" asked Cohen.

"Again, I do not believe you can apply standards created for humans to beings with superhuman ability." At this, for the first time, Cora felt fear creep into Miranda's voice. "I saw what they were capable of. I'm pretty sure I only saw a sliver of what they were capable of."

"And what did you see?" asked Cohen.

"I saw a van picking up speed and coming toward me. I saw the hood of a van crumple like it had hit an invisible wall."

"So what you are saying is," said Cohen, nearly cutting him off, "you saw a van charging a passive ETI, and either some invisible extraterrestrial force defended the ETI, or the ETI defended itself." Cora shuffled, itching a little that even the well-meaning Senator Cohen was still referring to Nikola as *it* instead of *he* or *they.* Even Miranda knew better than to describe Nikola as *it.*

"Yes," said Miranda. "If that force, that invisible wall, did indeed come from the ETI, what I saw was self-defense, but self-defense that comes from incredible power. We know little about what technologies could allow for remote electromagnetic manipulation, but many scientists agree that the ability to manipulate matter remotely would take an incredible amount of power. We're talking hundreds, maybe even thousands of nuclear bombs, just to stop a van from ten feet away."

Senator Cohen, his time allotment nearly over, put his glasses back on. "Indeed, people did die at Pershing Square, but none of them were at the hands, so to speak, of the ETI. We had three die in a helicopter crash—one pilot and two bystanders—as the direct result of a human-made EMP. Another innocent bystander was shot by the LAPD, and of course the gunman, Tony Cascio, who threatened the human Cora Sabino and the ETIs Jude Atheatos and Nikola Sassanian, was shot and killed by the LAPD. Indeed, I think there is credence to the idea that humanity needs to engage in some deep introspection with regard to how it responds to the foreign, the alien, the unknown. However, I do not see how, especially in a case like this, it makes any sense to place the legal onus on the individuals who were attacked—by men carrying illegal guns, no less—on the basis that humans are intrinsically discriminatory.

"As we all know," Cohen continued, "it would seem that their government caretakers have lost the two ETIs who were very nearly shot and killed after they were rendered incapacitated. But right now, it strikes me as inherently discriminatory to punish the victim, especially if they have not violated any rules we have in place. From a practical standpoint, given what happened in Pershing Square, I cannot say I blame Nikola Sassanian and Jude Atheatos for assuming the worst about humanity and wanting nothing to do with us. What surprises me, Mr. Miranda, on the subject of having a poor opinion of human nature, you and the ETIs appear to agree."

And with that, Miranda's testimony was over. The hearing, done for the day, dispersed. Cora saw Miranda get up, loosen up a bit from all the hours in the uncomfortable chair, and then turn to leave the chamber.

"I don't get it," she said. "I just don't get the appeal of his worldview. His whole platform is based on the idea that people are inherently barbarous and need a boot to hold them down."

"Well, yeah, baby fascists," said Kavch. "They love a police state, because it means party A has control over party B, and they are convinced they are in party A."

"Ampersand told me something like that once," she said. "That he believes that if there are two cultures, the dominant one will always try to reshape the less powerful one, and if they can't do that, they destroy them. And it's a pattern of human history, of their history, of nature, of everything."

Miranda walked by them as he exited the chamber, and neither side bothered to mask their contempt for the other. She caught Julian's eye as he was exiting the chamber, and he held it, clearly recognizing her. It wasn't just the look of an enemy on the other side of an ideological battle—he looked at her like he knew something she didn't.

"Are you going to eat?"

Cora started to shoot him an annoyed glare, then resumed her sentry at the window. *It's D.C.*, he thought. *There isn't even a skyline to gaze at.*

He looked down at the sad caprese sandwich he had ordered for himself, and the fettuccine Alfredo with a side of inoffensive white bread he'd gotten for her, barely touched. Kaveh had made his characteristic suggestion that the two go to an expensive restaurant, of which D.C. had a great many, but *someone* wasn't feeling it. So room service it was.

"You need to eat."

"I know," she said, and the guilt in her voice was starting to make him feel bad. They'd come up with a system that better worked for her food aversion, but even though she'd put on a couple of pounds in the last month, bringing her back up to the border of underweight, feeding herself did not come easy. Even the protein shake he'd gotten her, which he always had on hand as a last resort if other food made her sick, went neglected.

He got up off the bed, approaching her back and pulling her body to his, looking out the window over her head. He smelled her hair, brushed his fingertips over the soft skin of her neck. He felt her shiver under his touch.

"I know you're worried," he said. "I'm worried, too. That's why I'm trying to take your mind off it."

He started kissing her neck as he roved his fingers downward, around her shoulders, then her hips. She still wasn't responding, and he figured he might be getting close to crossing a boundary, and backed off.

"There isn't really anything else we can do right now," he said. "Besides, they don't get the last word, you do."

She sighed stiffly. "Just . . . I don't know, it almost felt like Miranda and Julian were in league."

"They *are* in league."

"No, I mean like . . ." She clenched her fist in front of her as if she were trying to pluck the right words from the air.

"You really need to eat," he said, whispering in her ear in his most seductive tone. "You need to eat before *I* can eat, if you follow."

"I mean like, he was looking at me like he knew something," she said, totally ignoring his overtures. He might as well have been a mannequin for all she was paying attention to him. "Like he had an ace up his sleeve."

"What kind of ace? Is there something in particular you're worried about?"

"Lots of things. Maybe something that happened when I was at work, or . . . I don't know, there's a lot that's not a matter of public record, I don't know what they might know, let alone how they might narrativize it."

"Wouldn't Porter have known the worst of it?"

She hugged herself tightly, head dropping to look at her bare feet on the hotel room carpet. "Maybe."

"What is it, specifically, that you're worried they might ask you about?"

He waited for her to answer, but all he got was tighter self-hugging.

"I was hoping I wouldn't have to read your mind," he said. "Is there something else that happened that they don't know about? That *I* don't know about?"

Still nothing. Normally, she'd been pretty good about honoring her agreement not to hide from him. It was understandable right now, all things considered, but it was hard not to be a little irritated by this backslide.

"Or are you worried about something . . . maybe a little more personal?"

She finally turned to him, her face a mask of guilt and fear, like he'd accused her of shoplifting. Okay, so maybe it *was* the fear that these goons might whip out something a little more personal and use it against her.

"It's not a big deal," he said, brushing her hair behind her ear.

"What's not a big deal?"

"If the personal side of things is what you're worried about."

"What am I worried about?" She was looking at him like he'd just revealed he was playing for the other team.

"Listen, I know . . ."

"What?" she snapped, backing away from him and up against the window. "What do you know?"

"I know you're in love with him."

Even as he said it, he wasn't sure why he did. It certainly wasn't out of spite or bitterness. It was just an observation, a statement of truth. At first she stared at him, incredulous, then without a word, brushed past him.

"Cora . . ."

She didn't look at him, marching straight into the bathroom and slamming the door behind her.

"Cora," he said, jimmying the handle to the door and finding it locked. "Please, open the door."

This went on for nearly an hour.

By the time the digital clock by the bed ticked 10:23 P.M., the situation had not worsened, nor had it improved. No sounds of self-harm, no indication she had ceased breathing. Kaveh sat with his back to the wall next to the bathroom door, arms resting on his knees, staring at the ceiling and thinking, *The twenty-one-year-old-ness was bound to resurface sooner or later.*

"Cora," he tried for the twelve billionth time. "Why are you doing this?"

Silencio.

"I hate to pull this card, but this hearing is really important. You need to eat, and you need to sleep. Think about what this could mean."

Niente.

"Think about Woodward and Bernstein. 'Andy and June.' This could be . . . Well, I don't *know* if it's life or death, but . . ."

Bubkes.

He sighed deeply, his eyes roving over the objects in their hotel room. Her open bag with clothes strewn out of it like a volcano had erupted, his suit for tomorrow hung neatly in the hall closet, and then there was the minibar. He felt an intense urge to tear into that minibar. An urge more intense than he had felt in a long, long time.

"You know, I never told you why I stopped drinking."

Silence.

He leaned his head back against the wall. "So Stephen King describes his alcoholic self as a fun drunk. The kind of guy you'd love at parties, and that was me. And the thing about being nice and functional and likable when you're drunk is it makes it a lot easier to justify your behavior. But that wasn't true 100 percent of the time because no one is in a good mood 100 percent of the time.

"You're my first relationship since I got sober. I've had flings, but no commitments. It's not allowed when you're in recovery. But I was in a long-term one before that. We were together for three years, and I assumed we always would be. I knew my drinking made her uncomfortable, and by that point, we'd fought about it a couple of times, but I was the Stephen King drunk. I'd never really suffered a tangible consequence. I put the 'fun' in 'functional alcoholic.'

"And then one night, I was angry, like about the Democratic primaries, of all things. I'd gotten in an argument with a coworker earlier that day and carried it home. But it escalated and started to bleed into other issues we'd been having. And I got angry. And then I got violent."

He ran his fingers over the knuckles of his right hand. "You know, the funny thing about drywall is you really have no idea how brittle it is until you punch right through it. I don't remember a lot from that night, but I do remember the look in her eyes when I did it. And then she left.

"And after that, I begged and pleaded for her to take me back. I was like, 'This isn't me, I'll go to rehab,' so I went to rehab. But by the time I got out, she'd already made up her mind. She said she loved me but she couldn't ever be with me. That maybe I was clean now but I've got this sleeping monster inside me that could wake up any minute. She couldn't stay in a relationship where she was always waiting for the other shoe to drop.

"My whole life, I was the *doodol tala,* the golden son, the nice guy, could do no wrong, always fun at parties. And I was the abusive one. I rang a bell I couldn't un-ring, and she never forgave me."

He looked at the bathroom door and let out a deep breath. "So now you know my deep, dark secret."

The door latch clicked, and the door swung open. Cora sat with her back to the bathroom wall on the opposite side of the doorframe, staring at the sink, and there they sat, yin and yang of the bathroom door.

He moved his hand toward her, walking his fingers toward her like a crab until he was at the end of his reach. She didn't move.

"What's causing this?"

She took a deep breath and, as she released it, said, "He did this to me."

"What do you mean?"

"He did this to me. I didn't have any say in it. This isn't my fault. I didn't want this."

"I know. I got that."

She hugged herself tighter, clamping her hands to her arms like two vises.

"When . . . did you start noticing these feelings?"

She kept staring ahead, eyes fixed on the porcelain throne in front of her.

"Because Nikola told me that while dynamic fusion bonding does bind party A to party B in a way that we as humans don't really . . . *do*, it doesn't necessarily incite feelings of love any more than being married to someone would. Like it's nice to love the person you're married to, but correlation doesn't mean causation."

She hugged herself tighter, hanging her head. "I guess the first time I saw him."

"So before any dynamic fusion bonding."

"I don't know, I just remember the first time I saw him having this instinct of like . . . 'This thing is alone, I have to protect it.' He called that 'maladaptive' but rolled with it, anyway, because it benefited him."

"And you'd describe that as feelings of love?"

She winced at the word *love* like it had pinched her. "Not really."

"When did that start?"

She took a breath, shuddering like she might start to cry. "A few weeks before Enola Gay, he told me he wanted to start studying me, my symptoms, to observe me while I slept to see what precipitated the nightmares. So he started staying with me every night until I fell asleep."

"Staying with you?" he repeated, trying to keep any judgmental tone out of his voice. He'd never asked, but he'd often suspected something along those lines.

"Yeah . . . like close. Physically close." She winced at that admission, keeping her eyes closed, refusing to look at him.

"Like touching."

Her face flushed. "Yes."

He braced himself. "Intimate touching."

"No. Well . . . intimate, yes, but not like that. Nothing sexual. He started staying with me until I fell asleep every night. He would just . . . hold me until I fell asleep. And I stopped having nightmares. Even during the day, I almost stopped having panic attacks. I just . . . I don't know. For this brief moment in time, he was like the family I never had." She opened her eyes, red and glassy. "But then Enola came, and he changed."

Kaveh bit his lip and crab walked his fingers toward her again. "So I do not pretend to understand the metaphysical underpinnings of your bond, but here's my read on the situation. You were suffering, and someone you cared about offered to help reduce your suffering. And over a period of time, you developed feelings for that person, because they were doing you a kindness."

She looked at him, the gray of her irises steeped in a pool of redness.

"So I may be off mark, but honestly? That doesn't seem like alien mind-meld magic; that seems like . . . normal."

"How is it normal?" she asked in a hoarse whisper.

"What the hell are we advocating for? I mean, if we really believe that Ampersand is a person, then how is what you're describing wrong? You're both adults by the standards of your respective species, you shared some emotional and physical intimacy, so you developed feelings for him. That's what happens. What's a better indicator of humanity, of *personhood,* than the ability to fall in love with someone?"

Her expression fell even further. "He doesn't love me."

"I don't think that's true. You don't go out of your way to help someone you don't care about. I get that he has scientific curiosity and you are his interpreter, and they seem to develop feelings more slowly than we do, but I don't buy that it was completely utilitarian." He scooted closer to her. "You can be a loving caretaker, and you can be cruel and neglectful. Both things can be true of the same person."

He walked his fingers the rest of the way, holding his palm open, inviting her to take it. She looked at him, then released the iron grip she had on herself and took his hand. "Why doesn't this bother you?"

"I guess because I'm not particularly threatened by him. Like, there are some things about being human he is never going to get. Like, he's never going to understand why 'Dick in a Box' is funny."

This elicited . . . almost a laugh. A proto-laugh.

"Do you miss him?" he asked.

Her already weak smile faded. "I miss the old him. The him I thought I knew. Before I found out he'd been lying about Obelus the whole time, before Nikola. I guess I miss this fictional construction of him, when I built him into something I wanted him to be."

Kaveh was already shaking his head. "But if he was literally there for you, physically and emotionally, was that a construction? He might have lied to you, and he might have also genuinely cared for you. Both things can be true. That's what sucks so much about . . . people." He couldn't help but laugh. "And that's how we know they're really people. Debate over, g'night, everybody!"

He moved closer to her, coaxing her body to his, until he had her in his embrace, kissing her on the eyelids, the nose, her cheeks. Then he whispered, "If he is a part of the package that is you . . . then okay."

She opened her eyes, and looked at him blankly.

"I can roll with it. We're in uncharted territory. But that's kind of fun in its own right. I said I know you're in love with him; that doesn't mean you don't love *me*. I know you love me differently than you love him." He paused, eyeing her. "I mean, I'm not saying you should *fuck* him. That's what you've got me for!"

She cracked a smile, and allowed a half laugh, half sob.

"No judgment, though. I don't think there's anything wrong with that, either," he said in a stilted joking-not-joking tone. "I'm not the jealous type, and exclusivity is not mandatory for me. If you're both consenting adults—"

"How would that even work?" she cut him off. She looked scandalized, but in a way that was forced. In a way that told him, oh yeah, she had definitely given this some thought.

"Honey, he can conjure a giant syringe out of the very cells of his being. I'm sure he could figure it out. I assume he's a consenting adult. How old is he, anyway?"

"He has a subjective age, like a lived age, and a relativistic age," she said, leaning into his shoulder. "Because of near–light speed travel. Like he was bor—well, he was *bred* over a thousand years ago."

"Holy shit. What's his lived age?"

"He's about 650."

"Years? *Wuahaha!*" He belly laughed so hard he half expected whoever was in the room next door to bang on the wall.

She cringed, but smiled despite herself. "Years."

He continued laughing. "Wow, you really do like 'em older, don't you? Next time I find a gray hair, I'll keep it to myself."

Her smile faded, and he began kissing her. Softly at first, then increasing in intensity. "If that's the thing you're worried about, if that's the worst thing you've got, it's okay. We're prepared."

He pulled her in, wanting to resume what he'd started, wanting to feel close to her, but she still felt distant, and a part of him wondered if this little revelation, this thing he had always deep down known to be true, wasn't actually the most damning skeleton in her closet.

49

"Chairman Leahy, Ranking Member Specter, members of the committee. My name is Cora Emiliana Sabino. I am twenty-one years old, and studied linguistics at the University of California–Irvine, and plan to continue my studies at Columbia University starting this fall. For three months, I worked as a communication intermediary for a subsidiary agency of the Department of Health and Human Services called the Refugee Organization and Settlement Agency, or ROSA."

She glanced up every sentence or so to the wall of old men and smattering of old women who lorded over her. She had been in near meltdown mode that morning, but by now the whole thing was so surreal, so heavy, her brain had quietly detached itself, and she was on autopilot.

"I must clarify that my mind is my own, because there are many out there who believe that it is not. I was not subpoenaed by Congress, nor was I compelled by any government agency, nor have I been compelled by any outside influence, human or ETI."

Cora's introductory speech, carefully tuned by herself, Kaveh, and a bunch of lobbyists, lasted about twenty minutes. Then the sharks began to feed. Kaveh had been right; her questioning did go on a good bit longer than Miranda's. It began with the chairman, then the ranking member, and on down the line.

To her surprise, the Third Option supporters on the committee were nowhere near as vicious to her as Cohen had been to Miranda. Some were more pressing than others, but none of them asked questions that were either incriminating or would force her to lie under oath. After the twentieth or so senator, her nerves were fried, but in a manner that felt like, if they really wanted to make this go on forever, fine. *I can take it.*

But the one she had been dreading the most was the one who got his turn toward the end, and that of course was Senator Todd Julian, Miranda's biggest supporter in the Senate and champion of the Third Option. The man who had given "Enola Gay" his first, infamous name.

"Cora Emiliana Ortega." It made her nerves itch. He had done that to disarm her, she knew, but it worked. "Many are deeply concerned about the potential superhuman capabilities possessed by the ETI species known as 'amygdaline.' There is some speculation that they may even be able to control human thoughts."

"To my knowledge, they cannot control a human mind any more than other humans can," she stated coolly. This was true, on a technicality. Ampersand had the ability to control human bodies through a form of hypnosis, and he certainly had the ability to erase short-term memories—but humans were also presently capable of both. Hell, a bottle of vodka could erase short-term memory. "Individual anecdotal evidence of people feeling like they are being manipulated by alien powers is not evidence that they have that capability."

Julian casually flipped through the briefs in front of him as if he were reading the morning newspaper. "If you were not under any form of mind control, why did you put yourself between Tony Cascio's gun and the body of the ETI?"

"I did it for the same reason I would do it for any person I cared about," she said without hesitating. "I'd do it for my friends, I'd do it for my sister, my brother—"

"Your father?" he cut her off. Her already itchy nerves spasmed at the word.

"So you consider the . . . 'amygdaline'"—he said the word with a slight chuckle—"to be on the level with family?"

"After a fashion, yes." *You knew this was coming,* she told herself. *Nothing to be ashamed of. This is the point.*

"So for an eight-and-a-half-foot-tall alien . . . we aren't even clear what they are made of. Is it alive?"

She wanted to believe that United States senators read their briefs, but as Cohen's staffers and the lobbyists had warned her, these people didn't really care about details, nor about what she said. They just wanted sound bites they could take back home to help with their reelection campaigns. "Yes, they are alive. Their bodies are synthetic, their brains are not."

"Well, speaking of bodies," said Julian boldly. "Another big part of this discussion is the question of how do we legislate their bodies? A person in the United States does have the right to bear arms, but the arms are not a part of their *person*, a part of their body, and in some circumstances, that right can be revoked. A felon cannot bear arms. An individual with extreme mental illness cannot bear arms. And we are talking about a being with, at minimum, profound defensive powers, and, as Brigadier General Porter testified yesterday, we do know those defensive powers can turn offensive. How do we legislate their offensive capabilities?"

Cora racked her brain for what he could be talking about. Was he talking about Ampersand's telekinetic shove when he had arrived at Pershing Square to clear the area? Had he considered that offensive, and not defensive? Given the information she knew to be available to the senators, she didn't know what else he could be referring to.

Julian shuffled his papers around and then pulled out one color printout. A portrait. "I would like to enter this into the record."

The portrait stared back at her, smiling jovially, creeping up on her like a light chill before morphing into a thick icicle stabbing her in the chest. The portrait was of a young Korean American man in his late twenties, his hair clipped short, his eyes sparkling with real pride. An official photograph taken from when he was still with the CIA. From when he was still alive.

Julian held up the photograph, making sure everyone in the room, including the cameras, got a good look at it. Then he looked at Cora, his lips curving into a satisfied smile. "Do you recognize the man in this image?"

Vincent Park.

Vincent Park hadn't even been publicly listed as killed in action. His star on the CIA memorial wall had gone nameless. Her mind splintered into a hundred directions, stampeding down a hundred different paths, trying to preempt what else they must know if they knew about Vincent.

Even Kaveh didn't know about Vincent.

"This man was Agent Vincent Park of the CIA. You were the last person to see him alive, were you not?" asked Julian.

Cora's throat had turned to cotton, her tongue to sandpaper. She tried to close her mouth, tried to swallow. "I can't answer that definitively."

"Then let me rephrase that—you were the last person to see him alive who survived the altercation that killed him, were you not?"

She knew she should say, "I don't know," because in an ecclesiastical sense, she didn't. She hadn't watched him die, she didn't know what else had happened in the couple of minutes leading up to his death.

Instead, she answered, "Yes."

Without taking his eyes off her, Julian shuffled his papers around, holding up more portraits in order. "I would also like to enter these into the record," he said. He shuffled through them quickly, each second an eternity. Portraits of two men and one woman. She only recognized one of the men, whom she remembered being the driver in the van that had been carrying her, Vincent, and the Genome. The other two faces must have belonged to the people who had been in the SUV directly behind them.

"These CIA agents," said Julian. "Do you know how they died?"

She thought of Obelus, his old body, that massive heft that carried with it the ability to unmake human flesh and bone with a thought. That monster that ripped apart the other Similar, Kruro, overpowered him, and disintegrated everything remotely carbon-based in his body. *Human bodies turning to ash.* She tried to swallow, tried to get some moisture into her cotton ball throat. "I don't know the specifics."

This seemed to anger Julian. "Four CIA agents were killed in action. You were there when they died. Can you tell us how they died?"

"I don't know the specifics."

Julian whipped out another ream of papers, glaring down at her. "According to this report, supplied to my staff by a whistleblower, they have an ability to instantly render organic flesh to ash. This ability was first observed by the specimen 'Scio,' who later adopted the name Jude Atheatos, during an autopsy of what 'he' described as his next of kin, the deceased specimen 'Čefo.' Team was unable to verify veracity of his 'next of kin' claim. Specimen Scio telekinetically removed the organic neural network of the deceased specimen Čefo, and then rendered the neural organic material to ash. A much more powerful version of this ability was observed by the specimens 'unknown stratocrats' AG-ETI-047, AG-ETI-048,

AG-ETI-049, and AG-ETI-050 attached to the event code-named 'Obelus.' You were present for this autopsy, correct?"

She scanned the panel, looking for one sympathetic face and finding none. "Yes."

"And according to this report, you were already active as Jude Atheatos's—né Scio's—communication intermediary, correct?"

"Yes."

"Therefore, you saw specimen Scio vaporize the organic material of his alleged next of kin, Čefo."

Stop, some distant part of her pleaded. *You didn't know this would be part of the testimony. You can plead the Fifth. You don't need to answer this.* "Yes."

"Have you ever seen any of these ETIs use this ability on a human body?"

"Yes."

When it came out, she heard the whole chamber erupt into chatter. She had all but forgotten there were people here, that she wasn't alone in a cold, white void being questioned. That this was being broadcast live to anyone who cared to watch.

"You were there when these four CIA agents died, but you got away. If you claim to have a connection to the specimen Scio, a much closer connection than any other human can claim, how were *you* able to escape the specimens 'unnamed stratocrats,' AG-ETI-047, AG-ETI-048, AG-ETI-049, and AG-ETI-050, and four trained CIA operatives were not?"

Shock mutated to horror. She was being accused of being *in league* with Obelus. That it had been her connection to Ampersand that had spared her, not the simple truth that she had run from the car crash as fast as her legs could carry her. "I wasn't deliberately spared," she said, her voice wavering like a flag in a violent storm. "I ran away."

"You ran, and they didn't." Julian's accusation was laced with cyanide.

He wasn't just implying that she had been spared because of Ampersand. He was accusing her of being complicit in their deaths. "The people in the car behind us were injured, I think. Vincent was injured. I just got out of the car and ran as fast as I could."

"What prompted you to run so immediately?"

"I knew what Obelus was capable of," she blurted. "I knew he wouldn't bother with a human if they weren't in his way."

"*How* did you know what Obelus was capable of?"

She could never have imagined that this man, this cosseted career politician, could sound so dangerous. *You need to shut up, plead the Fifth, you idiot, shut up shut up shut up!*

"Because I saw it. At NORAD."

"So you are telling the committee that in the early morning of October 7, 2007, you knowingly left these people, one of whom you knew personally, to die at the hands of an alien with superhuman physical abilities, because you already knew what it was capable of doing?"

She called forth an answer—*Just say, "No, it's not true"*—but nothing came. All she could do was shake her head in the negative.

"You consider Jude Atheatos your 'friend.' Your *family* member. Tell me, for the record, do you know where Jude Atheatos is now?"

She finally swallowed, but it felt like swallowing chalk. "No."

Julian eyed her like he was firing up to volley another round. Then he shot a glance at his watch. "My time is up," he said. "I have no further questions."

The instant she was allowed to move, she stood up, her legs not even shaky; the desire to flee was too strong. She eyed a staffer whom she had spoken to three days ago, one of Cohen's camp, and made a straight line toward her, ignoring the look the woman was giving her, a look of almost betrayal. "Please," she said. "I'm having a panic attack. Can you take me someplace private?"

The look of betrayal ebbed, and the woman nodded. "Follow me."

"Cora!" She heard Kaveh's voice and ignored it. She followed the woman as quickly as she was able, and the woman moved quickly, quickly enough that she lost Kaveh.

The staffer led her to a part of the building that wasn't open to the public, and Cora tore into the bathroom. She didn't say anything else to the woman, jamming the doorstop under the door, then shoving a garbage can under the door handle for good measure. She was breathing heavy and fast now, her skin trying to escape from her body.

"Please, please, Ampersand, *please*! Please come back, please take me away from here! I'll do anything, just please, take me away from this godfor-*fucking*-saken place!"

She fell backward into one of the two bathroom stalls, onto one of the toilets, slamming the old metal door and boxing herself in. She reached, tried to sense him, but her own emotions were too strong for her to sense anything. Could he feel her? Did he know what was going on, what had happened here?

Did he even care?

"*Please,*" she begged. At this point, she was just as much praying to God. "Please take me away from here, please, please."

"WOULD YOU LIKE ME TO TAKE YOU AWAY, LITTLE COUSIN?"

She nearly shrieked, and half imagined she'd heard the voice. "Nik!" She tried to quiet her breathing, tried to calm down so she could see or hear anything. "Oh, please still be here. Please, tell me you haven't left the planet."

"I AM RIGHT HERE, LITTLE COUSIN."

A shadow fell on the other side of the bathroom stall, and she tore open the metal door. There he was, in all his terrible, beautiful glory. His posture wasn't erratic; his eyes were still clear and bright. Despite everything, he hadn't been altering himself chemically. He hadn't been "using."

Cora stood up, breath still coming heavy and fast, spots beginning to form at the corners of her vision. "Please, take me away from here."

He lowered his head to meet hers and wrapped his fingers around her, not quite touching her, enveloping her like a birdcage. "I HAVE YET TO LOCATE OUR DEAR BELOVED. WOULD YOU ASSIST ME IN FINDING HIM?"

"Yes, I'll do anything you want. Just please get me away from here!"

He examined her, perhaps the only being in the universe that didn't see her as some sort of traitor. He pulled her close, and the sheet of his dark semiautonomous plating enveloped both of them.

April 19, 2008

𝕿𝖍𝖊 𝖂𝖆𝖘𝖍𝖎𝖓𝖌𝖙𝖔𝖓 𝕻𝖔𝖘𝖙

Search Underway for Missing Person Cora Sabino

WASHINGTON—The FBI has issued a Missing/Endangered Person Alert for Cora Sabino. Sabino was last seen on the afternoon of Wednesday, April 16, during a Senate hearing in which she testified in favor of personhood for amygdaline ETIs. Sabino disappeared after Senator Todd Julian (I-IL) revealed that she had been a witness to the previously classified death of four CIA agents allegedly killed by an unnamed ETI in October of last year.

As of Friday afternoon, Sabino has been missing for over 48 hours. Sabino is 21 years old with light brown hair and hazel eyes, stands 5′5″ tall, about 110 pounds.

No other information has been released at this point. If you have any information about this case, please call the FBI's missing persons unit at (202) 324-3000.

50

Kaveh packed his bag like an assembly line machine. He had been nervous about going to publication before, but never like this. He looked at the hard copy of the article he had readied for submission, wrapped in a neat manila folder like a rustic Christmas present. He'd had this conversation with his editor at *The New Yorker* several times in the past few weeks—is it ethical to honor this NDA? Should he "break his silence" regarding what he knew? They had agreed that it all depended on how the Senate hearings went, and in some ways, they could not have gone worse.

It was still too soon to really see how much the needle had budged politically; it would be another few days before any meaningful polling would be released, but the national mood had obviously changed. The world knowing about Nikola's defensive capabilities was one thing, the revelation that the government had covered up the deaths of, at minimum, four CIA agents was something else entirely. *At minimum,* four CIA agents killed by amygdaline ETIs. Probably, there were more that hadn't even been uncovered yet.

"It's a bust," said Paris from the living room. She'd only just gotten back from a long assignment in Seattle yesterday, and today was supposed to be their "catch-up hang." So much for that. "This sighting in Oregon. It's been debunked. It's not her."

Kaveh still hadn't decided what to tell Paris. If he told her what he was really planning to do, that might make her an accessory. If they tried and failed to bring the might of the U.S. government down on him, tried and failed to extradite him, they might punish Paris instead.

Then an even more nauseating thought: *They might punish her either way.*

"She'll turn up when she's ready."

"Kaveh . . . we need to take into consideration the possibility—"

"*Please,* no," he snapped, knowing where she was going. From a certain perspective, it made the most sense that Cora had thrown herself in the Potomac, and her body just hadn't been found yet. It wasn't even that he wasn't willing to accept the possibility; it was that he couldn't. His brain wouldn't allow it. "Please, not now."

"I'm sorry," she said. "I shouldn't have said that."

"No, you shouldn't have," he said bitterly, jamming his electric razor into his toiletries bag. As a rule, he always had one ready to go, so packing for trips, international or domestic, rarely took him more than a few minutes.

But this was different. This time, he didn't know if he would be coming back.

"I didn't mean to snap at you like that," he said, shaking fingers fumbling through the lotions and face wash he liked, checking to see which ones were less than three ounces. "I know it's a possibility. I can't humor it, not right now."

Paris didn't answer him, and then came the guilt. He'd never taken that tone with her before. He decided that the lotions weren't worth the time or attention; he might not come back, but hopefully one day he would, and even if he didn't, they were bound to open a Lush in Reykjavik one of these days.

"Kaveh?"

The voice was so small and squeaky it took him a moment to place it as Paris's voice, and he knew something was terribly wrong. He dropped his hand lotion into the sink, dashed through his bedroom and back into the living room, and nearly had a heart attack on the spot.

Paris was sinking into his couch in calcified horror, her ombre waist-length braids draped over the back of his white couch like a hand as she looked up at the apparition standing over her. There was Nikola, in the middle of his living room, regarding Paris as if she were a guest at a party he hadn't been properly introduced to yet. Kaveh clutched a hand to his chest, released a breath that was more of a cough.

"Nik," he whispered, stumbling toward him. Nikola crouched so that their eyes were almost level to each other, and Kaveh practically grabbed the sides of his head, pulling his muzzle to his forehead, allowing himself a moment to wallow in the relief that he was still alive, that he was still here, and that he seemed, for the moment at least, not to be medicated.

"Oh, Nik," he said, looking up into his eyes. Then he realized why Nikola was silent. "Oh, you'd been gone for weeks! I took the earbuds out. Hold on, let me go get them."

He looked at Paris, who was looking at him with a quizzical sort of horror. "Don't worry. He's harmless. Mostly harmless."

"That's not what we learned at the testimony the other day," Paris whispered.

"Hold still, both of you."

He ran back into his bedroom and tore open the satchel in which he had stuffed the pillbox he'd been using to store Nikola's earbuds. He returned to the living room to see that while Paris had obeyed the order to hold still, Nikola had not, and was not only looming over her but was using two of his long, spidery forefingers to fiddle with one of her box braids.

"Please don't do that," said Kaveh, taking the earbuds out of the pillbox. Nikola looked at him and withdrew his hand while Kaveh put in the bud to his right ear, feeling it conform to his ear canal. "It's not appropriate to touch a Black woman's hair without permission."

"Kaveh," said Paris, regaining her composure, "I think we can save the discussion on race and microaggressions for another day. Give him a pass."

Kaveh moved to put in the second earbud, but paused mid-motion, then gave it to Paris. "Put it in your ear. It'll conform to the shape of your ear canal."

While she hesitantly inserted the earbud, Kaveh turned to Nikola. "Please, tell me you know where Cora is."

"SHE IS UNDER MY PROTECTION, DEAR CLEVER CREATURE."

He thought he might be able to stay upright before deciding, *no,* so overwhelming was his relief, his legs buckled and he fell down on to the couch next to Paris.

"Holy shit," muttered Paris, presumably at the voice in her ears.

Kaveh wrapped an arm around Paris. He couldn't help but laugh as he wiped a tear. "She's alive," he whispered. Paris returned the hug, shaking out of her stunned stupor and pulling him in.

As though he remembered that he was much less intimidating to humans when he was seated, Nikola pulled his arms under his chest and lowered himself onto the rug.

"Nik," said Kaveh, wiping his eyes. "Where have you been? Why did you never contact me?"

"My dear Beloved disappeared from federal custody, and I left to find him. I could no longer engage with the government or the military, but I could not safely interact with you without their knowledge. I do not know where my dear Beloved is."

"'Dear Beloved' is Jude, right?" Paris deduced. Kaveh nodded.

"I intended to contact you once I had subdued him, but my attentions were diverted by the political situation. I was not aware of the damage noble Obelus had done, of the lives he had taken, nor the scale of it."

"So he's killed more than four people."

"Far more, especially if you include nonhuman persons. I have been monitoring the situation from a base I established not far from where you and I met. But I am at an impasse. My dear Beloved has been able to hide himself from me too well. However, I thought perhaps I might be able to exploit my little cousin's remarkable empathic ability to sense our dear Beloved. Therefore, when the opportunity presented itself for me to take her for myself, I did."

"What do you mean, 'the opportunity presented itself'?"

"She begged for me to take her away from the Senate building, so I did. She agreed to assist me in locating our dear Beloved, who I know is still on this planet, but she is far too distraught to sense anything clearly. It is for that reason that I have come to you, dear clever creature, you who love her so dearly, who takes care of her needs so well. My hope is that if you are able to soothe her, she will become less distraught, and we may be able to utilize her bond with our dear Beloved to locate him. Would you consent to this?"

"Nik, I need to tell you something. I . . ." He looked at Paris and squeezed her hand. "I need to tell you both something."

Realization dawned on Paris's face; she knew what he was planning.

"Nik, I've decided to break my NDA and write about you. I'm worried about how far the political situation has deteriorated. But you need to understand, even though we have a free press, I'll be exposing confidential information. So I'll be breaking the law to do this, meaning I have to leave the country. I don't know when or if I'd ever be allowed to come back. They may decide against pressing charges, they could strip me of my citizenship, they could try to throw me in prison for the rest of my life. Or, they could do nothing. I don't know what will happen. But I know that if I do this, I have to leave.

"I'm sorry, Paris," he said, looking at her. "I honestly hadn't decided whether to tell you the truth before Nik showed up. Knowing could implicate you."

She nodded and looked away from him to digest. "How were you going to do it?"

"I was going to drive to Canada tonight. Fly to Iceland first thing in the morning. Once I landed in Iceland, then *The New Yorker* was going to publish."

"I understand it is important for you to influence the political situation. I do not believe my request is mutually exclusive with your intent to publish. Aid me with my endeavor, and after we conclude, successful or no, I will take you anywhere you wish to go."

Kaveh had chosen Iceland not just because it would be nearly impossible for the United States to extradite him but also because at this point, full personhood was all but guaranteed to be the law of the land of that small island nation. "So if I do this, you'll let her go."

"She is not my captive. She may go as she wishes. But if you are asking if I will take her anywhere I take you, then I will."

"And if you find Jude, if you resolve whatever the problem is with him, you'll come with us?"

"If it pleases you, dear clever creature. If I am to honor our short-term agreement regarding our life spans, and if

WE ARE TO STAY ON THIS PLANET AND DIE HERE, I WOULD PREFER TO STAY WITH YOU AND FOR YOU TO CONTINUE TO BE MY LIAISON AND INTERPRETER. THE COUNTRY IN WHICH YOU RESIDE IS IMMATERIAL TO ME."

Kaveh nodded, took a moment, and then got up to go into the bedroom where he had been packing his bag. At least now he didn't have to worry about the three-ounce rule for liquids and gels anymore. He grabbed the manila folder from his satchel, returned to the living room, and held it out to Paris. "This is the hard copy."

She took it, handling it like it was some precious ancient relic.

"If anything happens to me, if I'm not able to deliver my copy to *The New Yorker*, or if we get detained . . . well, people have a way of disappearing where these guys are concerned. We learned that with the Sabino family." He nodded toward Nikola, who was lifting himself to his feet. "If anything happens to me, would you make sure this gets where it needs to go?"

"Of course."

He tamped down the swell of nervousness in his chest. "Yeah."

Paris stood, and then the two hugged, longer and tighter than they ever had in the time they'd known each other. Then she stood back, holding the manila folder to her chest like a teddy bear, and looked at Nikola. "Please, take care of him."

"I WILL LET NO HARM COME TO HIM."

"I'm sorry I reacted with fear when I first saw you."

"I UNDERSTAND THAT THE BODY I INHABIT IS INTIMIDATING TO HUMANS. I HAD NO MEANS OF COMMUNICATING PEACEFUL INTENT."

"I . . ." She laughed. "I wish we'd met under different circumstances. I would have liked to talk to you more."

"DEAR GENTLE CREATURE." Nikola regarded her, his eyes brightening with mottled blues and purples. Then he said, "WE WILL MEET AGAIN."

51

Kaveh had never experienced the preferred amygdaline mode of travel before, having only seen it in the form of what looked like a huge puddle of mercury on the ground at Pershing Square. It felt like being shrink-wrapped and put in sleep mode, like a laptop. One moment he was in his New York apartment, the next he was in the desert.

After he got his bearings, he released a consternated sigh upon realizing where he was. Even in the darkness, he could tell he was back in California, but not, like, the *good* part of California. The air was too clear, the sky too visible, and there was a disquieting lack of smog in the air. As his eyes adjusted to the dark, he could see that they were on some sort of complex, perhaps an ex-government complex, as there was no power anywhere. It looked abandoned.

"Where are we?"

"34°35'36.4" NORTH, II7°23'05.2" WEST."

"I mean, what municipality are we in? Or at least what county?"

"SAN BERNARDINO COUNTY. MUNICIPALITY OF VICTORVILLE."

Kaveh had to hand it to him; if he were to go into hiding, he probably would pick an abject shithole like Victorville. He looked over his shoulder, half expecting to see a group of squatters huddled around a fire burning out of a metal trash can. The only place worse he could imagine to hole up was Bakersfield.

Nikola led him to the entrance of a midsize airplane hangar, perhaps one built for private jets or Cessnas. He'd expected to enter into complete darkness, but once inside, he saw that Nikola had constructed a massive wall of television screens right in the middle of the building, a hodgepodge surveillance wall the size of a small billboard. *Human-made* television screens, and new LED flat-screens at that. A full half of them were tuned to news networks, every single twenty-four-hour one in the United States, as well as what appeared to be most if not all the major international ones as well—the BBC, Al Jazeera, Al Jazeera English, CCTV, and so on. The rest appeared to be security feeds.

"What the hell is this?" he breathed, stumbling toward the wall of talking heads, which had no sound coming out of it.

"Kaveh?"

He dashed toward the source of the voice, which was coming from the other side of a portable airplane stair that was functioning like a wall, and there she was.

She looked feral, curled up on a mattress on the floor, having lost her blazer jacket but still wearing her navy-blue pencil skirt and (formerly) white undershirt from the day of the hearing. If those TVs had been stolen, so, too, he assumed, had been everything in front of him. The mattress looked like it had been pilfered from an IKEA. She had food as well, if a box of single-serving Lay's potato chips could be considered "food," and several gallons of water in plastic jugs, though she didn't seem to have touched any of it except the water.

He practically fell on top of her, crushing her body to his, not waiting for her to give him permission. "Oh, baby," he said, burying his face in her dirty hair. "Oh, baby, I was so scared!"

"I'm sorry," she said, her voice muffled by his shirt. "I'm sorry, I'm sorry!"

"It's okay, it's okay. I'm just glad you're all right." He pulled her even closer. "He didn't hurt you, did he?"

"No," she said, finally unlocking her arms and allowing herself to hug him back. "No, he's been good."

He held her for a few minutes, breathing his relief into her hair, her skin. "Is this your room? Airplane stair as your bedroom wall?"

"So I don't have to see those screens."

"You're going to get some hop-ons." She didn't seem amused. "What the hell is all this?"

"He said he started building this about a week after Ampersand disappeared. He can't just instantly keep tabs on every news feed with whatever internal machinery he has—it doesn't work like that—so he set this up and created like . . . a system that collates all the info the news networks have and looks for patterns that might lead to clues."

"Has he found anything?"

"No, not yet. That's why he wanted me."

"Okay," he said, taking a moment to shake off the terror of the situation. "Why don't we . . . regroup back at the Yorba Linda house, freshen up, take a shower. There's no way they'll be looking for me here; I was in New York twenty minutes ago."

She opened her mouth as if to protest, considered, and then nodded in resignation. "Let me get my things."

"What 'things'?"

"Well, really just these things," she said, lifting up two items that could only be described as alien lumps. "Pill bug, pulse emitter."

"I remember this," he said, looking at the pulse emitter. "That's the thing that can take them out with an EMP. But what is that?"

"I call it the pill bug, for obvious reasons." They were indeed obvious. The thing looked like a squat, obese millipede dipped in silver. "It helps restart their systems if they've been taken out. So it's kind of like *Alice in Wonderland*. Drink this to grow smaller." She nodded to the pulse emitter. "And drink this to get bigger." She nodded to the strangely hideous magical pill bug.

He glanced around the airplane staircase, honestly impressed by this surveillance system Nikola had set up, no matter how obviously stolen the entire thing was. It gave a dispiritingly accurate snapshot of what was going on in the world.

Third Option going forward.

. . . strict definition of personhood.

The bill is being debated in Congress.

The vote is to be held on Monday.

"WHAT DOES SHE REQUIRE TO ENABLE MY SEARCH?" asked Nikola, ever sensitive.

"Being in a more familiar space would help." He looked toward Nikola, his massive frame silhouetted by the bright light of the screens. "What time is it?"

"9:10 P.M., PACIFIC DAYLIGHT TIME."

Kaveh bit his lip, thinking about that hard copy he'd shoved into Paris's hands, thinking about his editors downtown who were waiting for him. He knew it would be a bomb when it dropped, but if it was going to affect the vote that was about to take place in Congress, it needed to drop *fast*.

· · · · ·

Kaveh stood looking out his bay window, debating whether he should take a dip in the pool considering he might never get to do it again. It wouldn't be a *good* dip, he knew; it was still April, and the pool was not heated. It would be, putting it charitably, brisk, but it could also be his last. It wasn't that he was particularly attached to this house or this property, but it was of California, same as he was. He was going to leave without telling his family. There was a possibility he might never see them again.

"Is now an appropriate time to inquire?"

Kaveh turned to his guest, this creature who was always so wildly out of place inside his living room. Giger's xenomorph parked on a Macy's Black Friday Sale rug.

He wasn't sure if it was a good time, since the thing Nikola wanted Cora to do was, as he understood it, largely out of her control. She couldn't force it, she either sensed something or she didn't. He had taken her home the previous night, cleaned her up and fed her, and made his plea to get out of the country with him, which she'd refused. She was close, she said. She knew he was nearby, she just had to figure out where and what he was up to. They'd actually slept, which he had *not* expected to happen, but the following morning, she didn't seem any closer to her goal. It was already Saturday afternoon. The piece had to publish no later than Sunday morning.

He had to get out of the country.

"I'll go ask," he said and headed upstairs.

Cora was seated in the middle of his bed, looking through the glass of the balcony door, knees drawn to her chest, her bony arms around her legs. Any progress they'd made in the last couple of months getting her back to a healthy weight had crumbled in forty-eight hours.

"I can't wait any longer," he said. "I have to go. Please, come with me."

"No, not yet," she said, eyes still to the door. "I'm so close to figuring it out."

"Cora, do you not understand? *I have to go!*" He sat down next to her, delicately taking her hand in his. He could feel the bones sticking out of her wrist. "This piece has to publish. Whatever Ampersand does or does not do, the Third Option cannot pass, and the only way I have to fight that is with words. *Illegal* words. I have to leave."

She looked at him, piteous and even a little defensive, and he felt a hairline crack in his heart widening. "I'll join you later. Nikola won't let them catch me. He can take me wherever he takes you after I do this thing. I know something is about to happen. I know he's about to do something stupid."

He sighed, trying to blow out the hurt, how little she was considering his feelings in all of this. "What do you mean, 'something stupid'?"

She winced, shaking her head as though the answer were buried somewhere in her mind, but she just hadn't found the right patch of dirt to dig in. "You remember what I said? About Obelus needing a new body?"

Obelus. That thing's name hit like a slap to the face. She had known all about Julian's big revelation. She had *been there* when those CIA agents had died. Had she known there was a possibility that this could come up at the hearing?

"Yeah, Obelus," he said. "I wish I had known before the hearing."

Where a moment earlier she had been all fire, she turned cold. "I could have gone to jail for the rest of my life if I'd told you."

"I know. I don't want this to come across as blame. But I wish I had known. When we were prepping, when we were doing the murder-board . . . it would have been helpful. We could have prepared."

"What did you expect me to do? That information was beyond top secret; it wasn't even disclosed to most of the CIA! The president didn't even know. Did you really expect me to volunteer that to you?"

"I don't know."

She stared at him, her jaw tightening, but he could see that she was too tired, too distracted to find the energy to be mad at him, too. "Vincent's death was supposed to remain unidentified. He was going to be one of those unknown stars on the CIA memorial wall, same as the other three who died. I didn't even know their names."

Well, now you do, he thought, then a chill ran through him as he made a connection—*four* CIA agents dead in an event no one was supposed to know about. "Where did they die?"

"It was somewhere in Virginia. Southwestern Virginia."

"Bedford, Virginia?"

"I don't know. I think so. Why?"

The words he had sent Nils came back to him, clear as if he were reading them from a textbook: *I overheard Kaplan talking about losing agents in Bedford, VA the day after NORAD. Two vehicles were recovered. That's all I know.*

"What is it?" she asked. "What's wrong?"

"I . . ." He swallowed the bile forming his throat. "I heard something about an incident in Bedford. But I didn't realize—"

Had Nils been Julian's whistleblower? There could have been any number of ways Julian got ahold of that information. It didn't necessarily come through the Nils pipeline.

If Nils had found something, he wouldn't forward it to Julian, he told himself. *He would leak it. What benefit would it possibly confer to him to give it to Julian instead of leaking it?* No, it couldn't have been Nils. Julian had to have found out about this some other way.

Unless Nils wanted something from Julian, and Julian offered to give it to him.

"How many people has Obelus killed?" asked Kavch. "Four?"

"At least."

Julian is probably going to win the presidency. Nils knows this. There is a lot Julian could offer Nils.

"And NORAD?"

"I know people died there. I don't know how many."

The overlap of their rhetoric, how it had dovetailed in recent weeks, seemed so clear to him all of a sudden. The way they used almost the same wording, "debride the rot," "cut the corruption." The same lines. The same rhetoric.

Oh, God. Did I do this?

"And not just humans," Cora continued. "Also a couple of the Fremda group. They used to have two Similars. Now they're down to the one, Brako. Kruro's body was destroyed, but—"

She looked at him and gasped, then her face grew slack with epiphany. "Oh my God."

"What?"

"Oh my God, I am such a fucking idiot." She threw her legs over the side of the bed, looking at him urgently. "Brako isn't the only option."

"What's the other option?"

"Obelus's *old* body. The one in San Bernardino, the one that's on ice. Sol told me at the Senate hearing that the location was compromised. I didn't even consider it; I thought it was broken beyond repair."

"Why would he want a dead body?"

"The body itself didn't die; the living thing inside of it was removed to a smaller, more harmless body. But a Similar's body isn't alive; it can break, but it can't *die.*"

Kaveh considered this, connecting what she was telling him with things he'd overheard while he was acting as Nikola's interpreter. "Do you know when they're moving it?"

"Soon. Maybe even tonight."

"That might be our *dear Beloved*'s move," he said.

"What makes you say that?"

"He's afraid of humans in large groups, right?" said Kaveh. "And the location's been compromised; that means that on top of the military detail that's always surrounding the place, it's surrounded by Gadsden Liners, and they might have the EMP van with them. They don't have a way to take out that many humans without killing them, but the Gadsden idiots *know* how to take him down. He won't risk going near them."

She nodded in cautious agreement. "I think that's it. He won't go near the facility because they might have the ability to remotely take him out."

"But if the body is *removed* from the facility, if it's out on the open road . . ."

She looked at him, realization dawning as she followed his line of thought. "You don't need to go into a secured remote facility, if instead you can just wait for them to bring the body of an alien death machine right to you."

Cora was up in a flash, all but falling down the stairs, and Kaveh followed. By the time they reached the living room, Nikola was already on his feet, the door to the backyard already open.

"We think he's waiting for them to take out Obelus's old body from the San Bernardino facility," she said. "Can you take us there?"

"No."

She gasped. "What do you mean?"

"I THANK YOU FOR YOUR INPUT. I WILL SEEK YOU AGAIN IF THIS TURNS OUT TO BE A FALSE LEAD."

"Wait," she said, hesitantly approaching Nikola. He had never noticed how much more afraid of Nikola she was than he. "Take me with you."

"THIS MIGHT BE DANGEROUS FOR YOU, LITTLE COUSIN."

"He's not going to hurt me."

"IT IS NOT OUR DEAR BELOVED THAT CONCERNS ME."

"Please, take me with you. You know he's still terrified of you, right? You might need me to reason with him."

"I DO NOT BELIEVE HE IS AMENABLE TO BEING REASONED WITH."

He lowered himself to the ground, black ink flowing out of the carapace of his back, enveloping him in less than a second, and then he disappeared, a slight *whoosh* of wind slightly pulling Kaveh into the wake of his cloaked body zipping San Bernardino–ward.

"No!" Cora cried. "*Fuck!*"

Kaveh stared at the blank space where Nikola had been, the sudden lack of darkness playing tricks with his eyes. He thought of the manila envelope, the ticking of the clock beating in his mind like a war drum. "I think it's in God's hands, so to speak."

"No," she said, grabbing the car keys to the Roadster off the key hook.

"What are you doing?"

"I'm going, too. If you won't let me take your car, fine. I'll take a cab. I will fucking walk, but you can't stop me."

He stared at her, agog, feeling as if he were being torn in half, pulled on one side by his girlfriend and on the other by a manila envelope on the opposite side of the country.

She shouldn't have kept the information about the dead CIA agents from him, but at the same time, there was no mechanism by which she could have safely told him about it, either. Besides, what she had done was nothing compared to what he had done. He'd given Nils incredibly privileged information that he himself had not understood, and done it so carelessly. And he'd done it just as much to spite Kaplan as to protect himself and Cora from Nils's blackmail. All she'd done was keep quiet as she had been told to do. He'd done the opposite, and his indiscretion might be the cause of all of this.

You don't know it was Nils, the placating internal monologue assured him. *Julian has resources. You don't know it was Nils who caused this.*

But deep in his heart of hearts, in his soul of souls, he knew it was.

"I know I can't stop you," he said. "I'm not going to try to. I'm going with you."

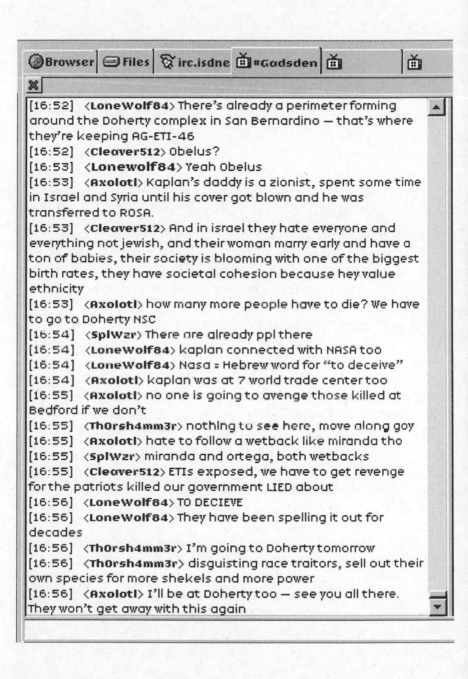

Browser | **Files** | **irc.isdne** | **#Gadsden** |

[16:52] <LoneWolf84> There's already a perimeter forming around the Doherty complex in San Bernardino — that's where they're keeping AG-ETI-46

[16:52] <Cleaver512> Obelus?

[16:53] <Lonewolf84> Yeah Obelus

[16:53] <Axolotl> Kaplan's daddy is a zionist, spent some time in Israel and Syria until his cover got blown and he was transferred to ROSA.

[16:53] <Cleaver512> And in israel they hate everyone and everything not jewish, and their woman marry early and have a ton of babies, their society is blooming with one of the biggest birth rates, they have societal cohesion because hey value ethnicity

[16:53] <Axolotl> how many more people have to die? We have to go to Doherty NSC

[16:54] <splWzr> There are already ppl there

[16:54] <LoneWolf84> kaplan connected with NASA too

[16:54] <LoneWolf84> Nasa = Hebrew word for "to deceive"

[16:54] <Axolotl> kaplan was at 7 world trade center too

[16:55] <Axolotl> no one is going to avenge those killed at Bedford if we don't

[16:55] <Th0rsh4mm3r> nothing to see here, move along goy

[16:55] <Axolotl> hate to follow a wetback like miranda tho

[16:55] <splWzr> miranda and ortega, both wetbacks

[16:55] <Cleaver512> ETIs exposed, we have to get revenge for the patriots killed our government LIED about

[16:56] <LoneWolf84> TO DECIEVE

[16:56] <LoneWolf84> They have been spelling it out for decades

[16:56] <Th0rsh4mm3r> I'm going to Doherty tomorrow

[16:56] <Th0rsh4mm3r> disguisting race traitors, sell out their own species for more shekels and more power

[16:56] <Axolotl> I'll be at Doherty too — see you all there. They won't get away with this again

52

"I think I see movement."

Kaveh put down his binoculars to get a better view with his own eyes. He was perhaps one of the few binocular owners who used them for spying purposes on the regular instead of birding or being a pervert, but it had been a while since he'd been in this position. Right now, that position was parked on the side of a hill about two miles away from the compound where Obelus's old Similar body was being held.

They'd been there for two hours, and while there were indeed a *ton* of Gadsden Liners surrounding the entrance to the complex, easily in the hundreds, there was no sign of extraterrestrial activity, nor any indication that anything had happened yet.

"What kind of movement?" asked Cora.

Kaveh put the binoculars back to his eyes. "Looks like the gate is opening. Oh, shit. That's National Guard. They're clearing the Liners off the road."

"Maybe it is happening tonight."

There was a large police presence as well, both county sheriffs and police from nearby towns. At least he didn't see any goddamn black vans with any goddamn Tesla coils on top, but even from this vantage point, he couldn't see everything.

The road was now clear, the entrance open, blocked on either side by National Guard. Then one helicopter rose from the base, then another, and finally the beginnings of a motorcade emerged from the gate.

"Oh, shit," Kaveh muttered. "I think it is."

Several military-grade vehicles emerged, then a few Hummers, and finally an armored car flanked in the front and back by police vehicles. The helicopters hovered over the procession like flies, flies with spotlights on the crowd.

"He's here," she said absently.

"I thought you said you couldn't sense proximity," he said, lowering the binoculars and turning on the Land Rover's engine.

"I can't, but I can sense other things. Like . . ." She crushed her eyes closed. "Like . . . the sound of people in a big crowd agitates him in a certain way. If he's not *down there*, then he's being agitated by a different crowd, which is not likely."

"Maybe we can follow the motorcade at a distance," he said. This complex only had a straight road about two miles long that connected the entrance with the main road. Kaveh had chosen this spot on the hill because it would be a simple matter to head them off, providing the motorcade didn't start tearing off down this little desert road at eighty miles per hour.

He put his binoculars up once more just in time to see that the two helicopters on either side of the motorcade seemed to have lost power, as did the SUVs flanking the armored car's front and rear, and every other vehicle on the road. The helicopters floated harmlessly to the ground, but the armored car sped up just as its driver and passenger either jumped or were flung from the vehicle. Then, it veered to the left and continued speeding into the desert toward the mountains.

"Follow it," said Cora.

Kaveh didn't move, one hand on the steering wheel, the other on his binoculars.

"Kaveh!"

"Okay!" he said, putting the car into gear. He raced down the hill, across the open road, turning onto the road the motorcade had been on before the armored car made its mysterious detour into the desert. He put the Land Rover into four-wheel drive and followed, checking to see if there was anyone else, human or alien, on their tail. The sun had almost completely set, and while the Gadsden Liners and the crowd that had gathered were well out of sight, the military caravan was not, and as best as he could tell, none of their equipment was working, indubitably the work of alien magic. Speeding through the desert, the brush of the untamed wastes scraping against the bottom of his car and a plume of dust spewing up in his wake, he had a suspicion that the same fate was to befall his Land Rover.

Almost the second he had that thought, it did, and the car rolled to a placid stop.

"Shit," he said, but inwardly, he was relieved. Of course he was worried about the situation, but whatever Ampersand was planning on doing with Obelus's body, the body that was responsible for a *minimum* of four human disintegrations, he had a feeling that neither he nor Cora could influence what was about to happen, and to run toward it was suicide.

But run toward it was exactly what Cora was already doing, out of the Land Rover before he could say anything, running toward the cloud of sand churned up by the armored car.

"Cora!" he bellowed, hopping out of the Land Rover. She was already in a sprint, running into the darkness. He knew he couldn't convince her to stop, so what else was there to do but follow her?

Perhaps it was desperation that fueled her, because he was not able to keep up. He jogged on and off for about five minutes before he saw that the armored car was stopped not far ahead. The sun had by now completely set, the sky now a cerulean rimmed with pink that was darkening by the second. The back of the armored car was hanging open. He couldn't see inside it, but he could imagine what was in there. An empty shell that, if inhabited, became Death, Destroyer of Worlds.

He continued toward the truck, seeing Cora on the other side, pleading with someone who was much taller than she was. It took Kaveh another few seconds to round the armored car, not daring to get near the open door. There he was, looking down at her calmly. She was speaking to him softly. Kaveh couldn't hear her words, only an incredible heaviness, an incredible sadness in her voice. Jude Atheatos, once known as Ampersand. At his side was a much smaller amygdaline, one that was no taller than Cora.

That must be Obelus.

"I TOLD YOU THIS COULD BE DANGEROUS FOR YOU, DEAR CLEVER CREATURE."

He gasped, split between relief and dread to hear Nikola's voice. Kaveh saw Ampersand look in his direction and go on alert, standing up straight, the crown on the back of his head splaying out like peacock feathers, and Obelus went still as a statue. Kaveh turned around, and there was Nikola, his monstrous silhouette black against the orange-blue sky.

"REMOVE HER," said Nikola. "GET BEHIND ME."

"Cora!" Kaveh resumed his trot, positioning himself right behind her but unable to take his eyes off Ampersand. He knew that Nikola could overpower the other two easily, but that didn't mean there wasn't danger for humans. He took Cora by the arm, every fiber in his being telling him that Ampersand was the one to be afraid of. Cora shrieked as she spotted something over her left shoulder, and Kaveh snapped his attention in that direction.

There were three Similars standing maybe thirty feet away, each bigger than Nikola, even bigger than the Similar Brako. He grabbed Cora by the shoulders and began backing away, keeping his face to the three of them. They seemed as interested in the two humans as the three they were ostensibly here for. One of them even started toward them when he was addressed by one of the others.

By Nikola.

"Nik," Cora whispered. "What have you done?"

"I HAVE MADE AN ARRANGEMENT," said the voice in Kaveh's ear. "THEY ARE HERE FOR OBELUS, NOT FOR US OR FOR YOU. I HAVE TOLD THEM I WOULD DELIVER OBELUS TO THEM, AND HIS OLD BODY, IN EXCHANGE FOR ALLOWING US TO DIE ON THIS PLANET ON OUR OWN TERMS."

But something already felt off. For the first time, he saw Obelus cut in, and he began speaking to his three former subordinates. Then Nikola's body language changed; antagonistic, alert, frightened, even.

"LITTLE COUSIN, DEAR CLEVER CREATURE, RUN."

"Did you hear him?" asked Kaveh, resuming the careful backing away.

"Nikola, what's happening?" asked Cora.

"THESE SIMILARS ARE TRYING TO CHANGE THE AGREEMENT. THEY WANT BOTH OF THEM, NOT JUST OBELUS. I AM EXPLAINING THAT THAT IS NOT OUR AGREEMENT. THEY CANNOT HAVE OUR DEAR BELOVED AS WELL. I FEAR THEY MAY HARM YOU FOR SHOW. PLEASE, RUN."

"You heard him," whispered Kaveh.

Then, as if emerging from his very nightmares, he heard the distant sound of truck engines. Still backing away, he turned to look and nearly stopped dead.

There were two of them, following the path laid out by the armored car, but it wasn't the military motorcade magically come back to life. This was all Gadsden Liners, a caravan of violent idiots charging blindly to their deaths. He could all but hear the redneck war whoops from nearly a mile away.

Kaveh continued pulling Cora away from the scene in front of them, but she stopped dead, keeping her mute gaze on the pair of headlights careening toward them. Surely, he thought, whatever alien voodoo had knocked out the motorcade and helicopters would envelop these vehicles, too. They were closer now, no more than a couple thousand feet. The light of their headlights had found the armored car, and they could probably see the silvery, iridescent skin of Ampersand and the Similars as well.

"They are going to kill every single one of those idiots," said Cora.

Kaveh looked back toward the Similars, who still had their attention on Nikola. Only one of them seemed to have taken a disinterested notice in the militia.

Cora wrenched free of his grasp and walked in the direction of the caravan. The trucks were closer still, no more than 1,500 feet. In a fluid movement, she reached into her pocket, and withdrew an object it took him a moment to recognize—the pulse emitter. She didn't look back at him, didn't ask for support, didn't hesitate; she just held the pulse emitter level and fired.

The headlights on both vehicles brightened like a flash of lightning before shorting out, and the trucks rolled to a harmless stop. He was too blinded by the now-shorted headlights to see clearly, the light from the sun by now almost completely gone, but he could make out at least four men. They were close enough now that without the din of the trucks he could hear their voices.

The instant the pulse went off, all six amygdalines in the vicinity either stumbled or collapsed entirely. The only one that seemed relatively unaffected was Obelus, who staggered slightly, and then, seeing an opportunity, tried to make a run for it. Kaveh couldn't help but admire him; he really did have a survivor's instinct.

Unfortunately for Obelus, the pulse's effect on the other Similars was less than what it had done to Ampersand and Nikola, who were both on the ground as they had been at Pershing Square, and Kaveh nearly melted into a panic that their sole defense had been knocked out until Nikola moved, struggling to get back to his feet. The three Similars were likewise struggling, seeming to pool what little telekinetic power they could muster to drag Obelus back to them.

Cora turned toward them and didn't even look at Kaveh as she marched past him, still holding the pulse emitter level, now at the three Similars. She walked past Ampersand and Nikola, standing in between them, keeping her pulse emitter trained on the three Similars and Obelus. "Leave."

The three looked at her, the leader of the group, now having regained his bearings, standing a bit straighter, as if trying to loom from twenty feet away. It was surprisingly effective. Cora didn't budge.

"Leave. You have what you came for. Now leave. Take him. Don't come back." She was stone still, hardly any tremor in her arm holding the pulse emitter.

Kaveh heard a noise coming from inside the armored car, of scraping as hundreds of pounds of biosynthetic mass was dragged out of it. It was only then that he saw the body, a broken, mangled thing that must have at some point resembled the three monsters standing in front of them. Then, as it dragged itself over the sand like a ghost, it seemed to reassemble itself, the innards closing like latches, the myriad spines and rods folding back into place like the hammers of a piano defaulting back to their resting places. The skin that looked like a lion had gotten ahold of it closed over the giant opening, folding back in on itself like wrapping paper. Then, it seemed to wrap in on itself even more as the Similars drew it closer—the head drawing in, the arms and legs folding up against it, and a film seeping out of it, not the liquid metal of the travel plates but a translucent material that flowed out of the back and around it like skin, wrapping it up until it resembled a cocoon.

Kaveh was so transfixed with what was happening to the uninhabited body that he didn't at first realize they were doing the same thing to Obelus's smaller, inhabited body, only this body was resisting. His arms and legs jerked out a few times before he resigned himself as the translucent wrap covered him, at first in strips like a mummy, then wider until it was one translucent sack, a spider's meal wrapped up to be sucked dry.

He noticed the lead Similar looking at Cora before it looked at Kaveh. It was hard to read any meaning into so alien an expression. If he had to label it as anything, he saw it as bemusement, maybe even curiosity. Humans were beneath contempt, perhaps, but it appeared that they had been bested by one. Their cocooned spoils disappeared from sight, and a few seconds later, the three Similars wrapped themselves in their own liquid metal transport system, and they, too, were gone.

Cora still had her hand level, but now it was starting to shake. Nikola continued struggling to stand, and Ampersand was still on the ground, but in a way that spoke to Kaveh that he was not incapable of standing up if he wanted to; this was the posture of someone who had been utterly defeated.

Then, a shot tore open the silence. Then another.

The sound made Cora shriek and drop the pulse emitter. "Shit, we have to go!" she said, kneeling next to Ampersand. "Get up! Come on!"

"Pill bug!" said Kaveh. "Do you have that pill bug thing?"

"Right," she said, fumbling it out of the other pocket of her jacket. She slapped it down onto the spot on Ampersand's back near the base of his neck, and it went off like a defibrillator, causing him to spasm slightly.

"Give it to me!" said Kaveh, and Cora tossed it to him without pause, continuing to shake Ampersand by his arms.

"Come on, come on!" she said. "We have to get out of here. There are more men with guns."

Kaveh placed the pill bug on Nikola's back and nearly dropped it in revulsion when it latched onto the "skin"; it moved like an actual bug, and the base of it had thousands of filaments that reached out and moved like the legs of a millipede.

He could hear the voices of the men now almost well enough that he could understand what they were saying, close, no more than a few hundred feet away. Another three shots rang out in rapid succession.

"Come on," he said, more to the pill bug than to Nikola. "What do I do? What am I doing wrong?"

Nikola didn't respond, still trying to stand up. Kaveh heard Cora cry out and turned to see that Ampersand had grabbed her, forced her to the ground, and had crawled on top of her like a soldier falling on a grenade. He watched dumbly, knowing Nikola was their best chance at self-defense but his instinct pulling him to get his girlfriend out from under the alien monster.

He pressed the pill bug to Nikola and felt nothing. "Come on, buddy, we need you!"

Ampersand had practically curled his head around Cora's, blocking the rest of her upper body with his hands like a cage. She was trying to reach out for Kaveh, but she couldn't get her arm out. "Get down!" she yelled. "Kaveh, he says you need to get down!"

Again, gunfire. One, two, three shots. There was a fourth shot, but Kaveh did not hear it.

Cora didn't see it when it happened; her vision was blocked by Ampersand's head and hands holding her down. She could see Nikola through his long, slender fingers, but not Kaveh. Nikola had almost stood back up to his full height, the pill bug on the ground next to him.

"Kaveh!" She scanned the ground for him, confused. Had Nikola already gotten him onto a plate, ferried him to safety? After another round of bullets, she looked at the ground and saw a black, rumpled mass half-sticking out from behind some brush. A mass that looked like a pair of human legs.

No.

"Kaveh! Answer me, Kaveh!"

"He is gone."

Nikola was standing now, had turned around and had his attention on the body that had collapsed next to the brush. Gunfire was ringing far too rapidly to keep count of the shots. Multiple guns. Multiple assault rifles.

"Save him!" Cora yelled, her voice tremulous with terror and disbelief. "Ampersand, I know you can do it. Save him!"

"I can't."

Cora noticed the air was thickening with bullets, not zipping by but stopping, caught in the air like flies getting stuck to flypaper, hanging in a cluster in front of Nikola.

"Please, you have to try! Please, I'm begging you, save him!"

"I cannot revive him. He is already gone."

There was a disagreement among the shooters. One of them was still firing, another several were yelling. Perhaps they knew that they'd not hit one of the invaders but a human. But whoever was still shooting did not care. The ends justified the means.

They were close now, perhaps fifty feet away. She could hear their voices, probably should have been able to make out what they were saying, but all she heard was gibberish. Nikola had not moved, was just staring down at Kaveh, all the while every round fired getting caught in the cloud in front of him.

Then Nikola's head snapped up toward the militia, his focus narrowing, what little light there was to be absorbed concentrating in his eyes like pulsars. The militiamen got a few more rounds off before, perhaps, they realized their mistake, that none of the bullets were connecting. But it was too late for all of them.

Nikola's posture became antagonistic, head down, fingers splayed out like barbs in a briar patch. The air itself trembled. Then everything lit up, every piece of brush within a hundred-foot radius ignited, and in seconds, they were surrounded by fire. The cloud of bullets was terrifyingly clear now in the light of the blaze, and then the cloud began to spin, turning into a tornado of fire and metal. The tornado at first took the form of a whirlpool directly in front of Nikola, but then the whirlpool spread. Soon the tornado enveloped all of them—Nikola, Ampersand, Cora. Kaveh.

The bullets continued building up momentum, swirling in a circle of fire and smoke and heat around them until they were going so fast she could no longer see them. Then Nikola released them, so fast she could hear them zipping overhead, cutting up the air in their wake. She heard several voices cry out, but only briefly.

And then, there was only the sound of the burning brush surrounding them. Nikola put his hands down, the focus of his eyes fading. He leaned over to examine Kaveh, and in her horror at what Nikola had done, she had already forgotten what Ampersand said.

"He's already gone."

No. No, it can't be true. He's wrong.

Nikola moved away from Kaveh toward the two of them and spoke something in Pequod-phonemic. Ampersand had not released his iron grip on her, despite the fact that the shooting had stopped. Then Ampersand's body moved, and for an instant, she mistook it for him standing up, rather than being dragged off the ground by a pair of giant black claws. He held on to Cora for a couple seconds before his grip grew flaccid, and he dropped her.

Cora shot up to her knees to get a better look at Kaveh. *No. No. He has to be wrong.* She looked back at Ampersand and at Nikola. Nikola seemed to have forgotten that she even existed. Ampersand lifted his head, the effort seeming to tax every reserve of energy he had in him, and his focus met hers. He looked at her, detached, like he was only seeing her for the first time.

"No!" she yelled, shooting up to her feet to grab him. Nikola was faster. In less than a second, he had wrapped both of them into a giant mass and had disappeared, pulling smoke into their wake. Cora launched herself toward them, but grasped only hot air.

Smoke filled her lungs, and already, she was finding it hard to breathe. She crawled over to Kaveh's body, turning him on his back and screaming at the sight of his face. It didn't even look like his face, the eyes open and glassy, his focus lopped to one side, his jaw hanging as though it might break off.

She lifted his head up into her lap; there was blood everywhere, pouring out of his head. She used her other hand to frantically feel around for a pulse, like she was just looking in the wrong spot. Nothing.

She ran her fingers through his hair, his beautiful hair that was caked with blood and brain matter and bits of skull. Then she felt it, felt the entry wound through his bloody hair, felt the hole in his skull, felt the edges of the bone. She screamed and jerked her hand away like she'd been bitten by a snake. She'd only felt the entry wound for milliseconds, but she knew that memory, that feeling, would stay on her fingertips for as long as she lived, and she was struck with the desire to cut her fingers off.

She let the body fall to the ground, and she screamed for a long time, hours perhaps. She screamed like if she screamed hard enough it might breathe life back into him. The flames nearest to her had burned themselves out, but the fire itself was spreading rapidly.

She was crying now, the screams having turned into heaving, weeping sobs, and she wrapped her arms around his chest. She pulled him closer, his head falling back in a way that was almost unnatural, and she pressed her face to his. It was already growing cool.

He's already gone.

She sucked in a breath of air, but it was more smoke and heat than air, and burned her throat, and she coughed violently. She became aware of how truly surrounded she was, they both were. She thought she heard a helicopter, perhaps saw a spotlight overhead, but it was becoming difficult to see. She pulled Kaveh's corpse toward her, wrapping her arms around his shoulders and dragging him to the middle of the small clearing they were in. The exertion made her body demand more air, and she breathed in fire. She looked at the armored car, half thought that it might provide some respite, but knew that would only cook her alive faster.

She let Kaveh go, rolling onto her back next to him. She looked into the sky and thought she saw a light shining down on her, but the heat burned her eyes, burned her nose, burned everything. She couldn't breathe.

He's gone.

April 20, 2008
Los Angeles Times

Reward Offered for Information on Whereabouts of ETIs

BY JACKIE SCOTT

SAN BERNARDINO—A $500,000 reward is being offered for information that will lead to the capture of the amygdaline ETIs Nikola Sassanian and Jude Atheatos, one or both believed responsible for the killings of anti-government protesters Paul Bird, William David Kovacevich Jr., Brendan Mooney, and Aaron Gittelman.

Kovacevich's wife, Margaret, said she feels "inconsolable."

"I didn't understand how this could happen," she said. "He warned us about the capabilities of the ETIs. We didn't believe him."

She said she still can't wrap her mind around Kovacevich's killing.

"Dave was always smiling," she recalled, saying he was a family man with a great sense of humor. His children did not respond for comment.

The four protesters all died from gunshot wounds that federal investigators believe were caused by their own bullets, which were reappropriated by one or both of the ETIs after the men fired on them.

Author and award-winning journalist Kaveh Mazandarani was also killed in the shoot-out, although FBI investigators believe his death was caused by one of the gunmen and not either of the two ETIs. Cora Sabino, who went missing after her shocking Senate testimony on April 16, survived the altercation.

· 54 ·

Consciousness bloomed a few moments before the memory of the pre-vious night did. For those few moments, Cora was confused as to where she even was and defaulted to the assumption that she was at home in bed. Home was New York now, home was Kaveh's Tribeca loft, his big king bed with the fluffy white duvet, with the morning sunlight that poured through the windows that ran alongside the entire wall. She liked to look out those windows in the morning onto Sixth Avenue, where the spring foliage was just starting to brighten the edges of the trees with green. Then came the stench of smoke that still clung to her. She opened her eyes, and for a few more seconds, her mind refused to accept where she was, what had happened.

He's gone.

Sol was standing next to the bed, and when he saw that she was awake, he sat down on the edge of it. Her face morphed to disbelief, and she drew in a painful breath, her throat still scorched from the hot air of the fire. "No," she said. The only word she could find. "No, no, no, no."

"I'm sorry," he said.

"Please," she said. "Please tell me you tried."

Sol shook his head. She'd never seen him look at her like this. "It was instant. He wouldn't even have felt it."

"Please, no," she said, her face growing hot, her dry lips cracking painfully. "This can't be happening."

"I'm sorry." He said it with a gentle tone she'd never heard from him before. He leaned toward her, leaned in like he was going to hug her.

"Don't you *fucking* touch me," she spat, recoiling. "Don't you dare fucking touch me."

Sol looked at her, stunned, and then drew away from her. The gentleness he'd exhibited for the shortest of moments vanished.

"You got what you wanted," she said, unable to contain herself.

"I didn't want this," he said coolly. He stood up and meandered toward the door. It was only here that she realized this wasn't home. She was in a hospital bed, but this was not in a civilian location. She was on a base, some government compound.

They were not going to let her go.

"He didn't always tell the truth about me," said Sol, keeping his back to her. "He told you he got me reassigned when he leaked my identity. He didn't. I requested to be transferred out of anti-terrorism months before they did their piece. I was gone before it even went to print. He didn't get me reassigned. I left."

He just stood there, his back to her. She hardened her jaw, forced the tears back. "But you still did those things."

Sol moved like he was about to turn to face her, but instead stuffed his hands into his pants pockets, and left.

As soon as he was gone, she wanted him back. Not because he comforted her but because he disgusted her. Imagine, him talking about *himself* at a time like this. Worse, trying to make himself out like he wasn't all that bad because he decided he'd had enough torture for one lifetime before his identity got leaked and he'd have been forced out, anyway. He made her fucking furious, and anger was vastly preferable to the kraken of grief that was just below the surface, bubbling, roiling, ready to pull her into the depths.

She didn't really believe it was true yet. He couldn't be dead. This incredible mind, this incredible person who had overcome so much—fleeing his home country, addiction, the death of his brother—and still accomplished so much. Scholar, writer, polyglot. This person who had seen the best in her, had shown her kindness when no one else had, and seen potential in her where no one else did. Had been her rock, her protection. Gone, all gone. Brain matter splattered on the desert. Rotting in a morgue somewhere.

This can't be real. This can't be happening.

The door cracked open, and Cora's entire body turned to steel, ready for a fight. She relaxed only slightly when she saw that it was not Sol but Luciana.

Luciana stood next to the door for a long time, looking at Cora like she felt like this whole mess had been her fault. Eventually, she spoke, voice barely above a whisper. "Cora, I'm so sorry."

Cora just glared at her. What did she expect her to say? *It's fine? The one person in my life who supported me, who saw any potential in me, who encouraged me, who didn't abandon me when things got difficult, is dead, but don't worry about it?*

Luciana inched closer to the bed. "How are you holding up?"

Cora coughed a little. How in God's fuck was she supposed to answer that? "I don't know." Her throat felt coated in rusted iron.

Luciana nodded, seeming to consider the wisdom of sitting on the side of the bed as Sol had, but refrained. Cora was all barbs, and Luciana knew it.

"I need to ask you something," said Luciana. "Did Kaveh ever say anything about me?"

Cora blinked, a little incredulous. First Sol, now Luciana? What was it about death that everybody had to make it about *them*? "Like what?"

Luciana made a face like the mere act of talking pained her. "Let me rephrase that—did he ever tell you that he and I had met before? A while ago, back when you were in high school?"

"No, he didn't say anything."

Luciana eyed her, searching for something. "Really?"

"Really."

"He didn't mention anything about meeting me in 2002?"

"No, nothing."

Luciana pursed her lips and braced herself, like forming words was an exercise in torture. "I need to tell you something."

"Not now—"

"No, please," Luciana cut her off, now on the precipice of tears. "Last year, when we parted on bad terms, I promised myself I'd make things right when I saw you again, and those two weeks you had disappeared . . . I honestly . . . I really, genuinely thought if you turned up dead, I couldn't survive that. And when they found you, I just wanted to make things right but . . . I never did. And I'm afraid if I don't tell you this now, what if the next time we part might be our last?"

Cora wanted to tell her, *Then I guess we'll never have it,* but held back.

"When I told you that I didn't have anything to do with leaking the Fremda Memo to Nils, that was the truth. When I told you that I don't know how he knew to go digging for it, that was also true. I didn't know, because I didn't remember. But to be honest, this isn't even about coming clean. I didn't lie. I didn't realize that I did know the truth, that I had forgotten it. You were right. It was me that did it. I was the one who told Nils about the Fremda group."

Cora's anger was starting to burn itself out, to fade to numbness. But she wanted it back, anything, anything to keep her from slipping into grief. She couldn't handle it.

Ampersand couldn't handle it.

She'd been so consumed with anger over the loss of Kaveh, she'd forgotten the loss of Ampersand. He was on a precipice of his own, she sensed it. He wasn't sharing her anger, wherever he was; he was mired in his own grief. And she knew, the second she slipped into her own grief, became consumed by it . . .

It would be too much. That would be the moment he decided, enough. I'm tired. I don't want to run anymore.

And with that, she remembered Nikola's decree, the very first thing he had said to Cora, the reason he was here on Earth at all: *And he will join me in death.*

"Kaveh told me—*reminded* me—what I did," Luciana continued. "The day you . . . The day the . . . self-harm happened. He reminded me of this one night in 2002, me and Nils and Kaveh and some of their other writer colleagues, we went to this bar in Culver City, and Nils got me drunk, and . . . apparently I told him the truth, thinking he wouldn't believe me. I swear, I didn't remember doing this. I was blackout drunk. And I'm sorry for the way I treated you. You were right. You were right the whole time. But the thing is, even if you were wrong, I was wrong to treat you like that. Wrong to distance myself, wrong to let you distance yourself."

She grabbed a handful of her copper-colored hair, pained by words that were clearly not coming naturally. "And I know I let you rely on him too much. Kaveh, I mean. And I should have reached out sooner, I should have fixed this sooner. And I'm so sorry. I'm so sorry this happened, but I'm also sorry that you *had* to rely on him as much as you did. I'm sorry to both of you, truly, I am. But I want to be with you through this. I don't know whether it's appropriate to ask for forgiveness right now, probably it isn't, but I don't think it matters. I just can't leave you to process this alone . . . this—"

Carefully, like she was afraid she might spook Cora, she moved closer. "Listen . . . it isn't just you. I've been diving into myself for a long time and denying that's what's happening. I lost all my friends at ROSA because they suspected me of talking to Nils, and it turns out they were right. I'm losing my mother to her own dementia. I've lost Demi. We don't talk anymore." She looked at her niece, and Cora saw tears pooling in her eyes. She had never in her life seen Luciana cry. "I can't lose you, too."

I can't lose you, too.

There it was. Every instinct, every fiber of her person, extending from this reality into the noumenal dimensions that bound them together, told her that she was going to lose him. Nikola had already convinced him of his original task; it was time to die. If she didn't act, didn't stop it right away, she'd lose him, too.

"Then you have to get me out of here," said Cora, sitting up painfully. "It's life or death. I have to go."

Luciana looked at her like that was exactly what she thought she'd say, but she was disappointed nonetheless.

"If you don't help me, I'll move heaven and earth to get out. I'll dig myself out with a spoon if I have to. But I have to get out. Please, I am begging you."

Luciana backed away from her slightly, looking at her with a strangely intense sadness. "Do you know where they are?"

"I think so."

"What are they going to do?"

"Nikola is going to kill himself and take Ampersand with him. And Ampersand is going to let it happen."

"Why?"

"Why do people ever take their own lives?" Cora laughed humorlessly.

Luciana's expression grew even more serious. "Why don't you tell Sol what's going on?"

"Because if I tell Sol where they are and the feds show up, Nikola and Ampersand will be dead before they even enter the room. They can't be forced to stop what they're planning. I only have a snowball's chance in hell of appealing to them, but I have to try."

"I'm guessing you see yourself, alone, as the only way to stop them."

Cora threw her legs over the side of the bed, relieved to see that she was still wearing her clothes from the previous night. "I don't see any scenario where either of them survive if I don't try to reason with them."

Luciana shook her head distantly. She knew she'd done the wrong thing so many times, she was trying to do the right thing, and she clearly did not know if this was it.

"If you are really sorry," said Cora, voice vibrating like a string on a harp, "you'll get me out of here. If you really want to make it up to me, if you really want a road to rebuilding this bridge, get me out of here. I just lost Kaveh, I cannot lose Ampersand, too." At this, her voice broke, and she barely held herself together.

Luciana closed her eyes as though she had lost a chess game she'd been playing for weeks. "Well, they've been firing me off and on for years. At least for once, it should be for a good reason." She pursed her lips, and looked at her niece. "Cora, if I get you out of here, how can I know you won't just disappear again? You'll be gone, and it'll be like last time. I won't know if you're alive."

"You won't," said Cora. "I can't promise you I won't disappear; in fact, I probably will for a little while. Nikola killed people."

"Nikola?"

"Nikola. Not Ampersand. Just Nikola."

Luciana nodded. Not the answer she wanted, but clearly an honest one. "Okay."

"I have to move fast."

"Okay!" Her voice hitched. "You can take my car, then. We'd better go now, before Porter finds out you're awake."

Cora forced herself to her feet, face stony as though the smell of smoke wasn't choking her, the flames weren't still kissing the back of her throat. She didn't have the emotional space to know what to do with Luciana's apology, what forgiveness looked like, if it was even possible, but she suspected that Luciana knew that it was too little, too late.

Cora hadn't known what to expect those couple of days with Nikola after the Senate hearing, nor had she cared. She'd offered herself up as a sacrifice, so who was she to care about what he would do with her? He wanted a tool to find his "dear Beloved" and nothing more; she knew the deal. Her horror at the Senate hearing had been so overwhelming, Nikola was welcome to do his worst.

But he hadn't. He'd been curious, respectful, but mostly he'd been absent. She didn't particularly crave physical comfort from him, but it didn't repulse her, either. She endured him even as he kept an eye on the world, the twenty-four-hour news networks, the beast with ten thousand heads.

She pushed the door to the hangar open, a largely empty space striped by decades of graffiti and decay. The windows had been blacked out decades prior, and the few that had been broken by time or vandalism provided the only source of light during the day, which was waning quickly. There was no electric light emanating from inside, which meant that Nikola's surveillance system was off. Why wouldn't it be? He didn't need it anymore.

"THERE YOU ARE, LITTLE COUSIN." The voice in her ear felt like an invasion, the aural equivalent of a clammy finger sliding up the back of her neck. It was even more echoed, more layered than it had been the first time she heard it. "ARE YOU HERE TO JOIN US?"

The same fear gripped her that grips young children at the thought of a monster in the basement. But there was a real monster in the darkness here, one that could not be reasoned with. Kaveh's Nikola was gone now, replaced with the same cruel id that she had first encountered in the woods all those months ago, Enola. His movements were erratic, jerky, sometimes so fast that gravity should not have allowed for them, like sped-up film. But it was his eyes that were the most damning tell that he had gone back to the medication, cataract and unfocused.

"Let me see him," she said.

"Shall you join us, little cousin?"

"No," she snapped. "No, you can't have me."

He approached her, not in the fluid way amygdalines normally moved but alternately too slow and too fast, like he skipped through time, appearing in front of her, eliciting a startled yelp. "Then I am disinclined to let you see him."

"I have as much right to see him as you do," she said, unconsciously leaning away.

"And what will you say to him when you see him?"

It was all she could do not to tell him, *You can't have him*, before she thought better of it. If Enola knew she was here to talk Ampersand out of this death pact, there was no way he'd let her in.

"He left me," she said, choosing her words carefully. "He left me alone without a word. He has to tell me why he did it. Will you let me talk to him alone?"

God, the way he held his head, never level, hands curled up in front of him like dead tree branches, was the very image of terror. "If it is his wish."

Enola sank back into the darkness like it was a pool of black ink. Cora entered, surveying the hangar as her eyes adjusted to the darkness, her hand gripping the pulse emitter in her jacket, more for reassurance than from any realistic expectation she could defend herself with it. Enola was already deep back in the mire and far too powerful for Ampersand to overpower. And moreover, she doubted Enola would let her catch him unaware with a pulse emitter a second time.

Ampersand lay in the middle of the hangar near the wall of screens, his eyes half-open and dark. His hands were curled up in front of him, his legs splayed out behind him. He looked like a deer that had been hit by a truck and left for dead. Cora turned to see if Enola was there, but saw only darkness.

"Ampersand?"

She lowered herself to her knees behind him, running her right hand under his neck and placing her left over his front, his "chest." She felt the carapace of his back, on the crest of his head, the tender, vulnerable "skin" of his neck. His shield was down. The shield he always had up, at any cost—he wasn't even bothering with it anymore.

What was the right thing to say? What had Kaveh told her? *You can't save someone who doesn't want to be saved.* He had lost everything, was by his own reasoning too far gone. How to talk someone down from that?

"I need you to come with me," she said, bowing her head. "Please."

She felt him resist, almost like she'd offended him by even asking. Offense based in resentment, she sensed, because of a wrong she had done him.

"I'm sympathetic about Obelus, really, but it was the only way. If we didn't give Obelus to the Similars, they'd still be here. They wanted you, too. It was the only way."

Eventually, he responded, "*You swore you'd never hurt me.*"

"What do you mean?"

"*You swore you'd never hurt me. Yet you attack yourself. You harm yourself.*"

She felt so far removed from that moment of violence, of self-harm, she hadn't even considered that might be the issue, and not Obelus being taken from him. "Yes. Myself. I didn't do it to you. I did it to *myself.*"

"*You said you'd never hurt me. You know I feel what you feel. Why would you hurt yourself if it was not your intent to hurt me?*"

She hadn't thought of it like that; it was just an impulse, energy that came out in the form of violence, violence that she deserved but no one else would mete out.

All the same, he was right.

"I . . . I didn't mean to hurt you."

"*You swore you wouldn't. Then you did.*"

"I was afraid," she said, tears welling. She was losing this battle already.

"*There will always be fear. It is in your nature to lash out because of your fear. You give your word not to cause harm, but your word is meaningless. You harm yourself with the intent of harming me.*"

"I didn't . . . It wasn't my intent to hurt you."

"*It was. You intended to hurt yourself, knowing it would hurt me.*"

She blinked hard, letting the first wave of tears fall out. "You're right. I acted on impulse. I wasn't thinking. But now that I know this about myself, I can work on the behavior before it becomes a pattern. It's not normal human behavior. I . . ." She reached out, feeling that there must be some magic words that she just needed to speak in the right order. That somewhere out there was the perfect thing to say to snap him out of this, to make him understand that now was not his time.

"I am twenty-one years old. You have to give me room to learn. You have to give me room to make mistakes!"

His big, waxy eyelids slid over his eyes like syrup as they closed. *"Our mutual trauma is too extensive. Our empathic bond is mutually destructive. One or both of us must die."*

"No!" she said sharply. "No, no, that's not how it works. We've only just started; you've only just gotten here. There's so much trial and error we haven't done. There's so much we haven't even tried."

"It is what's best for you. I cannot be your caretaker. You had a mate that provided for your needs better than I ever could. Your kind can care for you better than I ever could."

"It's what feels easiest right now, because Enola is pressuring you to do this thing. But it's a miracle you're here. It's a miracle that you tried to bind yourself to me, and it worked. It's a miracle that either of us are alive at all. We are the living embodiment of something so improbable it may as well be impossible. But we're here, and this isn't something you can undo. Please, don't throw it away."

"When I am gone, you will be free of the burden of my disease, every-thing I feel that you share. You will be free of it."

And there it was. As much as she'd been warned off anthropomor-phizing since she'd first learned of his existence, she didn't think she had ever heard such a human rationalization. *It may not seem like this now, but when I'm gone, things will be better. It may be painful in the short term, but ultimately, it's for the best. One day, you'll see.*

She'd had that thought herself so, so many times in the last few months. She'd only recently gotten herself out of the mire enough to see how much that was the sickness talking. *This isn't you,* she thought. *You could not have made it this far if this were what you really believed.*

"I hope you understand that I'll never be free of you. I . . ." She swallowed painfully, her throat feeling like it was coated in spikes. "Ka-veh's gone. I can't live through losing you, too."

"*Then you should come with me now.*"

At this, she felt that voice she'd spent so much work over the last few weeks beating back, the one that said, *It wouldn't be the worst thing in the world.*

"No," she said. "I'm going to live. Death is final. This isn't something you can undo. Stay with me. I'll take care of you."

Slowly, his eyes slid open, but the amber gemstones stayed sedate and dark. She wiped her face of fluids as best she could and then leaned her face into the smooth skin above the ridge of his eye. "You can't ever go home. You will never be the person you were before. But that doesn't mean there's no healing from this. That doesn't mean we can't make it better."

"*Enola refuses to witness the entire human superorganism meet the same fate as your lover, no matter how cruel some of them are.*"

"He is going to have to wait. It's not your time yet."

She tried to feel what was going on inside him and began tipping into despair when she felt that he hadn't budged. This wasn't working. Either she wasn't making a good case, or his alien mind just couldn't see things the way she did.

But then again, maybe there was a way.

She sat up straight, now aware of a string of hope to cling to, and she grabbed it. "Could . . . could you make me capable of high language?"

At this, his eyes opened further, a subtle fluid movement. The focus of his eyes eventually found her, but he didn't move.

She crawled around his body to face him. "You said you can't prove a negative unless you try. If you die now, you'll never find out. It might be possible. And if that's possible, who knows what else is possible?"

"*It would be extremely invasive. It will take months if not years for me to build an artificial neural network that might interface between our respective nervous systems, which would be incredibly taxing on you. And even then, there is still a good chance it might fail.*"

She wiped her face. "I can take that risk."

By now, his eyes were clear, his focus strengthening. "*And if it suc-ceeds, your mind may handle it poorly. My consciousness would be inside yours. That's a type of intimacy I do not think you are even capable of imagining."*

"I think you'd be surprised how vivid human imaginations can be," she said, hoping he wasn't picking up on the fear in her voice.

Ampersand's focus dissipated as if he were retreating inward. Considering what she was offering, she hoped.

"I don't know if it would end up meaning anything to either of our civilizations. Probably it won't, but maybe that doesn't matter. Wouldn't it be an incredible discovery in itself, if you found that it was possible? That I could communicate with you, or any of you, on your level?"

She closed her eyes and allowed herself to grip that little string of hope more tightly. "Do you still desire me like that?"

She opened her eyes to look at him, but he hadn't moved, his focus still hazy. He stayed that way for almost a minute, and then his focus sharpened on her, the crest on his head perked up, spread into his neutral stance. He pulled himself up into a roost, tucking his hands under himself and pulling his legs up and to his side.

"There is an ancient practice of our ancestors, obsolete within the Superorganism, but it may be relevant here. You might term it conservatorship."

"Conservatorship?"

"When one of a phyle is ill, or unwell, they give themselves over to the rest of their phyle, relinquishing their autonomy until both they and the rest of the phyle agree that their malady is sufficiently improved that the individual may live their lives with autonomy again."

"So basically, it's a form of guardianship. If you're unwell, you give up your autonomy and give custody of yourself to the rest of your phyle."

"Yes. This practice is obsolete because any one amygdaline of the Superorganism who fell ill or became mentally unstable would be treated by the state, not by their phyle. But we do not have that option here."

"Are you saying . . . you would give custody of yourself . . . to me?" she asked, her eyes growing hot. "You would trust me that much?"

"As you said, death is a decision that cannot be undone. Trust is immaterial; I have nothing to lose. If you will it that strongly, and if you genuinely desire to submit to a high-language experiment, then I will give conservatorship of myself to you. All I ask is, if after an agreed-upon amount of time—for instance, six months—if neither my nor Enola's conditions improve, or worsen, then you will be willing to let me go."

"That's a hard thing to agree to. You need to understand that in my culture, there's no circumstance where choosing to give up on life because it's hard and painful is permissible."

"*It is my condition.*"

"Okay." She reached out for him, and his hand enveloped hers, long fingers trailing down her arm like vines. "But I have a condition, too," she said, her voice finding its strength. "You don't lie to me anymore. You don't lie to me ever again. No more half truths. No more lies of omission. If I'm your conservator, then you have to trust me."

His eyes had split their focus, both on their hands and on her face. Within moments, his focus became singular, staring right into her eyes. "*I agree, dear one.*"

"This does scare me," she admitted.

"*Trust cannot be unidirectional. If I am to trust you with the truth, you must trust me with your body and mind. Trust that although the process may be difficult, I won't let harm come to you.*"

"I will," she said, voice small.

She saw Ampersand's gaze move back toward the entrance of the hangar, and saw a shadow move out of the corner of her eye, making her jump. It took a moment to make out the shape of Enola in the darkness, his eyes cloudy, lacking their distinctive reflection, his head jerking as he cocked it.

Ampersand stood up as Enola spoke to him. Ampersand responded, and a Pequod-phonemic back-and-forth ensued for a few seconds. She noticed his body language becoming defensive, the crest on his head rising like the hairs on her arm.

"*Dear one, you may need to use your pulse emitter.*"

Cora shot to her feet. "What's going on?"

"*Enola has refused to agree to your terms.*"

Ampersand's posture, no longer racked with so much hopelessness, had changed, and he had moved himself between her and Enola. Ampersand, as graceful as he ever was, was a stark contrast to Enola's movement, jerky and violent and fast, terrifyingly fast. If there was any conversation happening between them, it was in network language, not spoken Pequod-phonemic. What that conversation was she could not tell, but she sensed that Ampersand was trying and failing to reason with Enola, *Not now, I have made an agreement, please let me honor it. We just have to wait, but not now, not now, don't take her, too, don't punish her. Not now!*

Enola moved with that terrifying speed like a jumping spider, and Cora knew she wouldn't have the luxury of being able to coordinate or strategize with Ampersand. For this one instant, Enola seemed to have forgotten that she was even there, and she used that opportunity to reach for the pulse emitter in the pocket of her hoodie. She managed to tap it, not quite press it, before Enola's eyes found her, and a telekinetic hand smacked her across the room with the force of a truck, separating her from the pulse emitter, which flung itself all the way against the wall. There was a pulse, a tiny pulse, but not enough.

Cora tumbled so far, the wheel of a decommissioned airplane was the only thing that stopped her careening. Ampersand stumbled, falling down and trying to steady himself by rising up on his wrist joints. Enola stumbled, too, but seemed less affected by the pulse, calmly turning his head toward Cora like an owl, his eyes like television static. Cora braced for something else, another shove, or something out of Obelus's playbook, but nothing happened. He didn't have the power, not yet.

Most of their subroutines were still running, she figured, but the ones that required the most power seemed to be down—the remote electromagnetic manipulation, the telekinesis, and their shields.

Their shields.

She looked to where the pulse emitter had skidded over by the surveillance wall. Knowing that Enola couldn't grab her with his invisible hand at this instant, she lunged for the pulse emitter. In those eternal seconds, no more than two of them, she was propelled by the assumption that Enola would try to stop her. That he would either try to restrain her, or take the pulse emitter for himself. The lack of movement from the corner of her eye was what made her chance a look in his direction. He was not pursuing her, but was instead standing over Ampersand's body, one hand around his midsection, the other around his neck.

"IF THIS IS HOW IT IS TO BE," said Enola, "THEN IT CANNOT BE DONE HUMANELY."

She looked ahead to her goal, and in another second that lasted a year, she reached it. Just as she put her hands on the pulse emitter, she heard a ripping sound. She turned around just as Enola finished tearing out Ampersand's throat, nearly severing his head at the neck.

"*No!*" she shrieked, leveling the pulse emitter in a panic, but Enola was on her with the speed of a striking snake, smacking away the device and grabbing her around the torso in one swift movement, pinning her arms to her chest with one big hand. His fingers, sharpened to points, the biosynthetic fluid from Ampersand's body still coating them, sliced the air as they aimed for her neck, but stopped as he touched her skin.

"No," she repeated firmly, her breath coming hard and fast, looking him dead in the eye.

"JOIN US," he said. "DO NOT DIE ALONE."

His fingers were so sharp, she could feel them boring into her skin, sinking into the flesh like needles. "No," she said, keeping her voice low and steady. "You can't have me."

Enola cocked his head to the side, keeping both of his hands in place, his needle-sharp fingers still sinking into the skin of her neck like fangs.

"IF IT PLEASES YOU, LITTLE COUSIN."

In one movement so fast she could hardly see it, he removed his fingers from her neck, sank them into his own, and ripped his own throat out even more violently than he had Ampersand's. His other hand released her, and she didn't waste an instant, running to Ampersand, practically falling on top of him.

He had already stopped moving, and the mess on the floor was staggering. The fluid, his "blood," a translucent, oil-like substance, pumped from his open neck like a burbling spring. His open wound was a hundred strands of biosynthetic pieces in a puzzle she had no idea how to assemble. "No," she said, hands shaking as she tried to shove the body parts and blood and effluvium back into his body. "No, no, no!"

She recalled his ability to self-heal; like his telekinesis, it required a great deal of power, but it was possible. She pulled the pill bug out of her jacket and placed the bug on his back, begging, pleading for him to move.

"Please," she said, pressing it impotently against his skin. It didn't seem to be working. How much time had passed? Thirty seconds? A minute? A human would be dead by this point, but a post-natural amygdaline?

"Fuck!" She looked around the room wildly, looking for something, *anything* that might jump-start this goddamn pill bug to do its goddamn defibrillating job. A car battery, a gas generator, fucking *anything*. She could feel him slipping, feel him losing consciousness. She wasn't sensing fear anymore. No more pain, no more uncertainty. There was nothing.

Water. Water was a conductor. She spotted a gallon of water, one Nikola had brought to her after he'd taken her from the Senate, and dashed toward it. She tackled the gallon jug like a linebacker, and ran back to Ampersand, tearing the plastic cap off as she did and dumping it on top of his body. Still pouring out the water, she shoved the neck matter back into place as best as she could, and pressed the pill bug into him.

"Go!" she cried, her voice echoing into the big, empty hangar. "Fucking *go*! Do something!"

She poured out more water with one hand, trying to hold his neck in with the other, spilling water all over the floor, until she had used the entire gallon and was crouching in a pool that was spreading out all over the floor, all the way into the electrical equipment below Enola's monitors. "*Go!*" she screamed, pressing the pill bug desperately onto Ampersand's wet carapace one last time. "*Please!*"

She didn't feel it as the pill bug's current ignited into Ampersand's body, didn't feel it when the current contacted all the water on the floor, the pool she was crouching in. She didn't feel it when it stopped her heart.

Massive treetops framed the overcast sky, and it was silent, not even the rustle of wind in these massive trees. The treetops were green like the grass on the ground, evergreens in bright contrast to the red of their trunks. She'd never seen such a vibrant red on a tree trunk. She got up off her back, bracing for the act of sitting up to be agony, but her body was as light as air.

She stood up, tried to take a breath but found she didn't need to. She was in a grove of redwoods. She stood in a small patch of grass between the redwoods, the sun peeking through and illuminating the patch. This grove was dead silent, no birds, no bugs, no wind.

Then the grass in front of her carbonized, turned black as if it had burned and turned to coal, but there was no fire. She backed away from it to see that the small patch of grass in the middle of the grove had turned into a black patch like cooled magma, spreading over the forest floor. Some of the carbonized matter turned to white ash, and then the ash formed itself into the shape of a galaxy spiral. She looked at it in awe as it spun slowly, like a hurricane being viewed from space. She recalled some sense of urgency, some sense that she needed to get out of this forest, but she couldn't recall what it was or why it mattered. A gust of wind blew over the ash, scattering the image of the spiral until it dissipated.

"Hey!"

She turned, and there was a face she knew to match the voice. A face that pulled her out of her confusion. "Kaveh!"

He was walking along a sun-dappled path, hands in his pockets, smiling like this was a spot they came to meet regularly. He was wearing the same black denim jacket over the black hoodie and black pants he'd been wearing the very first time she had seen him.

"You came back," she said. "Why did you leave?"

"I didn't mean to," he said as he approached. His hair was silky and flowing, his facial hair clipped close, his jade eyes gleaming. She reached out for him, pulled him into an embrace. She tried to smell him, but there was no air. She didn't need it. He didn't have a smell.

"Kaveh," she said, pulling away from him. "I think we might be dead."

He cocked his head quizzically, but not confused. "I think you might be right."

She heard that voice, that insistence like a voice yelling through a thick wall, only now the wall didn't seem so thick, telling her there was somewhere she needed to go, somewhere she needed to be, someone she had to take care of. She looked at the patch of forest floor that had turned to black and saw that the patch was spreading, burning everything it touched to cinder without fire.

"You need to go," he said. He ran his fingers through her hair, but she couldn't feel anything. No warmth, no feeling of skin on skin. She looked and saw that the hills behind him were turning to black carbon, crawling up the trees and turning them to ash as well.

She thought of leaving the redwood grove, seeing what was yelling at her from the other side of that wall, but she knew what it entailed. Pain, burden, suffering. Maybe it wouldn't be the worst thing in the world if she stayed. "I think I'd rather stay with you."

He shook his head, the lines around his eyes crinkling. "No, not now. Not now."

Not now. But if I go back, he might hurt me again. I might hurt him again. What else was there to consider? She couldn't remember, couldn't see past the negatives, and she was tired. The fire without flame was almost on them now. She was so incredibly tired. She wanted to sleep now, sleep forever.

"No," she said. The giant trunks that surrounded them faded from red to black, began dissipating into ash, crumbling into the air. "No, I think I want to stay with you."

The warmth in his eyes didn't wane, but sadness crept in. "I have to go home now. But you're not done yet."

The oblivion was encroaching, and she knew if she didn't go now, if she let the oblivion take her, she'd get to stay with him, she'd get to sleep forever. She was so tired.

"You need to go," he said, releasing her and backing away. "You're not done yet."

Cora turned, forced herself to move, to go down the only path left that hadn't been burned to ash. She turned around to look at him one last time, to tell him that she loved him, but he was already gone.

· · · · ·

Air surged back into her lungs like it had been shot into her through a cannon. Her heart pounded, adrenaline firing through her, and she grabbed onto something, multiple somethings. Her eyes found focus, and her body fought wildly to take in the oxygen it had been deprived of.

Amber eyes looked down at her. It was his fingers she had grabbed onto, two of them. She reached out to him, but he was gone. Bright lights bore down on her, but these were neither peaceful nor pleasant. The light of LED screens, dozens of televisions. Surveillance feeds and news networks, frantic talking heads, noise that wasn't quite words, sounds with no meaning.

She rolled over in her confusion, still sucking in air, making incoherent noises as she tried to make sense of what was happening. For a second, she thought she'd imagined Ampersand was there at all, thought she'd roll over to see she was lying next to his corpse.

He was standing over Enola's body, frantically tending to it, doing what she had done to him earlier, shoving matter that had been violently ripped out of his neck back into his body, trying to save his life. A minute earlier? An hour earlier? A day earlier? How long had she been out?

How long had she been *dead*?

She fell onto her back, the adrenaline ebbing and allowing her to feel the pain in her chest. She was both freezing and on fire. She was still lying in a pool of water, water that must have done its job conducting energy, electrocuting her and flushing Enola's grid with power, turning every one of his surveillance feeds back on.

Each breath felt more and more like her lungs were turning to stone. She forced herself onto her side, and then pushed herself up onto her elbow. So many news networks, and the same images on all of them.

There were the faces of the men Enola killed. Their names. The photographs next to their names. Not photographs of crazed gunmen, of violence-obsessed conspiracy theorists, but of loving, smiling family men. Every one of those pictures the face of a dad-aged white man with a dad face, smiling a dad smile. These men weren't your enemies. These men were heroes.

And with the one side of the political fence claiming them heroes came the voices, the voices with their commentary.

Now we see a taste of what these alien beings are capable of.

We see an unprovoked attack and an alien defending itself and its human allies.

These men had every right to defend their country.

These men were vigilantes, careless, murderers. The alien had every right to defend itself.

What is to prevent beings this powerful from taking us over? From gaming our system? From overpowering us?

But those four men weren't the only ones who died. Even the most reactionary channels weren't able to spin it that Kaveh wasn't killed by human hands. They had his picture, too. The channels proclaiming the gunmen to be heroes used photos of Kaveh that made him look "foreign," his skin tone pitched darker, the skin around his eyes sallow.

Kaveh Mazandarani was a hero.

Kaveh Mazandarani was a tragedy.

Kaveh Mazandarani was a traitor.

This man was always a traitor. A collaborator with Nils Ortega, he weakened our military by exposing our secrets. Now he aligns with beings that threaten our very existence.

This is what you get when you let men like him into our country.

Refugee. Foreigner. Alien. Muslim. Traitor. We took his people in, and this is our repayment.

This is what you get when you let people like him flood into our country. They accept our generosity, and they spit in our faces. No more. No more. No more.

Never again.

Cora sat all the way up, her balled-up fists pressing into her cheeks, taking in the putrid horror of it all. Half the country had already narrativized Kaveh as a traitor, and they were drawing it back to his nation of origin. They had already labeled the alien as an existential threat, and had condemned this foreign man who hated America as an abettor. The other half, the half calling for reason, the half calling for a sense of perspective, the half waiting for more information before they made a judgment, was already on the losing side of the war.

She felt a presence next to her and didn't even wait for him to settle, to give her any indication; she turned from the wall of televisions and threw her arms around his neck, pulled him close, hoped he could feel her relief that he was alive.

"*Enola is in an induced coma. He will stay in it until I wake him.*"

He placed his fingers on her back, drawing them up to her neck and across her skin, the first comforting gesture he'd made in months. She held him close for a while, as if letting him go might mean he'd disappear. Like their surroundings would disintegrate into oblivion, and he would fall into the darkness, too.

His attention was not on her but the horror unfolding on the screens in front of them, the twenty-four-hour for-profit shit show, drumming up scandal and terror, both feeding on the fear of its audience and fattening it at the same time.

Kaveh Mazandarani was a tragedy.

The men who attacked Nikola Sassanian were vigilantes, outlaws.

Kaveh Mazandarani was a hero.

The men who defended our country were patriots, heroes.

Kaveh Mazandarani was a traitor.

We must defend our country. We must defend Western Civilization.

"*We could leave this place.*"

She looked at Ampersand. His body shook slightly as he lowered himself into a crouch, and then seated himself next to her, bright eyes still fixed on the wall of televisions.

"*I could remove us from this planet. You do not need to see this. I could take us to another life-sustaining place. I would protect you. We aren't obligated to stay here.*"

She looked at the chaos unfolding, the world crumbling before her. Already these talking heads were going on and on and on, not about human civilization but about *Western* Civilization. The misappropriation of Kaveh's face, a person she loved, now a hero, a tragedy, a traitor. The Third Option moving forward, gearing up for a machine designed to dehumanize and oppress. Thus perpetuating the cycle that was human civilization, over and over.

And she was powerless to stop it, powerless to change it, powerless to influence anything. She was a rat on a massive ship trying to push the rudder, deluding herself that she could budge it even a millimeter in either direction. *This is hopeless. There is no changing the direction of this ship.*

"*I can extract Nikola's ability to fold space,*" Ampersand continued. "*Anything we might be able to use, anything you may potentially want to rebuild, all we need is the data. We do not need to stay here.*"

It wasn't even despair that flooded her, it was something more akin to hatred. The way the Superorganism would see human civilization—bellicose, competitive, consumptive, dangerous, xenophobic—wasn't irrational, it was an accurate assessment. It wasn't just that humanity had built a civilization whose inertia toward its own self-destruction was too strong for it to change. This was a civilization that, in the face of adversity, turned on itself, devoured itself, ate its most vulnerable. *Flesh-eaters, pugilists, militarists.*

This was a civilization that did not deserve to be saved.

"Yes," she whispered.

"*Yes?*"

It was foolish to think they could ever really affect the direction the ship was headed. As people, they were tiny, nothing. The ship was too big, the inertia was too strong.

But Kaveh had been wrong about going down with the ship.

"Yes," she said. "Let's go."

A FICTION AGREED UPON

By Kaveh Mazandarani
April 20, 2008

T he date is February 2, 2008. This is the first time I see the
alien entity who will later be named Nikola Sassanian, by
me no less, and the mere sight of him turns my nerves to jelly
in a visceral, animal way that I have never experienced before.
This creature is beetle-black and over nine feet tall. His eyes
are the size and shape of footballs and glow in the dark. His
posture more resembles that of a carnivorous dinosaur than
my own. His fingers are long enough to easily wrap around
a human torso and more resemble the legs of a black widow
spider than human digits. I've never known such terror as the
first time I lay eyes on this alien being.

The date is February 4, 2008. Nikola has now been
restrained by one of his own kind, I am alone with him, and
he is vulnerable and frightened. By this point, he has found
a way to communicate with me, and uses it to beg me for
mercy. He knows how frightening he is to my eyes. He knows
I can't help but be afraid of him, and he fears I would do
what any animal might do to a threat: destroy it. I still find
him frightening, but he no longer turns my nerves to jelly, no
longer evokes the instincts of my tree-dwelling ancestors at
the sight of a predator to fight or flee. I communicate with
him in kind: "*I'm not here to hurt you. I want to help you,*" I tell
him, and he doesn't quite believe me, can't quite understand
why I would show compassion to something I instinctively
find so terrifying. This is the day I give him his "human" name,

Nikola, after the famed Serbian inventor Nikola Tesla. It never occurs to me that this name might be the one attached to him when the rest of the world first sees him.

The date is February 9, 2008, and humanity is getting its first disastrous glimpse of an ETI, and at the same time humanity is also getting its first disastrous glimpse of a human trying to reason with said ETI. That human, of course, is me, tugging on Nikola's forearm like he's a child refusing to leave the toy store after his dad said it's time to go. The people in attendance, at least those who are not in a panic, look on in bewilderment; the truly shocking thing is not the eldritch horror in the middle of Pershing Square, but the human berating him for being there in the first place.

The date is March 5, 2008, and I am sitting in a grove of sequoia redwoods in central California, sheltered by a fire scar that functions like a natural wood tent at the base of one of these living behemoths. This is one of several "field trips" taken at Nikola's request and at the American military's grudging expense. We are surrounded by chaperones, but this is the closest we ever come to being alone. I request these "field trips" on Nikola's behalf under the pretense of his own curiosity about our natural world, a good-will gesture on behalf of the American government to keep him from going on any more joyrides in major cities, but the main reason for these field trips is that we might speak in confidence.

As a student of science and a fan of biology, he can't help but be intrigued by the giant trees. He's seen living things this size before, he tells me, bigger in fact, but they were more in the vein of fungi—porous things with short life spans, not these massive, fibrous pillars that live for thousands of years. He is so distracted by the trees it actually takes him a little while to focus on those discussions that we don't want our government chaperones to eavesdrop on: the subject of his future, and of ours as a civilization.

It is at this point that Nikola sits down next to me inside the carbonized fire scar of the tree, which is big enough to fit both of us. Amygdalines have a rather prim and proper way of relaxing, and Nikola is no exception; he reminds me of a black swan. He's not two feet away from me, and confides, despite the serious nature of the conversation we're about to have, that he enjoys the opportunity to be here with me at all. He finds me "deeply intriguing." He likes it when I touch his "skin," not because he particularly enjoys the sensation of touch in the way a human might, but because he sees it as a gesture of trust on my part. Which, I suppose, it is.

As I sit inside a naturally formed shelter carved out by wildfire at the base of the largest living organism on Earth, Nikola by my side, my mind goes back to the first time I saw him, on February 2, 2008, when I was electrified by a primal fear that I had never in my life experienced. Now here we are one month later, relaxing in the woods next to each other like we've been friends for years. And it is in this moment that I am struck by the human ability to adapt to the foreign, the frightening, and the unfamiliar when the human mind endeavors to do so. When we make the conscious effort to take down the barriers put in place as a result of our culture, our upbringing, or even our natural instincts. I realize that I'd crossed the barrier of seeing him as a person a long time ago, probably within the first few hours of laying eyes on him. And by now I think of him not only as a person, but as a friend. I've thought of him as such for some time.

I know that I'm not unique. I know that if I have the capability to make this mental leap, anyone does. I decide that this will be the hope that I cling to; if I am able to go from pure animal terror at this alien to seeing him as a friend in such a short amount of time, then as conscious humans, as intelligent beings, we are stronger than our natures. My animal self saw Nikola as a monster, but my human self sees him as my friend.

W̶e are named human, derived from the Latin *humanus,* which itself is derived from a proto-Indo-European word meaning "of earth," or more specifically, "in opposition to the gods." They are named amygdaline, derived from the Greek *amygdale,* meaning "almond," for the shape of their eyes. Indeed their eyes are beautiful, awe-inspiring, like they reflect all the stars in the sky on the darkest night. But it is Pequod, the name that has been adopted for their civilization itself, that I find intriguing. Pequod is named for the ship on which Captain Ahab took his Pyrrhic voyage in Herman Melville's *Moby-Dick,* a ship whose mission to destroy a force of nature ended in its doom. The quote that sticks in my mind with regard to Melville's ship reminds me of Nikola himself: "A noble craft, but somehow a most melancholy! All noble things are touched with that."

The truth that Pequod had no knowledge of an advancing human civilization will come as a surprise to many; it certainly did to me. They are not here because of an interest in us, only our planet, which was remote enough from their civilization to not seem an obvious hiding place, but also temperate enough for them to survive in the short term. Owing to the vastness of space, they were aware of a growing population of hominids, but they were not aware that we had turned into an advancing civilization while they weren't looking. The few amygdalines who are here, twenty-four in total, did not run toward *us,* they ran away from something else.

Why are they here? It is a truth of which the American government is well aware, one that they are unsure when or even if they should share with the public. In some ways, they are in America for the same reason I am. The same reason so many of our ancestors came to this country. There was a genocide. The way they word it is "*genetic purge.*" The ones who are here are survivors.

The question most people have about the alien presence on Earth, understandably, is the question of whether their civilization poses a threat to ours. The simple answer is yes. Of course it does. Any civilization with the power to travel such vast distances possesses far more power than we do, and not in a way that can meaningfully be compared to anything we have experienced in human history. Comparing the scenario of their civilization meeting ours to European colonists meeting indigenous Americans is reductive, insulting, and childish for a number of reasons. When it comes to power discrepancies between our civilizations, the balance tips in their favor so far that to even entertain that comparison is absurd.

The question then becomes political—any culture has politics, and theirs is no exception. Is there a political motive for their civilization to come here? Of course there is. Nikola tells me that intelligent life is exceedingly rare, and that ours is the only advancing civilization outside those descended from their ancestors they have ever discovered. But the real question is this: Is there a political motivation inside this civilization that we know only as Pequod to do human civilization harm?

Yes.

Why, if Pequod knows nothing about our civilization, would anyone, human or amygdaline, assume that they might pose some danger to us? Part of it is based on their history, but most of it is based on what they can extrapolate about us. By nature, we are more competitive than they. We are more violent. We are more consumptive. We are more individualistic. We are more tribal. Most terrifyingly to them, we are omnivorous. Imagine being of a species descended from herbivores looking in on us humans, who eat nearly anything, but especially delight in the flesh of our fellow animals. We raise and slaughter them in factory farms, and that's not even the worst of it. We go to war with each other constantly. We continue to pump greenhouse gas into our atmosphere, knowing full well how future generations will suffer for it. We traffic and enslave our most vulnerable, and those who don't turn a blind eye to it. What intelligent being would look at a species like this and not see a potential threat?

Now imagine learning that these violent, competitive, omnivorous monsters had technologically advanced more quickly than you could ever have imagined possible, far more quickly than your ancestors did. Those traits you assumed would prevent the development of an advanced civilization—competitiveness, greed, gluttony, tribalism, bellicosity—in reality turbocharged their progression. These monsters may be only a few thousand, perhaps even a few hundred, years away from approaching your level of advancement, only a generation or two according to the life spans of your kind, and they are already looking to the stars with hungry eyes. What kind of threat might those monsters pose once they come close to your level of technological sophistication? What might you do to mitigate such a threat?

Nikola is, for the most part, resigned to what he sees as an inevitability. He sees our advancement as incredible, he sees our lives as precious, but he knows his fellows back home will not feel the same way, and he believes our long-term prospects are dire. He does not want to see our civilization die, but given that he has nowhere else to go, he considers his own journey near its end. Amygdalines are much more long-lived than humans, and as such they decide on their life spans, and choose when they die centuries in advance. Nikola has not come to Earth to live, but rather, to die, specifically to die with his last remaining "next of kin," Jude Atheatos.

Nikola claims he has no hope, either for his civilization or for ours, so he is ready to exit this life, and take Jude along with him. However, time and time again he betrays that he is not completely hopeless. He betrays this by taking care of his body. He betrays this by complying with the wishes of the American government. He betrays this by postponing this death he claims to desire. He betrays this by indulging his curiosity about our world. He betrays this by developing a friendship with me at all. Logically, he knows his civilization is unlikely to change, and will never welcome him back. He knows that the long-term prospects for our civilization are not good. But perhaps this is why he and I became such fast friends, despite such otherwise incredible differences—against all logic, we still have some hope that the inertia of the systems we were born into is not unchangeable.

There are people in this world who look at their fellow humans and see the worst in them, and their solution is a tilt to authoritarianism. They believe that human nature is immutable, not a construct, and therefore must be controlled with an iron boot. Calling the worst, basest impulses we possess a function of human nature excuses us from change and dismisses it as impossible. But this is the reality we now face—our survival as a species may depend on whether or not we are able to evolve past the foundation of cruelties on which our civilization is built, that we might prove both to ourselves and to nonhuman persons that we are capable of change, that we are not immutably stuck in our barbarous ways.

History shows us that liberal democracies and democratic norms are easily exploited when populists capitalize on mass fear for political gain, when they position a fearful majority into an "us" opposed to a nebulous, terrible "them." The Third Option is only the first step in a long process of dehumanization—one that will be applied first to nonhuman persons, and then eventually to human persons. This phase we are about to enter as a civilization may be our last, and already I am staggered at how shortsighted many have become. These fearmongers provoke the anxieties of an already insecure populace not because they have any strategy regarding our survival as a civilization, but because they desire power. They don't care about the cost, perhaps because they don't believe there truly is one.

My most ardent detractors have accused me of hating America, an odd contention, as it was America that took in my entire family after we fled our home country of Iran, and America that I have called home most of my life. We all have ways of showing our patriotism, and mine is holding my country to account. I want to dissuade her from her worst, cruellest impulses, for I truly believe that if she does not evolve past them, she will not survive.

In that way, America is synecdoche for humanity as a whole—capable of such feats of wonder, such innovation, such compassion, but also such greed, such exploitation, such consumption, such empire, and such cruelty. Are these truly traits of our shared human nature? Is this an inexorable, inescapable state of our being? Or is this all the result of a shared construct that we have erroneously agreed is a necessary evil of civilization, a fiction agreed upon, one that might be changed? If it is the latter, then perhaps we might be saved, but if it is the former, if our self-destructive tendencies arise not from construct but from our innate natures, then I truly believe that we will not survive. After a point, it is not even a question of surviving First Contact; outside intelligences need not be our own undoing if we can take care of our own destruction ourselves.

· · · · ·

I'm relaxing under a great sequoia tree, contemplating the way Nikola has described his civilization to me—a people that have grown to embrace fear, and to fear change. This was not always the case, he tells me. This is not some inescapable by-product of their nature, but a development as a reaction to outside forces that frighten them. This appears to be something our great ships have in common.

Sometimes he talks to me about his ideas on the Divine, which as best I can tell is his concept of God. The Divine is not religious to Nikola. The Divine is not a thing to be believed in; like gravity itself, it either exists, or it doesn't. But the Divine also encompasses everything outside of that which we can perceive, and, more frightening, lies outside of our understanding or control. The Superorganism seeks to control all that it encounters, mundane and Divine alike, which Nikola assures me is impossible, but that doesn't stop them from trying. We have a word for this in English, I tell him. It is from the Greek *hybris,* meaning "wanton violence, insolence, outrage," or more specifically, "presumption toward the gods."

"Hubris will be our end," he tells me.

He does not mean "our" in the collective sense—he means his own civilization. He doesn't think they will become some grand galactic empire, quite the opposite, in fact; their single-minded fixation on controlling everything they encounter combined with their rejection of the unfamiliar has led to a cultural and technological stagnation, which, he believes, will ultimately lead to their undoing.

If that is the case, then Pequod is a poetic name for the ship that is their civilization. The whale is the Divine, and the *Pequod* will sink itself in the pursuit of destroying it. "That inscrutable thing is chiefly what I hate," says Ahab of the white whale with which he is so obsessed and yet by his own admission does not understand. "I will wreak that hate upon him."

I look at this alien being next to me, the body he inhabits an incredible feat of engineering, technological advancement so sophisticated it may as well be magic. I reflect on what a miracle it is that either of us is alive at all, let alone here together on this tiny mote of dust in the outer Milky Way. That we, independent of each other, evolved from our respective primordial soups to a point that we are able to see and understand as much of the universe as we do, that we are able to inhabit the same space and to interact. Nikola finds our limitations a source of consternation; I feel that we are able to see and understand as much as we do as the epitome of true beauty. I don't know how many moments like this we will share together. Will this be one of many such moments, or is it both the first and the last?

I respond to him thus: "Hubris might be our end, too."

ACKNOWLEDGMENTS

I had a lot more help for this book than I did for *Axiom's End*, and I am grateful for everyone who gave me their time, energy, and support. First, to those who gave invaluable feedback on earlier drafts: my agent, Christopher Hermelin; TWO-time Hugo–winning editor Navah Wolfe; Stephanie Kroll; Lindsay Ribar; Elisa Hansen; Nick Hansen; and Emily VanDerWerff. (Audiobook listeners got to hear three pronunciations of her name in the first book. For the record, it's pronounced "VanDer-Werff.")

To my artists: Stanley Chow, who does portraits for *The New Yorker* and was kind enough to do a *New Yorker*–style "witness sketch" for my reporter-at-large, and Harry Brewis, who lent his handwriting talents to some hate crimes.

To Katharine Trendacosta and Devin "Legal Eagle" J. Stone, both of whom used their prestigious law degrees to help me explore the many legal questions at the heart of the book. Now Katharine's many long hours enduring congressional hearings can finally be applied to the question "What if alien rights got debated in congress?"

To Pete Wolverton, Lily Cronig, and the team at St. Martin's Press. A very special shoutout to the book's cover artist, Rob Grom, and the designer, Kelly Too, who spent a great deal of time working with me one-on-one to develop the book's aesthetic. I'm grateful to them for indulging my pedantry, and thrilled with the work they did.

To my audiobook narrators: Stephanie Willis, Abigail Thorn, and Kaveh Taherian. To Steve Wagner, Paul Schuler, and the audiobook team at Macmillan.

To others who gave feedback and support along the way: Kat Lo, Antonella Inserra, Ken "Todd in the Shadows" Munson, Angelina Meehan, and Alex.

· · · · ·

Kaveh Mazandarani was originally two characters, an older recovering alcoholic/mentor figure named Mark and a younger love interest for Cora whose name I can't even remember (it took me ten minutes of digging through Google Drive to even find it—his name was Reed). Both were basic white guys and neither had much personality. After I wrote half of an unsatisfactory first draft, Mark and Reed got merged into a single character around 2014, and around the same time I also decided that character would be Iranian.

At that point his name was Omid, but something about the shape of that name just didn't fit, so I decided to name him after this guy I knew from the USC School of Cinematic Arts, a fertile ground from which I've poached several character names (including from my classmates Hongsik "Vincent" Park, Satomi Mack, and Sev Ohanian, whose name I had to change to "Ghasabian" after the real Sev went and became a Hollywood famous writer/producer). Kaveh went through several surnames, but it wouldn't be until *Axiom's End* was nearing completion that I finally gave myself permission to name him what I secretly had always wanted to (readers of Gaston Leroux's *The Phantom of the Opera* will get it).

Kaveh Taherian was the producer of the advanced documentary project (CTPR 547, for those in the know) that I directed at USC, and by the mid-2010s he was one of those colleagues I saw once a year or so when he happened to be in New York. It's always awkward telling people you named a character after them, especially in this case where said character is not only the protagonist but a recovering alcoholic who has an affair with a girl fourteen years his junior. That is part of why the conventional wisdom is that you shouldn't name characters after your friends.

I didn't ask Kaveh Taheri
settled on using his name
musical theater, but t'
while I never expecte
became an invaluable re
acting as my "Persian con
like, "Do Persians do the 'n
lutely") and "Do you text your
of the Mazandarani family's Farsi/
ten suggested, by him, as were many
none of the actors who auditioned for th
chapters were quite clicking, in the end it w
would give Kaveh Mazandarani his voice.

But more important to me, in the last coup.
from a distant colleague to my good friend. At t
his Nikola, the Phantom to his Persian, the agent of
sanity, and there are few perspectives I trust more than
from the fictional Kaveh's life or backstory that was inf.
real one (he is, to my knowledge, neither a Rhodes Scholar
robber), but if Kaveh Mazandarani took anything from Kaveh
it was his good humor, his compassion, and his kindness. In the
arbitrary decision of borrowing his name, I have rediscovered a fr.
that I have grown to treasure. I love you, Kaveh, even if you are wron.
about *Phantom*.

Emily VanDerWerff

LINDSAY ELLIS is a *New York Times* bestselling author, Hugo Award finalist, and video essayist who creates online content about media, narrative, literature, and film theory. After earning her bachelor's in cinema studies from the NYU Tisch School of the Arts, she earned her MFA in film and television production, with a focus in documentary and screenwriting, from the USC School of Cinematic Arts. She lives in Long Beach, California. Her debut novel, *Axiom's End*, was an instant *New York Times* bestseller.